36

Strangers

Rosie Thomas

D0474638

arrow books

Published by Arrow Books in 2003

3 5 7 9 10 8 6 4

Copyright © Rosie Thomas 1987

Rosie Thomas has asserted her right under the Copyright, Designs and
Patents Act, 1988 to be identified as the author of this work

This novel is a work of fiction. Names and characters are the product of
the author's imagination and any resemblance to actual persons, living or
dead, is entirely coincidental

First published in the United Kingdom by William Collins and Company 1987
First published in paperback by Fontana Press 1988
Published in paperback by Penguin Books 1993

Arrow Books
The Random House Group Limited
20 Vauxhall Bridge Road, London, SW1V 2SA

Random House Australia (Pty) Limited
20 Alfred Street, Milsons Point, Sydney,
New South Wales 2061, Australia

Random House New Zealand Limited
18 Poland Road, Glenfield
Auckland 10, New Zealand

Random House (Pty) Limited
Endulini, 5a Jubilee Road, Parktown 2193, South Africa

The Random House Group Limited Reg. No. 954009

www.randomhouse.co.uk

A CIP catalogue record for this book
is available from the British Library

Papers used by Random House
are natural, recyclable products made from wood grown in
sustainable forests. The manufacturing processes conform to
the environmental regulations of the country of origin

ISBN 0 09 940646 2

Typeset by SX Composing DTP, Rayleigh, Essex
Printed and bound in Denmark by
Nørhaven Paperback A/S, Viborg

For Ruth Eleri Morris

The authors thanks are due to Susan Watt, Angela Coles, Jennifer and John Creer, Peter Harvey, and to Nick Evans for his generosity.

One

It was just starting to snow.

Annie stood beside the row of coats hung untidily on the pegs and looked out of the glass panel in the back door. The dark grey specks fell out of a paler sky, and the wind caught them and blew them up into a spiral before letting them drop on the path. They changed from grey to white, and then vanished. In a minute, Annie thought, the flakes would stop melting. The snow would stick. She would need to wear her boots to go shopping. She opened the door of the cupboard under the stairs and rummaged for them, sighing as she always did at the sight of the tangle of family belongings. Then she took her coat off the peg, disentangling it from a red anorak with the sleeves pulled wrong side out.

A boy came down the stairs, two at a time, thumping his feet. He swung around the banister post and vaulted the last four steps down to the lobby. 'Careful,' Annie said automatically. 'You'll break a leg doing that, one of these days.'

The child looked squarely at her, and she knew that he was wondering how forcibly to contradict her. Then he shrugged. 'No I won't.' He went to the door and pressed his face against the glass. 'Look, Mum, it's snowing. Can't I come out with you?' She buttoned up her coat and picked up her handbag, flipping through the contents to see if she had everything.

'Can't I?'

She smiled quickly at him, then glanced past him into the kitchen to see if her chequebook was on the table. She felt her attention being pulled two ways, fixing nowhere. It was often like that, nowadays.

'No, you can't. You hate shopping and you'll only nag me to come home as soon as we've got there. And I've got a lot to do today.'

She found her chequebook in her coat pocket, and put it into her bag with her purse. The boy was sitting on the bottom step now, still staring longingly out at the snow. A thought occurred to him and he looked up at her.

'Buying presents for me? For my stocking?'

His earnest gaze, a perfect replica of his father's, made her smile.

'That depends. And Tom, you may have grown out of Father Christmas, but Benjy hasn't. You won't spoil it for him, will you?'

Over the boy's head she saw the snow beyond the window, falling faster now, powdering the garden wall with the faintest rim of white. Perhaps it would be a white Christmas. She breathed in the scent of pine needles, tangerines, log fires. 'Okay,' Tom said grudgingly. 'He's such a baby.'

Annie gathered up her scarf and gloves. There were a thousand things to be done before Christmas, faithful preparations for the family myth of a perfect holiday. She hugged Thomas and went to the foot of the stairs.

'Martin? Where are you? I'm off now.'

There was a muffled thud from upstairs, two seconds of silence, and then the sound of a child's full-throated yelling.

A moment or two later Annie's husband appeared at the top of the stairs with Benjy in his arms. The little boy's face was scarlet and crumpled, but he opened his eyes for long enough to make sure that his mother was watching. The crying went on undiminished.

'He fell off the end of the bed,' Martin said.

Annie ran up the stairs, already hot in her outdoor clothes. She rubbed Benjy's head, feeling the round hardness of his skull under the silky hair. How resilient children are, she thought. Tougher sometimes than their parents.

'Poor old Benjy,' she said. Martin stood holding him, rocking him slightly, waiting for the noise to abate.

'You're going, then? What time will you be back?'

Martin was tall, with the rounded shoulders of someone used to stooping to reach the more general level. Annie was standing on the step below him and she had to stretch up to press her cheek against his. She didn't see his face, but she noticed that the label was sticking out at the back of his jersey. He patted her with his free hand and Annie turned and ran back down the stairs.

'What shall I give them for lunch?' he called after her.

'*I* don't know. Look in the fridge for something, can't you?'

The little ripple of domestic irritation washed after her all the way to the front door.

'Or take them to McDonald's, if you like.'

Thomas appeared in the kitchen doorway. 'Yeah, McDonald's. Dad? Are you listening? Mum said McDonald's.'

Annie turned back to look at the three of them.

It wasn't like Annie to turn back but today, for some reason, she did.

She saw Martin at the head of the stairs, his face so familiar that the features seemed to have been rubbed smooth, like a pebble by the sea. Benjy sagged in his arms, his head against his father's shoulder. He had stopped crying, and his thumb was in his mouth for comfort. A few feet below them Thomas swung in an impatient arc from the newel post.

And all around them, like an over-detailed picture, the evidence of family life came crowding in. There was a broken plastic car overturned in the hallway, a dim grey line of hand-prints all along the shabby paint of the wall, a basket of clothes waiting to be ironed, on the hall table a sheaf of Polaroid snapshots of the boys.

'What time will you be back?' Martin repeated mildly. Annie's irritation was disregarded. Sometimes it increased her annoyance, but she found herself smiling now.

'I'm not sure. The crowds will be awful, probably. But I want

3

to try and finish the last of the Christmas shopping today. Expect me when you see me.'

Annie opened the front door, and the cold wind blew in.

'Bye,' she called cheerfully. 'See you all later.'

The door closed again. It was quiet outside. Not the muffled silence that came with snow, yet, but the quiet of waiting for it to happen. Annie ducked her head into the biting cold, and walked on down the path. As she opened the gate the Co-op milk float came round the corner, its little electric hum barely reaching her. Annie reckoned up quickly in her head, how many pints, and held up four fingers to the milkman. The snowflakes patted against her face. The milkman gave her a thumbs-up sign as the float stopped. Annie set off towards the station, walking quickly. She knew that it would take her exactly eight minutes. Martin hadn't offered to drive her, even in the snow. They both knew without having to mention it that it was easier to walk than dress the children in outdoor clothes and persuade them into their car seats for the short drive. Annie was still smiling. That was the kind of telepathy bred by ten years of marriage, she thought, without bitterness.

As she turned the corner into the main road none of the few passers-by even glanced at her. Annie was just what she seemed, unremarkable, a housewife and mother intent on a day's shopping. It would have taken a close look to reveal that she appeared a little younger than her real age, that her face was smooth even though her expression was preoccupied, and that she had an air of being capable, and content.

It was still early when Annie reached the first big store on her route for the day. The windows along the street blazed their Christmas displays at her. She looked at them for a moment, savouring the sight of satin ribbons and fir branches frosted with dry, sparkling snow. The real thing in the street outside was already grey-brown, spraying in filthy plumes under the wheels of the traffic. Annie pushed gratefully in through the big glass doors and breathed in the warm, perfumed air. She took her

4

knitted hat off and shook her hair out, then turned towards the lift. She would start on the top floor and work her way down. Her list was ready in her coat pocket.

There was no one in the lift. She looked up at the indicator, congratulating herself on having arrived before the crowds. The doors opened at the top floor and she stepped out. A long counter heaped up with coloured balls faced her, red and green and silver and gold, and a pyramid of clear glass ones that held the iridescence of soap bubbles. She was drawn to the display and picked up a clear ball, turning it so that the colours changed in the light. Expensive, she thought regretfully. Nearly a pound each. But she took four, guiltily, putting them carefully into a wire basket. She moved across the department to the waterfalls of tinsel and buried her hands amongst the strands.

Two assistants waited at the nearest cash till.

'What time d'you finish?' Annie heard one of them ask.

'Seven, tonight,' her friend answered. 'Makes the day seem endless, doesn't it?'

The tinsel was coiled in Annie's basket now, a bright silver serpent. They needed some new stuff, she reassured herself. Theirs was tarnished from too many annual appearances. But she wouldn't spend any more money on decorations. She would go on down to the kitchen department and look for something for Martin's mother. Her own mother needed a new dressing gown. She would go on to Selfridge's for that, later. Annie's face clouded as if she had remembered something painful, and she turned quickly with her basket towards the cash desk.

Yawning, one of the assistants wrapped up her purchases in green tissue. The other tapped the till keys and the electronic total flashed at Annie. She counted out the notes, picked up her carrier bag and walked towards the stairs at the back of the store. They were nearer than the lifts. She would walk down two floors. Heavy swing doors led to the stairwell. A sign over them announced Emergency Exit.

Annie reached the doors. She was vaguely conscious of someone else heading the same way. It was a man, he had been standing beside her at the cash desk, and now he was right behind her. She half turned her head, and his arm reached past to push the heavy door open for them both to pass through.

'After you,' the man said. She didn't see his face. Nor did she ever say *Thank you*, although the words had formed in her head.

It was then that the bomb exploded.

It destroyed the staff cloakroom where it had been left overnight. It blew a hole up through the roof of the store, and the blast waves racing downwards into the heart of the structure ripped a great hole into which the floors tilted and fell. The terrible thunder of the explosion shook the surrounding streets and jolted the houses a mile away.

Annie didn't hear a sound. There was an instant, an instant as long as infinity, when gravity deserted the world. In total silence she saw a blur of red and gold as the counter threw its load of glass balls into the whirling air, and then smashed them into fragments. She felt a silent wind that tore her clothes and flayed her skin and lifted her up only to pitch her forwards, down into a deathly pit where broken beams and chunks of wall boiled around her.

The fierce, white light was abruptly extinguished, and the dark descended.

The noise came then, like thunder receding, and in the wake of it came the roar of falling masonry as the store was sucked inwards on itself, molten, a whirlpool of stone and steel.

Annie fell, and went on falling, into the dark.

The noise had possessed her, but now it abandoned her again, growing fainter. The roaring crash was finished and in its place was the rattle of chunks of stone and plaster falling down on top of her. That grew fainter too, until it was only a whisper of dust, trickling into the crevices and settling as gravity took hold of the world again.

The girls at the cash desk were both dead. So was the cleaner who had been working in the cloakroom and who had lifted the tartan holdall out of its hiding place. Annie didn't know it yet, but she was alive. She had fallen into the hole, with the heavy fire door half on top of her, like a shield.

Even the dust had stopped whispering now. The silence came again, long seconds, and nothing stirred. Then, up in the light, above the smoking rubble where tinsel and fragments of pretty glass were mixed with torn girders and other, terrible things, and where the snowflakes drifted and settled impartially, the first siren began to wail.

Annie couldn't hear it. Her head thundered with the echo of the explosion and her eyes burned with the white flash of light. She closed her eyes, opened them again, but the glare was undimmed. Where had the dark gone? Her own, private darkness, how could that have been taken away? Were her eyes open or shut?

She lay without moving for a long time, she didn't know how long. The roaring in her ears dropped in pitch, became muffled. The white blaze turned egg-yellow with a brassy point at the centre. The first bodily sensation to return was a wave of nausea. Annie tried instinctively to turn her head in order to be sick, but a sharp pain that seemed to be inside her head cut short the movement. She lay still again, staring up into the middle of the yellow glow. Slowly, like a fist unclenching, the nausea released its grip, and the light dwindled to a little point. Her eyes were opening and closing, she was sure of that now. It dawned on her that the light was inside her own head, and she could see nothing else because she was in utter darkness.

Annie's tongue moved, finding her lips. They were coated with dust, except for one corner that was clogged with sticky moisture. There was the brackish taste of her own blood. She was suddenly possessed by panic, more powerful than the nausea. She tried to roll sideways, to draw her knees up into the foetal position, and found that she could not. She was hurt, badly hurt, and she was trapped in total blackness.

Annie could hear screaming, a scream that went on and on, up and then down again as the sufferer gasped for breath. When it stopped she wondered if the screams could have been her own.

Where was she? What had happened?

Oh God, please help me.

The screams had been hers. She could feel another one, the voice of pure terror, rising inside her. She clenched her teeth, and felt the grit crunch between them. She tried to swallow it, to clear her mouth, focusing on the smallest thing to keep the fear at bay. She could feel it all around her, like a living thing.

Think. Try to work out what had happened.

Slowly this time, she tried to move. Her right side, arm and shoulder right across to her breastbone, and her hip and thigh, wouldn't do anything. She was pinned down by something smooth, sloping upwards at an angle. She discovered it by feeling cautiously upwards with her left hand. On her left side, higher up, there was something jagged that felt both hard and crumbling at the same time. She gave up her useless search and let her arm drop to her side again. Legs. Where were her legs? She could feel nothing at all in the lower part of them. It was as if her body was clay that had been crumpled up and crudely remodelled, stopping short at the knees.

And her head, the pain in her head. She rolled it, just a little, to one side and then the other. There was perhaps an inch or two of play before the pain gripped her. Suddenly Annie realized that her hair was caught underneath something. She had taken her knitted hat off – how long ago? – inside the doors of the shop. Now something very heavy was resting on her spread-out hair, and the pain she felt was the roots of it tearing her scalp. So even if there had been nothing else touching her she would still be trapped here by her hair, forced to lie staring upwards, into – into what?

There was only the pitch dark, not a sound except the threatening patter of falling fragments when she moved her arm. The fingers of her left hand fluttered, feeling the rough brick, splintered wood.

She was shuddering now, fully conscious, cold to her bones.

What would happen to her?

Annie screamed again as the fear lurched close and threatened to smother her. When the sound of it died away a voice said, very close to her, 'Stop. Stop screaming.'

It wasn't her own voice, she knew that. It was a man's. A stranger's.

At the sound of it, she remembered. Before the noise came, before even the silent wind and the shock that had spun her round into a rain of splintering glass balls, there had been a man. That was it. When she had still been Annie, walking calmly to the exit with a carrier bag of Christmas tree decorations, a man had come up behind her and pushed open the door. Out of the corner of her eye, in that last instant, she had seen his hand and arm.

Fear moved right inside her now. Where was the man, how close to her? Annie struggled to make her thoughts fit together.

He must have done this, whatever it was. And if he could do something so cataclysmic what else would there be, when he reached her? To stop the shuddering Annie bit her lips, and tasted salt blood again. She must keep still, or he would hear her. She lay with her head turned as far as it would go towards where the voice had come from, staring wildly into the impenetrable dark.

'Where are you?' he asked. 'I don't think I can reach you, but . . .'

'*If you come near me* . . .' Annie had wanted to scream at him, but her words were a gasp. 'If you come near me, I'll kill you.'

There was a long moment's quiet.

Then the man said softly, 'It's all right. Listen, can you hear the sirens? They'll reach us. They'll get us out.'

A solitary policewoman had been standing on the opposite pavement, checking the number plate of a grey van parked on the double yellow lines. The side of it had sheltered her from the blast, and she crouched in the gutter for an instant with her cheek against the cold metal. She heard screaming, and the traffic skidding wildly in the roadway, and the crash of breaking glass. Slowly, sliding her hand up the van's side, she stood up. Under a cloud of black smoke she saw the front of the store. The roof had been blown open to the sky and she could see the inside where the floors hung, pathetically exposed, tipping downwards. Chunks of brick were still falling. In the roadway people were running, some of them away from the falling bricks, others towards them. There were other people lying on the pavement.

The policewoman left the shelter of the grey van and made herself walk across the road. The broken glass crunched under her polished black shoes. She held up one black-gloved hand to stop the traffic, as she had been trained to do. Her other hand reached inside her coat for the pocket transmitter, to call for help.

The first squad car came, weaving up the street between the slewed cars and buses, its lights blazing. The policewoman was kneeling beside a man whose blood seeped through the clenched fist pressed to his cheek. There was suddenly an eerie quiet, and she thought how loud the siren sounded.

Two policemen leapt out of the car as it skidded to the kerbside. One of them carried a loudhailer, and he lifted it to his mouth.

'Get back. Get back and stay back.'

One by one the people who had been milling on the pavement began to move slowly backwards, a step at a time. They were looking up at the ruined façade of the store where the smoke still drifted in black coils.

'There may be a further explosion. Please leave the area at once.'

They moved a little further, leaving the injured and those who were helping them, bewildered groups on the littered pavement.

Down in the darkness the man's voice repeated, insistent, 'Can't you hear them?'

At last, Annie said, 'Yes.'

'I can't hear you properly,' the man said louder. 'Say it louder.'

She repeated, 'Yes,' and then, suddenly, 'What have you done?'

There was quiet again after that, and she heard something moving, close to her. Her skin crept in a cold wave.

'I didn't do it.' The voice sounded even closer now. 'It must have been a bomb, I think. Perhaps a gas explosion.'

A bomb.

In her mind's eye, imprinted on the terrifying darkness, the word conjured up flickering images. There were the television news pictures of violent death amongst the rubble, a half-forgotten impression of the reddened dome of St Paul's still standing amongst the devastation of the Blitz, and then the mushroom cloud over Hiroshima.

A bomb.

The images faded and left her in the dark again. Her eyes stung with the effort of staring into it. She understood that a bomb had gone off, and buried her along with the broken Christmas tree balls, the gaudy strands of tinsel and the heavy door she had been going to push open. It was the same door lying on top of her now, crushing her.

Annie was shivering violently.

'I'm afraid,' she said.

She sounded very shocked, the man thought. But she was conscious, and she had stopped screaming. He wondered if there was a chance of manoeuvring himself close enough to help. He eased himself sideways a little, reaching out with his right hand.

'What are you doing?' Her voice was sharp with the onset of panic.

'Trying to reach you. Listen to me, carefully. Where are you hurt?'

He could almost hear her thinking, painfully exploring the inner contours of her body, just as he had done himself.

At last she said, 'I can't feel my legs. My side hurts. There's something heavy on top of me. I think it's a door.'

'That's good. It's probably like a shield for you.'

'And my hair's caught. I can't move my head.'

She had long, thick fair hair. He remembered seeing it as she walked to the exit in front of him.

'Can you move any part of you?' he persisted.

'My arm. My left arm.'

Gently, he said, 'Reach out with it, then.'

He heard a tiny clink, perhaps the buckle of her watch against broken masonry, and the soft scraping of her fingers as they moved towards him. He stretched his own arm, further, until the muscles ached, and the splinters scraped his wrist. And then, miraculously, their fingers touched. Their hands gripped, palm to palm, suddenly strong.

Annie thought, *Thank God*. The hand in the dark was so solid, the feel of it gripping hers almost familiar, as if she already knew the shape of it.

The man heard the sob of relief in her throat. Her hand felt very cold in his.

'What's your name?' he asked into the blackness.

'Annie.'

'Annie. I've always liked the name Annie. Mine is Steve.'

'Steve.'

It was a reassurance to repeat the names, an affirmation that they were still there, still themselves after the cataclysm.

Annie felt his thumb move on the back of her hand, a little stroking movement. The fear began to loosen its grip, and her breath came easier. She turned her head towards him, as far as she could. Her hair pulled at her scalp.

'I thought you did it,' she said. 'I'm sorry. I was afraid of you.'

'I didn't do it. I was just doing my Christmas shopping, like you.'

Christmas shopping . . . the translucent glass balls that had been so expensive, the shiny ribbons and fir branches in the shop windows, the snow falling in the wintry streets. And now? To be buried, in this acrid darkness. How far down? She had the impression that she had fallen down and down, into a great pit. What was balanced above them, how many tons of rubble cutting them off from the sky and air?

Annie's hair tore at the roots as she struggled, involuntarily.

'Keep still.' Steve's fingers tightened over hers.

Annie heard the door creak over her face. Yes, she must keep still.

12

'And you?' she asked. 'Are you hurt?'

'I'm cut, here and there. Not badly. My leg's the worst. I think it's broken.'

Now Annie's fingers moved, trying to lace hers between his.

'Don't let go,' Steve said quickly.

'I won't. I'm trying to think. How can we get out?' She was collecting herself now, trying hard to keep her voice level.

'I . . . don't think we can.' The sound of the sirens came again, multiplying, but a long way off. 'They'll come for us, Annie. It won't be long, if we can just hold on.'

Annie thought, *They won't find us.* How can they? No one even knows I'm here. I didn't tell Martin where I was going.

'Who is Martin?'

It was only with the question that Annie realized she had been thinking aloud. All her senses were dislocated. She was looking, staring so hard that her eyes stung, but she couldn't see. There were noises all around her now, not just the sirens but other, rumbling sounds, creaking, and the rattle of falling fragments. Yet she couldn't tell whether they were real, or replaying themselves inside her head, like her own voice. And suddenly she had the feeling that she wasn't trapped at all, but falling again, spreadeagled in the blackness. Annie clenched her fists and tilted her face upwards, deliberately, ignoring the pain in her head, until her cheek met the solid, cold, weighty smoothness of the door.

'My husband,' she said, willing the words to come out normally. She wasn't falling any more. 'Martin is my husband.'

'Go on,' Steve said. 'Talk to me. It doesn't matter what. Lie still, and just talk.'

Leaving home this morning. There were the three of them, watching her go, little Benjy in Martin's arms and Tom swinging around the banister post. Before that, she had run to the top of the stairs, reaching up to brush her cheek against Martin's. A goodbye like a thousand others, hurried, and she hadn't even seen her husband's face. It was so familiar, rubbed smooth in her mind's eye by the years.

Suddenly, Annie felt her solitude. She was going to die, here, alone. But the hand holding hers was blessedly warm. Where had Martin gone, then?

I love you. They repeated the formula often enough, not out of passion but to reassure each other, renewing the pledge. It is true, Annie thought. I do love him.

Yet now, trying to summon it up in pain and fear, she couldn't see her husband's face.

In its place she saw the garden behind their house, as vividly as if she was standing in the back doorway. Only a week ago. Martin was stooping with his back to her, his head half-turned, reaching for the hammer he had dropped on the crazy-paving path. She saw his hand, the torn cuff of the old jacket he wore for gardening, and heard the music coming from the kitchen radio.

They were working in the garden together. Martin had at last found time to repair the larchlap fencing that separated them from their neighbour's voracious Alsatian. The boys had gone to a birthday party and they were alone, a rare two-hour interval of peace.

Annie was standing at the edge of the flower bed. The dead brown stalks of the summer's anemones poked up beside her, acid with the smell of tomcats, and the earth itself was black and frost-hard. Her arms ached because she was holding up a bowed length of fencing, waiting for Martin to nail it in place. Neither of them spoke. Annie was cold, and Martin was irritable because he was an awkward handyman and the setbacks in the task had brought him close to losing his temper. He picked up the hammer and jabbed it at the nail, and the nail bent sideways. Martin swore and flung the hammer down again.

Annie was thinking back to the days when they had first bought the crumbling Victorian house, long before Tom was born. They had worked endless weekends, painting and hammering, because they couldn't afford to employ builders or decorators. They would quarrel unrestrainedly then, launching themselves into blazing arguments over the coving that had been mitred wrong, the glaringly mistaken shade of paint, the tiled edge that rippled like waves on a lagoon. And then they would stop, and laugh about it, and they would go upstairs and make love in the bedroom where the last occupants' purple and orange wallpaper hung down in ragged strips over their heads. Nine, ten years ago.

A similar memory must have touched Martin too. He had kicked the hammer aside and straightened up to look at her.

Annie saw his face now, every line of it. She could have reached up and touched it in the darkness. He looked almost the same as he had when they first met, except for the deeper creases beside his mouth, and his frown.

He had put his arms round her, inside her coat, and kissed her.

'Let's ask Audrey to come in tonight, so that we can go and eat at Costa's.'

They always went to Costa's. Annie couldn't remember the last time they had been anywhere else. They shared a plate of hummous, and then they had dolmades and a bottle of retsina. The last time, after their work in the garden a week ago, they had come in late and Martin had taken the babysitter home. Annie had gone on up to bed and she had fallen asleep at once, before he lay down beside her. In the morning Benjy had woken at six, and for the sake of another hour's peace she had carried him in and put him between them. He had smiled in triumph, with his thumb in his mouth.

Martin had reached out across Benjy to rest his hand regretfully in the hollow of Annie's waist. They had looked at each other, acknowledging. That was how it was. They were tired, and then there were the children.

Something touched Annie now, colder than the cold that pierced her bones. She was shivering again.

'We always go to Costa's,' she repeated. 'I don't know why. Martin likes it.'

'I know,' Steve answered her. 'I know all about that, too.'

'Why?' Annie heard herself ask. 'Are you married?'

*

15

The street had been cleared. Out of the first desperate scramble to reach the injured the police had created a kind of order. They had unrolled orange plastic tapes to make a cordon around the store, and inside the circle the rescue workers were at work. The orange fluorescent jackets worn by the police seemed to spill their colour into the grey air, and the firemen's yellow helmets bobbed up and down as they unloaded their complicated equipment, pulleys and lifting tackle and strange, cumbersome cameras. They moved quickly, with practised efficiency.

Outside the orange line the rescue vehicles were drawn up. The high grey and scarlet walls of the fire engines made a solid wall, and beyond them an ambulance waited, drawn up beside the big white emergency first aid trailer. Another ambulance moved away with the last of the injured from the pavement outside the store. Sixty yards to the south two police constables opened the white tapes of the outer cordon to let it through.

The crowd, swollen with arriving sightseers, had been moved back beyond the fluttering white tapes. One of the uniformed constables at the cordon still carried a loudhailer, to warn back anyone who tried to come closer.

In the centre of a huddle of police cars drawn up between the inner and outer cordons stood an anonymous pale blue van with a domed roof. It was the major incident vehicle from Scotland Yard, and inside it the duty inspector from the local station was handing the direction of the operation over to the commander who had arrived with it. The bomb squad's equally anonymous control van stood close beside it.

A few yards away, at a special point in the white cordon, the press had already formed a restless knot. The first television news crew had set up, and their reporter was moving along the crowd at the tapes in search of an eye-witness to interview. But he turned away again as a senior police officer and a police press officer emerged from the control van.

'We don't have any idea, as yet,' the policeman told them. 'The store had only been open for a few minutes, as you know, so the chances are that there were fewer shoppers inside than there would have been later in the morning. We have a list of store personnel and it is being checked now against the survivors we have already reached.'

A dozen more questions were fired at him.

'No. We do not yet have an accurate figure for the number of casualties, nor will we for some time. The rescue operation has already begun, and it will continue until it is clear that no survivors remain.'

The cold, wet air was alive with the static crackle of police radios.

'No,' the officer said. 'We don't have any intention yet as to how many people may be buried.'

He turned away with a brusque nod, back towards the control van. At the cordon the press officer read out to the journalists the telephone number of the central casualty bureau set up at Scotland Yard.

Steve knew how it would be. He had been imagining it, using the picture in his mind's eye to convince himself that they would be rescued. He needed to convince the girl, too, make her believe in the precision of the rescue operation. Her hand was so cold, and he could feel her trembling even in her fingertips.

'I was married, for a while. Not any more.'

'Why?'

She wanted him to talk, too. She was reaching out in the same way, wanting to hold on to the sound of his voice. Steve tasted the dust in his throat.

Why? Cass had been waiting for him, that evening. She hadn't had a booking, and so she had been at home all day. It was very late when he came in, but it was often late. The irony was that that night he really had been working.

'Had a good time?' she had asked, without looking up. There was a bottle on the low glass table beside her, almost empty. So she had been drinking. And, as there always was wherever Cass went, there was a litter of other stuff as well. Two or three glossy magazines, a scarlet phial of nail-varnish with a plastic crest to the lid like a stiletto blade, her Sony Walkman with its leads trailing on the floor, a scatter of open cassette packs.

Steve had draped his jacket over the back of a chair and gone into the kitchen to make a cup of coffee.

'*Had a good time?*' she called after him. He had ground the coffee very fine, almost relishing the noise, and then he had gone to the kitchen doorway to look at her.

Cass was a model. She wasn't quite the youngest in the business now, but she was still successful. Cass's real name was Jennifer Cassady, but her agency had agreed when they took her on the books that her given name wasn't quite right. So they had opted simply for 'Cass'. There was the name, in the agency's folder, in her portfolio, on her cards. 'Cass. Hair, brown. Eyes, green. 5ft 10in. 35–24–34.' And all the rest of the information – her shoe and glove sizes, her particular modelling expertise, her willingness to 'do' underwear ads.

Like most of her model friends, Cass rarely wore make-up when she wasn't working. Her pale, triangular face turned towards Steve, expressionless under its straight-cut fringe of hair. Steve had often thought that with her wide-set eyes and her pointed chin, she looked like a Persian cat. She moved like a cat, too.

'Not particularly.' Steve answered her question deliberately slowly. 'I've been doing a reshoot for Fawcetts. I've had Phil Day on my back all evening.'

'That must make a change,' Cass said, carefully, not wanting to muff her line now that it had been presented to her, 'from having Vicky on hers.'

Steve hadn't said anything. There wasn't any point in saying anything, both of them understood that. He had gone back into the kitchen and rummaged in the drawers for the coffee strainer. He had poured himself a mugful of coffee and leant against the grey-painted cupboard, staring blankly at the newspaper, while he drank it.

When he went back into the living room, Cass wasn't there. He turned off the lights, went through into the bedroom, and found her.

She had made up her face, and changed out of her sweatshirt and track pants. Steve was used to her chameleon transformations, but now he stood still and stared at her. Later he remembered a black lace bra, French knickers slit high at the sides, suspenders and black stockings. Cass had painted pouting red lips over her own, but her black-rimmed eyes belied them. They met his, full of bewildered resentment. But she faced him squarely with one hand on her hip, posing.

'I'm sorry you didn't have a good time tonight. Shall I give you one now?'

'Cass, for God's sake . . .'

She came swaying towards him, reaching up to the catch of her bra but holding it over her breasts, sliding the straps off her smooth brown shoulders.

She was very pretty, tall and a little too thin, with hip-bones that jutted on either side of the soft concavity of her stomach. Against his will, knowing that she was manipulating him, Steve put out his hand to touch her. Her skin was warm, and he knew the intimate scent of it.

'Cass,' he whispered. 'What are you doing?'

'I am your wife, aren't I?'

'You are.'

He drew her to him and her half-naked body fitted against his. He kissed her, smudging the scarlet mouth, and she began to undo the buttons of his shirt. Steve tilted her sideways, down on to the bed. For a moment she lay looking up at him, then she rolled over so that she was on top. She undid the last button and her fingers moved to the buckle of his belt. She bent her head to kiss him and then looked downwards, dreamily, the soft ends of her hair trailing over his bare chest. For the moment Steve had forgotten the complicated sequence of their long-running battle. His fingers found the lace-trimmed edge of the provocative knickers. He slid them inside, reaching for her.

Cass pushed him away. She rolled out his arms and stood up. Without a glance back at him she went to her wardrobe, took out a coat and put it on over the black lace underthings. Then she lifted down a suitcase, opened a drawer and began to stuff clothes into it.

'What in God's name are you doing?' Steve felt the heat of his anger fuelled by desire.

Cass didn't look round. She put an armful of clothes on hangers into the case and slammed it shut.

'I'm leaving you,' she said flatly. 'I hate you. You disgust me.'

'Don't be so bloody stupid.'

He had lifted himself up on to his elbows to look at her, and he felt his awkward heat, the frustrated redness of his face. His anger intensified. Cass put her feet into a pair of suede boots. She swept a clutter of things, keys and her cheque-book and her precious Filofax, off the bedside table and into her bag.

She went to the door and then, finally, turned back to look at him.

'Goodbye, Steve,' she said. She hadn't been able to resist the final pose.

'Where the hell are you going?'

'Nowhere that concerns you.'

His wife walked out, closing the door behind her.

Steve lay motionless for a moment, and then he flung himself off the bed and went to the window. He tucked his shirt back into his trousers and opened the curtain. He saw Cass come out into the street and put her suitcase into her car. It was a little gold-coloured Renault 5, and Steve remembered that he had booked it in for a service later in the week. Cass revved the engine, backed the car up and then shot forwards. He stood at the window watching the street for a long time after the Renault had vanished.

She'll be back, he told himself. It won't last more than a couple of days. But she had never come back.

'I've never told anyone exactly what happened,' Steve said. 'I just said we'd split up. Out of shame, I suppose. But I'm telling you, now.'

'I don't think shame matters very much,' the girl said quietly, 'if you're going to die.'

Annie heard his quick movement, and then his breath catch as pain gripped him somewhere.

'We aren't going to die,' he said. 'Do you hear?' And then, when there was no answer, 'Say something, Annie. *We aren't going to die.* They'll dig us out of here. I know they will.'

'They'll dig us out,' she echoed him, at last. They lay still, their hands clasped.

Annie hated the quiet seeping around them. It seemed to be only a superficial quiet, masking all kind of noises, perhaps the first rumble of the avalanche that would bring the weight of rubble down to crush their precarious shelter.

'Do you want her to come back?' she asked quickly.

'I don't know. No, I don't think so.'

Not any more. He still saw Vicky, and one or two others just like her. He worked very hard – it was his own production company, and he had to – and when there was no Vicky or anyone else he came home to the empty flat.

'You sound sorry for yourself.'

Her words made him look into the blank darkness, wishing he could see her. He had had only the vaguest impression of her turning away from the counter and walking ahead of him towards the door. She had a pleasant, preoccupied face. Ordinary.

'And you sound like a schoolmistress.'

She did. There was a faint bossiness, a moral certainty. No, it wasn't a schoolmistress – it was a mother, used to delivering crisp reprimands. Steve heard something that might almost have been a low, painful laugh.

'Don't you think it's odd that we're buried here, holding hands and insulting each other?' the girl asked.

His answering smile flickered automatically before the pain in his leg made him wince again.

'I like the spirit, Annie,' he said. 'Nothing's *odd*, down here, is it? Say what you like. Talk to me some more. Tell me, are you happily married?'

What was the cold hand that had touched her, when she remembered the day in the garden? It came again now, tightening its hold, and she was already so cold. The shivering took hold of her and she went stiff, trying to stop it because it shook the pain deeper into her side, like a knife stabbing her.

'Yes. Yes, we're happy together. I am. I think Martin is.' She could hear herself gabbling and she made herself talk more slowly, shaping the words in her mouth before she uttered them.

Years, succeeding one another. Changing their texture a little, the colours fading from bright to dim, but all woven in the same, even way.

'I'm just a housewife. I've got two children, boys, eight and three.'

Oh, Thomas, Benjy, I love you so much. Don't let me die here without seeing you.

'My husband's a designer, interiors. His company does shops, that kind of thing. I used to do similar work, before Tom was born. Now I look after the children and Martin, and the house. I'm happy doing it. You can't imagine what it would be like, can you?'

I know you now, Steve thought. I've seen you, all of you, in the park with your kids, or struggling to get off the tube with one in a buggy and the other hanging on to your coat.

'Cass wanted to be like that, I think. For all her wild outfits and dotty behaviour. I think she really wanted to have dinner ready every evening at eight o'clock, get the holiday brochures in January and make plans for July, have a regular night out together every week.'

'And you didn't?'

'No, I didn't. It was the routine of being married that I couldn't bear.'

'Like always going to Costa's,' Annie said.

'I don't always want dolmades. I like to see different things on the menu. I like to eat in different restaurants.'

She listened carefully to the sound of his words, and felt his hand holding hers. His hand was large, and still quite warm.

Annie felt suddenly irrationally angry. 'I think you sound a bit of a pig.'

Steve did laugh this time, a spluttering cough of laughter. 'But I'm a pig who survives. And you'll survive too, my love. I'll make you.'

Annie's anger went away as quickly as it had come. Hearing his conviction, a man she had never seen, she believed him. It was important to believe, she understood that too.

'How long have we been here?' Her voice sounded childlike now. 'How long will it be before they come?'

'We might have been here an hour. Perhaps not even as long as that. Does your watch have hands?'

'Hands?' Annie could only think of their own, linked together.

'Mine's digital. But if yours has hands, and it isn't broken, we should be able to feel the time. We can keep track, then. It will help.'

He was practical, seemingly neither afraid nor disorientated. Annie closed her eyes. The pain in her head and her side made it difficult to think. All kinds of other impressions, memories that were more vivid than reality, came crowding in on her, but the simplest coherent thought slipped out of her grasp.

With an effort she said, 'My watch is on this arm.' She lifted her hand a little in his. At once the warmth of his hand let go. She felt him reach for her wrist, searching for the watch strap. It was a tiny buckle, and she heard the effort that the little, fumbling movements cost him. At last the strap loosened and the watch slid off her wrist. It dropped through Steve's fingers and there was a faint chink as it fell somewhere beneath their hands. It was as if a lifeline had been thrown at them, only to drift out of reach.

Steve gathered his strength and hunched his shoulders, trying to edge sideways, reaching down another inch. With his finger-tips he explored the rubble, to and fro, probing between the splintered wood and chunks of plaster.

Annie was silent, waiting. Then, miraculously, Steve's fingers found the leather strap again, still warm from her wrist. He lifted it and touched the smooth, convex watch face. The glass wasn't even broken.

Very gently he tapped it against a sharp edge of brick, then harder, and then harder still. The little circle of glass refused to break and he felt sweat gather under his hairline until a drop of it rolled down his forehead. It had suddenly become more important to know the time than anything had ever been. If he could find out what the time was they could hang on, counting the minutes together.

Trying to control his strength, he rapped the watch against the brick again. Then he felt the face again with the tip of his finger. The glass was shattered. He put the watch on his chest and picked the fragments of glass away. He touched the winder button and then felt for the hands. They felt tiny, like hairs, under his fingers. The second hand, moving against his skin, was like the touch of an insect on a summer afternoon. The watch was still going, then. He lifted his fingertip quickly.

'It's half past ten,' he said.

He had come into the store as it opened, only an hour ago. They had been lying here for only three-quarters of an hour, perhaps not even as long as that. He moved a little, as if trying to gauge how far down they were. It would take a long time, that was all he knew.

'Annie?'

'Hold my hand again,' she begged him.

He tucked the watch inside the fold of his coat and stretched out his hand. Their fingers touched at once, and they clasped hands.

'That's better,' she said. Steve wanted to take her hand and rub it between his own, chafing the warmth back into it, and his powerlessness struck home to him. She was badly hurt, and if she were to deteriorate before they came, he could do nothing to help her. At the same moment he realized how important it was that she was there. If he were alone, would he want to fight so hard?

'Tell me what you're thinking about,' he ordered her.

24

'Not thinking. I keep seeing and hearing things. So vivid.' Her voice sounded dreamy and distant now. 'All the old things. They say that happens, don't they?'

'No. What things, Annie?'

She had been seeing last Christmas, and the decorated tree in the front window.

Benjy was just two, sitting on the floor with his eyes and mouth wide open, reaching out for the shimmer of it.

'The boys. I was just seeing the boys. They grow up, and change all the time, but they still stay the same, themselves. If you haven't got children yourself you can't know what it's like. I don't think that even fathers have the same feeling.'

That was better, Steve thought, not really hearing what she said. Her voice was firmer now.

'I never thought about it before they came. Even when we decided to have a baby, when I was pregnant, I never understood what it would be like.'

They had driven to the hospital together, Annie and Martin, when she went into labour. That was the last time, she understood afterwards, that little drive through the night, when they were just themselves.

Thomas had been born, a mass of black hair and a red, angry face. He had opened his eyes and looked at her.

In the days afterwards the weight of responsibility had been like a millstone, and at the same time the love had buoyed her up so that she felt she was floating. Whenever the baby cried she felt it inside her like a knife, and his hours of contentment filled her with a satisfaction she had never known.

Steve was listening now, compelled by the tenderness in her voice. Yet with half of himself he thought, *Yes, I do know you*. She was the kind of woman who undid the front of her dress at dinner parties, and serenely breast-fed a milky-smelling bundle of baby. She almost certainly went to classes to learn how to have her babies in the approved way, and demonstrated her success afterwards to an admiring circle of women around the table. She talked about children all the time. She was talking about them

25

now, and the note in her voice held him. Yet she surprised him when she broke off and asked, 'Sounds desperate, does it?'

He almost smiled. She was quick, and that was good.

'Not desperate. I don't understand, that's all.'

'Cass wanted a baby, did she?'

Quick again.

'Yes, Cass wanted a baby. We talked about it, from time to time. Not much, in those last months, now I come to think of it. I was probably afraid that she might feel the same as you. No . . . I'm sorry, that didn't come out quite right. I didn't want to share her, perhaps. I wanted her to go on being Cass, not somebody's mother.'

'Somebody's mother,' Annie echoed softly.

Cass had sat cross-legged on the leather sofa, looking at him. She was wearing an armful of ivory and brass bangles and she turned them round and round, rattling them together.

'What about your work?' Steve had asked in exasperation.

'Other women manage, don't they? Quite a few of the girls I know do. We can always get a nanny to look after it while I'm working.'

'Why bother to have a baby at all, then?'

She had looked at him with her green eyes wide open and the bangles rattled and clicked under her fingers.

'Because I want one,' she answered at last.

'I don't.'

Once there was a baby, the responsibility shifted. Steve knew that; he understood that much of what Annie said. And not wanting to share Cass, was that the truth? He lay still, feeling the pain in his leg pushing its fingers up into his groin, and tasted the deception in his mouth. It was Cass who had had to share him, unwittingly at first, and then with increasing bitterness.

On the day that he had announced to his partner that he was going to marry her, Bob had rocked back in his desk chair and stared at him in disbelief.

'Married? *You?*'

'Why not? You're married, Phil is married, and so are most of my friends and all of our clients.'

'Yeah. Not you, though.'

'Perhaps I'm feeling the cold winds of solitude blowing around me.'

Bob had snorted with laughter. 'Wrap it round yourself for warmth, then. Should be long enough – you've given it plenty of exercise.'

'Fuck you, Jefferies.'

But Bob had only laughed even harder. 'What, me as well?'

Steve had married Jennifer Cassady two weeks later. He was thirty-six, moving easily along the business track that ran from comfortably off to rich. He was amused at the prospect of having a wife, and captivated by Cass's looks and abilities. They came from the same background and they were both busy climbing out of it. He thought they understood each other.

Cass was twenty-three and her career was blossoming. On the day that they were married, her face looked out across London from a hundred giant poster boards. It was suntan cream, that ad, Steve remembered. He had taken her out to dinner on the evening after she had been sent to the ad agency on a look-see for the same campaign.

On the day that they were married the party started at eleven o'clock sharp in the company's offices in Ingestre Place. Bob had masked his cynicism with an ad-man's enthusiasm, and had had every corner decorated with pink and white flowers. The bath in the directors' bathroom was full of ice and three cases of Bollinger.

'For starters,' Bob had said.

The bride and groom had planned to walk the two or three Soho streets to the restaurant they were to take over for their lunch party. But when they came out of their offices an open-topped vintage bus fluttering with pink and white ribbons was blocking the roadway. The bus was crammed with a cheering crowd of friends and clients, except for two empty front top seats. One of the videotape editors was driving, and the creative director of a medium-sized agency was dressed up as the conductor, complete with a polished brass ticket machine.

Steve had stopped dead on the pavement, but Cass had pulled him on.

'It's perfect,' she had breathed, half laughing and half crying. 'Did you ever see anything so perfect?'

The lunch went on all day and well into the night. Steve remembered it in hazy patches. He remembered the strippergram, and he remembered Cass looking at him, proud and proprietorial, down the long table.

The marriage had lasted for two years and eight months.

Quite soon after the wedding a day came when he had had lunch with a pretty girl, and he had bought her brandy afterwards. They had leant back against the green, velvet-padded walls of the restaurant booth to look at one another, and Steve had suddenly realized that they were sizing one another up in the old way. Afterwards they had walked along a sun-warmed street and the girl had looked sideways at him and said, 'Shall we go home for an hour?'

He had gone, almost without thinking, and he had enjoyed their rapid love-making more than he had done for months with Cass.

That hadn't been Vicky. Vicky had come along months later, when Cass already knew what he was doing. For a time there had been the two of them, and the tissue of deceptions and faked meetings and unnecessary business trips that went with it. And then, two years and eight months after the pink and white wedding, Cass had left him.

'I don't blame her,' the girl said.

The sound of her voice jolted Steve. For a moment, he hadn't been buried at all. He had been back at home, in the flat that Cass had had redecorated after their marriage. Then the darkness closed around him again, and he remembered whose hand he was holding.

'Feminine solidarity, is that it?' he asked.

'Partly.' Her voice was crisp.

It occurred to Steve that this girl wasn't so vulnerable. Then she added, 'Personal sympathy, mostly. Thinking how I'd feel if Martin did it.'

'And he doesn't?'

Almost to her surprise, Annie understood that it wasn't a taunt. He was asking a simple question.

'No, I don't think so.'

Martin came home between six and seven o'clock every evening. She was always glad to hear his bag thud on to the step as he dropped it to search in his pockets for the key. Tom would look up from his drawing, or the Lego, or the television, and say, 'Dad's home.' And if Benjy was still up he would slither in his pyjamas to the front door to meet him.

Seeing herself waiting with the boys, and a glass of wine, and the dinner simmering, Annie sometimes thought bleakly that they were like a family in a television commercial. Just as predictable. Almost as bland. Yet Martin did come home every night, to hug them in turn and to listen to the boys' recital of the day's events. After the boys had gone to bed they would sit down to dinner together, adding up in their talk the small change of another day. Annie knew the hours and the demands of Martin's job because he told her. She knew that there was no room in his life, between his work and the three of them waiting for him at home, for anyone else. She was glad of that.

And when the monotony of domestic life bored her, or the boys were awkward, or she was simply afraid that life was slipping past her in a succession of featureless days, she reminded herself carefully that her life was her own choice. She had chosen the smooth path that led round and round her family and her home.

Suddenly, with the pain like a hot band around her, Annie felt a longing for her life that hurt more than the pain of her body. It came back to her in every detail, the intimate pattern of their daily life. She smelt the freshness of clean sheets as she smoothed them out over the double mattress, heard the *ping* of the alarm clock on Martin's side of the bed, and saw the house

29

glow in all its worn, crowded, family-rubbed, patinated richness.

'I don't want to die,' she said.

Only a few days ago, she had sat over dinner with Martin and talked about what she hoped to do when Benjy went to full-day nursery. She would start work again, perhaps, just for a few hours a week. She had had the sense of wider avenues opening, giving new perspectives that would still let her stay in the places she loved. She had sensed her own good fortune like a jewel hanging round her neck.

'I can't bear to leave it.'

The man's hand holding hers was gentle.

'You aren't going to die.'

Out in the daylight it had stopped snowing, and it was growing steadily colder. The policemen manning the cordons moved to and fro across the strip of roadway to keep their feet warm, and their breath hung in front of them in grey clouds. The television crews, with the sightseers beyond them at a distance, huddled in their overcoats and waited as the minutes passed.

The slow, painstaking process of lifting the girders and rubble out of the hole had begun an hour ago. Now there was a flurry of movement amongst the firemen working under the tilted, ragged floors of the store. A broken beam was winched up and swung away to the side and one of the waiting ambulances started up and inched forward. A stretcher was carried across to where the firemen and doctors crouched in a circle, looking down. Then one of the doctors stood up and stepped backwards, over the heaps of wreckage. The firemen worked on until the watchers saw a flutter of something pale as another chunk of masonry was pulled away. A moment later a woman was lifted out of the hole. They laid her on the stretcher, and covered her face with a blanket.

The only sound was the crowd's sigh, as if it came from a single throat.

The cameramen swung their long black lenses with the

stretcher as it was carried, swaying and bumping, over to the ambulance. It was lifted inside and the heavy doors slammed. A moment later the ambulance nosed slowly away down the street.

'Fight for it, if you want it so much.'

Annie only half heard him. The sense of what she would lose had taken such a powerful hold of her. Her life seemed her own creation, not passionate or original, but warm, and sweet, and infinitely valuable. The threatening darkness, looming and shivering over her head, was unbearable. She wanted to move, throwing her limbs convulsively to fight her way out of it, and yet she couldn't. Her body hurt, and where it didn't hurt it didn't seem to exist any longer. Claustrophobia took hold of her and she felt a scream of terror rising again in her throat.

Annie opened her mouth and the scream came, and she heard the invisible mass around her swallow it up like a whisper.

'Don't,' Steve said harshly. 'Save that for when they might be able to hear us.'

Could they hear? Where were they? He felt the darkness as a weight now, too, heavy all around them. He strained his ears for a sound of the rescue that his reason told him must be under way, but he could hear nothing except the multiplying echoes of Annie's scream.

'Wait,' he whispered. He let go of her hand and moved his arm across his chest to feel for the watch. His fingers felt numb, but he stroked the face of it, trying to make sense of the tiny hands. He thought it might be half past eleven, and so a whole hour had passed, but then he realized that the hands might just be in the same position as last time. Perhaps he had misread them then, and the watch was broken after all. The dislocation frightened him. He had relied on being able to monitor the time passing, thinking that he could gauge how their strength was holding out. Then he felt the second hand brush against his fingertip again. He slipped the watch back into its place, reassured, and reached out for Annie's hand again.

'It's half past eleven. A whole hour has gone. We're doing all right.'

The relief in his voice and the touch of his hand pushed Annie's fear back again.

Fight, he had said, *if you want it so much*. To live. She moved her head and felt the door tilted against her cheek.

'You want to fight,' she said. 'It's precious for you, too, isn't it?'

Precious?

Steve tasted the word, trying it out against his memories of the last months. He began to understand it for Annie, listening to her talk about her children. The need to see them growing up, the fierce determination to protect them that he had glimpsed fleetingly in other women, that was part of her. He had nothing like that. Steve thought often, without much surprise or regret, that he was living at one step removed from life.

How long then, since the sharp edge of pleasure had gone? Not just pleasure, but anticipation, need, fear, even?

He thought backwards, a long tunnel of days and nights.

Before Vicky. He had wanted Vicky, but he had also been quite sure of getting her.

He had met her at a party, a party for a book that Cass had done some modelling for. Vicky worked for the publishing company. She looked frumpy, in a corduroy skirt and a thick, knitted jersey. They had been introduced and Steve had asked some polite questions and then looked past her, to see where Cass had gone. But Vicky had moved to stand squarely in front of him again. Then he had noticed that she had unusual dark eyes in a clever, challenging face, and that something was amusing her. He suddenly realized that he wanted to find out what it was, and at the same moment Vicky had shifted her weight, resting it on one leg with the other knee bent. She had tilted her head to one side, still looking at him, and he had imagined the line of her body under the thick clothes. They had talked for a moment or two more and then Vicky had licked the corner of her mouth, quickly, like a cat. She had put her hand up to cover it, like a schoolgirl trying out a kiss in the mirror. They had both laughed, then.

Steve had taken her to bed two days later. Her inventiveness, her energy and her exotic tastes had surprised him.

'Did you learn *that* at LMH?' he had asked.

'Some of it,' she grinned at him.

Yet even then he had been moving with the sense of inevitability, and their affair had unfolded in front of him as though he were watching it on screen.

Was he so used to the distance, then, that he couldn't remember when it had opened up? Steve lay still, feeling the cramp in his outstretched arm and listening to the painful, irregular indrawn breaths of the girl beside him. The girl was real, he felt her as close as if he were holding her in his arms. He was waiting for each of her breaths, willing her to draw the next, and the next. The blackness was real, and so was the dust that coated his mouth and stung in his eyes, and the pain was real too.

Steve felt a sudden frightening desire to laugh at the fact that it should take *this* to stir him. He understood the fragility of his life and the possibility of survival, the need for it, reared in front of him like a wall. He was afraid, as frightened as Annie was, but he forced himself to shake off the clutch of it with a determination that was almost pleasurable.

Precious, she had said. No, his life wasn't that. It was hollow and mechanical and faintly shameful. The need to laugh faded, and Steve saw as clearly as if a bright light had been turned on overhead that what was precious was the need to fight, and he had lost that long ago.

'I always wanted to be rich,' he said.

'And are you?'

He thought for a moment. 'It's a long time since I've had to live without something I wanted because I didn't have the money to buy it.' There was a pause before he added, 'The natural result is that you find yourself not wanting anything anyway. I've got a handsome, rather unlived-in flat and several quite good modern paintings. I've got a little house in the hills behind Draguignan that I hardly ever go to. I've got a BMW, more suits than I can get around to wearing, all sorts of *things*. What else is there?'

Annie listened, trying to picture what he looked like from the sound of his voice and the warmth of his hand. Something in what he said touched her. She knew that he had never said it before.

'Is that what you wanted?' she asked.

Steve didn't answer. To have answered would have been to peer into an abyss, gaping darker than the real darkness where they lay. It was suddenly so very far from what he wanted that he had completely lost his bearings. Wasn't there anything, then, waiting, if this weight was ever lifted off the two of them?

He lifted his head an inch or two, straining his neck muscles, as if the hopeless movement could push the wreckage and let the daylight come flooding down.

Was it still snowing? What were they doing up there, so long?

'I want to stay alive, like you,' he whispered. He did, and he wouldn't let himself ask, *For what?*

'We will be saved,' she whispered back to him. 'I know we will.'

Steve wanted to reach out and take her in his arms. It was the first flicker of her own determination, not cajoled from her by his own will. He felt the warmth of gratitude and it was like weakness because his eyes suddenly filled with tears.

No. Don't do that. It was important not to be weak. He must keep on holding her hand, listening to her breathing.

'And you, Annie? Have you got what you want?'

She was vividly aware of the truth that he had offered her. She could feel the intimacy uncoiling between them, incongruous, yet as important as the need to contain the pain, as important as holding on to her wavering consciousness.

She would offer him the truth in return.

Very quietly, so that he had to strain to catch the words, she said, 'I chose the easy option.'

Two

Martin waited until the kettle boiled and the automatic switch clicked back into the off position. He took the coffee jar out of the cupboard and spooned the granules into a flowered mug, then poured the water in so that the liquid frothed up in black bubbles. He opened the door of the refrigerator and peered in, frowning when he saw that there was no milk. Then it occurred to him that the milkman must have been and gone by now. He went up the steps from the kitchen into the hall and pulled the door open over the scatter of minicab cards and free newsheets that had been pushed in through the letterbox. His frown vanished when he saw that there were four pints of milk beside the doormat in the porch. He was whistling as he scooped them up and carried them back into the kitchen. He left three bottles on the worktop and splashed milk from the fourth into his coffee mug. Then, with his thumb hooked over the end of the spoon still standing in it, he carried his coffee through into the sitting room where the boys were sitting side by side on the rug. They were watching Saturday morning television.

As he came in Thomas jumped up and jabbed the buttons.

'Nothing on,' he complained.

Martin saw the news picture of the store with the jagged cleft struck through the middle of it, and he caught the reporter's words.

'. . . this morning just after nine thirty. One body has already been recovered from the wreckage, and the search continues. Police have not yet confirmed . . .'

The image vanished as Thomas impatiently prodded again. It was replaced by the test card of another channel, then by a commercial for breakfast cereal.

'I like this one,' Benjy shouted.

Martin stood for a frozen second, seeing his sons' heads bobbing up and down, hiding the little square of coloured screen. Then he lunged forward and the hot coffee splashed over his fingers. He stepped between the boys and crouched down in front of the set, fumbling for the channel button.

He heard Thomas protest, 'Oh, *Dad* . . .' and then the picture flickered and steadied itself again. He saw a reporter standing in a windswept street with a hand microphone held close to his mouth. Behind him Martin could see a corner of the store, its bulk oddly foreshortened. He knew exactly where it was without having to listen to the report. Annie had lived in a poky little flat in one of the little streets behind it in the days before they were married. They had walked past the high façade a hundred times on their way to a pub that they liked, just beyond the tube station. The tube was just opposite the store, away to the news reporter's right.

'No survivors have been found as yet, but one body was lifted out a few moments ago . . .'

What was he saying?

Martin knelt down, pressing closer to the screen as if he could draw a contradiction of the implacable picture from it. He saw the reporter's cold-pinched face dissolve into its component blips of colour, but the hideously altered shape of the big store never wavered.

'Hush, Tom,' he said.

What had Annie told him? He struggled to recall the casual words, seeing her run upstairs towards him as he stood with Benjy in his arms. She hadn't said exactly where she was going. But it was a direct journey from here by tube. And Annie often shopped there. It was almost 'her' store, from the days when she had lived so close to it. As he watched the camera panned away from the newsman to a limited panorama of ambulances and fire

36

engines. There were firemen working in yellow helmets, and policemen hemming them in.

Martin was cold, trembling with it, and the sick certainty that Annie was there. What had the man said?

One body was lifted out a few moments ago . . .

Martin stood up, almost stumbling, and the coffee splashed again. He put it down on top of the set and in the same moment the report ended. The picture changed to a solemn-faced studio continuity announcer.

'We will be bringing you more news of that explosion in London's West End as soon as it reaches us. And now . . .'

Martin turned away, moving so stiffly that Thomas looked up at him.

'What's the matter, Dad?'

He saw Annie's features printed on the boy's face and irrational fear gripped him in the stomach.

'Dad?'

'I . . . I'm going out to look for Mummy. I'll call Audrey and ask her to come and stay with you for a while.'

Even as he said it he knew that he should stay where he was and wait, but he couldn't suppress his primitive urge to rush to the store and pull at the fallen bricks with his bare hands. He snatched up the telephone and dialled the number. It seemed to take an eternity to explain to Audrey. He stammered over the neutral phrases that wouldn't frighten the boys yet would bring her, quickly. They stood in front of him, reflecting his anxiety back at him, magnified by their bewilderment.

'Why?' Thomas said. 'She's only gone shopping, hasn't she? Why do you have to find her?'

'I want to bring her home, Tom. I'll go and get her, you'll see.' He had a picture in his mind's eye of crowded shops with thousands of people milling to and fro, and then the bombed store, silent, as he had seen it on the television. How would he find Annie, in the midst of it all? He made himself smile at the boys. 'Stay here with Audrey, and we'll be back soon.'

Benjy's mouth opened, making a third circle with his round

eyes. 'I want Mummy.' He was frightened, picking the fear up out of the air. Martin didn't know how to soothe him while his own anxiety pounded inside him. 'I want *Mummy*.' He began to cry, tears spilling out of his eyes and running down his face.

Martin knelt down and held him. 'I'm going to get her, Benjy. I told you.'

Through the front window he saw Audrey coming up the path. He straightened up and taking Benjy's hand he led him to the door. Audrey was wearing an overcoat open over her apron, and Martin saw that she hadn't stopped to change out of her slippers. They left big, blurred prints in the dusting of powdery snow that lay on the path. Her urgency fanned his fear and he felt his hand tightening over Benjy's so that the child whimpered and tried to pull away.

Audrey came in, incongruously stamping her slippers on the doormat to knock off the snow.

'Do you know for sure that she was going down there?' she asked at once.

'No. But I think she might have.'

'You should stay here, you know. Wait for the news. You can't do anything there.'

'I know, Audrey, but I can't sit here. I want to be near, at least.' She was looking at him, her face creased with sympathy. Martin put on his sheepskin coat, feeling in the pockets for his keys.

'If . . . she telephones here,' Audrey said carefully, 'I'll tell her what's happened and where you've gone.'

'I'll ring in as soon as I can.'

He was ready now. He hugged the boys in turn, quickly. Benjy had stopped crying and was holding the corner of Audrey's apron. Tom followed Martin to the door and reached out to him as it opened, the cold air blowing in around them.

'Is . . . is Mum in that shop, the one on the TV?'

Martin's throat felt as if it were closing on the words as he lied, 'No, she isn't. But if there are things like that going on today, I think she should come home. Don't worry.'

He closed the door and left the three of them standing. He ran back over Audrey's slipper-prints to the gate, and to the car parked in the roadway. Inside was the familiar litter of crumpled papers and discarded toys. Annie used the car mostly, for taking the boys to and fro. The thought came to him: *What if she's dead?* and he leant forward over the steering wheel. He heard his own supplication – Please, let her be safe.

Then the engine roared and he swung the wheel sharply, heading the car towards the image of the store that he could see as clearly as he could see the road dipping ahead of him.

The police commander followed his opposite number from the fire brigade down the steps of the control van and across the few yards of pavement to the gaping, shattered windows. In the nearest one, on the corner, a tall Christmas tree made out of some green shiny stuff had been blown sideways. It lay amongst torn screens papered with scarlet satin ribbons. Broken glass lay everywhere, and the commander's shoes crunched in it as he walked.

They came to what had once been the big doors, and looked upwards. The grey sky showed overhead through the torn ends of girders and ragged floors. Dust still whirled in the air and it blew up in choking gusts behind the firemen as they inched under the tangle of brick and metal.

A young policeman stepped forward and handed the commander a protective helmet. There were two other men waiting. One, a big man in a waterproof jacket, was the borough engineer. He had been called straight out of bed and, under his waterproofs and sweater, he was still in his pyjamas. The other man was grey-faced and his silver hair stood up in unbrushed wings at the sides of his head. He held a helmet in one hand, and as the senior officers approached he put it on with an awkward, unpractised movement. He was one of the directors of the store, and he had arrived ten minutes ago from his home in Hampstead.

'Our main problem,' the fire brigade officer was saying, and he gestured upwards as he spoke, 'is that this portion of the frontage is almost entirely unsupported. There is a real danger that our work underneath will topple it this way.' He held his arm up to illustrate, flat-handed as if he was directing traffic, and then swung it graphically downwards. Even as they stood there conferring the crooked edifice above them seemed to creak and sway.

'It will take hours to bring it down from the top,' the engineer said. 'Erecting the scaffolding alone will take time. My works people can do it as quickly as is humanly possible, of course, but . . .'

The unspoken truth was that if there were any survivors underneath, they couldn't wait that long.

'Can you go on down as it is?' the director asked, 'whilst the work goes on to secure the frontage?'

The policeman and the fireman glanced at each other before the fireman said, 'Yes. At some risk.'

There was another pause. The policeman waited, touching the corner of his small, clipped moustache with a fingertip. At length he said, 'Is that the consensus, gentlemen? To continue the rescue operation and to work to make the façade safe, as far as possible, at the same time?'

The three men nodded. 'Good,' the policeman said quietly. 'Thank you.'

They waited side by side, sheltered from the wind by the threatening frontage. A medical team stood a few yards away, huddled together, not speaking. Everyone was watching the black-coated backs of two firemen who were kneeling side by side to lift chunks of masonry away from the lip of a black hollow.

'Heat camera pinpointed this one. They can see her now: It's another young girl.'

The commander glanced across at the medical team.

'Alive?'

'I'm afraid not.'

The minutes passed. Overhead a crane was being manoeuvred into position to begin the painstaking process of dismantling the toppling store front, piece by piece. The rescue workers in their helmets passed to and fro underneath it, never looking up. The commander waited until the second body was recovered. The girl's legs looked pitifully thin and white as they lifted her out and laid her on a stretcher. She followed her friend into an ambulance and then away through the cordons towards the hospital.

The commander ducked his head and walked back through the splinters of glass to the trailer. A preliminary report from the bomb squad was waiting for him. It had been a single bomb, sited on the third floor towards the back of the store, probably in a cloakroom. It appeared now that the possibility of another unexploded bomb hidden elsewhere in the store could be discounted.

'Thank Christ for that, at least,' the commander murmured. The explosives experts had been at work for an hour. One of them handed him a second report and he glanced quickly at it. Diagrams showed the probable direction of the blast waves following the explosion, and the sliding masses of rubble.

'Almost exactly the same as at Brighton, sir,' one of the officers murmured.

'Except that by a rare stroke of good fortune the PM hadn't slipped in there for her Christmas shopping.'

'No, sir.'

According to the calculations, the most hopeful place for survivors in the centre of the store was the basement, sheltered from the falling wreckage by the reinforced thickness of the ground floor. The commander stared through the trailer window at the tangled mountain resting on top of that floor. He put his finger up to his moustache again.

'Side access to the basement?' he asked.

'Almost entirely blocked, sir. They're working to clear it from both sides now.'

The commander looked down at his watch. It was eleven fifty-five. If there were any survivors in the basement, they had been buried for two hours and thirteen minutes.

*

Eleven years ago.

Annie wasn't cold any more. She felt almost comfortable, as if she was drifting in a small boat on a wide, dark lake. Steve's hand was her anchor.

She was trying to remember what had happened eleven years ago. It was important for herself, but it was more important still because she wanted to tell Steve. She felt him close to her, listening. The sensation of drifting intensified. They were both of them afloat, a long way from the shore.

'I chose the easy option,' she said again.

'And what was it?' His voice was as warm as if his mouth was against her ear and his fingers tangled in her hair.

'I chose what would be safe, and simple. Because it would be . . . wholesome.' Annie laughed, a cracked note. 'That's a funny notion, isn't it? As if you can turn your life into wholemeal bread.'

Her memory was clear now, the images as vivid as early-morning dreams.

The day she met Matthew was exactly eight weeks before her wedding day. She came up the stairs to the fifth floor of the mansion block where her friend Louise lived. The green-painted stairwell smelt of carbolic soap and metal polish, just as it always did. The lift was out of order, just as it always was and Annie was panting, the John Lewis carrier bag bumping against her leg, as she reached Louise's door. She rang the bell and when Louise opened the door Annie held the bag up in triumph.

'I got it. Ten yards, hideously expensive. You'd better like it.'

'Hmm.' Louise had taken the bag and peered into it. 'Oh, yes. I'll make you a wedding dress such as has never been made before. Annie, this is Matthew.'

He was sitting on the floor with his back against Louise's sofa and his legs stretched out in jeans with frayed bottoms. He had fair, almost colourless hair cut too short for his thin face, grey eyes, and his bare chest showed under his half-open shirt. He was in his early twenties, two or three years younger than Annie was.

He looked up at her and the first thing he said to her was 'Don't marry him, whoever he is. Marry me.'

Annie laughed, slotting him into her category *automatically flirtatious*, but Matthew hadn't even smiled. He had just looked at her, and Louise stood awkwardly behind them with the carrier bag dangling in her hand. They didn't talk about the dress that day. They had tea instead, sitting in a sunlit circle on Louise's rug.

Matthew had been living in Mexico for a year, working as a labourer on a peasant farm in exchange for his food and a bed in a lean-to shack. He told them about the long days monotonously working the thin soil, the efforts at summer irrigation using water brought on the backs of donkeys from the trickling river.

'Why were you there?' Annie asked. The self-conscious hippiedom would have irritated her in anyone else, but Matthew was perfectly matter-of-fact.

'I was thinking. I'm very bad at it. Can't do it when there are any distractions.'

'And why did you come home?'

He grinned at her. 'I'd finished thinking.'

They went on talking while the sun moved across the rug. Annie realized that it was herself and Matthew talking. Louise was sitting in silence, watching them. At six o'clock Annie stood up to go. Matthew stood up too, and she saw that he was tall and very thin.

'I'll come a little way with you,' he said.

'I . . .'

'I would like to.'

Annie left her bag of wedding dress material on Louise's floor. When she was standing with Matthew on the pavement outside she remembered that she hadn't even arranged to come back and look at Louise's design sketches. She hesitated, wondering whether she should go back upstairs, but a taxi came rumbling down the street and Matthew flagged it down. He opened the door for her and they sat side by side on the slippery seat, looking out at the rush-hour traffic idling in the sun.

'Where are we going?'

'To St James's Park,' Matthew said. She discovered later that he used his last two pound notes to pay the driver.

It was May, the first day of summer's warm weather. The grass was dotted with abandoned deckchairs, in secretive pairs and in sociable groups of three or four.

The setting sun slanted obliquely through patterns of curled leaves and glittered on the water. They walked under the trees, talking. It seemed to Annie that this hollow-cheeked boy had simply side-stepped the rituals of acquaintanceship and friendship, and had made her a lover without ever having touched her.

They stopped on the bridge to look down at the ducks drawing fans of ripples in their wake, and their shadows fell superimposed on the water.

Looking at the shape they made, Matthew said, 'You see? We belong together.'

'No. I'm going to marry Martin. We've known each other for seven years.'

'That's no reason for marrying him. Any more than you can dismiss me because you've known me for less than seven hours.'

She turned to look at him then, suddenly sombre. He had come to block the wide, smooth road she was walking down and he was pointing his finger down narrow lanes that turned sharply, enticing her. She felt angry with him, and at the same time she wanted to step forward so that their faces could touch.

'I meant what I said, you know.' Matthew met her stare. He put his hand out and stroked her hair, their first contact.

'Do you ask everyone you meet to marry you? Did you ask Louise when she offered to let you sleep on her sofa till you found somewhere else?'

He laughed at her. 'I've never said it before in my life. But when you came into the room, I knew you, Annie. I knew your face, and your walk, and your voice, and I knew what you were going to say.'

She couldn't contradict him, because she knew it was the truth. Matthew didn't invent or exaggerate.

'I don't know you,' she said defiantly. 'I don't know anything about you.'

He took her arm, drawing it through his and settling it so that her head was against his shoulder. They began to walk again with their backs to the sunset and their shadows pointing ahead of them.

'I'll tell you,' he offered. 'I'll tell you whatever you want to know. There isn't much, so it won't take too long.'

Matthew was the only son of an industrialist, a self-made tycoon with a newspaper name. The family assumption had always been that Matthew would emulate his dynamic father. But from the day he was old enough to begin to assert himself, Matthew had refused to conform to his father's requirements. His only interest at school had been woodwork, until he became really good at it – at which point he gave it up for ever. When his school contemporaries were heading for Oxford, Matthew turned his back on them and set out on the hippie trail to Afghanistan. He had supported his travels ever since with menial jobs, working in exchange for food, somewhere to sleep, for enough money to carry him on to the next place.

'What were you thinking about in Mexico?' Annie asked him.

'I was thinking about what I should do. And then I felt the pull to come home, so I came. And here you are.'

'Don't you think,' Annie said, 'that you might have seized upon me because you think you ought to? That you're trying to make me someone I'm not, to fill a need in yourself?'

He didn't hesitate for a second. 'No. You are the woman I want. You just are. I always knew I would recognize you, and I have. It's the truth, Annie. You know it too. Admit it.'

'I suppose you're going to tell me that we've been lovers in some previous life.'

Matthew dropped her arm and stared at her. 'Certainly not. What d'you think I am? I don't believe in all that mystical muck.'

They laughed until Annie wiped the tears out of her eyes and rested her forehead against his shoulder, and Matthew put his arms around her, still smiling. It was almost dark, and the cars swished rhythmically along the Mall under the thin glare of the street lights. She waited for him to kiss her. Matthew's mouth moved against her hair.

'I'm hungry,' he said.

So he wasn't going to kiss her. That made it easier, perhaps.

'Let's go and have something to eat.' Annie moved away a little, regretting the warmth of his arm. 'There's a little Italian place in Victoria.'

'I haven't got any money,' Matthew said.

'My treat,' she answered lightly.

They began to walk again and he caught her hand. Her ring scraped his fingers and he lifted their clasped hands to peer at it. The stones glinted coldly.

'Oh dear, diamonds,' he murmured. 'I can't give you any. Will you mind that? Will Martin want this one back?'

She was angry again then, her anger fuelled by a surge of guilt. She pulled her hand out of his and stuffed her clenched fists into the pockets of her jacket.

'I'm going to marry Martin,' she repeated. 'Eight weeks from today. With a ring that matches this one.'

'Very nice,' Matthew said icily. They walked over the grass together, silent, both of them angry. But when Matthew spoke again his voice had softened.

'What are you going to do, Annie?'

She shrugged her shoulders, suddenly bewildered. 'I don't know. Some thinking, like you. I just don't know.'

'I can wait,' Matthew told her, and she knew that he would.

It wasn't a double life, exactly. Half of it was a dream-world, and the other half was briskly real. She went to Louise's several times, and stood for hours having the dress pinned on her. The invitations came from the printers and she went through the lists with her mother, and then addressed and stamped the dozens of envelopes. She spent weekends with Martin in the flat they had bought, painting the window frames and helping him to put up cupboards in the kitchen. And whenever she could she ran away to be with Matthew.

He drew her into his world, and she discovered with a kind of fascinated fear that Matthew existed without any constraints at all. He didn't live anywhere. He drifted from a borrowed bed-sitter to someone else's sofa, and from there to an empty room over a shop where he slept on a blanket spread on the floor.

There was plenty of casual work in those days. He washed up in a café, and then spent a week labouring for a builder. He lived in the room over the shop because he was building display cabinets downstairs for the owner.

He never made plans, and he never worried about what might happen to him tomorrow. And so, Annie thought, he could give all his energy to enjoying whatever came. It was the quality of Matthew's enjoyment that she loved. Afterwards, she thought that the hours she spent with him were the happiest of her life.

When he had money, he spent it without thinking. He loved good food, and he would dig out his one presentable outfit and take her to grand restaurants where he insisted on spending almost a whole week's wages on a single meal. He derived such pleasure from the plush surroundings and the procession of exotic dishes that Annie couldn't refuse to go, or even persuade him to let her pay her share.

'You must know that it's only any fun,' Matthew said, 'if you can't afford to do it. My father eats lunch in places like this every day of his life, and all he ever wants is grilled sole and mineral water.'

When there was no money, Matthew was endlessly ingenious at finding free pleasures.

In his company Annie discovered tiny parks that she had never known existed, and she saw more pictures and sculptures and Wren churches than she had done in all her time as an art student. It didn't even matter what they did, particularly. As long as she had an hour or two to spend with him, Matthew was happy. He seemed to want nothing more than her company and their activities, whether they were free or costly, were simply an extra, pleasurable bonus. When she was married and thought back to the benches beside the river and the faintly stuffy smell of the National Gallery, the elaborate dinners and the sudden taxis, she wondered if the times with Matthew were the last in her life when she had felt young.

He made her feel other things, too. They made love for the first time in the room over the shop. Annie had come straight from work. It was a warm evening at the beginning of June and she was wearing a sleeveless blue cotton dress. Her hair crackled with electricity over her shoulders, and when Matthew opened the door he reached out and put his hand underneath the thickness of it, his fingers stroking her neck.

After the first evening in St James's Park, he had kissed her once or twice, lightly, almost jokingly. She had convinced herself that she was relieved that there was no more to it, and that she wasn't betraying Martin in any way. But she had also known that Matthew was simply waiting, according to some system of his own, for the right time.

He took her hand and led her across the bare floorboards to the grey blanket with a single sleeping bag spread out on top of it. Annie saw an electric kettle, the neat tin box where Matthew kept his minimal supplies of food, his spare clothes folded tidily in an open suitcase. He stood behind her, lifting her hair and bending down to kiss the nape of her neck. He undid the buttons at the back of her dress and drew her against him, his hands over her breasts.

'Here?' Annie asked. She looked at the uncurtained windows with the sun lighting up the coating of grime and throwing elongated golden squares on the floor. She could feel Matthew's smile curling against her neck.

'My layers of dust are as effective as your net curtains.'

'I don't have net curtains.'

'I expect your mother does.'

Her dress dropped to the floor and they stepped sideways, away from it, glued together. With the tip of his tongue, Matthew drew a line from the nape of her neck to the hollow at the base of her spine. Then, with his hands on the points of her hips, he turned her round to face him. Annie thought that she could see the sunlight shining straight through the taut skin over his cheekbones. Her hands were shaking but she reached out and unbuttoned his shirt, her movements echoing his. Then she looked at the shape of him, seeing the pale skin reddened from his labouring job, the bones arching at the base of his throat and the hollows behind them. She closed her eyes, and his mouth touched hers.

'You see? It doesn't matter where,' Matthew said. He took her hand and led her to the blanket, and they lay down together.

It was the most perfectly erotic experience she had ever had. Matthew moved unhurriedly, almost dreamily, and he kissed the thin skin between her fingers, and each of her toes, and then the arches of her feet. He was so slow that she felt he was torturing her, but when at last he came inside her it was so quick and powerful that she heard herself cry out, as she had never done before. When at last they lay still, with Matthew's arms around her and her head on his shoulder, she said softly, 'I thought it only happened like that in films, and books.'

He smiled at her. 'I knew objectively that it could probably happen in real life. But I've never known it like that before, either. We do belong together, Annie, my love. Listen to me. I love you.'

She felt real pain then, and she crouched in his arms trying to contain it. 'Matthew, I . . .'

But he put his hand up to cover her mouth. 'Be quiet,' he ordered her.

Martin knew, of course. He turned to her one day, tidily putting his paintbrush down on the tin lid so that it wouldn't drip gloss paint on to their kitchen floor.

'Who is he, Annie?'

He was trying to sound casual. Annie knew him so well that she understood exactly why. He would try to make light of the threat for as long as he could. But that didn't mean that it wasn't hurting him.

'You don't know him. I met him a month ago, at Louise's.'

They were standing shoulder to shoulder now, looking out into the well of the block of flats with its smudges of pigeon droppings. She couldn't see his face but she knew he would be frowning, the vertical lines deepening between his eyebrows.

Carefully, he said, 'Do I need to worry about it?'

There was a long silence. *Decide*, Annie commanded herself. *You must decide*.

At last, recognizing her own cowardice and with the sense of a light fading somewhere as she had been afraid it would, she whispered, 'No.'

Martin's hand covered hers. There were paint splashes on his fingers. She could feel the set of his shoulders easing with relief.

'I won't worry, then.' He squeezed her hand and let it go, and then picked up his brush to start work again.

'What is it?' he asked after a moment. 'Pre-marital itch?'

'I suppose so,' she said dully. She despised herself for reducing Matthew to that, even for Martin's sake.

The time trickled by. It was the hottest summer for years, and every day that passed seemed burnt into her memory by the blistering heat of the pavements and the hard blue light of the sky. Matthew finished his carpentry work at the shop and he moved out of the grubby little room. He was staying with another friend now, unrolling his sleeping bag on yet another sofa. Annie wouldn't let him come to her flat because Martin had a key to it too. They met when and where they could, and she was amazed by his ability to make her forget everything else that was happening. He made her feel irresponsibly happy. When she was with him, she knew that this was reality, and the other half of her life, the half that was occupied with shopping for clothes for her honeymoon and choosing flowers for her bouquet, was the dreamworld.

Then, only a week before the wedding, Matthew asked her again.

They were at yet another friend's home, but the house was empty for the weekend this time and so Matthew automatically made it his own. They were in bed, and Annie was lying with her hair spread out over the pillow. She was thinking exhaustedly, *This must be the last time.*

'Annie, will you marry me?'

Traffic noises from the street outside, and evening birds twittering in the trees in the square. She had a taste of her future with Martin as she lay there. There would be evenings like this in a house that was really theirs. Peace, and comfort, cooking smells and simple domestic rhythms, and Martin who she knew, and understood, and loved. She closed her eyes so as not to see Matthew's face, because what she felt for him went deeper than love.

'I can't jilt him,' she whispered. 'I can't marry you.'

'Those are two quite distinct and separate incapabilities,' he told her gently. 'Which is the real one?'

What would it be like to be married to Matthew?

There would be a succession of rented rooms, and Matthew would manage to make her feel that they were palaces. There would be the wild swings from penury to extravagance and back again, and no two days would ever follow each other in the same way. She was sure that they would be happy. Ever since she had known him he had made happiness blaze like fire inside her. What she didn't know was how long that could last.

She was afraid that a day would come when the discomforts would begin to matter, and pleasure would fade into resentment. The shortcomings were her own. She was cautious and predictable and careful, and Matthew was none of those things. She longed to be like him, to cut herself loose and sail with him, but she couldn't do it. She would live her life with Martin and it would be tranquil, and sunny, and safe. The peaks of joy would be out of her reach, but she didn't think that there were troughs of despair waiting for her either.

She made herself meet Matthew's steady grey stare.

'I'm a coward,' she said. 'I can't marry you.'

He bent his head. Their fingers were locked together and the knuckles of both hands were white. Then he looked up again.

'I know why you think you can't. You believe that married men have mortgages and salaries to meet them, and prospects and some kind of security to offer you. You're afraid that after a while you'll begin to resent me because I haven't. That's true, isn't it?'

She nodded miserably. There was more than that, but that was the stupid, pedestrian nub of it.

'Well. I went to see my father today. I asked him for a job in the company. There was a long lecture about having to start at the bottom like everyone else. Learn the business. Not expect any quarter just because I'm the boss's son. Work hard and prove my worth.' Matthew's face was a picture of resigned boredom. It made her laugh in the midst of everything, and he beamed back at her. 'I nearly threw one of his onyx inlaid executive toys at him, but I restrained myself for your sake. After the lecture he told me that he was glad I'd decided to pull myself up by my boot-straps . . . *boot-straps*, I promise you . . . and I could certainly have some simple tasks allotted to me within the corporate structure. So there, now.' His smile was dazzling. 'I'll be so exactly like everyone else that only experts like you will be able to tell the difference. I'll be able to buy you a diamond ring, and a three-piece suite and a Kenwood Chef, if that's what you really want.'

He was trying to make her laugh because he didn't want her to guess the magnitude of what he was really offering. He was holding out everything he valued, his freedom and his independence, for her to take and dispose of. Annie felt the tears like needles behind her eyes.

'I don't want you to do anything for my sake. I don't want to see you go off every morning in a suit. Thank you for offering to do it, but I'm not worth it.'

She hadn't meant to let him see her crying, but the tears came anyway. Matthew made a little, bitter noise.

'I can't win, can I? You won't marry me when I have no

prospects. You won't marry me when I do, because Matthew with prospects isn't Matthew.'

A space had opened between them, mocking their physical closeness, and Annie knew that they would never bridge it again.

'I'm sorry,' she said hopelessly. She felt smaller, and more selfish and more ashamed, than she had ever done in her life.

'Tell me one thing,' he said. 'Tell me that it isn't just because you haven't the guts to cancel your wedding and send back the horrible presents and shock all your mother's friends.'

Annie lifted her chin to look straight at him. 'If I was courageous enough to marry you, I would be courageous enough to do all that.'

Matthew let go of her hand. He slid away from her across the bed and lay looking through the window into the trees in the square.

'All the time,' he said softly, almost to himself, 'all the time until tonight I was sure that I could win.'

There was nothing else to say. Heavy with the knowledge that she had disappointed him Annie slid out of bed and put her clothes on. When she was dressed she went to the bedroom door and stood for a moment looking at him, but Matthew never turned his gaze from the trees outside the window. She closed the bedroom door and went downstairs, and out into the square where the day's heat still hung lifelessly over the paving stones.

She never saw Matthew again.

She went home to her flat, and found Martin sitting at the kitchen table waiting for her.

'I'm back,' she said simply. Her face still felt stiff with dried tears.

Martin stood up and came across the room to her, then put his arms around her and held her against him.

'I'm glad, Annie.'

They were married a week later on a brilliantly bright July day. Their approving families were there, and the dozens of friends they had accumulated over the years of knowing one another, and they had walked out under the rainbow hail of

53

confetti to smile at the photographer who was waiting to capture their memories for them. The photograph stood in a silver frame on the bow-fronted mahogany chest in their bedroom. Eleven years later, when she picked the photograph up to dust it and glanced down into her own face, Annie had forgotten how painful that smile had been.

'I had forgotten,' she said. 'But it's so vivid now. I can see his face so clearly.'

The boat was rocking gently on the dark water, and in that movement Steve's hand had become Matthew's, holding hers, pulling her back. His voice was different but she knew his face, and the way he moved, and she could remember every hour that they had spent together as if she was reliving them.

For an instant she was suffused with happiness. *It isn't too late*, she thought. *Why was I so sure that it was?*

She smiled, and then felt the stinging pain at the corner of her mouth where the blood had dried.

Not Matthew's hand. This man was Steve, a stranger, and now more important to her than anyone. She felt another pain, not physical now but as quick and sharp as a razor slash. It was the pain of longing and regret.

'I wish I could reach you,' she said. 'I wish we could hold on to each other.'

Tears began to run out of the corners of her eyes and she felt them running backwards into her knotted hair.

'We are holding each other,' Steve said. 'Here.'

The pressure of his hand came again, but Annie ached to turn and find the warmth of him, pressing her face against his human shelter. She was afraid that the weeping would take possession of her. It pulled at her face with its fingers, distorting her mouth into a gaping square and the blood began to run again from the corner of it.

'It's too late,' she cried out, 'too late for everything.'

This was the end, here in their tomb of wreckage. The tidy plait of her life stretched behind her, the stridently glittering threads of the past softened by time into muted harmonies of colour. Martin and she had woven it together. She thought of her husband and of Thomas and Benjamin left to look at the brutally severed plait, the raw ends uselessly fraying. Sobs pulled at her shoulders, and her hair tore at her scalp.

'Don't cry,' Steve said. 'Please, Annie, darling, don't cry. It isn't too late.' If they only could hold each other, he thought, they could draw the shared warmth around them like armour. He tried to move again, and knew that he couldn't pull his crushed leg with him.

'My mother's ill,' Annie said abruptly. 'She's got cancer, they've just told her. It must be just the same.'

Steve could follow her thoughts, unconfined, flickering to and fro. The extra dimension of understanding was eerie but he took it gratefully. 'No,' he contradicted her. 'Not the same sense of loss. No waste. Your mother has seen you grow up, marry. Seen her grandchildren. Illness isn't the same as . . . violence.'

He wouldn't say *violent death*, but he sensed Annie's telepathic hearing as clear as his own.

'Perhaps . . . perhaps everyone's death is violent, when it comes.'

They were silent then, but they were unified by fear and they could hear one another's thoughts, whispered in childlike voices quite unlike their own.

'If they come for us in time,' Annie said, 'and there is any life left for us that isn't just lying here, I won't let any more of the days go. I'll count each one. I'll make it live. I've shrugged so many days off without a single memory. Dull days. Resigned days. Just one of them would be so precious now. Do you understand, Steve?'

'Oh yes,' he answered. 'I understand. Annie, when we're free we can do whatever we like.'

Steve tried to think about how it would be, and nothing would come except confused images of Vicky, and of unimportant restaurants where he had sat over lunches, and of preview theatres where he waited in the dark for clients to watch their

55

fifteen- or thirty-second loop of commercial over and over again. 'Run it through a couple more times, David, will you?' His own voice. 'Did you learn all that at LMH?' The self he had been. Work and play, alternating, undifferentiated, spooling backwards. And now the tape snapped, and the film he had only been half-watching might never start up again.

Steve opened his eyes on the real darkness. He seemed to have been groping backwards for hours, failing to find an image that he could hold on to amongst so many that flickered and vanished.

'Annie?' he called out, seized with sudden panic. 'Are you still there?'

'Yes.'

She sounded drowsy, too far away from him.

'*Annie?*'

He could hear the effort, but she responded at last. 'Yes. I'm still here.'

'Talk to me again. About your mother. Anything, just go on talking.'

'I . . .' she sighed, a faint expiry of breath and he knew that he was only imagining the brush of it on his cheek. 'I can't talk any more. You talk, Steve. I like to hear your voice.'

When was the last time? That was what he wanted to catch hold of before it was too late, the last time he had felt the rawness of wanting something very much. The last time he had wanted something in the way that he wanted to live now, because he wouldn't be defeated by a maniac's bomb. Was that the key to it? *Because he wouldn't be defeated . . .*

Steve felt his head thickening, the thoughts and memories beginning to short-circuit. He forced his eyes open wide, willing himself to hold on to consciousness, and he began to talk.

'A long time ago. So long I'd forgotten how important it was. I wanted to get away, that was it. My Nan's flat, Bow High Street, three floors up. From the moment I went to live there, I wanted to get away.'

It had taken long enough, but he'd made it in the end. When the day came he went into the little room that led off Nan's kitchen and stuffed jerseys and shirts into his blue duffel bag. Nan was sitting in the kitchen watching the television. He could see her bulk past the half-open door, and the tablecloth half-folded back over the Formica-topped table, and the brown teapot and milk bottle, and her cup and saucer waiting to be refilled with thick brown tea.

'Off again, are you?' she shouted over the din of the television.

There had been trial getaways before this. Plenty of Saturday-night stopovers in overcrowded flats when those who were left behind after the part petered out had just fallen asleep wherever they fell down. There had even been a week, not long ago, when he had stayed with a girl up near Victoria Park. That had been too good to last, of course. She'd seen through his assumed adult suavity all too quickly.

'Sixteen? Is that how bloody old you are? *Sixteen?* Go on, get back to your mother before they come and lock me up for corrupting infants.'

Nan had welcomed him back, and the sharpness of her tongue didn't disguise her relief. 'Where the hell d'you think you've been? Not a word from you for a week. Didn't you know I'd be worried stiff? You'll end up like your Dad, Stevie, after all I've done.'

He put his arms around her. She was fat, but she was also frail and she could only move stiffly across the poky kitchen.

'I will *not* end up like my Dad. You know that.'

Nan had shifted her dental plate with the tip of her tongue and said acidly, 'Perhaps not. But there's plenty of other ways of going to the bad. I daresay you'll manage to find one that suits you.'

There had been calm after that for several months.

Now, as he closed the empty drawers in his bedroom one by one, he tried calling out, 'Nan? Nan, I'm going to live up West . . .'

She couldn't hear him, of course. The television obliterated

57

everything. So he had finished his methodical packing, even taking down his childhood posters of West Ham United and Buddy Holly and folding them up. Then he went into the kitchen and put his assortment of bags down on the cracked lino floor. He crossed to the vast television set and turned the volume knob, and silence descended.

'Eh? I was watching that, Stevie. Don't play about, there's a good boy.'

'Nan, I want to talk to you. I'm going to live up West. I've got a room and everything. I'll be all right.'

He had been so callous in those days. Nan had just sat and stared at him, with her big pale fingers twisting in her lap.

'Eh? Live up there? What for? You live here, love. Ever since you were that high.'

She held her palm out, a couple of feet off the lino, and Steve thought, *Yes, I do remember. And ever since I've wanted to get out.* 'I can't live here for ever, Nan. I want to get on. I'll come and see you weekends, I promise.'

Her face went sullen then. 'After all I've done,' she murmured.

She had done everything, of course. Mothered him and fended for him, and bought his food and clothes for ten years. He couldn't pay her back for her devotion, he knew that with chilly sixteen-year-old detachment.

'I'll come and see you often,' he repeated. 'And as soon as I've made it I'll buy you a better place, up near me or here, whichever you like.'

'Make it?' she snapped at him. 'How are you going to do that? What about school? You could go to college. Mr Grover told me himself.'

Patiently he had tried to explain it to her. 'I don't need to go to college. It's a waste of time, all that. I've got a job, Nan. I'm not going back to school.'

She was too angry to listen to him. So he had hugged her unyielding bulk, picked up his belongings, and marched out.

All he felt was relief as he left the Peabody Buildings. He

bumped past each pair of heavily-curled brown-painted balcony railings, down the tight spiral of stone steps to the road. He walked briskly up the street to the bus stop and then stood peering eastwards into the traffic for the first sight of the bus that would take him up West for good.

The job was as a messenger for an advertising agency, and his home was a second-floor bedsitter with a restricted view straight down into the Earl's Court Road. As soon as he arrived, Steve knew that he would never look back. After eighteen months as the Thompson, Wright, Rivington messenger boy he was offered the humblest of jobs in the media buying department. That job led to another and then another, and then to the huge leap upstairs to the circus of the creative floor. From Thompson, Wright, Rivington he was headhunted by another agency, and he began to enjoy money for the first time in his life.

Then, Steve remembered, I wanted everything. I was so busy making sure I got it that I never thought about anything else.

There were plenty of other people like him, and the time was ripe for all of them. His agency career began with the first shy appearances of pink shirts at client meetings, and it blossomed all through the sixties and into the seventies between lunches at the Terrazza and afternoons at the Colony Club, punctuated by parties swaying with girls in miniskirts and location shoots in exotic places and creative crises when somebody, usually Steve himself, managed to come up with a headline in the nick of time. Perhaps it hadn't really been like that at all. It felt too far back to remember. But it had seemed easy and so congenial that for a long, long time he had gobbled up everything that came his way.

Some time during those years, Nan had died. Steve had been in Cannes at the time of the funeral, doing business, and he couldn't fly back home for it. But he had paid for everything to be done properly. And he had sent a wreath, which was more than Nan's only daughter, Steve's mother, had bothered to do. If she even knew that her mother was dead. Steve himself had hardly seen her since she had taken him, at the age of six, to live with his grandmother.

'Poor Nan,' he said softly. And then, is remembering always feeling ashamed?

No, it wasn't so for Annie. Annie had fulfilled all kinds of promises that he had broken himself. Steve felt the slash of regret and telepathically she whispered, 'It isn't too late.'

His reaction to the pain was anger instead of fear now. He heard himself shouting, 'Where are they then? Why don't they come for us, before it *is* too late?'

The mass hanging over them swallowed the sound and gave nothing back. They couldn't hear anything at all.

'*Oh, Jesus,*' Steve said.

'It's all right.' Annie soothed him as if he were Benjy. 'You believe that they'll reach us in time. You made me believe, too. They'll come. We must just hold on . . . What are you doing?'

Steve was disentangling his hand from hers.

'I want to find out how long it's been.' His fingers felt swollen and hooked with cramp as he fumbled painfully for the watch.

'We must hold on,' Annie repeated, as if she was obediently reciting a rote lesson, 'until they come for us.'

Steve realized how much of her strength she was drawing from his reassurance, and wondered how long that could last. He felt much weaker now, and the pain from his leg clawed across his hip and stomach. He drew the watch out and laid it face upwards on his chest. Again he traced over the tiny hands with his fingertip. Suddenly dizziness enveloped him as he struggled to make sense of what he could feel. The hands were almost vertical, opposite to one another, and he touched the winder button to make sure.

Six o'clock . . . it could be six o'clock. If it was six o'clock it would be dark outside too. How could they search in the dark? Lights. Of course, they would bring emergency generators. They wouldn't stop looking until they had found the two of them. Steve struggled to draw sense out of the tiny, baffling circle and suddenly realized with a wave of relief, *not six o'clock* . . . It was half past twelve. Saturday lunchtime. Out there people would be cooking meals, telephoning one another, driving past twinkling shop windows on the way to warmth, doors closing against the wind, the sound of voices. The dizziness disorientated him, and he was shivering.

'Annie . . .' He moved involuntarily, too quickly, and the watch dropped out of his grasp. He heard it rattling and then clinking to rest somewhere beneath him. It was gone.

'I'm here,' she said. 'Go on talking.'

'I'm very thirsty,' Steve answered. He was sleepy too, but he wouldn't let that take hold of him. He began to talk again. His voice sounded slurred and he breathed deeper to control it.

What had happened? Some time during those agency years, without Steve ever having time to recognize it, he had stopped wanting anything. He had stopped feeling hungry. He almost laughed at the obviousness of it now. But the pleasure of being in the thick of such a business, where huge sums of money were treated so anarchically and still successfully, had faded too. It wasn't just his own appetite that had gone.

By the mid-seventies most of the parties were long over. Budgets were being cut back and unprofitable companies were toppling everywhere. The lunch-tables were ordered by a new breed of accountants, and to describe something as 'Mickey Mouse' was no longer a kind of inverted, admiring compliment. Steve's job was never threatened, he was too good at it for that, but most of what he had liked about it was gone. Holding company decisions and corporate images and long-term business projections bored him. He liked making commercials, and his freedom to do so was increasingly restricted.

He had known Bob Jefferies for two or three years before Bob suggested that they might set up on their own together. Bob was shrewd enough, and he was also unusually clever. He had been. at the LSE while Steve was riding his Thompson, Wright, Rivington scooter around the West End delivering packages of artwork. And Bob's proposal came at the tail end of a particularly dreary week.

Steve looked at him across the table in Zanzibar and shrugged. 'Yes, I'll come in with you. Why not?'

Bob exhaled sharply, irritated. 'Christ, Steve, don't you ever think anything out?'

Steve grinned at him. 'You do that. I'll make the commercials.'

That was how they had arranged it, and it had worked.

At the beginning, when there were just the two of them and an assistant and a girl to answer the telephones, it had even felt important. Not as exciting as the old Earl's Court days, because Steve knew exactly what success would buy him if it came. But interesting enough to absorb his attention and energies for a while. Then the studio diaries filled up, and they took on new staff, and moved to the offices in Ingestre Place.

After that the images slid together again. There was Cass's face looking down at him from the hoardings, and Vicky in her thick jersey and unflattering spectacles, his office with half a dozen people sitting around the table, and nothing that he could pick out and hold on to while the dizziness swooped down around him.

Annie's voice came out of the darkness. 'You sound important.'

She sounded stronger than he did now, and he took hold of that gratefully.

'No. There are plenty of companies like ours. I made some money, if you think that's important.'

'Steve?'

'I'm listening.'

'When all this is over, will you give me a job?'

A job? He turned his face towards the sound of her, caught short in his disjointed recollections by the recognition of her casual courage. For a moment the dizziness lifted and his head was as clear as a bell again.

'I don't think I've got a card with me. But I'll give you my number . . .'

'And I can leave my name with your secretary . . .'

'I'll get back to you if there's anything suitable on the books . . .'

They laughed in unison, crazy-sounding but it was real laughter, and it set the dust billowing in invisible clouds around them.

The traffic stood motionless in every direction. Martin peered ahead down the long line of cars and buses, and then over his shoulder at the blank faces waiting in the vehicles crammed behind him. In his panicky rush he hadn't stopped to think that the streets surrounding the bombed store would be thrown into chaos. He sat with his hands rigid on the steering wheel, trying to decide what to do. The news bulletins on the car radio told him hardly anything more than he already knew, yet his conviction that Annie was there deepened with every minute.

The press of cars moved forward a few yards and then stopped again. Martin could see the junction a hundred yards ahead of him now, where a solitary policewoman was diverting the traffic northwards, the wrong way, and he was still nearly a mile from Annie's store. He looked quickly from side to side, searching for a way out of the dense, immobile mass. He saw a narrow turning twenty yards ahead, on the wrong side of the road across three jammed lanes, but as soon as the next inching forwards began Martin turned on his headlights, rammed his finger on the horn and swung the car sideways. Oblivious to the storm of hooting that rose up around him he forced his way through the maze and shot down into the mews. He abandoned his car against a garage door and began to run.

The network of little streets at the back of the store were eerily quiet with the usual press of traffic. Once, ahead of him, Martin saw a patrolling police car nose across a junction. Instinctively he ducked sideways down another turning, and ran on until a stitch stabbed viciously into his side.

His feet seemed to drum out *Annie, Annie,* as they pounded along, but it was a relief to be moving, coming closer to her.

The streets nearest to the store had been cleared once by the police but there were still people passing quietly, in twos and threes. They turned to stare at Martin but he didn't see them. At last, with the blood pounding in his ears, he turned the last corner and saw what was left of Annie's store. He pushed through the people who still stood gaping outside the police cordons, and stared upwards. Terrified fear for her froze him motionless.

Some of the giant letters spelling out the shop's name that hadn't been blown away hung at crazy angles. One of them swung outwards, buffeted by the wind. On either side of the name Christmas trees hung with golden lights had stood on ledges. There were a few tattered shreds of green left now, and the lights had been blown out with all the others. High above the remains of the trees the shop was open to the sky, because the roof had gone. The front of it looked as if a giant fist had smashed downwards, ripping through the floors like tissue paper, and as he looked at it a jagged column of masonry seemed to sway, ready to topple inwards.

On either side, away from its ruined centre, the façade was a blinded expanse of broken windows. Decorations had spilled out of the windows and they lay ruined in the street on top of the shattered glass. Everywhere, beneath the buckled walls and in and out of the smashed windows, rescue workers swarmed to and fro, pathetically small, like busy ants over some huge carcass.

Martin stared at the torn-out heart of the shop. It was impossible to imagine that anyone could be alive in there.

He heard the words of the radio announcer repeating themselves endlessly inside his skull. *A second body has been recovered from the store in London's West End, severely damaged by a bomb explosion this morning.*

Not Annie, please, not Annie. If she is in there . . .

Martin's limbs began to work again. He stumbled forwards, elbowing his way brutally until he came up against the cordons. He clambered through them, thinking blindly that he would run forward to stand beneath the twisted letters and call out her name.

A police constable moved quickly to intercept him, putting his black-leather hand on his arm.

'Would you move back behind the barricade, sir. This way.'

'I'm looking for my wife. She's in there somewhere.'

The policeman hesitated for a moment in propelling Martin backwards. Martin saw the young face twitch with sympathy under the helmet.

'Do you know for sure that your wife was in there, sir?'

Martin thought, he didn't know anything. Annie could be anywhere in London. But yet he was sure, with sick, intuitive certainty, that she was here.

'Not for certain. But she could be.'

The policeman's brisk manner reasserted itself. There was a procedure to follow. He guided Martin back across the tapes, and they faced each other over them. The officer pointed away down the displaced street.

'If you will go to the local station, sir, down there on the left . . .'

He knew where it was. Once, when he and Annie had been out shopping, they had found a gold earring on the pavement. She had insisted on taking it to the police station, and he had waited impatiently beside her while the desk sergeant wrote everything in the lost property file.

'. . . they will take down your wife's details. And there is a number you can ring at Scotland Yard. They'll give you more information there.'

I want to help her. Over the man's shoulder Martin looked at the devastation again, and felt his own impotence. His fists clenched involuntarily, aching to reach out and pull at the rubble, to uncover her and set her free.

He shrugged uncertainly and turned away from the barrier. The watchers stood aside to let him through, and he walked down the road to the police station.

They showed him to a corridor lined with hard chairs. There was an office at the far end with a frosted glass panel in the closed door. Two or three people were sitting in a row, waiting, not looking at one another, and the stagnant air smelt of their anxiety.

Martin sat down in the empty chair at the end of the line.

The minutes ticked by and he thought about Annie and the boys. Whenever the question *What would we do, without her?* reared up he tried to make himself face it, but there was nothing he could see beyond it. It was impossible to envisage. He couldn't think beyond the diminished figures of the firemen that he had seen, working away up the road. He thought about them instead, willing them to uncover her, as if the intensity of his longing would spur them on.

The door at the end of the corridor opened and a woman came out. Someone else from the silent line went in in her place, and the rest of them went on helplessly waiting. A fat woman in a checked overall came past and asked if anyone wanted a cup of tea from the canteen. Martin shook his head numbly.

At last, after what seemed like hours, it was his turn. The office was cramped, lined with steel filing cabinets. A police sergeant sat behind the desk with a young WPC beside him. They nodded reassuringly at Martin, and the sergeant asked him to sit down.

As Martin answered their questions, the girl filled in a sheet of paper. He gave Annie's name and age, her general description. They asked him why he thought she had been in the shop and he answered, unable to convey his fearful conviction, simply that it seemed likely.

'I've got a photograph of her here,' he said.

Martin took out his wallet. In a pocket at the back there was a snapshot of Annie playing in the garden with the boys. She was laughing, and Benjy was standing between her knees, twisting the hem of her skirt. He pushed the photograph across the desk to the sergeant and then demanded, 'Do you know anything? Can't you tell me anything at all?'

The policewoman turned her pen over and over in her fingers while her colleague spoke.

'As you must know, everything is being done that can be done to explore the shop for possible survivors, and the operation will continue until it is quite certain that no one is left inside. One survivor has been located in the last hour, using thermal imaging equipment, and they should reach him very soon.'

The wild, hopeful flicker was extinguished almost as soon as it had shone out.

'Him?'

'Yes. It's a man, apparently not badly hurt.'

So it was possible, then, for someone to survive under that landslide of rubble. The hope it gave him helped Martin to confront the next question.

'And the two . . . bodies that have already been recovered?'

'Both have been positively identified. They were store employees.'

He wanted to put his hands up to cover his face, letting it sag with relief, but he sat still, ashamed to feel so grateful for the news of someone else's death.

'I would go home, sir, and wait there. We'll contact you immediately if there is any news of your wife.'

The interview was over. Martin got up reluctantly and then stood holding on to the chair back.

'Or you could wait here,' the WPC said. It was the first time she had spoken and she glanced nervously at her companion. He nodded, and looked past Martin at the door.

'Thank you,' Martin said. He had never intended to go home while Annie might need him here.

'When your wife does come home, sir,' the sergeant called after him, 'would you be kind enough to let us know at once?'

Martin nodded and went out into the stale, chilly air of the corridor again. Instead of sitting down he found his way by the scent of fried food down the stairs to the canteen in the basement. There was a public telephone under a blue plastic hood beside the swing doors. He dialled the familiar number and counted the rings. One . . . two . . . Audrey answered before the second one was complete. She sounded breathless, as if she had run to do it.

'It's Martin. Have you heard from her?'

In the background he could hear Tom's voice calling out, '*Is it Mummy?'* Martin closed his eyes and hunched his shoulders, as if he were waiting for someone to hit him.

'No,' Audrey said.

Martin looked at his watch. It was ten to one. Wouldn't Annie have telephoned, by now, to make sure that everything was all right? He knew there was no particular reason why she should, but the knowledge that she hadn't reinforced his conviction. She was in the store. Every minute that passed made it more certain.

'I'm at the police station,' he said. 'They can't tell me much. None of the . . . ones they have found is Annie. They don't know any more than that. I'm going to stay here and wait.'

'Yes,' Audrey answered, 'you'd best stay there. We'll be all right here . . .' The dialling tone cut her short. Martin had already hung up and gone. He ran up the stairs again, and walked out of the police station into the street. In front of the store the yellow latticework of a crane stood idle. He walked towards it, into the wind, shivering. He passed the enclave of television cameras and waiting pressmen and thought, with unreasoning savagery, that they were like vultures hovering before the kill. He walked on around the outer edge of the barriers until he came to the point where the policeman had blocked his way. He looked up, over the heads of the crowd. It seemed impossible that the crumpled front of the store could remain standing. As he watched it seemed to sway, curling inwards with a shower of falling fragments that drew clouds of whitish dust down with them.

Martin shivered, and he realized that the wind was strengthening. It swept across the street, lifting a torn paper wrapper into the air before pasting it to the wet roadway again. Even above the noise of the wind, Martin thought he could hear the creak of broken girders as the concrete weight shifted and then settled itself for another moment or two, before the next gust came.

A police van inched along the inside of the cordon. Behind it the police were moving the watchers back, all the way back up the road. More steel barriers were lifted out of the van and pushed into place. Looking backwards, as he was ushered out of range with everyone else, Martin saw a group of men in protective helmets moving under the threatening frontage. The crane swung slowly round. He understood that they were going to try to push the wall outwards so that it collapsed into the street.

They would have to do it quickly, before it fell of its own accord the other way.

Three

Annie was thinking about the wedding picture. Not her own and Martin's this time. Theirs was as bright as a paintbox with the splashed colours of the girls' dresses and the vivid blue sky behind the church. She was thinking about her parents', in a big, old-fashioned leather frame, standing on a table to the left of the fireplace in their sitting room. Theirs was black and white with a faint brownish cast that was deepening with age. It was wartime, and her mother was wearing a two-piece costume with square shoulders and a little hat perched on one side of her head. Her hair was in a roll to frame her face. Her father was beaming in his army uniform. His face had hardly changed, except for thinning hair and lines dug beside his mouth and around his eyes. Her mother was barely recognizable. She had had full cheeks then, and her smile was lavishly painted with dark, shiny lipstick.

Annie was very cold.

The drifting sensation was still with her, but it wasn't like being in a boat on a calm lake any more. She felt that she was floating towards the big, blank mouth of a tunnel. She didn't want the tunnel to swallow her and so she gripped Steve's hand as if he were reaching out from the bank to pull her out of the rushing water.

'It's so cold,' she said.

Steve was straining to hear. He had thought for a moment that he caught the clink of metal overhead, a harsh scraping, and the sound of voices not his own or Annie's.

If they were really coming . . . If it was soon, they would be all right. Time had lost its meaning now, and Steve cursed the watch irretrievably lost somewhere underneath him. He could hold on himself, but he didn't know about Annie. He couldn't hear the noises any more.

'It won't be much longer,' he promised her. 'Talk to me, if you can.' He wanted to hear her voice, but he wanted to listen for the other sounds too. He felt himself shaking with the effort of it, his eyes wide open and staring as if he could hear with them in the dark.

'I was thinking about my father and mother,' Annie whispered. 'I didn't suffer anything when I was a kid, Steve. Not like you. It was all smooth. They made it smooth for me. They always believed in routine, and their lives run like clockwork now. I wonder . . .' she breathed in painfully, 'how happy they've been.'

The water stopped rushing forward and seemed to eddy in a wide circle, swinging her round with it, so that all her perspectives changed. She had been thinking about her mother and father as a way of keeping a hold on herself, building them into the bridge of words that linked her to Steve. But now she caught a reflected image of marriages, seeing how hers mirrored theirs, and her parents' back to her grandparents', the same coupled conspiracies perpetuating themselves.

What had her mother missed, Annie wondered, that she would never recapture? Not now, when there was nothing to do but wait for the disease to get the better of her. *Like me down here*, she thought, and the mirror images reflected one another down a long, cold passageway.

She saw her mother's house, and remembered her totems. Polished parquet floors, and guest towels put neatly beside the basin in the downstairs cloakroom when visitors came. Her store cupboard was always well filled, and there were best tablecloths carefully folded in the drawer underneath the everyday ones. Annie had a faint recollection that there were even certain teatowels kept for best, but the caked blood at the corner of her mouth dried the smile before it began.

The thirties house on the corner of a quiet, sunny street was too big for her parents now, but it still shone from daily polishing and it still smelt of formally-arranged flowers, even though most of the rooms were unused.

Seeing it, Annie felt a sudden, infinite sadness. All her mother's adult life had been devoted to servicing a house, and when she died her husband would sell up, new people would move in and knock down walls and laugh at the outmoded décor, and there would be nothing left of her. How hollow it was, Annie thought, that her house should be her memorial. It had contained her like a shell and inside it she had waited for her husband's comings and goings. From the shelter of it she had watched her children until they grew too big and went away.

Annie realized that she had no idea about the marriage that had kept it polished. The house had been its emblem, tidy and clean, and she had assumed that the one stood for the other. Like their house, her parents' marriage had seemed decent, and respectable. What else?

The sense of how little she knew shocked her.

Martin and me . . . The same, or different?

The house was no totem, but she loved the things that they had done in it together, and its warmth lapped around the four of them. Yet perhaps she was making the ways of it stand in the place of something else, something once fresh that had faded with middle age. Was it the lost sense of that that had made her think of Matthew?

Annie stirred, turning her face in the sloping space under the door. The smoothness of it felt as cold as a sheet of ice. The reflections had gone and she couldn't recapture the chilling insight. Everything was confused – her childhood home with the house she shared with Martin, rooms superimposed and faces blurring together. She only knew that she had been happy with Martin. A weak longing for him washed over her like a wave.

Where was he? Wouldn't he know what had happened, because he knew her well enough to read her thoughts, and so come for her?

72

She closed her eyes and lay thinking about him. Her felt very close, as if his body was part of hers and sharing the same pain. It was his hand holding hers, not Matthew's, and not the stranger's.

Man and wife, Annie thought, knitted together by time and habit. The full span of their years seemed to present itself for her recollection, measurable. Annie felt a new throb of terror with the speculation: *Is that because it's finished?* The weight above her pressed malevolently downwards. Completed. No, not completed but severed. The image of the plait, blunt ends fraying, came back to her. Yet, she thought sadly, yesterday she had had no sense that she and Martin were constructing anything together, not any more. They had made their marriage and were sure of it. They were busy with the small tasks of maintenance now, not preoccupied by the grand design. It was time that was not fulfilled.

It was to be cheated of the years of calm living in the structure they had created that was bitter, Annie understood. She had taken the promise of years for granted. There would be the boys growing up, Martin and herself moving more slowly together, in harmony. Or there would be nothing. Only death, and the people she loved left behind without her.

She wondered if there would be the same bitterness if she had simply fallen ill like her mother, and been gently told that she had only a little longer. She would have had time, then, to make her goodbyes. To neaten those terrible ends, at the very least. But it would be just the same, she thought. She would feel the same loss and the same fear. Annie had a sudden unbearable longing for life, for all the promises she had never made, let alone never kept, all the conversations unshared, all the bridges of human contact that she had never crossed and never would. The vastness of what she was struggling to confront was ready to crush her. I'm going to die, Annie thought.

The blackness was utterly unmoving but she felt it poised, greedily ready to consume her and to push the tiny coloured pictures out of her head.

I'm sorry. The words swelled, dancing above her, dinning in her ears. Surely they were loud enough? I'm sorry. She wanted Martin to hear them, somehow. She had failed him, and their children, and she knew how much they needed her. 'I'm afraid,' Annie said again. 'I'm afraid to die.'

Steve lay rigid, thinking, I don't know what to say. He had been absorbed in trying to imagine it as one more thing to get the better of. He felt it facing him, as tense as an animal ready to spring, but it was he who was cornered. *I don't know what to say to her.* I've always known what to say. I've been so bloody sharp. I've cut myself. He heard Nan warning him, back in the kitchen three floors up behind Bow High Street. And now. Now there was this.

'I'm afraid too,' Steve whispered.

The confession of their fear drew them close, and the spectre of it moved back and let them breathe a little. Steve and Annie couldn't huddle together and keep it at bay but they felt one another in their fingertips. Their hands became themselves.

'Thank God you're here,' Annie said. And then, after a minute, 'Steve? If it comes, will you be here with me?'

If death comes, that's what she means, Steve thought. Will I be with her through it?

'Yes,' he promised her. 'I'll be here.'

We'll wait, together.

Annie took the reassurance, and Steve's admission of his own fear, and built them into her barricades. The terror receded a little further. She used the respite to look at the pictures that whirled in her head like confetti, examining each one and setting it in its place. It became very important to make a logical sequence of them. Annie frowned, gathering the ragged edges of concentration. So many little pieces of confetti.

There was Martin, on the day that they met. That's right, that one would come first. She looked at the fragment carefully. He was sitting at the next table, in the coffee bar in Old Compton Street favoured by students from St Martin's. Annie was in her foundation year, and Martin was two years ahead of her. She had seen him before, in the corridors and once across the room at a party, without noticing him in particular. He had long hair and a leather jacket, artfully ripped, like everyone else's. Today he was drawing on an artists' pad, his head bent in concentration. She remembered sitting in the warm, steamy atmosphere listening to the hiss of the coffee machines behind the high counter. The boy at the next table had finished his drawing and looked up, smiling at her.

'Another coffee?' he asked.

He brought two cups over to her table, and she tilted her head to look at the drawing under his arm. Obligingly he held it out and she saw an intricately shaded pencil drawing of the coffee bar with the chrome-banded sweep of the counter, the polished levers of the Gaggia machine and the owner's brilliantined head bent behind it. At her table, close to the counter, he had drawn in her friends but Annie's chair was empty.

'Why haven't you drawn me?' she demanded and he answered, 'Well, that would have been rather *obvious* of me, wouldn't it?'

He's nice, Annie thought.

She felt the intriguing mixture of excitement and anticipation that she recalled years afterwards as the dominant flavour of those days. Everything that happened was an adventure, every corner turned presented an enticing new vista.

'What's your name?' the boy asked her. 'I've seen you at the college, haven't I?'

'Anne. Annie,' she corrected herself. Since leaving school she had discarded sixth form gawky Anne in favour of Annie, freewheeling art student with her Sassoon bob and cut-out Courrèges boots.

'I'm Martin.'

And so they had met, and the strands had been picked out and pulled together in the first tentative knot. Martin had taken a crumpled handbill from his pocket. It was the term's programme from the college film society.

'Look. *Zéro de Conduite*. Have you seen it?' And then when

75

Annie shook her head, 'You really should. Would you like to come with me?'

For all their protestations of freedom they had still been very conventional, all that time ago. He had invited her to see a film and she had accepted, and he had taken her for supper afterwards at the Sorrento.

But there was no fragment to illustrate what had happened next. She simply couldn't remember. All she could see was herself, trudging through the rain in the streets beyond Battersea Park, with Martin's address burning in her pocket. He must have taken her out once or twice and then moved on to someone else. Was that it?

Perhaps. And perhaps she had been smitten by the anguish that was as much part of those days as the enchantment. She had determined that she wouldn't let him go, and had boldly gone to the registry to find his address. But she could see her nineteen-year-old self so clearly, in her white plastic mac dotted with shilling-sized black spots, splashing through the puddles wearing her tragic sadness like a black cloak. Just as Jeanne Moreau did, or Catherine Deneuve, or whichever French actress was providing her model for that week. She was going to confront him, beg him to listen to her because she was lost without him. There was a bottle of wine in her carrier bag, and when the time came they were going to drink it together, all barriers down at last.

There, that little piece fitted there.

She had reached his door and rung the bell, her face already composed in its beautiful, sad, brave lines. Martin opened the door, brandishing a kitchen ladle. He beamed at her, and her heart lifted like a kite.

'Oh, Annie, it's you. Great. Just the person we need. Come in here.'

She followed him into the kitchen and stared around. It wasn't what she had planned, not at all.

The room was packed with people, mostly ravenous-looking boys. In the middle of the table, amidst a litter of potato peelings and bottles of beer and cider, there was a slab of roast pork, half carved, with blood still oozing from a round pinky-brown patch in the centre.

'We were going to have a house feast,' Martin explained. 'But the meat looks wrong. What d'you think?'

'I think it needs about four more hours in the oven,' Annie retorted. It was hard to maintain her Jeanne Moreau expression confronted with a piece of raw pork and a dozen hungry faces.

Martin shrugged cheerfully. 'Oh well. Let's stick it back in the oven and go to the pub.'

They went to the pub, and came back again much later. At some stage they ate the pork, or what was left of it. Somebody else drank Annie's wine, and later still threw it up again. Annie didn't care about anything except that she was with Martin. He took her upstairs to his room and put his arms round her, and they looked into each other's eyes as if at a miracle.

'Why did you come down here, this evening?' he asked her and she answered, with daring simplicity, 'Because I can't live without you.'

'You don't have to,' Martin said.

It was the truth.

After that, for a long time, all the pieces of confetti that she put into the proper sequence belonged to them both. Slowly, by the same stages that many of their friends were passing through at the same time, Martin and Annie became a couple. They explored each other, awkwardly at first on the mattress in Martin's room, then with daring, and then with skill that turned quite quickly into tenderness. In the same way, but even more slowly, their life in the world found its pattern, echoing the private one. The discovery of one another's likes and pleasures was consolidated by sharing them. They launched themselves into the endless, fascinated talks that convinced them they were identical spirits. They went everywhere and did everything together, exchanging the romantic isolation of adolescence for the luxury of mutual dependence. They became, to all their friends, Martin-and-Annie.

For a while in Martin's last year they lived together, sharing a chaotically disorganized house with three other students. There were lots of little, disjointed pictures of that time, of faces around the kitchen table and skinny legs sprawling in broken-backed armchairs. Where had all those people gone? Perhaps, Annie thought sadly, they had become Martin. Become him because all the memories of that time were crystallized in him, part of the cement that held them together. In those days, at the age of twenty, Annie had proudly acted out the role of housewife. Here was the image of herself heading for the local launderette with two bulging blue plastic carrier bags. She had cooked meals too, and folded Martin's shirts for him.

Did I ever, she wondered, see my mother in myself? Was I never afraid that it would be the same for me, too?

No, not that. We thought we were different, so busy making new rules. We thought we had turned the world upside down because Martin used to clank about the house with a mop-up bucket. Because he used to take his turn at cooking dinners that were never ready until midnight, and left every saucepan in the house dirty.

They had been happy . . . There was a lot of laughter printed on those confetti fragments. Lying numbly in her tiny space with Steve's hand her only warmth, Annie wished that she could breathe life into them again.

At the end of that time Martin had gone to work in Milan. Here, Annie saw herself with him at the airport, her face crushed against the leather shoulder of his coat as he hugged her. For two years they had separated, because they had grown out of play-acting married life.

Annie remembered the flat that she had taken. It was close to here, above the creaking weight that pinned her like a butterfly to a board. She followed the turns of the streets that would take her there, and up the stairs into her rooms. She saw the colour of the walls – had she really painted them aubergine? – and the fringed Biba lampshades. The flicker under the skin of her face might have been a smile.

At the end of two years Martin had come home from Italy. They had found each other's company all over again, as comfortably fitting as a winter coat left on a peg all through the summer, and then gratefully put on with the coming of cold weather. Within a year they were engaged. Their parents met and approved, exchanging drinks in their similar houses, pleased that their children had found the way at last. And a year after that, with Matthew's still face watching from inside her head, Annie was married.

'I thought that we would be gentle to each other,' Annie said. 'And we have been.'

'You're very lucky,' Steve answered her softly.

That made her turn her head to him, as far as it would go.

'Why do I feel ashamed, then?'

Steve thought, I hardly glimpsed you, walking in front of me towards that door. How long have we been lying here? Talking. I know you now. Better than I knew my own wife. Better than I'll ever know anyone again, if there is anything beyond this day.

'You haven't anything to be ashamed of, Annie.'

'I made a choice, an easy choice. And now it's too late to take the other path. I feel that . . . everything has faded. For Martin, too, do you think? And now it's too late.' Annie was too tired to cry any more, but she felt the fine muscles pull at her eyes, the little mechanisms of her body still unbelievably functioning. 'It's too late to turn and run and draw it back again, and make the colours shine all over again.'

'If you and I weren't lying here, if this thing had never happened, would you have changed anything then?'

Annie said, very quietly, 'No. I would have gone home with my tree baubles and the toys for my kids, and I would have hidden them and put the boys to bed and Martin and I would have eaten dinner together, just as we did every night . . .'

Did. More pieces of confetti, fresh and unfaded now, mosaic of a life, a family life. She longed for it, aching where her hurt body was numb.

'You haven't anything to be ashamed of, Annie,' he repeated. 'You have loved your family, mothered your children. Ordinary, admirable things. You should take hold of those.'

'Take hold of them,' Annie echoed. And then, abruptly, 'Everyone is ashamed.'

Steve felt her closeness, closer in the touch of her cold fingers than he had ever held anyone.

'I am ashamed too,' he said. 'Of a thousand things. Business subterfuges. Social evasions. Lots of lies, so many I couldn't begin to count. I lied to my Nan, to Cass, Vicky, everyone I've known and should have cared about.'

Annie could hear his breathing, shallow gasps as he sucked in the stagnant air. 'I'm ashamed because I've never loved anyone. Never, in all my life. If there isn't anything after today . . . I will have lived for nearly forty years without making anyone happy. And you say that you are ashamed.'

The bitterness in his voice cut her as sharply as any of the physical pain.

'No,' she said, so loudly that he wondered whether somehow she had managed to bring her face closer to his. 'I know you. I know that isn't the truth.'

Out in the street the wind was bringing snow again, tiny flakes of it driven horizontally into the faces of the small groups of watchers. The wind tore at the orange tapes so that they strained and flapped and the policemen guarding them turned their backs into it and moved uneasily to and fro. Martin stood motionless, watching the store front. Along with everyone else, he had been moved so far back that the effort of staring into the distance made his eyes ache, and they watered with the cold blast of wind.

The crane had moved round once, very slowly, and was now stationary again. The fireman had brought their ladders forward in its place, fragile-looking metal probes reaching up against the buckled frontage. Martin could see the yellow helmets swaying at the ladder tips. Everything seemed to move so slowly. What were they doing? *Please hurry up.* The words beat in his head with the throb of blood. Why so long?

Through the tears that the wind scoured out of his eyes Martin saw a chunk of brick fall from the raw edge of the façade. It plummeted downwards in a shower of smaller fragments and he heard the sharp indrawn breaths of the people pressing around him. Amongst the wreckage the rescue workers scattered and, involuntarily, they turned their faces up to look at the sagging wall and the patch of sky seeming to press down on top of it. Then, when the dust had blown away, they bent to their work again. Painstakingly the chunks of concrete and splintered beams and broken shop fittings were still being lifted away. Part of what had been the ground floor was exposed now, its carpets whitened with thick dust. The tiny flakes of snow settled and vanished, and settled again unnoticed.

In the big control trailer that had joined the line of police vehicles, the police commander was watching the time. It was just after three o'clock, and the light was already fading. The power supply to the store had failed with the explosion, but generators had been brought in and the emergency lights had been hauled into place, ready to be switched on. The work would go on for many hours yet.

Three ten p.m. The commander moved abruptly to the trailer door and looked out at what the bomb had done. He knew with a degree of certainty now where the bomb had been planted, what type it was, how much explosive it had detonated and who had been responsible for it. He didn't know whether there was a chance of reaching any survivors in time. They had been buried more than five hours.

'Three,' he said aloud, without turning away from the door.

The thermal imaging cameras had located three heat sources, human bodies. They were in the basement of the store, lying four storeys directly below the point where the bomb had exploded. Two of them were very close together and the third some yards away. They could have been in the basement at the time of the explosion, or they could have fallen into it as the store collapsed inwards on itself. The policeman put his finger to his moustache, the only sign of anxiety that he ever revealed. It should only be a matter of minutes, an hour at the most, to reach them now.

But the broken façade hung over them, unsupported. It had taken precious time to discover that it couldn't be knocked outwards to fall harmlessly into the street. There was no time to erect scaffolding and bring it down piece by piece. The only hope was to work faster, to uncover the remaining three bodies before it fell, or the wind brought it down.

For the hundredth time since early morning the commander offered up thanks that the bomb had gone off almost as the store opened. Instead of hundreds of casualties in a store packed with Christmas shoppers, the total so far was eight deaths. In the last hour two people had been brought alive from the wreckage near the main doors. One of them was a store commissionaire and the other a teenage boy, both seriously injured. There were thirty or so further casualties, some of them passers-by who had only been cut by flying glass. And there were three more people, perhaps alive, to be recovered before the teams of rescuers could be pulled back and the frontage knocked down into the tangled mass already lying beneath it.

Unless, the commander thought, the wind does it first.

He went down the trailer steps, settling the protective helmet on his head, and felt the full force of the wind in his face. He walked quickly, with his head bent, past the ruined windows again. The bobbing yellow helmets and the orange fluorescent jackets of the police seemed to be the only spots of colour in a world that had been drained of it.

A screen of tarpaulins had been rigged up and the constables stood aside to let the commander through. Behind the store front, over the spot where they were digging into the basement, they had made a kind of shelter. Lengths of scaffolding had been roughly bolted together and roofed with planks, as makeshift as a child's play house. Beneath the flimsy protection the rescuers went on burrowing downwards. One of them glanced upwards for an instant, his face coated with grime.

The commander crouched in the dirt and the chunks of debris were prised loose and handed backwards past him. When the bodies were recovered and the site was safe once more, every piece would be examined by the forensic teams.

The commander gestured that he wanted to move forwards and the firemen made way for him to inch forward under the planking. Looking down he could see a coloured edge of carpet in the store's colours, and the thickness of floor beneath it sliced as neatly as cake. Below him two firemen were working like machines, hauling out the rubble. And beneath them, the commander knew, eight or ten feet down, were two of the three bodies.

The space the rescuers were working in, cramped as close as they could under the hopeful protective umbrella, was tiny. The commander delivered his brief word of praise and encouragement and squirmed backwards again to leave them to their task. His opposite number from the fire service was waiting inside the curtain of tarpaulins.

'We should reach them within the hour, God willing,' he said. The policeman nodded and they stood in silence watching the work, the mounting piles of debris as it was feverishly dug out and set aside.

'From the look of all that . . .' the commander murmured, and they both knew that he meant *no one could survive under all that*. The fire officer's brief glance upwards revealed his anxiety for his men, working under threat of burial themselves to reach victims who were almost certainly dead. But neither of the senior men spoke again, and the slow process of cutting and lifting went on as the firemen fought their way downwards.

Steve heard it first.

It lasted only a few seconds but it was the unmistakable high whine of a power drill. It was cutting through the darkness. It meant that they really were coming for them, at last.

'Annie. I can hear them. Listen.'

As if to prove it there was another noise at once, the sharp ring of metal on stone and then the whine of the drill again, dropping in pitch. Steve felt relief and gratitude numb the pain inside him like a powerful drug. When Annie didn't answer he was furiously angry with her.

'Can't you hear?' he demanded. The darkness swallowed his words and Annie listened for something else, longing to hear. What would rescue sound like, when she had longed for it so much?

Then it came, no more than a tiny metallic scraping, once and then silence, and then again, louder. *It sounds like music*, she thought wildly. 'Yes,' she whispered. 'I hear it.'

'*Now* we can shout,' Steve exulted. 'I'll count three. Then scream as loud as you can.'

He counted, one, two, three, and they screamed together. It sounded so tiny, the only noise that they could make, eaten up by the hateful dark. Annie's head fell back and she closed her eyes. It was no good. Of course it was no good.

Steve was thinking, a power drill of some kind. That means they've brought the power in, cables, floodlights, everything possible. He had an image of the black cables snaking over the rubble, the intent faces of the rescuers with the harsh shadows from the lights across them. There had been silence for so long, since the first wailing sirens, that he had been afraid he had imagined the other noises. He had begun to fear that there was no rescue at all. He had even wondered – he could confront that terror now, now that he knew it was unfounded – whether it had been a different kind of bomb, and there was no one left outside to come to their rescue. Horror prickled at his spine until the sounds started up again.

'They're right overhead, Annie. Do you know what that means?' Still she didn't answer and he shouted at her, 'Don't you know?'

'Tell me,' she said. He heard her exhaustion, and knew that she was near to giving up, now, after so long.

'Annie,' he begged her. 'Hold on for just a little while longer. They're right overhead. It means they must have found where we are. They've used heat-seeking cameras, and they can come straight to us. I'd forgotten that's what they'd do.' Steve shook his head, weakly surprised by his own stupidity. 'We must make them hear us,' he said. 'I'll count again. Shout, Annie.'

Again, the thin sound rising and evaporating into the limitless dark.

'It isn't any use,' she whispered, but Steve's fingers dug into her hand like a claw.

'Again,' he commanded, and then, 'Again.'

One of the firemen held up his hand. He lifted his head to listen and the others froze into stillness. The silence seeped from the torn hole that held them and spread outwards. The next time it came they all heard it. It was a cry, very faint, but a human cry. They stood still for another moment, then heard it once more.

'Someone's alive down there.'

The word was carried backwards like a torch. It reached the senior officers waiting inside the tarpaulin screen, and the medical team waiting with the ambulances.

The commander stepped quickly forward and looked down at the filthy faces ringing the hole. 'As fast as you can,' he said quietly, and they stooped to work again.

Martin was chilled to the bone and his face was stiff with being turned into the wind, watching the unchanging scene in the distance. Abruptly he turned his back on it, but the sight of it was still clear in his mind's eye. He knew that he would never forget the distorted shape of the store against the cold sky. He began to walk northwards, his feet painfully numb in his thin indoor shoes. The nearest tube station was closed, he had seen that when he passed it on the way back from his interview with the police. He would have to walk on to the next one. There would be a telephone there.

He felt a little warmer as he walked, but his feet stung as the circulation started up again. He began to walk faster and faster, imagining how he would pick up the receiver and dial the number. Perhaps Annie would answer it. Perhaps she had come home long ago. He was almost running now, wondering how he could have stood stupidly for so long without telephoning. Perhaps she was waiting for him to call, sitting with the boys and Audrey, comfortable in the warm room.

The blue and red tube station sign drew him on and he ran the last hundred yards, panting and slithering on the greasy pavement. In the ticket hall there were two payphones in malodorous wooden cubicles. He snatched up the receiver in the nearest booth and listened between his gasps for breath to the thick silence of a dead line. In the same instant a fat man wedged himself into the next booth and began leisurely dialling. Martin planted himself in the middle of the man's field of vision and held up his coin, but the man turned his back and settled himself to talk.

Martin stood counting the seconds off, thinking what he would say to her. *Annie? You're safe? Thank God . . .*

The fat man hung up abruptly and eased himself out of the cubicle. Martin cradled the warm receiver and dialled.

'Hello?'

It was Audrey's voice. The pips cut into it and Martin pushed in the coin, but he already knew. Annie hadn't come home.

'No,' Audrey said. 'There's been nothing. But she could still be shopping . . .'

Martin looked out of the square mouth of the tube station entrance. It was getting dark. He could hear music somewhere, a jazzed-up carol. He thought it must be buskers playing at the foot of the escalators. Annie wasn't still shopping. He knew where she was.

He said, 'They've brought two people out alive so far. Both men. I asked one of the policemen on the cordons. I don't know anything else. But they're still working there, dozens of them. They're still expecting to bring people out.' Martin looked at the scribbled graffiti over the cubicle walls, names and telephone numbers, *phone Susie . . . Kim & Viv woz 'ere*. Millions of people, filling the sprawl of London, moving to and fro. Why should it be Annie, there, today?

'I don't know anything else,' he said again, helplessly. 'I'll stay here until they stop looking.'

Audrey's voice was quiet. He knew that she didn't want the boys to hear what she was saying.

'I haven't had the TV on, Martin, in case they saw . . . something. But I heard on the kitchen radio. They think there are still three buried.'

'Alive?'

'They said it was a possibility. I think it was only the reporter, you know, guessing. There's been eight killed.'

He knew that, too. He had pushed his way as close as he could get to the control trailer and asked. The officer had been sympathetic, like the ones at the station, but uninformative. Eight bodies had been recovered and identified. None of them was Annie. But he wouldn't say whether the rescuers were still expecting to find anyone else, however hard Martin had pressed him. The radio reporter, whoever he was, had done rather better, he thought dully.

'I'll go back and wait then,' he said. 'Can you stay, Audrey?'

'Of course I can.'

Martin noticed that she didn't try to say that Annie would be back soon.

He hung up and pushed through the stream of people pressing into the station with their loaded carrier bags. Most of them looked over their shoulders as they plunged into the lighted space. He felt how their buzz of shocked fascination overcame their irritation at being diverted to a different station, and it made him angry. He went out into the icy street and began to walk back. The shape of the store, sideways on against the sky, looked mockingly almost as it always had done.

Martin was pulling his coat around him and wishing that he had wellington boots on his feet when the noise came. It was a vicious gust of wind first, making him duck his head into his collar. He heard the full blast of it funnelling past him down the

87

long street. But then the wind dropped a little, and the noise should have subsided with it.

Instead it was augmented by a different sound, unplaceable at first, but it made the hairs prick at the nape of his neck. It was a low rumble like thunder, but much closer to earth than thunder. After the first crash it became the distant roar of surf breaking and, drowning in the sound of it, Martin heard people shouting. In a terrifying split-second he thought, *Another bomb*. He was waiting for the blast to hurl him sideways but it never came and he stood, frozen, staring into the sleet-thickened darkness. Surely it was *there*, before the noise, that the blue and white lights had been reflected under the store front? He couldn't see them now. A pall of thick, coiling dust hid everything.

Martin began to run.

There had been no warning.

The police commander had been standing with a group of bomb squad officers close to the trailer. He felt the gust of wind and looked up in alarm. As he watched, the broken edge of the façade trembled and swayed inwards. He opened his mouth to shout a command and heard the sharp rain of falling chunks of brick.

'Back,' he yelled. 'Get back.'

There was a scrambling rush of men, scattering away over the pavement to the shelter of the vehicles. He glimpsed a fireman rooted to the spot, and from the tilt of his helmet knew that he was staring upwards.

And then there was a deafening roar as the height of the façade crumpled inwards, seeming to hang unsupported in mid-air for an instant, and then fell into the wrecked centre of the store. The dust billowed outwards, thick with the acrid smell of pulverized brick. Choking, with his hands up to cover his nose and mouth, the commander stared into the clouds of it.

The blue tarpaulins had been torn down. The shelter of planks and scaffolding was buried, and half in and half out of what had once been one of the festive display windows a fireman was lying face-down, his legs twisted beneath him.

In the darkness the noise was another explosion, the first terror renewing itself. It took hold of them, eating them up as it swelled louder so that their bodies shook with the vibration and their lungs filled with the smell of it.

'*Steve.*'

He heard Annie scream his name, just once, and then the scream was extinguished and the roaring went on. The sensation was like falling again, but it was more terrible because there was nowhere to fall to. Instead, everything else was falling. Steve turned his head until his neck wrenched, hunching his shoulder as if that could shelter him. There was a pounding rain of red-hot rocks all around him and he knew that he would drown in this solid sea of noise and grinding stone.

There was no pain then, except the agony of terror. On and on.

Still the noise, but muffled now. An angry, diminished roar.

The solid rain was still falling, but it was finer now. It had washed away all the air.

The air.

Steve choked as the filth swept into his lungs. Gasps for breath convulsed his body and he writhed until the pain in his leg swept back again. He would have screamed but there was no breath. There was no breath to cough, no air to breathe.

The blackness grew heavier, pressing its pain all around him.

Steve closed his eyes and then there was nothing, oblivion as sweet and comfortable as a child's sleep.

He didn't want them to come back again, the pain and the smell and the air that lay like a mask over his face. But they came anyway, dragging him back into consciousness. Each breath tore his chest and yet wouldn't fill his lungs.

He lay in the silence, moaning. The silence. The noise was over now. The thing, whatever it was, had come and gone and left him alone again. Then something else pecked at his unwelcome consciousness. He groped after it in the fog of agony and remembered, *not alone.* He made his mind work outwards, to the limits of his body. His shoulder and arm were still part of him, his arm outstretched. His fingers were still there, and he was still holding the girl's hand.

'Annie.'

The word was no more than a croak, but it left him gasping. The hand in his felt limp and cold as ice. He lay for a moment, trying to gather his strength, and then called her name again.

'Annie.'

The silence was hideous now. There was something different. Steve slid his hand from hers and found her wrist, thin and bare. His fingers moved up her arm, meeting the rough edge of her coat sleeve, and a woollen cuff underneath it.

Something different. What was it?

His fingers moved again, scraping the gritty cloth.

Cloth.

His head hurt so that each thought took a separate, punishing effort. Before, surely, there had been only her hand? His shoulder still ached from stretching out to reach it. Yet now he could feel her arm, all the way up to the elbow, slightly crooked. In the silence Steve could hear his heart's terrified drumming. He opened his mouth to try to pull more oxygen out of the thickened air.

He was capable of only one thought, and it gripped him for long, shivering seconds. He was holding her arm, but it was no longer part of her. Something had severed it. Fear and nausea swelled inside him and he crouched within a shell of pain, longing for unconsciousness again. But his head defied him and the thought clarified, until it was certainty, and he knew that he must confront it.

He took his lower lip between his teeth and bit into it, to stop himself screaming when the discovery came. Then he slid his hand down once more to clasp the fingers in his. Slowly, he pulled their linked hands towards him.

The arm moved, not easily because the coat sleeve snagged on the roughness beneath it. But it moved, and he drew it closer until his fingers could crawl up again to the elbow and beyond, inch by inch, his lip held beneath his teeth to help him to bear the discovery of sticky flesh and bone.

But there was only the reassuring weave of the cloth, and then the rounded hump of the shoulder.

Suddenly, as though his consciousness could only dole out one at a time, another thought came to him. Her pulse. He could feel for her pulse. His fingers slid back again and fumbled under the woollen cuff. He turned her hand so that it lay wrist upwards and touched his forefinger to the vulnerable skin. Nothing, and nothing, and then he found the place. A little beat quivered, tick, tick.

Steve breathed out, a long sigh that stirred the stench of brick dust again. She was still alive. This was Annie's arm, her hand still touching his. He held on to it like a lifeline.

Think again, then. What had happened? He must work it out, establish a thread of hope for Annie again . . .

He tried to remember the noise and then the avalanche that had followed it. They hadn't fallen, but everything else had fallen around them. Steve had the sudden conviction that the limits of their black world had redefined themselves. As the weight fell something had shifted.

He had heard Annie scream his name, and then what? Had one of them rolled sideways, involuntarily, to escape the avalanche? If that had happened, something had moved to release one of them from the weight that had pinned them down. Steve tried to move now, willing his leg to follow the jerky spasm of his other muscles. The pain intensified, shooting across his stomach, but he found that he could lift his hips and drag himself to the right by an inch or two. His left leg slithered uselessly with him. He could reach out and touch Annie's side now. His fingers explored the folds of her coat and then moved upwards, vertically. He found a button, and then another alongside it, and he knew that he was right. The discovery comforted him like a shot of painkiller.

91

Annie had rolled towards him as the falling began. She had been lying on her back before, with her hair pinning her down. Now she was on her side, much closer to him, still with her arm stretched out towards him. She had rolled with all her remaining strength, and she must have torn her hair free.

She had been trapped by the heavy, fireproofed door. That's what she had said. He remembered – how long ago? – trying to push it open for her. It had been lying at an angle on top of her, pinioning her right side. Now he reached upwards as far as his arm could stretch, but he couldn't feel even the edge of it. So whatever it was that had fallen had tipped the door further and freed her. But the door had been a shield as well as a pinion. What was protecting them now? Steve looked into the unyielding darkness. If it fell again, he thought wearily, it would extinguish them too.

For the first time Steve thought that he could reach out gratefully for that extinction.

And then, like a feeble blue flame, came the determination: *No.*

His fingers moved to Annie's wrist again and felt the little slow ticking of her pulse.

Martin ran faster, his legs pumping up and down.

The cloud of dust swirled outwards, the colour of its underbelly in the lights fading as it drifted away.

The spectators at the cordons had thinned out as darkness fell and the cold intensified, but Martin could see people turning, running back to see as the echoes of the crash died away.

He ran without thinking and reached the line of people, standing with their faces upturned and staring at the blue and orange smoke reflections where the façade had been . . . He looked each way and then pushed through them. He scrambled through the barriers and ran again, down the length of the store front. The space was full of other people running and the sound of their boots crunching on brick and glass. Two men with a stretcher passed in front of him and Martin saw a group of others bent around a fireman lying on the ground. As the stretcher was unfolded and they lifted him up his heavy helmet fell and rolled unnoticed in the debris. Martin looked past it into the centre of the store and saw a smoking mountain of stone and planks and scaffolding. A blue tarpaulin was draped like a cloak around its base.

Martin stumbled forward with his hands outstretched.

Annie was under there. He would launch himself at it and dig until he reached her. There were uniforms all around him, police in helmets, and firemen with their brave silver buttons. He went forward with the surge of them, through the gaping hole where the busy doors had stood, and into the thick dust and the blizzard of fragments that the wind blew off the broken walls.

They were already working at the wreckage, with shovels and picks and their bare hands, to clear a space. He pushed further forward, and the broad blue back in front of him turned and heaved a chunk of stone into his hands. Martin never felt the weight. He swung round and passed it on to the next link in the chain and then reached out for the next. His lips drew back from his teeth in concentrated effort and he felt the tension of the day's idleness evaporating.

He was helping her now, working with his strength to reach her.

Hold out, brace for the weight, swing with it, let go and reach again.

I won't let her go. I won't let it take her. The words beat in his head, synchronizing into a desperate chorus with every heave and stretch of his body. Instead of the rubble at his feet and the legs of the men struggling in front of him, he saw Annie.

He saw her at home, waiting for him to come in at the end of the day, and the way that her face softened with pleasure at the sight of him. He saw her frowning, with her head tilted a little to one side as she sat reading with Thomas, and then laughing, with Benjy as a fat, tow-headed baby slung on one hip.

He thought of the warmth of her beside him in their bed, the softness and familiarity of her curled against him. The warmth

93

seemed to spread around him, insulating him for an instant from the desperate rescuers.

He could feel Annie's generosity and strength, and the reality of her love for the three of them, like a living thing fighting beside him. If she was dead, and all her warmth and life had bled away, how could he bear it? And if she wasn't dead, but buried, injured, what must she be suffering? Her pain stabbed into him, becoming his own, and he doubled over it. Like an automaton he took the next chunk of masonry that was thrust backwards at him.

If it could be me down there, instead of you, Annie. I love you. Did you know that? I wish I'd told you. I wish I'd let you know how much.

He knew that he could have worked for ever and he found himself trembling with impatience, sweat glueing his hair to his face as he waited for the next load. But there were more uniforms pushing past him now. He dimly heard the blare of sirens. Martin let his arms drop to his sides and he ducked sideways, into a corner of shadow. The lights carved out a pallid room inside the skeleton store and the rescuers milled within the room. Martin tried to slip out beyond the walls of it. He went down on his hands and knees and tried to pull at a piece of plank that stuck up at an angle. The illusion of superhuman strength had deserted him and he wrestled feebly with his piece of wood. The sweat dried icily on his face.

Then he felt a hand on his shoulder.

'Who are you?'

It was a policeman, of course, in a greatcoat and peaked cap.

'My wife is under there,' Martin said. He looked at the policeman and saw the official expression fading for a moment, and sympathy peering out at him. He was very young, Martin thought irrelevantly, the old cliché. Not more than twenty, surely? A year or so older than Annie and he had been, back at the very beginning.

'Will you come this way, sir?'

Martin nodded, helpless now, although his torn hands still

twitched involuntarily, reaching out for more stones. He followed the policeman to the steps of the parked trailer. Inside it he saw telephones on a bench, a little group of men waiting. It was very warm and stuffy after the cold outside.

'My wife,' he explained to them. 'I want to help to get her out.'

'Do you know for sure that she is down there?'

Martin shook her head, but then he babbled, 'Yes. Yes, I'm sure she is. There's nowhere else she could be, not after all this time . . .' The words petered out as they looked at him.

'The façade is unsafe still,' the senior man said gently. 'I can't allow anyone except rescue personnel anywhere near it. The most helpful thing you can do for your wife is to leave her recovery to those trained for the job. *If* she's there, of course.'

'I want to help,' Martin repeated.

'I know. But what will happen if I let you go in there and a chunk of rubble falls on you?'

The policeman pinched the bridge of his nose between his fingers. Martin could see that they wanted to be considerate, but they were also irritated by his persistence.

'If you would like to go down the road to the local station,' the other one suggested, 'you can have a cup of tea in the warm. I'll send a WPC to keep you company, and we can contact you as soon as we know anything at all.' He tapped one of the telephones with his fingertip.

'I'd rather be here, as close as possible,' Martin insisted.

'I'm afraid, then, it will be a case of asking you to wait at the cordon. The inner one, at the point closest to here.' The commander gestured backwards over his shoulder. 'Would you like a constable to come with you?'

Martin thought of the young faces he had seen today, blotched with cold under their helmets.

'No,' he said. 'Thank you. I'll be all right on my own.'

They nodded, waiting for him to go and leave them to their work.

'It said . . . it said on the radio that there are still three people in there. Is that true?'

The officer hesitated for a moment and then he said, 'Yes. Before the collapse at least one of them was alive. We heard a shout. There's still hope, of a sort.'

Martin stood up, painfully, like an old man.

Annie, was it you, screaming down there?

They escorted him back to the cordon. Martin walked to the place closest to the control trailer and stood once more to watch as he had watched since midday.

There was a disturbance behind him but he didn't hear it. It took a tap on his shoulder to make him half turn his head, never taking his eyes off the store.

'Hello. Mike Bartholomew from the BBC.' It was a man with a microphone, a camera crew trailing behind him. 'I saw you come out of the control trailer back there. Is there anything you can tell us?'

Martin whirled round and struck out, almost knocking the mike out of the man's hand.

Annie, was it you, screaming down there?

'No,' he shouted. 'I can't bloody tell you anything.'

And he turned his back on them, staring helplessly at the circle of lights around the store front, tears blurring his eyes.

Steve lifted his shoulders, gathering what was left of his strength, and then dragged himself another inch to the right. He had to rest afterwards, lying with his lip still drawn between his teeth until the claw of pain released a little. Then he tensed his muscles again for another effort.

If he could get close enough to her, he thought, he might be able to do something to help her. Annie lay very still and silent, and the beat of her pulse seemed frighteningly weak.

To move across the last few inches separating them took everything Steve had. His head flopped down and his ears filled with the sound of his own gasps for breath.

At last he had done it. He was still holding on to her hand, and he clung to it while he fixed all his will on the next breath, and then the next. He had kept the worst fear at bay while he struggled to reach her – the fear that the airflow, wherever it had come from, had been blocked off by the fall. But now that he could think about it he realized that the clogged air was settling. Each breath came easier, and although the dust still choked him there was oxygen filling his lungs. He even had the impression that a draught of clean, cold air touched his face.

He lay on his side facing Annie. He could feel her close to him, and he had the sudden sense that they were like lovers in the dark. Gently he disentangled his fingers from hers and felt for her pulse. The little beat was still there. He laid her hand down and then reached out to touch her face.

With his fingertips he followed the contours of it, trying to see her through his hands. Her hair was tangled over her cheek and he stroked it back. Her forehead was cold, but he knew that she was alive. When he touched her upper lip and traced the line of it through a crusted patch at the corner, her mouth opened and he felt the faint exhalation of breath on the palm of his hand.

His fingers moved again, over her chin and then to cup the point of her jaw. Except for the dried blood at the corner of her mouth her face was untouched.

He rested for a moment. Steve was thinking, his confused mind still only admitting one thought at a time, *What happened?*

He tried to recall the exact quality of the noise. It had been a long, diminishing roar. Not an explosion, but a collapse. It must be that more of the store had fallen in overhead. Perhaps the rescue work had undermined it. Perhaps the rescuers themselves were pinioned, somewhere in the weight above . . .

Steve headed off the thought. They would come in the end, but how much longer could it be? He thought of the watch again and knew that it was gone for good. They had both moved, and he had lost his bearings.

Annie's cheek had grown a little warmer under his hand. He began his slow exploration again. Her hair was matted with dust, but that was all. He combed his fingers through the ragged length of it, but he could find no trace of blood. Very slowly, as gently as he could, he lifted her heavy head and slid his right arm under it.

Her skull felt hard and round. There were no soft places, nothing sticky. Steve felt the first flicker of real hope. No head injuries. He settled her head once more so that it was pillowed on his arm. Then, with his free hand, he stroked her hair.

As if to reward him Annie stirred a little, and then murmured something. Thillren? He strained to hear, and then to make sense of it. *Children*, was that it?

'Annie?'

He whispered her name at first, then repeated it, louder and more insistent. There was no response, and she didn't move again.

Doggedly Steve slid his hand down from her head to her throat, and then over the crumpled stuff of her coat.

At the level of her breastbone his fingers stopped moving. There was a stiffness at first, a difference in the texture of the cloth. He reached further, and then met the stickiness he had dreaded. Blood, here, a patch that had soaked right through her clothes. It was warm on the side she was lying on, and he couldn't stretch far enough beyond her waist to discover how far the blood had seeped. He trailed his fingers downwards to touch the rubble underneath her and there was blood there too, mixed with the grit and dust. He lifted his hand and put it to his own mouth. There was the taste of blood in the dirt, and when he put his hand down to feel it again the patch seemed bigger.

In despair, Steve let his head drop back. A shower of powdery dust fell on his face and he thought of the earth scattered on a coffin lid. Annie was bleeding, and she would bleed to death in his arms.

He opened his mouth and shouted upwards into the black firmament. 'Why don't you come, you bastards? Why don't you come for us?'

The shout was no more than a croak, and he felt the dry ache of thirst in his throat.

There was no point in shouting. 'Annie,' he murmured. He turned his head again so that they lay face to face, their foreheads almost touching.

'I'm here,' he told her.

Suddenly he felt weak, languid and almost comfortable in his exhaustion. The thick air was like a blanket. It if wasn't for the thirst, he thought, he could fall asleep. Like a lover, with Annie in his arms. If he just inclined his head a little he could kiss her cheek . . .

Annie. Not Cass, or Vicky. A stranger, but he knew her face now.

Steve forced his eyes open again.

Not fall asleep. Not.

He made himself think, remember, anything, just to keep his consciousness flickering on.

Overhead the lights made a harsh ellipse in the dark cave of the store. There were more of them now, and the work in the light was faster, and fiercer. The collapse had come, injuring two men, but the danger was past. Even the injured were forgotten, now that they had been taken away to safety. The rescuers worked on, grimly, digging from the point where the scaffolding shelter had been. The tarpaulins had been rigged up once more, providing a rough screen against the wind and sleet, and from inside them the police guarding the store front could hear the multiplying bite of picks and the juddering whine of the drills.

It was ten past five. Forty-two minutes since the frontage had collapsed. Already, seemingly incredibly, the ground floor had been exposed all over again. They were working downwards, once more, into the basement.

Annie lay with her head in her mother's lap. It was a warm day, and she had been playing in the garden. She knew that, because she could still smell the scent of crushed grass where the rug had been spread out, and the musty geranium leaf smell from the window boxes. Then she had hurt herself, somehow. Perhaps she had fallen on the path and cut her knees, or perhaps she had bumped her head on the kitchen door as it swung outwards in the breeze.

99

She had run in tears to find her mother, and her mother had bathed her cuts and dried her face. Then they had gone together into the cool sitting room. There were photographs on the piano and on the low table by the fireplace, Mummy and Daddy when they were young, Annie herself and her brother on seaside holidays. It was very tidy, very quiet. Annie was lying on the sofa. She was wearing sandals with a rising sun pattern punched in the toes and white ankle socks, a green cotton dress and hair ribbons. Once or twice her mother stroked her hair back from her cheek.

Annie smiled contentedly. As she lay there she had a huge, luminous sense of something that was puzzling, because it felt so strange and important, but yet was also utterly comforting and warm and safe. For a brief moment she held the whole of childhood, the summer afternoons and birthdays and holidays and winter bedtimes, all distilled in the recollection of one single day. She turned her head a little, feeling the touch of her mother's fingers, afraid that the vision would evade her. She wanted to hold it, but she knew that it would burst like a bubble as soon as she touched it.

It stayed with her for a moment longer, and then she felt her smile of joy fading. So complete, so perfect a vision of childhood could never visit a child. A child's view of its own life was a mass of fragments, frustrations and fleeting pleasures and unexplained loose ends.

She was cold, not pleasantly cool any more. She wasn't a child, and the precious, glowing vision had vanished. From a distance, Annie saw herself sit up and swing her legs down off the sofa. She ran to the door, with the hair ribbons fluttering like white butterflies. Her mother sat with her hands in her lap, watching her go, and her face was sad.

It wasn't her mother, then, but Annie herself and she was watching the open door and the sunlight making long squares on the parquet floor of the hall. Pain was stabbing into her side, and there were tears behind her eyes that hurt in a different way. She heard children's voices in the garden. Somehow she got up and went to the window. It wasn't the little girl with the hair ribbons playing out there. It was Thomas and Benjamin, Benjamin in his pedal car and Tom clambering up into the branches of the pear tree. They were calling her and she couldn't run, or even answer them.

'Children,' Annie managed to say.

Someone was listening to her, she knew that. It was comforting not to be alone in the dark, with the pain. He was very close to her, and she heard him say, 'I'm here.'

Annie wanted to ask him, 'Come outside and see the children,' but she couldn't. She watched them herself, instead, knowing that he was close enough to see whatever she saw.

They were absorbed in their play. Benjy came hurtling down the path, his face a concentrated frown. Tom hung out of the tree, his legs dangling as he pretended to fall, just to frighten her. She waved to them, but they didn't wave back. Watching, she knew that she should have felt the same calm sweetness as when she had recaptured her own childhood. But it was cold in this garden. The trees were bare of leaves and it had been trying to snow. There was a white powdering of it on top of the walls, and the wind was like a knifeblade. The boys were on their own, out there.

Annie knew why she felt so cold and sad. She was afraid of leaving them. She felt her weakness, and the sure sense that she was failing them. Her love for them took in every minute of their lives, interwoven with her own for eight years, unshakable. It couldn't end, could it, cut off in the darkness?

Annie left the garden window and walked through the house, touching the memories accumulated in the rooms. In the playroom they crouched beside the model train layout, their heads almost touching. In her bedroom Annie saw the wicker crib that he had put Tom into when she brought him home as a baby. He lay under the white covers, a tiny, warm bundle. Their faces turned up to her from the kitchen table, Benjy's mouth rimmed with jam. The sounds of their voices drifted up the stairs, and she heard running footsteps overhead.

There was nothing of herself left in the house. She wanted to be there, but something terrible had happened to stop her going back. She felt her sons' love, and their need, and the brutally snapped edges of the circle that had held them together. The dream she had had of her own childhood had contained another circle, unbroken. She had wanted so much to duplicate that circle and to set others moving outwards, ripples on a pool.

The loss hurt unbearably. Annie moaned, and at once the arm holding her tightened.

'Tom,' she said, 'Benjy.'

'Annie,' the man's voice said, very gently, like a lover's in the most secret darkness. 'Hold on. They're coming for us. I can hear them.'

Annie didn't know what he meant. She had been in the garden, watching her children play.

Steve had been listening. The ring of spades and drills was louder now, and he felt himself shrink from the sharp metal biting over his head. But he was frightened by how quickly Annie seemed to be slipping away from him.

'Go on thinking about your children,' he said. 'You'll be with them soon. I wish I had children. I've never felt that before, but I do now.' *Now it's too late.*

The scraping overhead was much closer, but he felt himself at a distance from it, further with every minute. Another irony. Steve found himself smiling, but couldn't remember why. He put his hand out to touch Annie's cheek, strengthening their contact.

'If I had children,' he rambled, 'I'd make it different. Not like for me. It would be so different. I'd make sure of that. Perhaps that was why I didn't want any with Cass. I never thought of that.'

Annie turned her head a little, perhaps to hear better, perhaps reaching for the touch of his fingers again. He cupped her cheek in his hand.

'Shall I tell you? I've told you everything else. There isn't much, anyway.'

He began to talk and Annie listened, dimly confusing the little boy he was describing with her own sons, so that Steve and Tom and Benjy ran together down the paths ahead of her and their voices were carried back to her on the wind.

He had been to that flat before, of course. He knew it, on the day that his mother took him there with his suitcase, almost as well as his own home. Three floors, up the hollowed stone steps that had mysterious twinkly fragments embedded in them. Into the living room, where his Nan was waiting for them. Beyond was the kitchen, with the cracked lino floor. There was a grey enamel stove on legs in there, with a little ruff of grease around each of its feet, and the sight of the hairs caught in the grease made him feel sick in the back of his throat.

'Here we are then, Mum,' his mother had said, in the too-cheerful voice that always told him she was about to do something he wouldn't like.

His Nan had simply jerked her chin and muttered, 'I can see that.'

He had stayed with Nan before. He didn't like sleeping in the little room beyond the kitchen because there was no window in it, and it was dark in the mornings when he woke up even when the sun was shining down on the High Street.

His mother had taken his case through into the room. He had seen her putting his things into it; too many, surely, for just one or two nights?

Nan had put the kettle on and made a pot of tea and his mother had drunk hers standing up by the kitchen window, smoking and looking out of the window. She wouldn't look at him, and that made him afraid.

Then, when she had finished her tea she had come across the room to him and hugged him. She said, 'Steve, are you listening to me? I've got to go away for a bit. Will you stay here and be a good boy for your Nan, and then I'll come soon and take you home again?'

He had nodded, miserably, knowing that it was pointless to argue. And so his mother had gone and left him with his Nan, and he had gone into his bedroom and taken his toy cars out of his suitcase. He made a line of them on the kitchen lino, taking care not to look at the grease around the feet of the stove.

His mother had come back from time to time, less and less frequently. At first she had brought money, and Nan liked that.

'Perhaps next week,' she always said, when Steve asked her when she was going to take him back home. Then she began coming without money, and that made Nan angry.

In the end she didn't come at all.

In the dark Steve lay holding Annie and trying to remember what it had been like, then.

It was hard, because it had been so featureless. There had been a long, long time when everything stayed exactly the same except that he grew bigger. He would recall the places clearly enough. Outside the flat there was the high, grey-brick school surrounded by a fenced yard. After school he had played between the lines of prefabs at the end of the street, and on the bombsites where the willowherb sprouted cheerfully. It had been the same for him, more or less, as for his friends. And if he had felt anything much, he had forgotten it.

Once, when Nan was angry with him for some reason, he had shouted at her, 'I'm going away from here. I'm going to find my Dad, and tell him.'

All Nan had said was, 'That'll take a better detective than you are, my lad.'

At about the same time, he had learned that his mother had gone to live in Canada, with a friend.

Perhaps a year later, after months of silence, she had sent Nan some money in an envelope. There had been a letter with it, and in the letter his mother had said that part of the money was for a Christmas treat for Steve. Nan was to take him up to the West End, to Selfridges – she had stressed that, Selfridges, underlined – to see Father Christmas.

'I was eight, or nine perhaps. Too old for Father Christmas. My mother had forgotten I was growing up. She must have thought I was still six. But we went, anyway. All the way, on the bus. I remember everything about it.'

He hadn't been very interested in Father Christmas. An old boy with cotton wool stuck all over his chin. But the rest of it had been like a vision of Paradise. They had ridden on the escalators past mirrored pillars that reflected the stately lines of shoppers gliding upwards. He could look down at the floors below him, acres of things spread out for him to admire, lit and scented and brilliantly coloured. No one else, even Nan, had seemed to be surprised by it.

'It's all right for some,' was all Nan had said.

But he could have stayed there all day, just wandering about, looking at things. And at the people, all brushed and glossy and furred. When Nan dragged him away at last they had walked along Oxford Street, looking into every glittering window. They had tea in Lyons', and he sat at a table in the corner by the door so that he could look out at the taxis and big cars.

It was then, on that day, that Steve decided where he would live. And how he would live.

'I can remember, when we got back to Nan's, how grey it looked. Grey and bare.'

After that, it was just a matter of how long it took to get away.

Annie was so quiet. He stroked her hair again and whispered, 'Did you hear all that, Annie? Are you still here?'

She had heard it, and she could see the children ahead of her. They stopped running to look in at a shop window. There was a Christmas tree in the window, hung with clear glass balls that captured the colours of the rainbow. There were presents all around the tree, wrapped in shiny scarlet paper and tied with scarlet satin ribbons.

She couldn't see their faces, but the children looked so small and vulnerable, silhouetted against the bright, white lights. She wanted to reach out and draw them into her arms, but she couldn't. She couldn't even put her arms around the man in return for his warmth and the comfort of his voice. She turned her head a little and felt him tense, listening to her.

'Children,' she said again.

Steve nodded in the darkness, exhausted.

'That's right, Annie. Hold on to them. They're coming for us. Can't you hear?'

She could see them, still looking at the Christmas tree, but she couldn't hear their voices. There were other noises, scraping and rattling, drowning them out. But she said, summoning up her strength, 'Yes.'

They were working in silence now. They bent in a circle under the glare of the lights. Every minute or two they stopped work and listened, and when the silence settled around them, unbroken, they began again, burrowing downwards. In his trailer the police commander waited with his finger touching the corner of his moustache. Martin waited at his point on the barricade, never taking his eyes off the tarpaulin screen.

Children, Steve was thinking. *If I had a daughter.*

His face was wet, and he thought how stupid it was to cry for her because she had never been born.

I'd buy her a pony, he thought. And ballet lessons, and white satin shoes with ribbons to go dancing in. And when she's seventeen I'll buy her a car, and take her downstairs on the morning of her birthday to see it parked outside the house. I'll open the front door, he thought, and say, *There it is* . . .

As the door opened inside Steve's head, he saw a beam of light.

It shone straight down on to his face and the brightness of it was as sharp as pain. He closed his eyes because the light hurt so much and he saw the dazzle of it inside his eyelids. When it had faded a little he opened his eyes again, and the patch of light was bigger, and still brighter.

He opened his mouth and through the dust caked in his throat he shouted, 'Here. Down here.'

The light blinked and went out and he felt a second's terrible disappointment, but then he understood that it was a head, blocking the light to look down at them.

'Down here,' he said again. And then, 'Please. Come quickly.'

'You're all right,' a voice came back to him. 'We'll have you out in no time.'

'Come quickly,' he begged. 'She's bleeding.'

He turned his head to look at Annie. Her eyes were closed and she looked as if she was deeply asleep. Her eyelashes showed dark against the dust that masked her face.

'Annie,' he whispered to her, 'we're all right. They're here now.'

She didn't answer but he held her tighter and with his free hand he tried to brush the coating of filth off her face.

The ragged circle of light grew wider. He could hear people talking, giving orders, and the quick movements and the clink of their tools as they worked. The girl in his arms looked so defeated. He was afraid that now, after all, it was too late.

'Please hurry,' he begged them.

They wanted him to talk, and now that it was over he was too weary to speak. The questions came one after another as the men came closer. Steve saw the light glinting on their helmets and their shiny boots.

'What's your name?'

'Is she your wife?'

'Do you know the woman's name?'

'I'm thirsty,' Steve said.

A moment later they lowered a little bottle of water down to him. He reached up with his free hand and then lifted his head just enough to tip the bottle to his mouth. It ran out between his lips and down his chin, clear and cool. He let his head fall back again.

He told them his name. 'Her name is Annie. I think she's badly hurt. When the collapse came.'

'That's all right, don't worry.' They were trying to soothe him, he knew that. 'We're going to try to put a doctor in beside you.'

A moment later someone came sliding downwards and the dust rose chokingly. Steve braced himself, waiting for the extra shock of pain from being touched. Since the light had come, the pain had intensified. He wondered if he could bear it without screaming out.

The doctor crawled into their tiny space.

'I'm Tim,' he said, and Steve thought it was just like at a party. He would have laughed, but for the pain in his leg. 'And there's Dave, and Tony, and Roger and Terry up there. They're all wonderful diggers. They'll soon get you out.'

They lowered a bag down to the doctor. He had a torch, too, and the light burned into Steve's eyes. It was so bright that he couldn't see Annie's face any more, and he didn't see the flash of the hypodermic either as the doctor slid the needle into his arm.

The pain receded after that. Steve lay and watched the doctor's black shape hunched between them. He bent over Annie, touching her, and the sticky patch in her coat. Steve heard him rummage in his bag and the tiny, metallic clink of his instruments.

'She won't die, will she?'

After a moment the doctor said quietly, 'I don't know yet.'

Hurry up, damn you all. Why does it take so long?

'Okay, Steve,' someone called out to him. 'Hold on just a few minutes longer.'

The police commander crouched at the lip of the hole. Under the lights he could see the colour of the woman's coat. It was blue, and she was wearing black boots.

'The descriptions tally, sir.' One of his men had checked the computer-stored descriptions of people reported missing through the long day. 'And the man is conscious. He says her name is Annie.'

The commander nodded. For a moment he had been thinking of his own wife, and seeing her crumpled amongst the debris.

'How long?' he asked the fire chief.

'Ten, fifteen minutes.'

The men were working in frantic silence now. There was a girder to be lifted and hoisted away before the smaller chunks of rubble could be moved. Once that was done the victims could be lifted out on to stretchers.

The commander looked down at the doctor's head, and then glanced at the stretcher party, waiting. The ambulances were drawn up beyond the tarpaulins.

'Her husband's waiting at the barrier,' he said. One of his men was already moving, but the commander said, 'Wait. Leave it for another five minutes, until they're ready to bring her up. He'll be in the way here, and if she's unconscious he can't help her. Take him into the trailer and tell him, will you?'

Steve didn't know how long it took, in the end.

The doctor waited beside him, holding up a bag and tubes that ran into Annie's arm.

The firemen tried to joke as they came closer.

'You'll be tucked up in bed with a nice nurse in good time for "Match of the Day", mate.'

'What time is it?' he asked them.

'Ten past six. You'll have to leave now, the store's closing.'

He was laughing now, weak laughter that didn't begin to express his happiness. He loved all the firemen, and the doctor. It wasn't all ending. There were still chances.

When the men in their boots and helmets were almost beside them, Steve turned his head to look at Annie again. Her eyes were open, fixed on his face.

'You see?' he said, and smiled at her. 'I knew we'd be all right.'

He saw her look at the doctor and the fireman and the whites of her eyes showed startlingly in her dirt-blackened face. Then she came back to Steve again. Her lips moved and he heard her say his name, just once.

'Ready?' the fireman asked. The doctor nodded, his mouth tight with anxiety.

'We're taking Annie out first,' they said to Steve. 'You're fit enough to wait another minute or two.'

It must be hurting her. Steve clenched his fists, futilely trying to absorb some of her pain as they slid the harness under her

109

body. He wanted to hold her hand, but the doctor's fingers were at her wrist. They began to winch her upwards and he saw the dark, ugly mark where she had been lying. Her eyes were closed again. She swung for an instant before the doctor and the firemen steadied her and the tubes dangled at her side.

Her hair fell back and he remembered how he had seen it brushed back over her shoulders, so long ago, when he had reached to open the door. It was grey with dust and ragged where she had torn it free.

Everything was dark again, and he had an instant's recall of the hours they had clung together.

They were taking her away now.

Steve blinked up into the painful brightness of the lights.

'Annie,' he said. 'I love you.'

Martin followed the policeman down the trailer steps.

He knew, now. She was here, and she was alive. Just.

His fists clenched in his pockets so that his fingernails dug into the palms of his hands. The blue tarpaulins made a blur in front of him. They held the stiff curtain aside and he ducked between them. There were cold, bright lights here and people intently watching a knot of men clustered around something that came up into the light. Martin stumbled forward and saw Annie on a stretcher. There was a doctor supporting her head and her arm lay pale and bare where they had cut her coat sleeve away.

Martin looked down past her and saw a man lying on his side. The space where she had been was tiny. The man's hand clenched and unclenched, on emptiness.

They were carrying Annie out of the terrible place. Martin ran to the other side of the stretcher and walked beside them, his heart thumping out wordless prayers.

Please. Let her live. Let her live. Please.

Back through the blue screen.

As they came out of the ruined store front Martin was assailed by different lights. These were the cameras, flashing after them. He felt the upsurge of anger but there was no time for it. They were into the ambulance and the double doors thudded shut. He saw the reflection of the blue light beginning to turn over their heads as they slid away.

They were working on her already, two nurses and a second doctor, but Martin found a place at her side.

Annie opened her eyes again. They were glazed with pain, but they moved and then settled on Martin's face. He saw the flicker of bewildered disappointment. It was as if she had expected to see someone else.

He took her hand and held it, but it lay limp and cold in his.

Four

The doors of the accident department swung open ahead of the ambulance. Annie's stretcher was lifted out and laid on the waiting trolley. Martin ran beside it with the doctor. He felt the brief coldness of the sleet on his face and then the hospital closed around them like a white tunnel.

They were wheeling Annie away out of his reach. He stepped awkwardly forward and saw her face. It was so white, so withdrawn into itself, that he was afraid she was already dead. A little involuntary shudder of fear and grief escaped him.

A sister wearing a blue dress with white cuffs put her hand on his arm. 'Are you her husband?'

He nodded, unable to speak.

'Come and sit in my office. I'll get you something while you're waiting.'

They put him in a wooden-armed chair in the corner of the little room. The sister brought him tea in a plastic cup, and Martin sipped it without tasting it, grateful for its warmth.

She won't die, will she? The words kept hammering in his head, but he didn't speak them yet.

The casualty consultant and his senior registrar were with Annie.

The consultant had been off duty when the hospital put out its special major accident alert to everyone from the pathologists to the porters. He had arrived in his unit thirty minutes later, and he had been at work ever since. With his team he had treated forty-five people, and he had heard from the police that another casualty would soon be on his way. They had just confirmed that he would be the last. There was another man still buried in the wreckage, but he was dead.

'The last but one,' he told his colleague. He rubbed his hand quickly over his face and then pulled his gloves on to begin the examination.

Annie's skin was pale and clammy, and her breath was coming in shallow gasps.

'Blood pressure?'

'Seventy over nothing.'

Her pulse was fast. One-forty.

The consultant pulled Annie's coat open and undid her blood-stained dress. Her stomach was dark with bruising, and it was rigid to the touch. The doctors glanced at each other and then the consultant said quietly, 'O-neg blood up at once. Urgent cross-match. Theatre immediately.'

He went to the telephone to alert the surgical team who were waiting upstairs.

Five minutes later Annie was on her way to them.

She was already gone by the time they brought Steve's stretcher in. The pain in his leg was biting through the blur of morphine, but he twisted under the blanket they had covered him with, trying to see where she was. The accident unit looked quiet, almost ominously peaceful. Then suddenly the examination cubicle seemed full of people, their faces looming over him.

'Annie,' Steve said distinctly. 'Where is she?'

They murmured amongst themselves and then someone said, soothingly, 'She's in good hands. On her way to theatre. Now, let's take a look at this leg.'

The pain jabbed into him. Steve stared upwards at the bright circles of the overhead lights. They bled outwards into rainbow wheels and then contracted, hard and sharp again. He bit his teeth together to stop himself from crying out. At last the doctor straightened up and left his leg alone. 'You've got a nasty fracture in the upper bone in your left leg,' he said smoothly. 'I think we'll whip you up to theatre as well and get it pinned for you. We can tidy up one or two other things while you're under the anaesthetic.'

The pain made Steve helplessly angry. He thought, *Why do they always talk like that?*

But he was too weary to try to say anything. He closed his eyes, thinking about Annie's white face under the rescue lights, and waited for them to put him to sleep.

The consultant finished what he had to do to Steve and then went out into the corridor. He was stretching to ease his muscles and thinking longingly of a whisky in the bar across the road from the hospital, but the duty sister was waiting for him. She told him briskly that Annie's husband was still waiting in her office.

The doctor looked puzzled, glancing backwards to where Steve was lying. 'I thought he was her husband.'

The sister shook her head. 'Her husband is sitting in my room. He looks very shocked.'

The doctor sighed. 'Well. I'd better go and tell him, then.'

When Annie opened her eyes again there was light streaming all round her. The brightness was shapeless at first, but then it began to form itself into long rectangles with dimmer patches separating them. She tried to turn her head and found that she couldn't. The discovery brought a cold spasm of terror that made her eyes snap wider open, staring into the light. The light was reassuring, but she wanted to see more, to see what was beside her, and she couldn't. She tried to gather her strength to do it but all she could feel was pain, pain everywhere, as if it had possessed the air surrounding her. Annie felt a moan rise in her throat but it was stifled because there was something blocking its way.

Then someone's face slid forward, blotting out the rectangles of light. Annie looked carefully at it. It was a man, wearing a white coat with a high collar. Like a barber's jacket, she thought. The man's mouth was moving, and she realized that he was talking to her. When he stopped talking he smiled, but his eyes were watching something behind her head.

She tried to ask him what he was doing. Her tongue moved, and then she felt that she would choke. There was a tube going down her throat, and her stomach heaved against it.

The man's face moved again, and now she could hear what he was saying. 'Just to help you with your breathing for a little while longer, Annie. You're doing fine now.'

She was in hospital, then. Steve had said that they would come for them before it was too late. Annie wanted to reach her hand out to touch Steve's hand again. Her fingers moved, but her hand was too heavy to lift. There were tubes there too. She could feel the rubbery kiss of them against her wrist.

She was very tired. Annie closed her eyes again and the bright rectangles vanished.

'She won't die, will she?'

Martin had waited at the hospital all through the evening. It was midnight before they brought Annie out of the operating theatre. The surgeon came to find Martin in the stuffy waiting room where he had sat for hours, staring at the rubber-tiled floor. He told Martin that Annie had crush injuries to the abdomen. They had found that her spleen was ruptured and so they had removed it, and they had repaired a deep tear in her liver. The operation had revealed no other serious internal damage, but there were fractures in her right shoulder and upper arm, and deep cuts and extensive crush bruising on her legs and thighs. She was in the recovery room now, and they hoped that her condition would stabilize.

'Can I see her?' Martin had asked.

'We'll be taking her along to intensive care shortly,' the surgeon had answered carefully. 'I don't think there's anything to worry about tonight. We want to try to bring her blood pressure up. Go home and try to get some sleep now, and come in to see her in the morning. Sister will call you at once if there's any change.'

Martin had gone home.

His mother had arrived to take care of the boys, and she was sitting at the kitchen table waiting for him. Martin shook his head wearily at the familiar sight of everything. Was it only this morning that Annie had been there? He relayed the news that the surgeon had given him, and then he went upstairs to look at the boys. Benjy looked as he always did, curled up with the covers pulled close around his head, but Tom was restless, turning and muttering anxiously in his sleep.

Martin went and lay down on their double bed. He dozed fitfully, waking up constantly because he thought he heard the telephone ringing.

In the morning he went straight back to the hospital. On the telephone before he set out the sister told him that Annie was *rather poorly*. The doctor was with her now.

Martin's car was still in the little mews near the wrecked store where he had left it yesterday. He went to the hospital by tube. All the people travelling to work held up their newspapers, and the pictures of the bombed store and the outraged tabloid headlines danced in front of his eyes. Martin turned his head and stared through the black window, thinking, *Annie, Annie.*

In a bleak little room beside the double doors of the intensive care unit, Martin saw the doctor. Annie's surgeon had gone home to sleep, and this man introduced himself as a renal specialist.

Martin listened numbly. In the early hours of the morning Annie's kidneys had begun to fail, and they had put her on a dialysis machine. Her blood pressure had fallen further, but they had stabilized it now.

'It's a question of waiting, I'm afraid,' the doctor said.

'She won't die, will she?' Martin repeated. He saw the muscle twitch under the doctor's well-shaven cheek, and he thought, He must hear this all the time, people asking, *Will my wife die? Will my husband die?* Suddenly the enormity of what had happened struck him, and the random horror of it. Why did it have to be Annie?

'Your wife is young and healthy. I think her chances are good. But we won't know for a day or two.'

'Can I see her now?'

'Sister will take you.'

They gave him a white gown to wear, and plastic covers to pull over his shoes.

Martin followed the sister's blue dress and starched cap through the double doors. He had a brief impression of a long room, brightly lit, partitioned into cubicles. As he passed he saw, in each bed, an inert shape fed by tubes and guarded by machines. Then the sister stopped. He looked past her and saw Annie. He knew it was Annie because of the colour of her hair on the pillow. But her face seemed to have shrunk, and her cheeks and the skin under her eyes looked bruised. There was a tube in her mouth and another in her nose, there were tubes taped to her wrists and another to her ankle. She was wearing a white cotton hospital gown and through the open front of it Martin could see a line fixed into her chest. Her bed was hemmed in by the square, hostile shapes of machines and a bag of dark red blood hung over her head, trailing its colour down into her arm. Under the gown her shoulder was strapped with white tape, and there was another taped dressing over her stomach. Looking down at her Martin felt how cruel it was that she should be so reduced. Her body looked so dispossessed, as if the machines had taken it and Annie herself had gone away somewhere, a long way off.

There was a male nurse in a white coat watching the three monitor screens at the bedhead. Martin looked away from the flickering dots that read Annie's life out second by second.

The nurse nodded at a chair a little to one side of the bed.

'Would you like to sit with her for a while?' he asked cheerfully. He was Irish, Martin noted automatically. The unit was full of quiet, deftly moving people. It seemed strange that they should have individual characteristics like an Irish voice or a dark skin, and yet be part of these machines and their winking eyes.

'It's a pity you weren't a minute earlier. She was awake for a little while, there,' the nurse told him. 'She's dropped off again now.'

Martin sat down beside her. He reached out to take her hand, but he was afraid of dislodging the tubes. He just touched his fingertips to hers.

Martin sat with her for an hour, but Annie didn't move. He thought of her as she had been at home, moving briskly around the kitchen or running up the garden with the boys whooping ahead of her, and he shifted on the uncomfortable chair to contain his anger. He was angry with the people who had done this to her, and he was shocked to recognize that he was angry with Annie, too, because she had gone away and he couldn't reach her. Martin looked at the machines as if they were rivals, cutting him off from her.

'What are they for?' he asked, nodding at the monitor screens.

'Pulse, blood pressure and ECG,' the nurse said. 'This scale monitors her central venous pressure through the line in her chest. These shunt tubes are for the dialysis machine.'

And so they held her, keeping her alive, a long way away.

After an hour he stood up stiffly and said goodbye to the nurse. Benjy and Tom were waiting at home. Martin went away down the ward without looking left or right.

'How is she?' Steve asked.

'She's holding her own,' they told him. 'Her husband's with her.'

Steve had been thinking about the hours that they had lived through together. The darkness of them was still almost more real to him than his curtained segment of the bright ward. He could hear the nurses going to and fro beyond the curtains, but he could hear Annie's whispering voice just as clearly. It was Annie he wanted to see, and talk to, now that the darkness had gone. Annie and he knew each other. In the long hours she had become his friends, his family, and he knew that he had become hers. But Annie was lying upstairs in the intensive care unit, and her husband was waiting beside her.

By the time the evening came Steve had recovered from the anaesthetic. He knew he had, because although the memory of yesterday hadn't loosened its claw-hold, he could distinguish quite clearly between the memory and the reality of now, in the hospital ward. As if to confirm it a nurse with a little starched frill pinned to the top of her head came and pushed the curtains back, smiling at him.

'There now. We'll give you a bit of a view, now that you've woken up properly.'

Steve saw four beds opposite, and the occupants peering across at him. The table in the middle of the ward was banked with a great mound of flowers. He lay against the pillows looking at them, hypnotized by the generosity of the colours.

Annie woke up again, and she saw that the bright rectangles overhead had been dimmed. They were lights, she understood, and if they had been turned down it must be night-time now. How many nights had gone? She swallowed on the tube that stuck into her mouth, and felt the nausea rising behind it again.

Another nurse was looking down at her. This one was a woman, and Annie saw with intense clarity the contrast between the black skin of her face and the whiteness of the cap that covered her hair.

'Hello, dear,' the nurse said. 'Your husband has been here all evening, but he's just gone off home. He told me to tell you that everything is all right. Tom and Benjy send their love, and you're not to worry about anything. So you won't, will you?'

The nurse smiled at her, and Annie looked at the warm, reassuring contrast of light and dark again. She tried to say, *Martin*, but the tube gagged her. She realized all over again that she couldn't talk or move, and the pain that had attacked her down in the darkness was even more intense here. She knew that she must be safe here under these lights. The nurse's smile was so wide and white and confident. But still the fear came back and clawed at her. Where had Steve gone? She couldn't even turn her head to look for him. Steve would understand what was happening. He had been there with her, every minute. She could hear quite clearly what he had said to her. She could even see through his eyes his Nan's hunched figure shuffling to and fro in her cramped flat, Steve's own flat with its big, abstract paintings on the white walls. Why wasn't he here then?

She tried to speak again, this time to call his name as she had done in the terrible darkness. But he didn't answer now, and the black nurse put her warm hand on Annie's arm.

'Lie nice and still, there's a good girl. You don't want to upset all my machines, do you?'

Annie tried to think, *What machines?* The answer hovered somewhere beyond the edge of her understanding, like the outer edge of one of the lights overhead that lay out of her field of vision. Its elusiveness seemed more unbearable than the pain, and Annie felt the tears gather behind her eyes and then roll out at the corners.

The nurse bent over her and dabbed them away.

'Oh dear, now,' Annie heard her murmur. 'There's no need for this. You're doing just fine.'

Early in the morning two officers from the anti-terrorist squad came to see Steve. They sat stiffly beside his bed with their note-books, sympathetic but persistent.

'I'm sorry,' Steve said. 'There was nothing. I just held open the door for the girl, and then the bomb went off. I didn't see anything, I wasn't aware of anyone else.'

It happened, he thought wearily. It happened and Annie and I were there, that's all. Annie and I and the others. The two of us were lucky. We're still alive. Annie, are you still there?

But he had no sense of luck, yet. He felt numb, and he simply remembered the two of them lying side by side in the darkness, without being able to think any further. The officers had thanked him, folded up their notepads and creaked away again.

Steve's next visitor was Bob Jefferies.

At the beginning, in the accident unit with the pain fogging everything, they had asked Steve for the name of his next of kin.

Cass? he had thought. No, not Cass.

'Or just someone we can contact to let them know where you are,' they had reassured him. In the end he gave them Bob Jefferies' name, more because Bob was his business partner than because he was a closer friend than any of a dozen others.

And now Bob came down the wards towards him, bulky in his expensive overcoat, carrying one of Steve's Italian suitcases. He stopped at the end of the bed and looked at the dome of blankets propped over Steve's leg, at the dressings covering his hands and chest, and then at his face.

'Jesus, Steve,' he said at last. 'Was the prospect of the staff Christmas party as bad as all that?'

Steve let his head rest against his pillows and, with a part of himself, he laughed. But the laughter jarred his bones, and it died quickly.

Bob looked at his grey face. 'Is it bad?' he asked.

Steve said, 'No. Painful, but no lasting damage.' The orthopaedic surgeon who had come in to see him earlier had told him that the compound fracture of his femur had been pinned. In time, new bone formation would begin, and he should be able to move quite normally. 'I won't be able to walk on the leg for a bit. Months, perhaps.'

Bob hoisted the suitcase on to the end of the bed. 'Mmm. What about getting it over?'

Steve didn't risk laughter this time.

'I didn't ask about that.'

'No kidding?'

They were uncomfortable together, Steve thought, because Bob's awkward urge to extend unobtrusive sympathy and his own determination not to need it had shaken their arm's-length, flippant intimacy out of true.

Bob busied himself with unpacking the suitcase. Steve saw that he had brought in his bathrobe, pyjamas, sponge-bag. It was odd to see Bob handling them.

'Sorry to land you with this,' Steve said.

'Wish there was more I could do.' Bob wasn't looking at him now. 'I couldn't find your electric razor.'

'Not much of a next-of-kin, are you? Don't you know I wet-shave?'

'You apply that frayed bunch of animal hair that's crouching in your bathroom cupboard to your *chin?* Well, don't worry. I'm sure you can get one of these lovely girls to shave you.'

Suddenly Steve wanted to close his eyes. The effort of trying to be the person that Bob knew was too tiring, and there was nothing else he knew how to reveal to him.

Bob saw the weariness, and rapidly unpacked the last things. There were books, and a bottle of Johnny Walker Black Label.

'Can I have some of that?' Steve asked. Bob emptied the water out of the glass on his bedside table and poured two inches of whisky into it. Steve drank some and the familiar, worldly taste of it seemed to link him back to Bob again.

'That's better. Thanks.'

Bob stood back a little, holding the empty suitcase.

'They wouldn't let anyone in except me, and they're only allowing me ten minutes. But they all send their love. Everyone, you know.'

Steve knew. He meant all the people they worked with, colleagues, the business. He could imagine how the news would have travelled.

'And Marian, of course. If there's anything we can do, Steve . . .'

Marian was Bob's wife. Steve nodded.

'Thanks. Thanks very much.'

'D'you want me to get in touch with anyone? Anyone in particular?'

Steve thought for a numb moment. 'Well, Cass, I suppose. And Vicky Shaw. Numbers are in the book on my desk, Jenny'll find them. Tell them I'm all right.'

'Yeah. Okay. Look, can't we fix you up with a private room, at least? Somewhere with a TV and a phone?'

Steve looked round at the ward with its half-drawn curtains. He hadn't spoken to any of the occupants of the other beds, but he liked the feeling of their company. And the glory of the flowers massed in the middle of the room had come to matter as much as anything.

'I'm fine here. Bob, I was supposed to meet Aaron Jacobs yesterday about the fruit-juice commercials . . .'

'Don't worry about the damned business, Steve. Don't worry about anything.'

Bob was a kind man, Steve realized. They had worked together for years, spent countless hours and eaten numerous meals together, but the thought had never occurred to him before. He saw him now, fussing with his coat as he got ready to leave, wanting to do something helpful or say something comforting.

'There is one thing you could do,' Steve said. Bob turned at once, pleased and relieved.

'There was a girl. Her name's Annie. We were down there together, all that time. We talked to one another. We could just touch hands. It would have been . . . terrible, without her.'

'Yes. There was a bit about it in the news. Not very much.'

'She's here, somewhere. They brought her in before me. I've asked, but they won't tell me anything much. Will you find out how she is? How she really is?'

'Leave it to me.'

Bob would do as he asked, Steve was sure of that. He only had to wait, now, until he came back with the news of her.

They said goodbye then, and Bob went away and left him to himself again.

Annie was very ill.

After the emergency operation she had developed pneumonia. The surgeons had taken the ventilator tube out of her mouth and cut a hole for it directly into her windpipe. The machine breathed smoothly for her, and they pumped anti-biotics into her veins to counter the lung infection. Her kidneys had failed completely, but the dialysis machine at her bedside did their work. For another day she lay inert, knowing nothing. Then, as if her body had no strength left even to start the struggle to heal itself, Annie began to bleed. She bled from her operation wound, from her cuts and grazes, and from the holes where the tubes and drips punctured her skin.

Martin sat by her bedside watching her face. He couldn't even hold her hand because the lightest touch brought up big purple bruises under her skin. Her face was so dark with bruising that she looked as if she had been beaten over and over again. He sat and waited, almost in despair.

The doctor in charge of the intensive care unit had told him that Annie's blood had lost all its ability to clot and stop her wounds from oozing. From their battery of tubes and plastic packs they were filling her with all the things that her own blood couldn't produce. Martin watched the packs emptying themselves into her bruised body. Even her hair seemed to have lost its colour, spreading in grey strands against the flat pillow. Her lips were colourless, and leaden circles like big dark coins hid her eyes.

Steve waited too. Bob's determined enquiries had led him to Annie's surgeon, and the surgeon had come down himself to talk to Steve.

'How is she?' Steve asked.

The other man had looked at him speculatively, as if he was trying to gauge how much he should be told.

'I held her hand for six hours,' Steve said. 'I want to know what's happening to her.'

'She has pneumonia and kidney failure. She is also suffering from disseminated intravascular clotting. That is in addition to the usual post-operative effects and her other, more minor injuries.'

'Will she live?' Steve watched the doctor's face. But he didn't see any flicker of concealment, and after a moment the man told him, 'I think her chances are about fifty-fifty. The next two or three days will tell.'

'Thank you,' Steve said.

Two days went by.

The third was Christmas Eve, and the hospital hummed with the sad, determined gaiety of all hospitals at Christmas time. The staff nurse on Steve's ward wore a tinsel circlet over her cap, paper streamers were pinned from corner to corner, and Steve could see a big Christmas tree in the day room that linked the ward to the women's ward across the corridor.

The double row of beds with their flowered curtains and the narrow view through the doors at the end had become perfectly familiar. It struck Steve that he already knew the other occupants as well as he knew Bob Jefferies or any of his other friends outside the walls of the ward.

On the day of the bombing the eight-bedded ward and its women's counterpart had been cleared to receive the victims. They had been brought in one by one, and they had found that their experience was a stronger bond than years of acquaintanceship. By unspoken agreement, they almost never mentioned the bombing itself. But there was a wry, grumbling kind of determination to overcome its effects that linked the newspaper seller, whose pitch outside the store had been covered with falling rubble and glass, the teenage store messenger, the five other Christmas shoppers, and Steve himself. In the handful of days that they had been enclosed in the ward, Steve had unwittingly become a kind of hero. It was only partly because he was the most seriously hurt, and because he had been trapped for so long. The real reason was the tide of presents that flowed into the ward for him. Flowers and cards and gifts arrived for all of them, every day. It was Christmas. The world felt guilty sympathy for them, and the loaded table in the middle of the ward clearly showed it.

But Steve's tributes, from advertising colleague and friends and clients, were set apart by their lavishness. There were complete sides of smoked salmon, champagne and whisky by the case, boxes of chocolate truffles and fruit and flower displays that came in great hooped wicker baskets. Steve had been embarrassed at first by the procession of presents, and he had wanted none of the luxuries except flowers to look at. He gave the rest away, to the other men and the nurses, and then he saw the delighted interest that greeted each new delivery, and he began to enjoy them too.

On Christmas Eve, from Bob Jefferies and some friends in the film industry, a television set and a video recorder arrived. With the machines was a box containing tapes of two dozen of the newest feature films, some not yet even released.

The young messenger-boy shuffled over to Steve's bed and gaped into the box. 'I haven't seen *one* of these before.'

'You've got plenty of time to see them now, Mitchie.'

That was the accepted level of reference to what had happened to them all. They shied away from anything more. Steve thought of Annie lying somewhere upstairs, and wondered what they would say to one another if she was here, instead of this assortment of strangers precipitated into companionship.

At six o'clock one of the nurses inexpertly opened one of Steve's bottles of champagne. The cork popped and bounced over the polished linoleum floor and the silvery froth foamed into hospital glasses. The nurses handed the glasses round and the old newsvendor next to Steve sipped at his and smacked his lips.

'Well,' he pronounced. 'I've known worse Christmases.' He looked appreciatively at the staff nurse with the tinsel wound around her cap. 'But I wish I was your age again, Stevie.'

To be called Stevie, and the way that the old man spoke, reminded Steve of Nan. The thought of her, with the determined paper streamers over his head and the winking fairy lights and his image of the old man's Christmases, filled him with sadness.

I wish I was your age again.

For what? Steve thought.

He hadn't cried since he was a little boy, but there were tears in his eyes now. He wanted to get up and walk out of the room, defending himself with solitude as he had always done. But his broken leg and the pain under the blanket cage pinned him down. He felt his own weakness, and the way it exposed him to the need for other people to be tactful. Steve put his champagne glass down on the locker and turned his wet face into the pillows.

The others saw, and looked away again. Steve knew that they were raising the pitch of champagne jollity amongst themselves to shield him, and he felt the strangeness of what was happening more sharply even than the pain.

He lay and waited for the tears to stop forcing themselves out of his eyes, and thought about Annie. He knew Annie now better than he knew anyone else in the world, and he was afraid that she would die.

You mustn't die, he whispered, as though they were buried again and she could hear him in the dark. You won't die, will you?

The coldness of his fear for her dried up the weak tears.

Deliberately he turned his head back to face the other beds and reached out for his beaker of champagne.

Later, the hospital medical students came to tour the wards with their portable Christmas pantomime. They put on an extra lively show for the bomb victims. Steve lay and watched the clowning with a smile stretched over his face.

It was later still, when the overhead lights had been dimmed and he could hear the nurses rustling and giggling at the end of the ward, when Steve opened his eyes again and saw a man standing beside his bed.

He had a square, pleasant face with lines of tiredness pulling at his eyes and cheeks. He was tall and stooped a little, and he was looking down from his height at Steve lying in bed, as if he wasn't sure whether to tiptoe away again.

'It's all right,' Steve said distinctly. 'I wasn't asleep.'

The man's hand rubbed over his face.

'The sister said I could come in and see you for a minute.'

Steve reached up and clicked on the lamp over his bed. The circle of light enveloped them within the curtained space.

'I'm Annie's husband,' the man said.

She's dead. You've come to tell me that she's dead.

Steve tried to haul himself upright against his pillows so that he could meet squarely what Martin had come to say.

'How is she?' he asked flatly. And then he saw that the lines in her husband's face were drawn by exhausted relief, and not by defeat at all.

'She's going to be all right,' Martin said. 'They told me this evening.'

Steve closed his eyes for a minute. He saw Annie as she had been, lying beside him when they shone the rescue lights down on to her face. Then, superimposed on it there was another, suddenly vivid image of her as she must have been before the bombing. She was laughing, with colour in her cheeks and her hair flying around her face. Steve opened his eyes abruptly.

'Thank God,' he said.

In his own relief he saw Martin's exhaustion more clearly. He pointed to the chair beside his bed and Martin flopped down into it.

'If you look in the locker,' Steve said softly, 'you'll find a bottle of Scotch.'

He took it from Martin and poured a measure into his water glass. Martin wrapped his fingers round the glass and then drank half the whisky at a gulp.

'Thank you,' he said.

Steve waited until Annie's husband looked up again, and then he asked gently, 'What did they say? The doctors?'

Martin shrugged his shoulders inside his coat, as if he couldn't believe now that she was indeed going to live in the face of the terrifying list of things that had threatened her.

'She had pneumonia, but they're beating that with antibiotics. She's been on a ventilator machine that has been breathing for her, through a hole cut in her windpipe, but they say now that they'll be able to take her off that in a couple of days. And her kidneys are starting to work again. They showed me. It's all shown on the screen and marked on the charts at the end of her bed. Her blood wouldn't clot, you know. She had bled so much that it couldn't do what it was supposed to do any more. They filled her up with plasma, and all kinds of other things, and now it's functioning for itself again. The wound from her operation will start to heal now. She'll get better quite quickly from now on, they think.' Martin's hands rested on the sheet, with the glass held loosely in them. 'It was so terrible to see her, in there with the monitors and machines all around her as if she belonged to them and not to me. I couldn't even touch her hand, because it bruised her poor skin.'

Martin's head was bent, and Steve waited again. The image of Annie was too clear and pitiful. But then Martin looked up, and Steve saw that he was smiling. He shrugged his shoulders once more.

'But now she's going to get better. She was awake, tonight. She can't talk, because of the ventilator. But she smiled at me.'

Steve had to look away to conceal the stroke of jealousy.

He made himself think, *Her husband*, and then to remember that Martin had waited all through the day and the night of the bombing, and all through the days ever since. But even his understanding of that, and his sympathy, didn't lessen the shock of his jealousy.

Unseeing, Martin drank the rest of his whisky. The relief was so profound that he wanted to share it. He could have stood up and announced it to the curtained ward, and to the nurses squeezed hilariously into the sister's office at the far end. He felt a wide, stupid smile breaking through the stiffness of his face, and the whisky burned cheerfully in his head and stomach.

'She must have wanted to live, you know,' he murmured. 'She must want it so much.'

Steve remembered. 'Yes,' he said. 'She did. She was very courageous, down there.'

Martin's hand moved a little, as if he had been going to hold it out to Steve and then found that he couldn't.

'I wanted to tell you that she's getting better, of course.' The smile, again. 'And I wanted to . . . thank you. For helping her.'

Through the glow of relief that had bathed the hospital corridors as he made his way down to the stranger's bedside,

Martin found himself watching Steve. He saw the bomb site again too, and himself peering down into the tiny space where the two of them had been lying together all the fearful hours.

It was smaller than a bed. It was like a grave, he thought, and he remembered a medieval tombstone that Annie and he had seen in a cathedral somewhere. They had been on holiday. Long ago, before the boys were born. The stone lord and his lady lay shoulder to shoulder on their stone slab, with a stone replica of their favourite lapdog asleep at their feet. Annie and Martin had deciphered the Latin lettering on the slab together. *In death they were not separated.*

Annie had sighed and said it was very romantic, but Martin had been struck by the intimacy of the narrow place beneath the slab for them to lie in.

They had both shivered a little and then laughed, and had gone on down the side aisle, hand in hand, to look at the stained glass windows.

The image of the same terrible intimacy came back to Martin now.

'I'm so glad she's getting better,' Steve said.

The lame words didn't begin to express the knot of his real feelings, and that was good. 'I've been thinking about her a lot. Wondering. There's no need to thank me, you know. We helped each other. Taking it in turns, one to be afraid and the other to pretend that there was no need. I know that I couldn't have . . . couldn't have held on as long, without Annie.'

It was very quiet on the ward, Steve noticed. Annie's husband was looking at him. In ordinary times he would have a relaxed, humorous expression, and his eyes would be friendly. A nice man. Almost certainly a good man.

Quickly, Steve said, 'What about your children? Benjy, and Tom? They must be . . . missing her.'

'Yes,' Martin said. 'They are.'

Steve said quietly, 'We talked, you know. For a long time, before the wall collapsed. We talked about all kinds of things. She told me about you, and the children, and your house. About how she didn't want to die, and leave you all.'

Martin put his hand up to his eyes and then rubbed them, digging into them with his fingers. He was stupid with exhaustion and relief, wasn't he? 'I know she would say that. Annie wouldn't give up. She wouldn't give up up there, either. In that room with all the machines.'

'I'm glad.' Lame words, again.

Martin stood up. 'The boys are all right. It's harder for Tom, because he knows she's ill, and he can't see her. They won't let anyone go up there, except me.'

Steve felt the movement of jealousy again. He wanted Martin to go now, but he still hovered at the bedside.

'What about you?'

Steve shrugged. 'Broken leg and cuts and bruises. Nothing much.'

Martin was looking at the dimly-lit ward. 'It isn't much of a Christmas for you, either, is it? What about your family?'

'I'm not married. It isn't exactly my favourite time of year, in any case.'

Martin nodded. 'Annie loves Christmas,' he said. He did hold out his hand then. Steve took it and they shook hands.

Martin smiled. 'I'd better go. The kids will be awake at five a.m.'

'Go and get some sleep.'

'Yes,' Martin said. 'I'll be able to do that now.'

After he had gone Steve lay awake for a long time. He took the fact that Annie would recover and held it close to him like a talisman. He didn't think beyond that.

The house was quiet when Martin reached it. His parents had already gone to bed, so he sat in the kitchen and drank another whisky. He thought about the other Christmases he had shared with Annie, and her pleasure in the rituals that must be observed every year. It was Annie who had sewn the big red felt stockings for the boys to hang up, and Martin knew that when he went upstairs he would find them draped expectantly over the ends of their beds.

If she had died . . .

The terror of it struck him all over again and he clenched his fist around the whisky glass.

But Annie wasn't going to die. He was still afraid of her injuries, but he was sure that she was going to live.

He felt a moment of simple happiness. It was Christmas, and their children were asleep upstairs, and Annie was going to live.

He put his empty glass down and went to the boys' rooms. He collected the red stockings, turning the covers back for an instant to look at the sleeping faces. Then he went into their own bedroom where Annie had stacked the presents neatly at the back of their big wardrobe. He took them out one by one and filled the stockings. He was touched and impressed by the care she had given to choosing even the smallest toys. It was so obvious which of the boys each of the things was intended for. He recognized how smoothly and lovingly Annie had orchestrated their simple, domestic affairs. Why had he never told her, or even really noticed it?

When he had finished he laid the bulging red shapes back on the beds. Then he carried their big presents downstairs and put them with the others under the tree.

The fairy lights made a glowing coloured pyramid in the dim room. Martin saw that on the hearth the boys had left a glass of whisky and a mince pie for Father Christmas, and a carrot, neatly peeled, for the reindeer.

That was always at Annie's insistence. 'Why shouldn't the poor old reindeer get something?' he heard her demanding.

It must have been Thomas who had reminded his grand-mother to arrange the little offering tonight.

Martin was smiling as he poured the whisky back into the bottle. He ate the carrot and the mince pie, suddenly ravenous. He realized that he had eaten almost nothing since the bombing.

'Come on, Father Christmas,' Annie would have said now.

'Let's go to bed.' He missed the warmth of her hand taking his, and the sweetness and familiarity of lying down beside her.

Martin turned off the tree lights and went upstairs. He would make this Christmas a happy one for the boys, however little he felt like it himself. For Annie's sake.

The boys woke up very early in the morning, as Martin had known they would. First Benjy and then Thomas came creeping into his bed, the stockings bumping behind them.

'Look!' cried Benjy. 'He's *been*.'

'Is it all right?' Thomas whispered.

Martin lifted the covers and the two of them scrambled in beside him, a wriggling mass of sharp elbows.

'Shh. Don't wake your grandparents. Yes, Tom, it's all right. Everything's all right.'

'Hey, Dad. Happy Christmas.'

He held them for the minute that they allowed him, and they listened breathlessly to the crackle and rustle inside the stockings.

'Well, then,' Martin said. 'Aren't you going to look and see what he's brought you?'

They dived in in unison.

Martin watched, and then, even though he had done the filling what felt like less than an hour ago, their delight drew him into the excitement of unwrapping. For Benjy, who loved to draw and paint and make things, there were fat round fibre pens in fluorescent colours that fitted into his awkward fist, and scribbling pads with orange and black and purple pages, and colouring books. There were building bricks that snapped together with a satisfying click, and puzzles to colour and cut out himself.

For Thomas, quick-witted and pugnacious, there were pocket quiz games and a miniature robot. There were toys that could be changed into other toys by turning and flipping the right parts, and there was a model aeroplane to slot together that twisted unerringly back to the sender's hand. For both of the boys there were the space-age death weapons that they coveted, and Martin heartily disapproved of. But he was too absorbed in the burrowing discoveries even to smile at the evidence of Annie's principles succumbing to her soft heart.

At last the three of them sat back in a drift of discarded paper and packaging, glowing with pleasure.

'How *brilliant*,' Thomas observed, sitting back with a sigh of satisfaction. Then he remembered, and a shadow crossed his face. 'I wish Mum was here.'

Martin put his arm around him. 'She will be,' he promised him, 'before long. She was much better last night. I'll be able to take you to see her soon.'

The shadow lifted.

'And then I'll be able to *zap* her with my new gamma gun.'

'And I will,' Benjy chipped in.

'Go on,' Martin said. 'Zap into your own rooms. I'm going to make a cup of tea for Granny and Grandpa, and tell them about Mummy.'

He waded through the debris with the boys hopping and firing around him.

It's all right, he reminded himself. It's going to be all right.

He opened the curtains, and saw that the light was just breaking on Christmas morning.

Christmas Day was exactly as Steve had imagined it would be. The women from the opposite ward who were well enough to walk came in in their pink and turquoise housecoats and wished each of them a merry Christmas. They were followed by flurries of other visitors, from the hospital padre who came with the hospital choir to sing carols, to the consultants, some of them with their wives and children. The smaller children were obviously bored and ran up and down the ward, sliding on the polished floor. After the doctors came a television crew, to film the bomb victims' Christmas celebrations.

At what felt to Steve like just after breakfast, but was in fact the dot of noon, the Christmas dinner was wheeled in. The accident unit consultant carved the turkey from a trolley in the middle of the ward and the nurses swished to and fro with plates. They brought wine too, from Steve's impromptu cellar, to add to the glow from the morning's surreptitious consumption. After his dinner the old newsvendor lay back against his pillows with a smile of beatific contentment and fell noisily asleep.

At the start of the afternoon visiting the families came trooping in one after the other, wives and children and grand-parents, to make a rowdy circle round each of the beds.

When he heard the *click, click* of very high heels Steve knew who it was before he looked up.

Cass was wearing the fur coat she had bought on an assign-ment in Rome. The pelts had been shaved and clipped and dyed until they looked nothing like fur at all, and they were only reminiscent of animals because of the tails that swung like tassels at the shoulders. A fur hat was tilted down over her eyes so that almost nothing was visible of her face except her scarlet lipstick. Cass had adopted her dressed-up look, as striking and as unreal as a magazine cover. Her entrance had an electrifying effect. The family parties turned round to stare for a long minute. Cass stood beside Steve's bed and looked down at him.

'Hello.'

'Cass,' he said. 'And on Christmas Day, too.' He was trying to remember the last time he had seen her, but he couldn't. Months ago, now. How many months?

Cass shrugged off her furs. She was wearing a tube of cream-coloured cashmere underneath it. It looked as smooth and silky as the pelt of a Siamese cat, emphasizing her resemblance to one. Steve knew that her eyes had the same intriguing smoky depth as a cat's because Cass was short-sighted, and too vain to wear spectacles.

'You look well,' he said, and caught himself smiling inwardly at the bathetic understatement. Cass was, as always, perfectly beautiful.

'That's more than I can say for you.'

'Thanks.'

She swayed forward and sat on the edge of the bed. Her legs

under the short knitted hemline were very long and smooth in pale stockings.

'Oh, darling, I didn't mean that. I meant that it looks as though it was grim.'

'It's all right. I know what you meant.'

There it was, confronting them already, Steve thought. Their almost deliberate inability to understand the first thing about each other. It was hard to believe that this pretty girl with her wide, unfocused eyes had ever been his wife.

She looked around now, and shivered a little. 'Ugh. I hate hospitals. How are you bearing it?'

'Oh, I can bear it. I lie here and listen to people talking. Watch the nurses. There's one very watchable redhead. I think, and sleep. There are worse things.'

Cass laughed and re-crossed her legs. 'I can't think of very many. Poor love.'

Steve was thinking that he found her just as attractive in just the same way as when he had first met her. If she was lying down beside him he would run his hand from the hollow of her waist over the satiny hummock of her hips. He knew how she would sigh with satisfaction, her wide-set eyes fixed dreamily on his.

Steve shifted uncomfortably under the bedclothes, feeling the heavy weight of the plaster encasing his leg.

'Is your leg hurting?' Cass asked innocently.

'No. Not my leg.' She heard the note in his voice and she laughed, pleased with the effect she created. Yet he had hardly known her, Steve reflected. Any more than Cass had known him. Annie and he knew one another intimately, and he had done no more than hold her hand and cradle her head to try to comfort her.

Watching him, Cass asked sharply, 'Has Vicky been in to see you?'

'Vicky? Yes, she came the day before yesterday. When they lifted the next-of-kin-only restriction. She's gone home to Norfolk for Christmas now.'

Cass pouted a little. 'Why did you have to name Bob Jefferies as your next of kin? It made it look as if you didn't have anyone else.'

Steve sighed. 'I couldn't have named you, my love, could I? We haven't seen each other for months. I didn't even know if you were in the country.'

'I was here. I would have come right away.' Cass picked up his hand and bent her head, looking at their laced fingers. 'Didn't you know that?'

After a moment Steve said, 'No, I didn't know. You were the one who left, remember?'

Cass turned her head further, so that a wing of creamy-blonde hair fell and hid her face. Further down the ward someone had turned on the radio. It was a recording of the Nine Lessons and Carols, and they heard the achingly high notes of a boy soprano.

'Steve, I . . .'

He moved quickly, knowing that he couldn't listen. He opened his hand and let her fingers fall back on to the bedcover.

'Bob came. Bod did everything that was necessary, which wasn't a lot.'

Cass turned her face squarely to him then, and he read the mixture of hurt and irritation in it. Just as there had always been, almost from the very beginning. 'It's no good, is it?' she asked. He wanted to reach out and touch her then, but he knew that he shouldn't do that either. There was no point in beginning again, because there was nowhere that he and Cass could go together.

'No,' Steve said at last, and the word fell into the stillness between them.

After a moment Cass looked up brightly. 'Well. I'm not going to dash off at once, having come all the way in here. Let's talk. What shall we talk about?'

'Tell me what you've been doing.'

She launched into a spirited listing of her bookings and her travels to assignments. She had been to New York for six weeks, to Singapore, and to Rome and Sicily. She was busy and successful, and she was still moving in the same fashionable world that she and Steve had once moved in together. At last, however, she ran out of bright anecdotes and they looked at one another again in silence.

In a different voice Cass said abruptly, 'You look so wretched. Why don't you talk about what happened?'

'It happened. I don't remember all that much about it. Except that it hurt, and it was very dark.'

He longed to talk to Annie about it. No one else.

'I saw the news pictures on television.' Cass shuddered. 'Before I knew you were there. There was someone trapped with you, wasn't there?'

'Yes. A woman. We talked, to keep each other company. It made it easier.'

It was impossible to say any more. Somehow Cass understood that.

'I'm sorry,' Steve said. 'I'm very tired.'

She stood up at once and slung her fur coat over her shoulder so that the animals' tails swished to and fro.

'I know. I'll go now. I didn't even bring you a present, did I?'

Steve grinned crookedly at that. 'No need. Everyone in the business has sent things. Half the stock of Harrods.'

Cass laughed. 'I can imagine.' It was the first completely natural note that they had struck between them, and they smiled at each other. Suddenly Cass leaned forward and kissed him, her hair falling against his cheek. Steve was reminded vividly of the night she left him. Cass in her black lace bra and French knickers. He put his hand up to hold her head down to his and kissed her in return. It was Cass who eased herself away in the end.

'Behave yourself.'

'No option, in this plaster.'

Cass sketched a model's little pouting gesture of mock-disappointment. It was all right, Steve thought. They had steered themselves safely through the visit. Cass pulled the fur cloud of her hat down over her forehead.

'Goodbye, my love.'

'Goodbye, Cass.'

Her confident, graceful walk set the tails swinging around her. She didn't look back from the doors.

The old newsvendor leant forward as soon as they had closed behind her.

'Who was that, son?'

'My ex-wife.'

He chuckled throatily. 'Didn't look all that ex to me.'

Steve laughed. 'Appearances can be deceptive, Frankie. Especially with Cass.'

'Well.' The old man settled himself down gain. 'I wouldn't say no myself, I can tell you that much.'

Steve looked around the ward. It had the appearance of the end of a party, with empty chairs abandoned at odd angles, strewn wrapping paper, one or two lingering guests. The smell of cigar smoke drifted in from the day room. Steve was smiling when he closed his eyes. He fell asleep at once.

The lights overhead were clear now. Annie could see the line of rectangles with the neon tubes more brightly defined behind the opaque glass. She knew the faces of each of her nurses, and the eight-hour cycles that governed their appearances made sense because she could see a big, white-faced clock on the wall opposite her bed. The Irish male nurse called Brendan was on duty now. Annie liked him best, because his touch was light and he never hurt her when he changed her dressings or slid a needle into her skin. She watched him in his white jacket as he took a reading from a scale beside her and wrote a figure on one of his charts at the foot of her bed. Behind him Annie could see the senior nurse sitting at her desk on the raised platform in the middle of the room.

Brendan finished what he was doing and leant over her. 'There you are, my love,' he said. 'That's that for another hour. Are you comfortable?'

She could move her head just enough to make a little nod. She tried to smile at him too, feeling the quivering in her swollen lips.

'That's my girl,' Brendan said. He stood still for a moment with his head to one side. Then he said, 'Listen, can you hear?'

It was a long way off, but she could hear it. It was people singing, a warm and familiar sound. It was a Christmas carol. *Hark, the Herald Angels Sing*. The sound of Christmas Day.

'Ah, that's beautiful,' Brendan sighed. 'Our hospital choir, it is. As good as anything you hear on the radio.'

Annie wished that Martin were there to hear it too. He had been sitting beside her bed earlier, but he had leant over to kiss her and then he had gone away. She liked it when he was there. Sometimes he talked, telling her little, ordinary things about the boys and the house. At other times he sat in companionable silence, and that was comforting because it was tiring to listen. It was only when he held her hand that Annie felt uncomfortable. She wanted the other man to be there, then. Steve. The man who had held her hand in the dark. The thought puzzled her, and she turned herself away from it.

Annie lay and listened to the singing until she couldn't hear it any more. Then she let the warm wave of drowsiness take hold of her again. Sleep was so safe, except when the dreams came.

A week later, in the absurdly early hospital morning, Steve was sitting in the armchair beside his bed. He had been up for several days now.

They had hauled him out of bed and given him crutches that fitted under his elbows, then helped him to stand upright. There was a little knob embedded in the heel of his leg plaster. When he was ready to take the first awkward, swaying steps with the crutches, he was allowed to rest it on the floor to balance himself. Never to put any weight on it. For several days one of the nurses and a physiotherapist had made him walk up and down, a little further every time.

Frank and Mitchie and the other men cheered and called out as he struggled to and fro.

He was resting in his armchair now while the nurses made his bed. One of them looked backwards over her shoulder at him as she worked.

'I've got some news for you, Steve. One of my friends works

in the ICU. She told me when she came off last night that they're bringing your friend down today. There's a bed for her in there.' She nodded across the room to the door that linked the day room to the women's ward. 'So you'll be able to see each other.'

'Aw,' the other nurse said, 'isn't that nice?'

Steve looked at the door, and at the reflections of light from the windows on the floor separating him from it. His fingers moved on the metal shaft of the crutches propped against his chair.

'When?' he asked. 'When will they bring her down?'

The nurses looked at each other. 'After rounds, I should think.'

Now that the time had come, Steve was afraid. He could feel the flutter of fear in his stomach. Annie was so important. She was important because she was herself, but also because it was only through Annie that he could learn to come to terms with what had been done to them both.

He was waiting to see her, waiting to begin it together.

Yet he was afraid. What if Annie looked at him with the blank, polite face of a stranger?

She mustn't do that.

Steve curled his hands deliberately round the crutches and held them tight while he sat looking at the door of the ward.

Brendan and another nurse helped Annie up from her bed. They had put one of her own nightdresses on her, and she looked down at her legs under the frilled hem of it. They looked unfamiliar, very thin, their whiteness veined and mottled with blue, as though they belonged to someone else. Brendan brought her blue wool dressing gown and helped her left arm into the sleeve. Her right arm was strapped up and so he draped the dressing gown over it and tied the sash around her waist.

A wheelchair was waiting beside the bed. They lowered her into it, then put her slippers on her feet.

'There you are, now,' Brendan beamed at her.

A person again, Annie completed for him.

For a week, since she had heard the carol singers on Christmas Day, her body had been reassembling itself. It was defined now, within its own skin. It no longer blurred at the edges through tubes into incomprehensible machines. She had become an individual again, dressed in her own clothes, colours and materials she had chosen for herself. She was well enough to be taken out of this quiet, humming room with its bright lights and immobile bodies.

Brendan took the handles of her chair and pushed.

Annie was suddenly frightened. She was used to the room. She had given herself up to it, and the nurses and doctors and their machines had done everything for her. Now they were thrusting the responsibility back at her. The doors came closer, and she was afraid of what lay beyond them. Annie's hand clenched in her lap, and she felt the weakness of her grip.

The nurses in their white coveralls came to the door to see her off. Even the sister left her observation platform for a moment.

'Good luck!' they said.

'Be good, downstairs where we can't keep an eye on you!'

'What does she want to be good for?' Brendan pouted.

The doors opened.

Annie took a deep breath. She had come this far, and to stop was unthinkable. This afternoon, she told herself, she would be able to see Thomas and Benjy.

Annie turned round to smile at the circle of nurses.

'Thank you,' she said. They waved, and the doors closed behind her wheelchair.

Annie faced the hospital corridor as they rolled along. Brendan was whistling behind her. She saw the little cream-painted curve where the wall met the maroon vinyl floor, and the scuff marks in the paintwork. A porter passed them and she noticed a tiny three-cornered tear near the hem of his overall coat. A group of student nurses in pink uniform dresses were as bright as figures in a primitive painting. It was as if the light were brighter than she had seen it before, or as if a thin veil of mist had lifted to define sharper contours and strengthen the colours that sizzled around her. It was a grey, lowering day outside the windows but Annie thought that the utilitarian corridor had been illuminated by bright sunshine. She could hear with perfect clarity, too, the separate sharp notes of Brendan's whistled tune, the clash of a trolley, footsteps and voices, traffic, even distinguishing the diesel sputter of a taxi in the street outside.

At the lift doors she watched mesmerized as the light flicked upwards over the indicator buttons. The doors opened with their pneumatic hiss and inside the green-painted box the musty, metallic smell was so strong that Annie looked round to see if it affected Brendan too.

He smiled at her. 'Okay, my love?'

He pressed the button. As they swooped down the sensation was so intense that Annie was briefly afraid that she might faint. But now, with bewildering speed, the falling stopped and the doors hissed open again. Annie blinked in the shafts of light that fell around them and they swung along another echoing corridor. At the end of it she saw a ward. They were moving so fast that she wondered if Brendan was running.

The doorway yawned and they swept inside. Annie gasped at the jungle of flowers and flower-printed curtains, the scents and the profusion of colour, and the light and dark shadows dappled over the vivid red floor. It was as if there had been only the terrifying darkness, and then a world bled of all its colour, and now the light and vividness of it had all come flooding back at once.

'It's beautiful,' she whispered.

Brendan laughed. 'Ward Two's been called a lot of things. Never beautiful.'

A bed was waiting for her. The sheets were as white as a hillside under thick snow. Brendan was talking to the ward nurses. Annie could distinguish the separate cadences of all their voices but the impressions were crowding in too thickly for her to be able to hear what they were saying. Through the window behind her bed she saw a vista of red-brick walls, more windows, drainpipes, and pigeons sitting on a ledge, an intricate network, each part of it defined with spotlit clarity.

On the bedside locker there was a poinsettia in a pot. Annie had always disliked the assertive red flowers. Now she thought she had never seen anything as lovely as the flaring scarlet bracts with their ruff of jagged bright green leaves beneath. She wanted to touch their sappy coolness with the tips of her fingers. There were more flowers waiting in a great cellophane-wrapped spray on the bed. One of the nurses held the bouquet out for Annie to see. The flowers were chrysanthemums, every shade from pure white to deepest russet bronze. The curling yellow satin ribbon bows crackled with the shiny cellophane. They held out the card to her too, and Annie read the florist's unformed handwriting.

With love and best wishes for a speedy recovery, from everyone at Rusholme.

Rusholme was Thomas's school.

Without any warning, the kindness of the gesture made her cry. The rush of sensation seemed to have peeled away a protective layer of her skin, and Annie felt how vulnerable she had become. She sat in her wheelchair with tears running down her cheeks.

'I'm sorry,' she said. 'I don't know why flowers should make me cry.'

'Don't you worry,' Brendan told her.

Another of the nurses took the flowers. 'I'll put them in water, shall I? Mind you, I'm no flower arranger.'

They helped her into bed. The sheets felt crisp and smooth under her feet, and the pillows were soft behind her head. The tears were drying stiffly on her face and Annie sniffed a little.

'That's more like it,' Brendan said. When they had made her comfortable he kissed her on the cheek and waved at her as he left.

'You've done well. We're proud of you, upstairs.'

'That Brendan,' the other nurse exclaimed when she brought back the chrysanthemums in a tall vase. She pulled the curtains tight around Annie's bed. 'Shall I leave you to get your breath back now?'

Annie lay in her quiet space. She looked around it, examining each detail as though she had never seen anything like it before. The light from her window lay thickly on the white covers and the cream-painted curve of the bed-frame, and on the flowers in their place on the locker.

Very slowly, Annie put out her hand. With the tip of her finger she traced the waxy curve of a chrysanthemum petal. The intense yellow of the flower seemed to trap the light, and then to beam it out again, as rich and buttery-warm as burnished gold.

In that instant Annie felt a beat of pure happiness. The charge of it diffused all through her body, warming it and weakening it with its glow until her hand dropped to her side and she lay back helplessly against her pillows.

The world had never seemed so beautiful or so simple. She understood not only that she was going to live, but how precious life was. Gratitude for it took hold of her. It swelled in her chest and throat until she could hardly breathe, it danced in the light and dazzled her eyes, and it sang in her ears and blocked out the mundane clatter of the hospital ward.

Annie was smiling. She was awed by the munificent beauty of the gift that had been presented to her, and the reflected glow of it bathed and transformed everything around her. Even her own hands were beautiful, stretched out on the sheet in front of her. Her vision was so penetrating that in her mind's eye she could see the tiny threads of capillaries as they branched away, full of resourceful life, under the bruised and discoloured skin.

Annie was weak, but she was also unshakably strong again. *I am alive*, she told herself. *I won't be afraid any more.*

Annie was still smiling when the curtains parted a little at the foot of her bed. She had heard murmuring voices beyond them, and now a nurse's cheerful invitation, 'Go ahead. She's quite decent.'

The curtains opened wider and a man came through them. He was moving awkwardly, on crutches, and one of the flowered hangings caught over his shoulder. The man shrugged it off without taking his eyes from Annie's face.

Annie saw his slight frown of concern or concentration. His

eyebrows were very dark, darker than his hair, and they drew close together over his eyes. There were deep lines beside his mouth and she saw that his hands were clenched too tightly on the arms of his crutches.

She had never seen his face, but she knew him as well as she would ever know anyone.

'Steve,' she said softly.

His frown disappeared then.

Annie put her hand up to her bruised face and then, with the recollection that she had nothing to hide from Steve, she let it drop again.

At last, still looking at her, he said, 'You look so happy.'

'I am,' she answered. She held out her free hand, the same hand that had held on to his all through their hours together. Steve balanced upright as he put his crutches aside and then, holding on to the edge of the bed for support, he swung himself slowly along until he could take her hand.

The memory that the touch brought back caught them and held them. It was a long moment before either of them could move.

Then Steve came closer, perching on the bed beside her. He lifted his other hand and reached under the torn ends of her hair to touch his fingers to the nape of her neck. Then, quickly and quite naturally, he leant forward and kissed her cheek.

Annie felt the colour rising into her face as if she was a girl again.

'You look so happy,' he repeated and Annie found herself laughing.

'I look dreadful.'

'No, Annie, you don't.'

Steve didn't see the bruises, or the unhealthy pallor of the rest of her skin, or the half-healed graze blurring the corner of her mouth. He saw the Annie he had imagined when her husband told him that she was going to live. Laughing, as she had been a moment ago, with her fair hair loose around her face. She had blue eyes and warmly coloured skin. She wasn't beautiful, or even particularly striking, but she was full of life.

'Look,' Annie said.

She held out their linked hands to touch the tightly furled petals of the yellow chrysanthemum.

They looked at the flowers, and then at the simple things all around them, a plastic water jug and a glass, the chipped wooden locker, the curtains and the dingy view from the window. They were both thinking about the pain in the darkness, and their fear that they would never see anything so ordinary and beautiful again. Annie felt her happiness rising once more, rippling and ballooning outwards until she could have floated with it. She looked at Steve's face and saw from the light in it that he felt it too.

They smiled at each other in their triumphant pride that they had survived. Steve lifted her hand and touched his mouth to her knuckles. For a moment there was nothing to say. They knew everything already, yet they had to begin all over again, here in the warm daylight.

When they did speak again the questions came spilling out together and they broke off together too, half embarrassed and half laughing, like adolescents.

'Go on.'

'No, you go on,' Steve said.

'I was just going to ask how you are. Is your leg bad?'

He told her briefly, shrugging it off. As he talked Annie listened to the familiar sound of his voice, trying to piece it together with his face and the shape of his head. His attractiveness surprised her. In her mind's eye, down in the darkness, he had been a bigger, bulkier man with blunt, assured features. But this Steve was lean, and she guessed that before the accident he must have been very fit. His dark hair was cut short over his forehead, which made him look younger than the age she knew he was. There were marked frown lines between his dark eyebrows and more lines beside his mouth, but the mouth itself curled humorously. When he smiled, she found herself smiling back.

'I know how you are,' Steve told her.

'How come?'

'I've had regular bulletins. Mostly from the nurses, once from your surgeon. And your husband came to see me on Christmas Eve.'

'Martin did?' Annie was startled.

'He told me that you were going to be all right. He said that you smiled at him.'

'I don't remember.' Annie was thinking about the blur of the overhead lights and Brendan's face looming over hers, the possessive pain. 'I remember hearing the carol singers. My nurse told me afterwards that it was Christmas. What else did Martin say?'

'He wanted to thank me for helping you through.' There was an expression in Steve's eyes that Annie couldn't fathom. 'I told him it wasn't necessary, because we helped each other.'

'Yes,' Annie said.

The raw recollections gathered around them. Annie knew how badly she needed to talk to Steve. Not to Martin, because to tell him how it had been in the darkness would be to start at the beginning. It was only Steve who could exorcise it.

'Are you still afraid?' he asked, his voice gentle.

Annie looked around again, at the flowers on the locker and the curtains' pattern. The radiance of the light had faded.

'No, I'm not afraid. We're safe in hospital, aren't we? You said all along that we would be. Do you know what? The first thing I remember thinking, when I came round afterwards, with a tube in my throat, was, *Steve said that they would come for us in time*. I tried to reach out for your hand again, but I couldn't move. I was afraid then. There were more tubes in my wrist. I could feel them touching my skin.' Annie put her fingers up to touch the corner of her mouth. 'I'm only afraid now when I dream. I dream that we're buried again, and that we won't be rescued. And that there's no air, so we can't breathe. I wake up choking, then. The worst dreams, nightmares, are the ones where I'm alone. You aren't there.'

Steve took her hand and held it. He fitted his fingers between hers and clasped them to hold their palms together.

'Remember?' he demanded. 'I was there. I'm here now.' And then, as if she might reject the intimacy that that implied, he said quickly, 'The dreams are only dreams. They'll go away.'

'Will you stay?' Annie asked suddenly. 'To talk?' They had already talked so much. 'Not now, I mean. But some time?'

'Yes,' he promised her. 'I need that, too.'

He could hear someone walking down the ward. *Not too long*, the staff nurse had warned him when she showed him in. Steve let go of her hand. He tapped at the solid leg plaster under the folds of his bathrobe.

'I'm going to be here for weeks,' he said cheerfully. 'Long after they've sent you back to the real world. I should think we'll have plenty of time for conversation.' He nodded past the curtains. 'I'm in the next door ward. It links to this one via a charming day room. There are a great many vintage magazines and a dozen or so videotapes of bloodthirsty films. I can't wait to show you round.'

Annie smiled at him. 'I'll look forward to that.'

The staff nurse came and began briskly pulling aside the curtains. Annie saw other beds across the ward, women looking over at her, more flowers.

'Don't tire her out, will you?' the staff said. She looked pointedly at Steve and added, 'Wouldn't you be more comfortable in the chair?' Meaning, Annie translated silently, 'Don't sit on the bed.' She sensed Steve's amusement answering her own.

'I would,' Steve said regretfully. 'But I couldn't lower myself into it. I'm going to hobble back now and leave Annie in peace. Will you help me?'

Annie recognized his charm. The nurse moved happily to take his arm.

'I'll be back as soon as they let me,' he promised Annie. They began to shuffle slowly away. Without knowing why she did it, Annie told him, 'Benjy and Tom are coming this afternoon. I haven't seen them since it happened.'

Steve paused, looking back at her.

'I'm glad they're coming,' he said gravely. Then the nurse led him away through the day room doors.

There were three hours to wait until afternoon visiting time. Annie made herself be patient.

One by one the women in the ward came over to talk to her. Two of them had been injured in the bombing. Others had already been discharged, and new patients unconnected with it had taken their places. Annie had the sense of other tragedies and losses, piling up within the hospital walls, each one obscured in its turn by the next.

She remembered that she had wanted to ask Steve if he felt angry. She looked towards the door, thinking about him. He had said that he would come back. The knowledge was a firm, steady point in the thoughts that moved like fish, directionless, inside her head.

At two-thirty exactly, Martin and the boys came in. They must have been waiting outside for visiting time to begin. Annie saw them immediately. They stood at the end of the new ward, looking around for her, Martin stooping protectively behind the children. Tom's face was anxious and serious, but Benjy was swinging Martin's hand and staring along the beds. Suddenly he pointed and called out.

'There's Mummy. There she is.'

Annie's happiness swelled up again. She held out her free arm.

Tom came first. He ran to her and then stopped just short of the bed.

'Are you all right?' he asked, looking at her face.

'Yes, Tommy, I'm fine.' The sound of her voice reassured him. He put his arms around her and she hugged him, rubbing her cheek against his hair. She kissed the top of his head, smiling, with the heat of tears in her eyes.

'I'm so glad you're better,' he murmured against her shoulder.

'Christmas wasn't nearly so much fun without you.'

'I know,' Annie whispered. 'There'll be next year, you know. Lots and lots of Christmases to come.'

Benjy was hanging back with his head against Martin's leg. He was watching her, half-eager and yet reluctant. Annie had never been away from him for more than a day of his life before, and she knew that he was distrustful of her now.

'Come on, Ben,' she said gently.

Martin lifted him on to the bed beside her and Annie took his hand. She wanted to squeeze it in hers and then kiss his round face, pulling him to her so that no one could ever take him away. But she made herself suppress the intensity of feeling in case it frightened him. She smiled and hugged him, and said cheerfully, 'I'm sorry you couldn't come to see me in the other ward. The doctors were very strict. It's much better in here, you can come whenever you like.'

'I want you to come home,' Benjy said. 'Straight now.'

They laughed and the little boy squirmed closer to her, reaching out to touch the marks on her face.

'Is that a bad hurt?' he asked and Annie said, 'Not very bad. Benjy, I'll come home just as soon as I can. I promise I will.'

Over the boys' heads she looked at Martin.

'You look much better,' he said.

'I know.'

Annie wanted to share the glistening happiness she had felt. She wondered for a moment how to express it, and then gave up the attempt to make it sound rational. She let the words come spilling out. 'When they brought me downstairs this morning it was like waking up after a long, disturbed night. Or like recovering my sight after being blind. I could see everything so clearly, colours and shapes and people's faces.'

Steve's face, she remembered.

'I felt so happy. As though there were no flaws, no ugliness or misery anywhere. Just for a minute. I'll never forget.'

She thought that Martin didn't understand what she was saying. He was listening, but not responding, and so she couldn't share the miraculous delight with him. If joy in the simple rhythm of the ordinary world didn't touch him, then it must be her words that were inadequate. Regret and guilt touched her briefly with their light fingers.

'Do you see?' she asked humbly.

'It's natural relief,' Martin answered. 'After what's happened. Don't take it too fast, Annie, will you? Don't expect too much of yourself too quickly.'

So cautious. Not to seize on the happiness? Annie thought. Why not?

'I won't ever forget,' she murmured, almost to herself. Then she made her attention direct itself outwards, beyond her own selfish concerns.

'How is it at home?' she asked. She felt the house, too, so clearly.

'Oh,' Martin shrugged with a touch of weariness, 'we're managing. Aren't we, Tom?'

He told her that his mother was helping wherever she could, and Audrey was coming in every day. But Annie knew that the responsibility for the boys' daily life, always hers in the past, would weigh heavily on Martin. He had less patience, and in two days' time he would have to go back to work after the Christmas break.

'McDonald's every day?' she asked Tom, and he grinned at her.

'Just about.'

Benjy was lying quietly with his head against her good shoulder, his thumb in his mouth. Annie was still thinking about the house. It was so much part of her, she realized, that it was like an extension of her body. She could see the tiles in the kitchen, two or three of them cracked, the patches on the walls, the ironing basket overflowing next to the washing machine.

'Can we get someone in? A temporary mother's help?'

'Very expensive,' Martin said stubbornly. 'Don't worry. We'll muddle through.'

Annie felt the ties of responsibility beginning to pull at her.

She felt both guilty and relieved that she couldn't respond to them yet. The hospital felt, momentarily, like a haven of peace and she remembered the brilliance of light that had illuminated it. It was a sanctuary from the demands that had followed her since the boys were babies. She loved them, all of them, but she couldn't respond to their needs. Not yet.

'What about my Mum?' she asked. 'How is she?'

'Um. About the same. She wants to come in and see you. Are you up to it?'

Annie picked at a thread in the bed sheet.

'Tell her to come. Whenever she can.'

They talked, the four of them, for a few more minutes. The boys told her about Christmas, shouting one another down as they listed their presents.

'How marvellous,' Annie said. 'I *wish* I'd been there.'

Family. Gathered around her, needing her to pick up the threads again. It was hard to be all things, she thought, even some of the time.

Her head and back ached overwhelmingly now.

Martin stood up at last. Reluctantly she let the boys scramble away from the warmth of her hug.

'Come back soon. Tomorrow?'

Martin kissed her, and she put her hand up to touch his cheek. 'Thank you for being here.'

'Where else could I be?' he whispered.

They held hands for a long minute. Then, remembering something, Martin reached for a bag he had put down at the foot of the bed.

'I brought you these. Essentials of life.'

Annie peered into the plastic carrier. There was a jar of Marmite and another of anchovy paste, both of which she loved. There was a big box of Bendick's Bittermints. They always gave one another the dark, bitter mints as a consolation or a gesture of reconciliation. There was the latest copy of her gardening magazine, and the plant encyclopaedia that Annie often sat poring over on winter evenings. Every winter she drew up lists of the plants she would stock her garden with; every spring she failed to put her elaborate plans into force.

The little things were an expression of how well they knew one another, of how their lives had woven a pattern together.

What else? Annie wondered. The question pricked her, disturbing.

'I love you,' she said deliberately.

'I know. Me too.' He was gathering up the boys' anoraks, helping Benjy into his. 'Come on, you kids.'

'See you tomorrow. See you tomorrow,' they called to her. Annie waved to them. Martin took Benjy's hand and with Tom scuffling beside them they went out in the tide of departing visitors.

Annie lay stiffly against her pillows.

She was wondering why she hadn't mentioned Steve. She should have told Martin that they had met and talked.

But then, answering herself, she thought, *No*. That was separate. The thing had happened to them together, and it didn't touch on her family. It was important that it didn't because of the fear, and also because of the other things that she had felt with Steve today.

When it was over, when the dreams had stopped and she was well again, he would be a stranger again too.

Five

Annie stood at the window of the day room. Three floors below her was a narrow side street lined with parked cars. On the corner was a sandwich bar, and she could see office workers from the surrounding buildings going in and out. They looked a very long way off, as if she were watching them in a film about another place.

The dislocation of time increased her sense of separation from the outside world. She knew that it was lunchtime for all the people passing to and fro in the street, but in the hospital wards their meal had been served and cleared away an hour and a half ago. The tea trolley with its rows of clinking white cups and saucers and big enamel teapot had just circulated. Annie didn't want tea, but she had taken a cup anyway and carried it into the day room. The nurses encouraged her to walk around now. She moved very slowly, slightly hunched, but every painful step gave her pleasure too. A chain of them linked her to the happiness that she had felt on the day when they brought her down from the intensive care ward, and she knew that she would survive.

Annie put her cup down on the window-sill and looked around the room. There were plastic-covered armchairs and a pair of sofas, low metal-framed tables piled with magazines, and the cream-painted walls were haphazardly hung with institutional posters and prints. The curtains and the carpet and the air itself smelt of cigarette smoke. At the opposite end of the room from Annie's window two old men were smoking determinedly and staring at the screen of the big television. Annie guessed that they were waiting for the day's racing coverage to begin. A woman in a flowered housecoat was reading a magazine, and another in the chair beside her was knitting ferociously, a long knotted pink coil.

Yesterday, and the day before, Annie and Steve had met in here.

They hadn't said anything yesterday, when they stood up to walk back to their wards, about meeting for the third time. They had looked at one another instead, and they had smiled, understanding each other perfectly, at the thought of making a date in such a place.

But before she had left her ward today Annie had looked in the mirror. She had looked at the hollows in her pale face, and she had even thought of lipstick. Then she had imagined how the colour would make a too-vivid gash in the whiteness. She had simply brushed her hair out so that it waved loosely and hid her cheeks, deciding that she must find a pair of scissors to trim the jagged ends.

She was standing with her hand on the window-sill, looking out into the street again, when Steve hobbled in. He saw her against the light, and the brightness of it shining through her cloud of hair gave it a reddish glow.

She turned towards him at once.

'Did you get your five bob on, Steve, like I told you?'

It was one of the old men in front of the television, calling out to him.

Steve stopped, thinking, *She was waiting for me.*

'Merrythought,' the old man prompted. 'Two-fifteen, Kempton.'

Steve shook his head. 'No, Frank, I'm afraid I didn't.'

The newsvendor clicked his tongue. 'You'll be sorry, son. It's a cert.' He swivelled back to face the screen.

Annie and Steve looked at each other and felt the laughter rising again. They had laughed yesterday too, like school-children, at almost nothing.

Trying to keep a straight face Annie asked, 'How's the leg today?'

'Itching. Right down inside the plaster.'

The woman with the knitting peered up at him, then held out one of her steel needles. 'Here. Poke this down inside and have a good scratch with it.'

Steve looked gravely at the implement.

'I'd have to take my pyjamas down to get at the top of the plaster.'

The woman beamed at him. 'Feel free, my duck.'

Her friend smothered her laughter behind her magazine.

'The itching is probably safer,' Steve murmured. He reached Annie's side and turned a chair with its back to the room. They sat down in their corner, facing each other.

'This place,' he sighed.

'You could afford to get yourself transferred to a smart private clinic,' Annie reminded him sharply. 'Peace and privacy. Menu food and real art on the walls.'

She wondered if Steve knew that she was voicing her fear that he might really go. He was sitting with his hands curled loosely over the arms of his chair, his crutches laid neatly at his feet.

'No, I couldn't,' he said. 'I want to stay here, because this is where you are.'

Annie felt the tightness of joy and panic knotted together under her ribs. It took her breath away, and the blood beat in her throat. She felt the closeness of his hand on the chair arm, and her own lying in her lap. She would have reached out, but panic suddenly overwhelmed her happiness. She lifted her arms and slotted her hands into the opposite sleeves of her robe, hugging them against her chest, shutting him out.

Steve saw the gesture and read its implication. She knew, and regretted it at once. She saw his handsome, haggard face and the grey showing in his dark hair. Steve was more than a man sitting in a hospital day room. He had been her friend and her comforter, her family and her lifeline all through the hours that still came back, renewing their terror, almost every time she slept. The memory and the fear were still potent, and Steve belonged with them, inextricably.

But he meant much more than that, because he was the man he was. Nothing to do with the bombing.

Annie was certain that it would be wrong to add fear of what Steve might demand from her to the pantheon of all the rest.

He was, and would be, her friend.

She slid her hands out of her sleeves again. She couldn't reach out to him now, and she made an awkward little gesture instead.

'I am here,' she said simply. 'Don't go to a clinic.'

Over Steve's shoulder she saw the woman with the knitting look up, curious. And with the intuitive quickness that seemed to link them now whether they wished it or not, Steve intercepted and understood Annie's glance.

'When did they unstrap your arm?' he asked casually, nodding at it.

She took the opening gratefully. The progress of their injuries and illnesses was the common currency of ward conversation. Annie and the other women exchanged their latest details first thing in the morning and last thing at night, after the doctors' rounds, and in between times when the nurses brought round the drugs trolley and the dressings packs.

'This morning,' she told him. 'When the physio came round. It's still strapped at the shoulder, but at least I can use the hand and elbow.' Annie held out her arm, turning it stiffly. The woman looked down at her knitting again, uninterested. She had heard the details already.

'That's good news,' Steve said. 'They took me down to the physiotherapy room this morning. They had me pulling weights to and fro for hours, to get my arms and shoulders working.'

And he went on, talking blandly about his treatment.

But Annie knew that he wasn't thinking what he was saying any more than she was listening. He had taken her hand as she held it out. He turned it over in his, looking at each of her fingers and at the shape of her nails. He touched his fingertips to the marks that the needles and tubes had left in her wrist. She felt the light touch as if it had been his mouth against her throat. She knew that he was looking at her, but she couldn't raise her head to meet his eyes.

'It's very clever, they make the muscles work against one another, you know . . .' Annie felt afraid to move in case he came closer, or let her hand drop.

Stupid, she thought dimly, *don't you know what you want?*

There were half-healed cuts on Steve's hands too. She could remember the length and shape of his fingers so clearly. Was the tactile memory so much stronger than the visual, then?

'It's very important. Otherwise they just fade away from lack of use . . .'

Annie made herself look up. She met his eyes and saw the question in them, but she couldn't even have begun to frame an answer. Behind them the two women had left their seats. The younger one with the magazine was holding the door open for the knitter. They went out together, and the door swung to with its gust of medicinal tasting air.

'They've gone,' Annie said.

The two old men sat with their backs turned, intent on the racing. It occurred to Annie that she was alone with Steve for the first time since the bombing and the blackness. The first time that they had been effectively out of sight and out of earshot of the nurses or the other patients.

Together the two of them seemed infinitely isolated, even within the tiny, cut-off world of the two hospital wards. For a moment Annie could have believed that reality extended no further than the stuffy air enclosed in the day room. She looked down again at their linked hands.

'It's very strange,' she whispered.

'What's strange, Annie?'

'This.'

Her hand moved in his, no more than a faint tensing of the muscles. Steve was wishing that she could have brought herself to say, *You and me*, or *Us, here.* He remembered her telling him about Matthew. I chose the easy option. The safe option. That's what she had said. He looked at her, trying to take the measure of her courage. But Annie had infinite courage. He knew that.

'I want to ask you such a lot of things,' Annie said. The words tumbled out in a rush. 'All sorts of things. Ends, to tie up everything you told me when we were buried. I think about them instead of going to sleep. Cowardly, because I'm afraid of the nightmares.'

'Ask me,' Steve said.

Annie smiled. 'I wanted to ask you if you felt angry,' she said. 'About what they did to us. Whoever they are.'

He had been looking at her eyes. The blue was intensified by the dark shadows around them.

'Angry?' Steve thought for a moment. 'No. Sad, for the other people. Not angry for myself. How could I be?' That movement of her hand in his again. 'It happened and we were there. That's all. It's hard to direct anger into a vacuum. I think what I feel most, now, is happy. I caught that from you, the other day. Do you feel angry, Annie?'

'No. Not for myself. Sad for the others, like you. I feel angry for the boys' sake, for Benjy, because he needs me. And for Martin. It was worse for him.' Annie looked back at Steve. 'I can't imagine what I would have felt, or whether I would have been able to bear it. Waiting to know if Martin was alive. Waiting afterwards to find out if they could keep him alive.'

Her blue stare was level now, holding his.

'I think you would have borne it with great courage,' Steve said after a long moment. 'I know how brave you are.'

'You helped me to be brave down there.'

There was a pendulum swinging between them. It swooped from its high point, down and then up again, stirring the close air with its arcs. The bombing and their hours in the dark had set it swinging, Steve thought. Time would slow it down, and in the end it would stand still. Then they would know. He couldn't ask her for anything while the pendulum still swung.

They sat facing each other, their hands still linked.

'Did you think we were going to die?' Annie asked him.

'I was afraid, at the end, that they might not come in time.'

'Yes. I can't remember the end. Only you talking. You were telling me about your Nan, and when you were a little boy. You all got mixed up together, you and Thomas and Benjy. I could see you running away from me, the three of you, and I was afraid that I would never catch up with you again.'

'And now you have,' Steve said softly.

'Now I have,' she echoed.

Annie held out her other hand and he took it, folding both of hers between his own. Annie had the sense that she had been afraid of choices, and also that there was no choice now. The hours underground had changed all the neat, straight lines of her life, and the perspectives would never be the same again.

'If we hadn't been afraid that we would die,' Annie said, 'we wouldn't have told each other all the things we did.'

'Do you regret them?'

She looked up at him then. For a moment she saw a stranger's face, a face as she would have seen it if she had glanced round in the doorway of the store. If nothing had happened then she would have gone on down the stairs.

But then. There had been the wind, and the thunderous noise, and the pain that held her in its fists. They had escaped from that. Relief renewed itself inside her and she felt the weightless brilliance of happiness again. It made her smile and she read the answering smile in Steve's eyes.

He knew her thoughts. He was as close to her as her family; he was a part of herself. Not a stranger.

'No,' she told him. 'I don't regret anything.'

His hands moved over hers, warming them. Annie wanted him to reach forward and put his arms around her. He had held her in the dark, and she wanted to feel his touch again. She saw their joined hands, and the blue woollen weave of her dressing gown over her knees. She was clearly conscious of the whole of her body, patched and stitched as it was, and the slow movement of blood inside it. She felt her scars, and the new skin rawly pink at the margins. She was regenerating herself. She was suddenly almost drunk with the giddy pleasure of it, and the glow of it spread through her fingers to Steve's.

'Annie,' he whispered.

They looked at each other still, motionless, silenced by the sudden need that drew them closer.

Another hermetic world, Annie thought wildly. The hospital enclosed them, just as the tangled girders and broken walls and floors had done. *Did that make it all right, then?*

Her skin prickled. Steve's face was very close to hers. She looked in his eyes and saw the dark grey irises, flecked with gold.

Annie's awareness of her body's workings made her feel naked. The colour flooded into her cheeks and she looked down to hide the heat of it. Steve moved too and their heads bent. For a moment their foreheads touched.

At the opposite end of the room one of the old men levered himself out of his chair. There had been a muted, distantly hysterical racing commentator's voice in the day room background, but a control button clicked on the television now and there was silence.

Steve raised his head. The circuit broke and Annie thought, *No, don't do that.*

But at the same time she felt relief wash through her, cooling her skin.

'Did your horse come in, Frank?' Steve called. He squeezed Annie's hands in his and then let them go. She folded them in her lap, empty.

'Nah,' Frank grumbled. 'The bugger ran like a one-legged ostrich.'

He shuffled across the room towards them, peering at the clock on the window wall.

'Five to visiting time. They'll all be pouring in here with their talk, talk. I wish meself that they'd leave me in peace with the racing. Still,' he winked across at Annie, 'I wouldn't miss the sight of Steve's visitors. You should see 'em.' His hands outlined explicitly in the air before he stumped off towards his ward.

Annie and Steve were laughing. Their laughter was another link, almost a safety valve.

'He has me cast,' Steve explained, 'as a kind of hybrid between Warren Beatty and Frank Harris. Nothing could be further from the truth, I promise.'

'Who's coming to see you today?'

'Vicky.'

'Hm.'

Acknowledgement flickered between them, humorous, unexpressed. As if they were partners, Annie thought. It was easy to laugh with Steve. The warmth of it was comfortable.

'And you?'

'Martin's mother, bringing Tom and Benjy.'

Steve reached awkwardly for his crutches. Annie could move more freely so she bent down and retrieved them, holding them upright while he fitted his elbows into the padded cups and then let the metal legs take his weight.

'Thank you.' He half turned, then looked back at her. 'Doesn't this strike you as absurd? Crutches. Bandages. All the rest of it? A pair of battered bodies . . .'

'It will pass,' Annie interrupted him.

'Soon, I hope.'

Annie let his challenge lie. Infirmity was a protective shield, and with her old caution she shrank from confronting what lay beyond it.

They moved slowly away towards the opposite doors. Annie imagined the outside world, reaching its long fingers into theirs to draw them apart. The image disturbed her but she still stopped in the doorway.

'Tomorrow?' she asked.

Steve nodded gravely. 'Naturally.'

But then his face split into a smile, a smile that brought the fierce colour into her face again because it was as intimate as if they already lay in one another's arms. Annie drew her blue robe around her and pushed through the door into the women's ward.

Martin's mother and the two little boys came down the length of it towards her.

'Mummy!'

Somebody's mother, Annie remembered. Steve had said that about his wife wanting a baby. Just somebody's mother. The recollection made her angry and she was grateful for it. He was arrogant, and he possessed all the male characteristics that she had turned her back on long ago, when she married Martin. Annie bent down to hug her children, drawing them close to her.

When she stood up again her mother-in-law kissed her and then stood back to look at her, exclaiming, 'Annie! Darling, you look so much better. You've got pink cheeks again.'

'I am better, Barbara,' Annie said deliberately. 'I'm working really hard at it. I want to get home just as soon as I can.'

'I wish you would come home. Dad won't let us do *anything*,' Thomas complained. 'Life's very hard, right now.'

'Poor boy.' Annie put her arm round him. 'Poor Dad, too. When does term start again?'

Thomas stared at her. 'Monday. You *know* that.'

'Of course I do. I'm sorry.' She had forgotten. The slip of her memory made her aware again of the two worlds, one trying to draw her back and the other enclosing her here.

School terms. The neat pattern of days, the boys needing to be driven to and fro, her own routines of cooking and shopping and attending to them, and the quiet evenings when she sat with Martin opposite her at the table, exchanging the small snippets of news. And here, the high white beds in their curtained boxes, the terrifying fingers of her dreams, the peaks and troughs of pain. And Steve. Annie put her hand up to the corner of her mouth. The cut there had almost healed. Her body renewing itself. She felt the life in it.

'Mum, are you listening?'

'Yes, love, of course I am.'

They settled themselves around her bed. Benjy had brought her a series of drawings, and he wanted her to guess what every crayoned shape represented. Thomas wanted her to read a new book with him. She listened carefully to what they had to say, trying to share her attention between them with scrupulous fairness, suggesting and reassuring.

Barbara wanted to talk, too. She was an indefatigable talker, a friendly, outgoing, ordinary woman to whom Annie had never been particularly close. The bond with her own mother was too strong.

Annie struggled to spare some attention and make the right responses to Barbara's recitals of how Martin was coping, what the neighbours in her street had said and thought, how the boys were behaving for her, the emergency domestic arrangements. She wished that her own mother were well, and that she were here instead of Barbara.

She remembered how she had imagined that she was a girl again, in the dark with Steve. Lying with her head in her mother's lap, in their cool living room. Annie's mother had come to see her twice since they had brought her out of the intensive care unit. They had been short visits, no more than ten minutes, and all through them she had held on to her husband's arm with thin white fingers. She had been cheerful, painfully bright, for Annie's sake.

Listening to Barbara's stream of talk, Annie felt the vibration of anxiety for her mother, love and fear mixed together. With the anxiety came a sudden, sharp resentment of the demands that the other world made. The dues of love, she thought bitterly. Payable to parents, husbands, children.

Her selfishness startled and shocked her.

In pointless expiation she praised Barbara fulsomely for everything that she was doing. She bent her head over the books and drawings, trying to give of herself as generously as she could.

The visit only lasted an hour, but Annie was glad when it was over. Her head ached fiercely, and the long scar in her stomach burned. She knew that her goodbyes sounded hasty and irritable, and when the boys had gone she ached with guilt and longing for them.

She pushed the tray of supper aside as soon as they brought it to her, and lay dozing against her pillows until Martin came on his way home from work.

He stretched his long legs out in front of him as he sat in the hospital armchair. 'You look tired,' he said.

'I am a bit. But I felt wonderful this afternoon. A tower of strength.'

'That's good. How was your day?'

The eagerness in Martin's voice reproached her. My husband, she thought. Half of me. Annie sat up straighter against the pillows, watching him. She would tell him that she had talked to Steve. Tell him truthfully, now, while there was nothing to tell.

The words didn't come.

She tried the beginnings of them in her head, and couldn't voice any of them. Instead she heard herself saying brightly, 'They took the strapping off my arm. Look.' She held it up and Martin took her hand, linking his fingers with hers.

'That's wonderful.'

Annie's guilt bit more sharply. She tried to tell herself that there was no reason for guilt. But she knew that there must be, just because it was there. 'Barbara came in with the kids, you know that. Ben had a stack of drawings, and Tom wanted to read. Barbara talked without drawing breath once, and the boys needed all my attention. They were here an hour, and it gave me a headache. I feel bad about it now.'

Martin drew his chair closer to the bed so that he could put his arm around her.

'Poor love,' he said. 'You're bound to feel like this, to begin with. Well enough to cope, and then too tired as soon as you try to. Don't worry so much. We're all managing perfectly well at home.'

Annie nodded, resting her head against his shoulder.

'What else?' he murmured. 'Any other news?'

'No,' she answered. 'Not really.'

She closed her eyes. He was so kind, she thought. Kind and good, and she loved him. Perhaps it was an unflamboyant, muted love, but it was infinitely valuable. *Don't risk it*, she warned herself, and then could almost have laughed wildly out loud. The idea of risking anything, buried alive under tons of rubble and then shuffling in bandages around a hospital ward, was so absurd. She pushed the thoughts aside.

'Tell me about your day,' she begged Martin. 'All about it. Every detail.' Her fierceness surprised him and to explain it she said, 'I feel so closed up in this place. Separate from you and the world and everything that matters.'

'It won't be long now,' he soothed her. 'I saw the sister on the way. She says you're doing brilliantly.'

Home, Annie thought, not knowing truly what she felt about the prospect. She would be going home, soon.

'Tell me,' she insisted.

He settled his arm more comfortably around her.

'Well. Let's think. I went to a meeting this morning with the new hotel people in Bayswater. They want to open the place in time for the summer. There isn't a chance of that, not with the level of work that they want done . . .'

Annie listened, with her eyes shut, imagining that they were at home. They would be sitting on the shabby chesterfield in front of the fire. The cat would be asleep on the bentwood rocking chair opposite them. The boys asleep upstairs. Newspapers and magazines stacked up on the lower shelf of the television table. The grandmother clock that stood in the hall ticking comfortably. The curtains would be drawn, shutting out the threats that stalked in the darkness outside. Martin went on talking softly while Annie conjured up the certainty of home.

At last he whispered, 'Are you asleep?'

She shook her head. 'No. Just thinking.'

Annie opened her eyes and he leant over to kiss her. He fanned her hair out with his fingers and turned her face so that their mouths met.

'Hurry up and get better. I want you back home. I need you so much, Annie. I love you.'

Love. Need. The dues to be paid.

Annie nodded, unable to say anything.

When Martin had gone she lay still, looking at the flowers on her locker and at the faded, flat shapes on the curtain behind. The fresh ones were so vivid. She could feel the sappy strength of the stems between her fingers, and the green, pollen-rich scent held amongst the tight petals was stronger than the reek of the hospital. It was only by contrast that the curtain flowers seemed drab. The colours and shapes would have been satisfying enough, if they had been allowed to stand alone.

Annie looked away from them, turning her back on the flowers and the unwelcome analogy that they forced upon her.

She made the decision, as she lay there, that she wouldn't go to the day room tomorrow. There would be no need, then, to shoulder any guilt. She would stay in the ward all day, and so she needn't see Steve at all. She could stop what was happening, stop what she was afraid of now, simply by not seeing him at all.

Martin walked out of the main doors of the hospital. The cold wind funnelling between the high buildings seemed sharper still after the airless ward, and he ducked his head and moved briskly. His car was parked in a side street nearby, but when he reached it he made no move to drive away. His attempt at briskness had petered out, and he sat instead staring through the windscreen into the darkness, his hands loosely gripping the wheel.

Annie was getting better. Every day he could see the changes, and he looked carefully for the latest proof that she was stronger. Yet the new strength didn't bring her back again. He had believed it would, while he sat holding her hand among the possessive machines, and now he saw that the expectation had been too simple. The bomb had done more than tear Annie's body. It had blown a crater between the two of them, and Martin knew that he couldn't fling himself across it.

Annie had suffered the pain and the fear, and he had not. However much he willed himself to allow and understand, he did not and he accepted that he could not.

The man did. Steve did, because he had shared it with her. It was absurd, Martin thought with sudden bitterness, to envy him for that.

Martin's hands slipped off the wheel and hung at his sides. The fingers opened and clenched, as if he wanted to reach for something, but it eluded his grasp. He was thinking of the way that Annie had slipped away from him. She was there, the shape of her filling out every day, but she had gone away somewhere.

Just for a few seconds, Martin let his head drop forward and rest against the wheel. His own concerns were with the mundane double load of business, and of keeping himself and the boys fed and clean. How could he guess from that vantage point what Annie's concerns were, who had nearly died? And who had shared that almost-death with *him?*

With Steve, Martin made himself repeat.

He jerked his head up and groped for his car keys. He drove home again, too fast, trying to deny the current of his thoughts.

Annie was dreaming.

The darkness had absorbed her again and it stretched all round her, limitless. It wasn't empty darkness. Rather it was tangible, heavy and threatening, and sharp with broken edges that pressed against her. The darkness was utterly silent, but at the same time it held the threat of a terrible cataclysmic noise that might erupt at any instant. The noise would bring the weight, crashing downwards, to extinguish her. She wanted to move, to raise herself on to all fours and then to crawl, to stagger upright and then to run, lurching away, in all her terror. But there was no possibility of movement, no hope of escape. The silence was absolute. There was only Annie herself, trapped in her weakness. No one would rescue her, because no one else existed. No one could comfort her, and when the noise came at last she would be utterly alone. She felt the icy cold in her chest, deep in her heart, and the stick-like fragility of her outstretched arms and legs.

And then she heard the noise begin.

It was a low rumble, a long way off, beneath her and over her head, terrible and implacable and final.

Annie woke up with her scream frozen in her throat. It was always the same dream, and she always woke at the same instant.

She lay with her knees drawn up and her fists clenched, shivering in the grip of terror, waiting for it to relax as she had learned that it would. Her back and her shoulders were clammy with sweat.

Steve.

The thought of him filled her mind. She longed for him to be with her, with a desperate, almost unbearable longing. She wanted him to lie down beside her and put his hands over her eyes. She wanted him to put his mouth to her ear and whisper, as he had done in the darkness that now seemed less fearsome than the darkness of her nightmare. Steve saw and understood, and it was unthinkable that he should not be with her now.

Annie sat up in bed. Her nightdress clung icily to her skin, and she pushed the damp weight of her hair back from her face.

She stared across the ward to the day room door. Beyond it was the day room itself, in darkness, with the television's eye briefly extinguished. And beyond that, in the ward that mirrored this room, Steve would be lying asleep.

She saw his face, every line of it clear. She felt his hands holding hers, and the touch of his forehead making a circuit that she had wanted never to break. She thought of how he had kissed her cheek, that first afternoon, and today he had smiled at her like a lover.

She fought against the longing.

She let her head fall forward against her drawn-up knees, hugging herself, almost welcoming the stab of pain from the wound in her stomach. They couldn't possess one another now. That they had done so already, tenderly and brutally in the darkness through the touch of their hands, that was only the cruelty of the trick that circumstance had played on them.

A trick, an irony. Life's little irony, in the face of death.

Annie raised her head again. The sweat on her cheeks had

dried and they shone with tears now. She stared down the ward as if she could see through the walls and doors that separated her from Steve.

'Damn you,' she whispered helplessly. 'Damn you.'

A student nurse checking the ward had seen that Annie was awake. She came and stood beside Annie's bed in her pink dress.

'Are you all right?'

'Yes,' Annie said. 'I had a dream. Just a bad dream.'

The girl moved to straighten her pillows and the crumpled bedclothes.

'Shall I bring you a drink? Some hot milk, and something to help you sleep?'

They had taken the flowers away for the night. The chintz flowers of the curtains looked like nursery hangings, reassuring in the dimmed light.

'Yes,' Annie said. 'Thank you. Something to make me sleep.'

She slept at last, and it seemed that almost at once they came to wake her up again. The ward routine was already numbingly familiar. A group of doctors came and examined her, and then mumbled amongst themselves at the foot of her bed.

Annie was used to that now.

Their senior beamed at her, once the consultation was finished.

'You're doing very well, you know. Your kidney function is normal, and everything else is healing nicely.'

'I *want* to do well,' Annie told him, irresistibly reminded of school interviews with her headmistress. 'I want to go home.'

'Oh, I'm making no promises about that. Two or three weeks more with us, and then we'll see, mmm?'

Annie nodded patiently. Her recovery, going home again to Martin and the children, that was in her power now. That was what she would focus on. She stretched out under the bedclothes, feeling the pull in the tendons as she moved her feet, and the ache in her shoulder.

The hours of the morning crept by. The lunch trays were brought round and then cleared away again, the tea trolley clinked up and down, and the ward settled into its early-afternoon somnolence. Annie lay against her pillows, watching the woman in the bed opposite with her knitting, trying to doze. Unable to sleep, she settled the radio headphones over her head and listened for ten minutes to an incomprehensible play. Another ten minutes passed, then twenty, and Annie found that she was staring at the day room door. Then, without being aware of having made any decision, she found herself pushing back the bedclothes. She put on her blue dressing gown, tied it carefully, and walked across to the door.

Steve was sitting in the day room. He had been watching the sky through the tall windows. It was a windy day, and towers of grey cloud swept behind the roofs and chimneys of the buildings opposite. There were half a dozen other people in the room, their voices competing with the sound of the television.

Annie stood beside his chair and he looked up at her.

How stupid, she thought, to try to deny him. She wanted to put her hand on his shoulder but she stopped herself.

'I thought you weren't coming,' Steve said.

'I wasn't going to.'

He nodded, and she wondered if he did understand why. A chair had been drawn up close to his, ready for her, and she moved it back a little way before she sat down. Steve studied her face. The colour and light that he had seen in it yesterday had faded. It looked closed up now, as if the Annie he knew had retreated somewhere.

'But you did come?'

She bent her head and her hair fell forward. Steve saw the line of her scalp at the parting, and the childish vulnerability touched him.

'It seemed . . . mulish, not to.' Then she looked up again, her eyes meeting his directly. 'Steve. If I seemed to make you a . . . promise, of some kind, yesterday, I'm going to tell you now that I can't keep it.'

He saw the resolution in her face. Annie would be resolute. The certainty of that increased his regard for her.

'It wasn't a promise. I thought it was an acknowledgement.'

She moved her hands, quickly, to silence him.

'It seemed to me that we were going beyond what we could naturally be. Friends.'

Steve smiled crookedly. 'Is there any definition of natural, in our circumstances?'

In the quiet that followed Annie felt the quicksands shifting around them. She thought of the ground that they had already covered together and the ways ahead, unmarked. There was only one path she could allow herself to take, and that led her away from Steve. Her face changed, showing her uncertainty.

'Or any definition of friends?' he persisted.

'Oh, yes,' Annie said. 'I can define friends. Friends are less than we were, yesterday.' She pressed on, talking rapidly, before he could interrupt her. 'The doctor told me this morning that I'm getting better very quickly. I shall be able to go home in two weeks, perhaps. When I do go, it will be back to Martin, and our children. I love my husband.' She lifted her chin as she spoke to emphasize the words. 'I don't want to deceive him, or hurt him. When I go home, I want to make everything the same as it was before.'

'Annie. It can't ever be the same.'

Steve was sure that her words were a denial of what she felt. He looked at her thin, pale face, trying to read her thoughts, but she had closed it up to him. She looked very small, hunched up in her chair, her physical frailty seeming at odds with the importance that she held for him.

He wanted to reach out for her. He wanted to make her say what she was denying to herself, and in his turn to tell her how much he needed her. Steve remembered, too vividly, the blankness of his life that had confronted him in the darkness. Listening to Annie, and talking to her, had given him his own reason to hold on. Now, hardly believably, they were here together. Steve's eyes left Annie's face and he looked around the ugly room. The other patients seemed fixed in their chairs, resigned and hopeless. He felt the luck, by contrast, of simply being alive. It was sad that these motionless people with their pinched faces couldn't share the exultation. He knew that Annie felt it, and he experienced a shock of anger with her for her refusal, now, to admit the chance of happiness.

But then, to admit their own chance of happiness was to deny her family's. His anger disappeared as quickly as it had come. Annie was unselfish, that was all. Steve's crooked smile lifted again. He had been selfish all his life, and it would be ironic, now, if by being different he was to lose her.

The air in the day room was stale, and the windows were firmly closed. Beyond the glass the grey masses of clouds whipped past, the noise of the wind only emphasizing the stifling stillness inside the hospital.

Whatever came, Steve thought, he wanted Annie to know how much he cared about her. That much selfishness, at least, he would allow himself. He listened to the voices of the television and a woman three chairs away, complaining about her treatment. The wind battered at the hospital windows, and Steve sat silently in his place. He wanted to stumble forward to reach Annie, taking hold of her and drawing her back to him. His hands tightened on the arms of his chair, stopping himself. He could only have done that if they had been alone, if they had been fit, if everything else had been different. Nor could he find the words, here in the day room, that didn't sound over-used, shop-worn. For all his adult life, Steve had known what to say to women. He had told them what they had wanted to hear and they had accepted it. He had asked for what he had wanted, and it had been given to him.

Steve wondered, now, whether he had been disliked as much as he had deserved. Perhaps. Or perhaps the long procession of girls had used him, too. He thought of Cass and her half-puzzled, half-defiant air. Cass hadn't used him. Steve tasted the sourness of dislike for himself, thick on his tongue.

And now, confronted with Annie, he didn't know what to say.

He was afraid that everything he could try would sound like a gambit. All the words had a coarse, locker-room echo.

He looked at her, sitting withdrawn from him in her blue dressing gown. A fair-haired woman with blue eyes that changed colour with the light. Not young any more, without Cass's loveliness or Vicky's direct female charge. But Annie possessed a kind of beauty that Steve had never seen before. At the thought of losing her, of letting her walk away from him, anger and longing and jealousy boiled up inside him. He shifted in his chair, feeling his physical weakness and his incapacity to reach her.

I love you.

No, not even the simplicity of that would do. The words were too fragile to say aloud in this listening room with its teacups and ashtrays and dog-eared magazines.

'Annie.'

He was reduced to repeating her name, as he had done to keep her conscious in the darkness. He had said the other words to her then, at the end, but she hadn't heard them. They had been lifting her up and away from him, bumping her in the tight harness, up into the circle of lights rimming their hole.

'Annie. It can't ever be the same,' he said again. 'You can't make what has happened un-happen.'

'I know that.' Her voice was too clear, as if she were trying to keep it steady. 'We're here together, in this room, because of a circumstance, a trick of fate. I mean that we can stop that circumstance from rolling on and changing everything that comes after it.'

She wouldn't look at him now because she didn't trust herself, but she sensed that he was leaning forward, straining to catch the nuance of what she said.

'If you and I had met anywhere else, at a party, say, there would have been nothing to draw us together. We'd have passed on by, just like we would have done in that doorway if the bomb hadn't exploded. It did explode, and we were lucky because we lived and other people didn't. But it was a circumstance, still. We can't let it be anything more than that.'

Annie knew that he was still looking at her. She felt the intensity of his stare. She could even feel, through her own hands, his grip on the arm of his chair.

'It *is* more, my love.'

'I'm not your love,' she whispered. 'I can't be.'

Annie's head fell forward and she covered her face with her hands. Her hair swung with it, showing the tips of her ears. Steve wanted to lean forward and kiss them, and then to push the hair back and kiss her cheek and her throat, and the palms of her hands where they had covered her eyes.

He made himself look away, then. The television was still blaring, incredibly, and old Frankie and his friend were set squarely in front of it. Mitchie was reading a newspaper, and Sylvia with the knitting was interminably talking. No one was looking at them, but Steve resented their intrusion with unreasonable intensity.

Annie didn't look up. She pushed her hair back and sat still, looking at the floor.

'So what shall we do?' Steve asked.

She shrugged, suddenly weary.

'Nothing. Get better and go home, I imagine.'

'Look at me, Annie.'

She raised her head. She knew that he expected more of her. He expected courage in place of the rooted loyalty to Martin that was all she had to offer.

'Is that really what you mean? What you want?'

His face could look very cold, Annie thought. She nodded, her neck as stiff as a column, seeing his disappointment in her clearly in his face. But to have said it was a relief. She felt the weight of anxiety lift a little, although something else, chillier and more final, slipped to take its place. Regret, Annie thought. She could almost have smiled at the inevitability.

'And in the meantime?' Steve asked quietly.

'We can go on seeing each other in here, and talking.' She faltered then, seeing the fallacy. 'As friends. Why not? We are friends, aren't we?'

His hand shot out and took her wrist, holding it too tightly.

'What shall we talk about, as friends? The racing?' He nodded towards the television. 'Sylvia's knitting? Nothing too close to home, I imagine. In case it leads us on to dangerous ground.'

Annie heard the bitterness in his voice. He doesn't like to be denied, she thought. He isn't used to it. But even as the thought occurred to her, she knew that she was doing him an injustice. She felt the bitterness of loss as strongly as Steve did. She looked past him at the room and knew the artificiality of being confined in it. To get home, that was the important thing. Perhaps then the dreams would stop. Perhaps, in the ordinary world, the potent mixture of happiness and regret that Steve stirred in her would fade away too. It was the unreality of hospital, Annie told herself. Isolation magnified feelings that she would have dismissed outside.

She made her voice light as she answered, 'We can talk about anything. We already have, haven't we?'

As she spoke, she knew that she was a coward. Was it the old dues, she wondered, that she was dutifully playing? Or did she use them as an excuse for not meeting a greater challenge?

Annie thought briefly of Matthew.

Matthew had gone. Steve knew that. She had the sense of choices again, multiplying, and a great windy space all around her from which all the familiar landmarks had been lifted up and tumbled away. And then regret, sharpening, because after all she lacked the courage to enter the space herself. Steve let go of her wrist. His hands settled on the chair-arms again. Annie was close enough to him to feel the tension from inactivity that vibrated in him.

But he simply said, 'Thank you for saying what you feel,' and smiled at her.

No, Annie thought. *What I ought to feel.* Regret, again.

'Look.' Steve nodded towards the television. 'The afternoon movie is *Double Indemnity*.'

'I've never seen it. Martin will know everything about it. Who the second cameraman was, who built the sets. He's the film buff, not me.'

'You should see it. Shall I move our chairs?'

The oddness of their knowledge of one another struck her all over again. They had never shared a meal, or seen a film or a play together, never even properly seen one another in day clothes. None of that mattered, she understood that now. Perhaps, in her life with Martin, she had set too much store by it. What had mattered to them, to Annie and Steve, was the recognition and understanding that had come and grown in the darkness.

Annie stared at the grey images on the television screen.

Was it enough, then, to fall in love by?

She knew the answer without asking herself. It was enough.

They stood up, helping one another to their feet, and positioned their chairs side by side, behind Frank and the others.

Annie wanted to turn to Steve, to say, *Wait*. He stood until she was sitting comfortably and then lowered himself awkwardly into his chair. He was close enough for her to feel his elbow touching hers.

After a moment, he turned to look at her. The bitterness seemed to have evaporated and he smiled again.

'We can watch television together. Just like real life. That's safe enough, isn't it?'

'I don't know,' Annie said softly. And she thought, He sees quite clearly, the difference between what I say and what I feel.

She made herself sit perfectly still and they pretended to watch the film together, counterfeiting the ordinariness of real life.

Afterwards, when it was over, they stood up again and went in their opposite directions, back to the wards.

The day of *Double Indemnity* set a pattern.

Annie's body healed rapidly. The doctors and nurses began to call her Wonderwoman, joking elaborately about the rapidity of her progress. Every day she felt a little stronger. The walk down the ward became routine instead of a challenge. She walked down to the physiotherapy department, and upstairs to pay a visit to Brendan. He pursed his lips when he saw her, and walked in a circle around her before whistling his admiration.

'Not bad at all. I wouldn't like to have had a bet on it, you know. I was anxious, back there, just for a day or two.'

Annie laughed at him. 'You should have had a bet. I'm pretty tough.'

'Is that so? Tell me now, how's that handsome friend of yours?'

'Steve's doing okay. He's impatient, that's all.'

Brendan sighed. 'Some people have all the luck, love, don't you? Take me, then. If I'd been buried alive, it would have been with some little old lady. Not your hero.'

'I didn't plan it that way,' Annie protested.

'Luck, I said.'

Annie rested, and slept as much as she could, welcoming unconsciousness except for the fearful dreams that still came. She dutifully ate all the food that was presented to her, and her face lost the sharp angles of sickness. She submitted to tests and exercises and the routines that were imposed on her, and she was rewarded with returning strength. Her family and friends came to visit her, and every evening Martin sat beside her bed and told her the day's news. She tried hard to feel the intimacy of home in the hour of evening visiting, with the over-familiar flowered curtains enclosing them.

She felt closest to Steve, aware of him near to her when they didn't meet, keeping her manner deliberately neutral when they did. It was hard, and she knew that they both felt the falsity of it.

When they met in the day room they talked about the books they were reading, the progress they had made, the day's newspapers, but the artificial distance that Annie had imposed made no difference. Sometimes she thought that the casual talk did no more than emphasize another, silent dialogue.

One morning Annie was sitting reading in the chair beside her bed. At the ward sister's suggestion Martin had brought some of Annie's clothes in for her, and she had dressed herself in a skirt and jumper. The clothes felt thick and strange, and dowdy with her feet in slippers.

It wasn't visiting time, and Annie was startled to look up and see her mother making her way slowly towards her bed. She relied on a stick now, and her knuckles stood out sharp and knobby as she grasped it. Annie stood up and went to her mother, putting her arm around her shoulders.

Anxiety made her demand, 'What is it? Is something wrong?'

'Nothing at all,' she answered. 'Your father dropped me off on his way somewhere. The ward sister kindly let me in. Here I am.'

Her mother was proud of herself, Annie saw. The little solo journey from the hospital doors to the ward was a triumph. The mother and daughter smiled at each other, and a little hopeful flame flickered between them. Perhaps, after all, she was getting better. Annie hugged her.

'Thank you for coming. Sit down in this chair, Tibby.'

Annie's mother's real name was Alicia, but from childhood she had been called Tibby. Thomas and Benjy used the name now.

'It sounds better than Granny. Sort of furry,' Thomas said.

'Like a cat, of course,' Tibby had agreed. She was close to the two little boys, and it was an added sorrow for her that they tired her too much now to spend more than a few minutes with them. Before her illness Tibby had taken them on day-long expeditions, planning them in advance with Thomas and packing careful provisions in their picnic boxes.

'It was clever of you to get them to let you in,' Annie said. 'They're quite strict about it.'

Tibby was tired, and she sat down gratefully. 'Couldn't really turn me away, could they? Once I'd landed myself, stick and all. I wanted to see you. They're asking me to go into some place, for a rest, that's what they call it.'

The flame of hope went out, at once, and Annie saw the darkness. She felt cold, and pointlessly angry.

'When? Why didn't either of you say anything?'

'Nothing to tell, darling. Jim agreed with me. Just a rest.'

'Of course,' Annie said numbly. 'It will do you good.'

Of course. Tibby was sixty-five, but she looked older. Her hair was thin, and her arms and legs seemed fragile enough to snap under her tiny weight. Annie wondered, How long? Her mother's pleasure in having reached the ward by herself stood out in a different, colder light.

Tibby was leaning back in the chair, looking at her daughter. 'I'm glad to see you in your clothes. What about your hair?'

She was striving for the painful brightness that she had adopted for her other visits. Annie had weakly accepted it then, but she was well enough now to look beyond Tibby's determined smile. She felt almost too heavy-hearted to answer, but at last she said, 'I'll have it cut when I get home. It won't be long now, they've promised me.' She was thinking that she would be going home almost well again, her own strength confirmed in her. But Tibby wasn't going to get better. Annie remembered that she and Steve had talked about it as they held hands and looked up into the blackness. She had wondered if her mother felt the same anger, confronted by death, the same sense of regret for everything left undone. *No*, Steve had said. *Your mother has seen you grow up. Seen her grandchildren.*

She sat down beside Tibby and took her thin hand between hers. Annie was filled with a longing to be close to her, and to make the most of the time that was left to them.

'Tibby, what do they say? The doctors. Tell me honestly.'

'That you're doing fine.' Tibby's smile was transparent.

'You know that I didn't mean me. What is this rest? How long is it for?'

Suddenly Annie heard in her own voice the same demanding, indignant note that was familiar from Thomas and Benjy. You're my mother. You can't leave me. I need you, and you belong here, with me.

More dues, Annie thought.

Tibby shrugged and said gently, 'Well, darling. You know this disease. It doesn't go away. They can't predict what course it will take. They do what they can, and they tell me what they do know, because I ask them to. One doesn't want to be deceived about the last thing of all, does one? A rest will help, they say. And it makes a break for your father, too.'

'I should be helping,' Annie said dismally.

Tibby surprised her with her laughter. 'What could you do?'

'Help Pop out in the house, or something.'

'Darling, are *you* offering to come and clear up in *my* house?'

Annie laughed then too. In her mind's eye she saw the polished, formal neatness of her mother's rooms in contrast with the rag-bag of family possessions that filled her own. Annie's indifference to domestic order hadn't always been a joke between them.

'I'm sure the house looks immaculate.'

Tibby nodded, her smile fading a little. 'It does. And will, as long as I have anything to do with it.'

Annie wondered, without speaking, how long that would be. She couldn't imagine even now how Tibby could polish the parquet tiles and scour the big old sinks. She had thought with Steve how sad it was that her mother's life had been dedicated to a house. How happy had she been? Her hand tightened on Tibby's.

'I was thinking about you, and the house, while we . . . while I was waiting for them to come and dig us out. I could remember it all as clearly as if I was really there. I thought I was a girl again, wearing a green cotton dress with a white collar, and white ribbons in my hair.'

'I remember that dress,' Tibby said. 'I remember the day we bought it for you.' She leaned forward, closer to Annie, and her fingers clutched more tightly. 'It was very hot, the middle of a long, hot summer. You were six or seven, and you had gone to play for the day with Janet. Do you remember Janet? You were inseparable, and then the family moved away and you cried for a whole week, insisting that you would never have another best friend in all your life.'

'I don't remember her at all,' Annie said.

'Your father and I went shopping, and we bought you the

green dress. When we came to pick you up you and Janet were playing in the garden, pouring water over each other with a watering can.'

'Go on,' Annie prompted her, and Tibby smiled. She began to talk. Some recollections made her laugh, and she sighed at others. She told stories about Annie's childhood and babyhood that Annie had never heard before. She remembered the day that her daughter was born.

Annie listened, watching her mother's face. She felt Tibby's need to recollect and to make the patterned strands tidy, as she had remembered herself, with Steve. As she listened the layers shifted over one another to give altered perspectives, her own memories, rubbed painfully brighter while she lay beside Steve, her mother's additions to them, stretching back beyond the reach of Annie's own recollection.

'You were a funny, good little girl, always,' Tibby said at last. 'Isn't memory a strange thing? I can remember you at eight, nearly thirty years ago, better than I can remember Thomas from last week. And I can't remember at all whether I paid the milkman last Saturday, or the name of the girl in the book I've just read.'

'I know,' Annie smiled, seeing the truth in the truism. 'Tibby, I wish we could talk more.' She had meant *like this, while we still can*, but her mother made a little startled gesture and peered at her watch.

'Oh, my dear, I said I would meet Jim downstairs a quarter of an hour ago. He didn't think the sister would let us both in. You know what he'll be like.'

Impatient, Annie knew.

'I'll walk down with you.'

'Can you manage that?'

'Of course I can.' *I'm* stronger, Annie thought sadly. Much stronger than you are.

They stood up, Annie much taller than her mother. Tibby seemed to be shrinking into herself. With her hands on Annie's arms she said, suddenly, 'I can manage everything else. Other people do, after all, with reasonable dignity. But I don't think I could have borne it if you had died. Not now, Annie, after all.'

Her face creased, vulnerable, with the beginning of tears.

Your mother has seen you grow up. Seen her grandchildren.

'Tibby.' Annie wrapped her arms around her. She rested her cheek against her mother's head. 'I didn't die,' she whispered. 'I didn't want to die.'

For a long moment, they held on to each other.

Then Tibby sniffed hard.

'I came to cheer you up,' she said, her voice wobbly.

Annie let her go, briskly gathering up her mother's coat and bag. 'That's Barbara's chosen role. I should leave it to her.' She felt that her mother's bright, tight smile had transferred itself to her own face, but Tibby responded hearteningly. Their faint disparagement of Martin's mother had always been a little, contained joke between the two of them.

'Poor Barbara . . .' Tibby protested.

'. . . She does mean well,' Annie completed automatically. 'Come on. Let's start shuffling downstairs, or Pop will stamp off without you.'

Arm in arm, they set off for the ward doors.

Annie saw Tibby safely into her father's care. He was waiting amongst the WRVS drivers in the main hall, looking at his watch every few seconds. He kissed Annie and then he and Tibby began to fuss each other about the time, adopting with clockwork precision the roles that they had fallen into decades ago. Tibby was always very slightly late, and Jim chivvied and agitated to bring her up to schedule. Annie felt the irritation that she always felt, and she recognized that that was her own role. She reassured her father that they had plenty of time, suspecting that they had nothing pressing to do for the rest of the day, and equally aware that her father would insist on a strict timetable for a week in bed.

Perhaps, she thought, Tibby's rest was a rest from her husband's precision. They said goodbye, and from a curve in the stairs Annie watched them wander away together. They would still be arguing about the time. She could see Tibby's head pecking to and fro as she defended herself. The patterns of a lifetime, set long ago. She found herself wondering again whether her parents had really been happy at all, caught up in their own pattern.

And Martin and me? How different now? How different in twenty years?

Annie walked slowly because her legs were heavy. It took her a long time to reach her bed in the ward again.

It was two days later when they told her that she could go home on Friday. That was three days away.

'You'll have to come back to out-patients for tests. We don't want you to escape that easily,' her surgeon told her jovially. 'We want to keep a close eye on those kidneys of yours, and there will be blood tests and so forth. But I think that by the weekend you will be well enough to be at home with your family.'

'Thank you,' Annie said.

She went to telephone Martin immediately.

'That's wonderful news,' Martin said.

'It is, isn't it?'

In her own ears, her voice sounded thin.

They talked for a few minutes more. Martin was making euphoric promises and plans. 'We'll all take care of you. All you have to do is rest. Audrey and Barbara will manage the boys between them, and I'm going to take some time off. Annie?'

'I'm here.'

'Then when you're stronger we can have a break together, just the two of us. Barbara says she'll have the boys to stay. We could go to Paris. Or Venice. What about Venice?'

'Yes,' Annie said. 'We could do that.'

She was looking down at the red-tiled floor and at the toes of her slippers. She tried to imagine beyond *here, now,* and found that she couldn't. At the same time she tried to make her voice stronger, as full of conviction as Martin's.

'In a few weeks' time, it'll be as if all this never happened,' he said.

That was what Martin wanted, of course, Annie thought. He wanted their lives to be the same as they had been.

You can't make it un-happen, Annie. What did that mean, then?

'I've got to go, sweetheart. I'll be in tonight, at the usual time. I can't wait to get you out of that place. I love you, Annie.'

'Yes. Yes, I love you too.'

She replaced the receiver and walked slowly along the corridor. She worked out that it was five weeks and two days since the bombing. For all those days the hospital had stood in for the world. She realized now that she had hardly thought beyond it. Her determination to recover had focused on the point of being well enough to leave, and now the vista of *afterwards* opened coldly up in front of her.

Annie passed the ward kitchen where the trays of meals were unloaded from trolleys. She caught the scent of boiled greens mixed with antiseptic scrub, and realized too that it was the first time for weeks that she had noticed a hospital smell. The day sister from the men's ward crossed her path at right angles, smiling at Annie.

'Good news,' she called cheerfully. 'Well done.'

Annie noticed the shape of her calves in black stockings, and the high polish of her black shoes. She knew that she was already looking at the hospital as a visitor, not as an inhabitant. Annie went on into her ward. Sylvia came across at once, eager for news.

'Going home at the weekend, I hear. Looking forward to it?'

'Oh yes. I can't wait.'

Giving the expected answer made Annie more sharply aware of the truth. She was afraid to leave. Hospital had been a protective cocoon, and illness had been an immediate obstacle to conquer.

Steve had known that, of course, and he was waiting. Annie smiled wryly. She had fought to be allowed home, and now she didn't want to go anywhere without Steve. She had willed herself better, so that she could go home safely to Martin. Now she saw that imprisonment in hospital had been their real safety, and when she and Steve were both outside there would be choices infinitely more complex than whether or not to go to the day room.

Annie shivered. She had the sense of open spaces surrounding her again, and an unfamiliar, salty wind blowing.

That day, and the next, she sat with Steve in the day room and didn't tell him that she was going home. More vividly than ever, she was aware that they talked on two levels. There was the banal, public conversation that she had led them into. It was innocently audible to any of the other patients who passed their corner, or who drew up their chairs to join them.

Then there was the other, silent dialogue that grew steadily louder in Annie's head. *Listen to me, Annie,* Steve said. *You must, sooner or later.*

And she babbled back, *Wait. I don't know what to do. I'm afraid. I'm afraid to stay and I'm afraid to leave.*

On the third day Steve was irritable and restless. She watched him as he sat tense in his chair and then impatiently levered himself to his feet, hobbling to the window and staring down into the street before turning back to her again. She knew that he was chafing against boredom, and against the frustration of their holding apart. Her sympathy swelled with wishing that she could stay with him.

'How long will it be?' she asked. 'They must have some idea, surely?'

'You know as much as I do.' His voice was sharp. 'Not until the X-rays show new bone formation. Six weeks, perhaps. Therapy. Muscle rehabilitation. Jesus, Annie, how can I survive another six weeks? Without you?'

'They've said I can go.' The words came out flatly.

Steve swung round, awkward, very close to her. Annie felt her heart lurch.

'I thought it must be soon. When?'

'Tomorrow.'

He stood still, then. She saw the denial in his face and her own longing to deny it too, answering him.

'Why didn't you tell me?'

'I suppose,' Annie said softly, 'I was trying to pretend that it wasn't going to happen.'

Their eyes fastened on the other's face, hungry, importunate.

'I don't want you to go.'

'I don't want to leave you.'

The words spoken aloud, at last. How many days have I made us waste? Annie thought, despairingly.

Steve turned on his crutches again. He looked up and down the room, at the interminable television and the rain-streaked windows, the incurious, sick faces of the others.

'Come here,' he said.

Annie stepped forward, unable to question. If he had undone her clothes, then, and asked her to lie down with him on the institutional floor, she would have done it because he wanted her to.

But he led her away, to the door that opened into the corridor. With all her senses painfully sharpened, Annie heard the tiny metallic creak that his crutches made under his weight.

A few steps beyond was another door, this one with a little round window in it. Steve looked in through the window, and then eased the door open. Annie knew what was inside, because the room was the twin of the one over on the women's side.

'Where are you going?' she whispered.

'Come on,' he repeated.

Annie followed him, and Steve closed the door behind them.

The room was unoccupied. It was a single-bedded side ward with a tall, narrow slit of window that looked out at a dark angle of the red-brick hospital walls. There was a high bed, made up with stiff, smooth white sheets and pillows set perfectly straight. The bed table was pushed away to the foot, bare of the usual clutter of belongings. The only other furnishings were two upright chairs, a folding screen and a basin with long-handled taps like metal ears.

As they faced each other in the silence, footsteps passed by the door.

'No one will come,' Steve said.

'I know.'

Steve disengaged himself from one of the crutches and propped it against the wall. He took Annie's hand and used the other crutch to hobble the few feet across to the bed. He drew her with him, and she followed, without hesitation. Steve reached the bed and rested himself against it, then let the second crutch fall. Then, gently, he took her other hand. She stepped forward, close, and then so close that their bodies touched. She saw the shape of his face and his mouth, the line of his top lip and a muscle that pulled at the corner of it. Her chest was tight with pain and happiness.

He lifted their linked hands and his mouth brushed her knuckles. Annie felt the softness of his tongue between his teeth. Her own mouth opened and she drew the breath in, sharpening the wonderful pain in her heart.

Then Steve let her hands go. He lifted his to cup her face, looking levelly into her eyes, through her eyes and into her head. And then he leant forward, slowly, and his mouth touched hers. He turned her face to one side, and then to the other, and kissed the corners of her mouth.

For that moment, Annie knew nothing except the happiness. She smiled, with her lips curving upwards under his, and he drew her closer still, until her body arched backwards as he kissed her.

His arms came around her and they clung together, greedy, admitting their hunger at last in silence. Annie forgot her physical weakness and the bleak room that enclosed them, and the world waiting for her outside. There was no one but Steve. Her mouth opened under his as she answered him, candid, and his sudden roughness bruised her skin and sent the shocks of sweetness racing all through her.

Annie heard her own voice, wordless, caught low in her throat, *Oh*.

Steve lifted his mouth from hers, and looked into her eyes again. His eyelids were heavy and she saw the gold-flecked irises. Annie was shaking. Behind Steve's shoulder she saw the white cover of the hospital bed, drawn up now in rumples like long pointing fingers. She turned her face away from the fingers and rested it against Steve's shoulder. She brushed the tiny raised loops of his towelling robe and felt the warmth of his skin under her cheek. A pulse beating at the base of his throat answered her own heartbeat. She closed her eyes, giving up all of herself, and put her lips to the little flicker under his skin.

'*Annie*.' His voice crackled.

'I'm here.'

Their kiss was gentle now, and for a second behind her closed eyelids Annie saw the lit threads of tiny veins that netted her head, as beautiful as winter trees and all the firmaments of stars shining behind them.

When they moved apart at last it was slowly, and their fingers reached out to curl together.

Annie opened her eyes to see again. Behind Steve there was still the high white bed, and the ugly, cream-painted bed table on its black rubber wheels. She looked carefully at the folding screen, the door with its single black eye, and then through the window at the brick walls stained with damp and the black humps of drainage pipes. She thought of the hospital, the nurses, and the other patients with their inquisitive stares, and it was like a microcosm of the world that separated her with Steve into this bare room under the blind eye that could see at any moment. The joy was still vivid inside her, but the pain and uncertainty came back to tangle inseparably with it.

Steve watched her face and she knew that he was reading it, and her thoughts flickering behind it. He lifted and smoothed back a fine strand of hair that had caught up at the corner of her mouth, and then his fingers slid under the thickness of hair at the nape of her neck.

'You know, Annie,' he said, 'that we started at the end, you and me. The two of us, stripped down in the darkness, nowhere further to go. It's hard to go back and fill in the steps.'

She saw his crooked, amused smile as he ticked the steps off. 'How do you do? What do you do? How, and where, and what for? I wonder. Another drink? You feel the same? We must be kindred spirits. Let's talk some more, your husband isn't looking. Am I boring you? Monopolizing you? No? I'm glad we met. Very glad. Yes, another drink. More talk. Is it so late already? Could we perhaps meet again? Lunch. Yes, lunch some time very soon.'

'You must be very practised,' Annie said. Steve shook his head to answer her, and she saw his truthfulness too.

'At that. Not at this. This hasn't happened, never. I don't know, any more than you do, how to explain the strangers we were and what we are now. I can't deny it, Annie, and now that I'm holding you like this I know that you can't deny it either. Nor can I justify it, because of what it means to your family. *Wait.*'

She had tried to move backwards then, to disengage herself, but he held her too tightly.

'There hasn't been any neat social two-step between you and me, my love. We came together without anything except ourselves, the parts of ourselves that were real in that bloody wreckage. It was real then, and it is still real now.'

He turned her chin with his fingertips to make her look up at him, and at last she returned his clear gaze.

'I've never taken you to dinner. We've never met for a clandestine drink, and so I don't know whether you prefer white wine spritzers or vodka martinis. We haven't take those particular steps together and we won't do, now. I'm glad, because I don't believe you tread that path in any case. And we haven't made love, although I want you now more than I've ever wanted anyone in all my life.'

Annie knew that that was the truth. She felt the colour hot in her cheeks, but her eyes held his.

'I'd lie down with you here, now, this minute, if only we could,' she whispered.

Steve leant forward and for a second his lips were hard against hers.

'Thank you,' he said. He was smiling, but the pulse was still beating at the base of his throat. 'I will remind you of that. For now, I just want to tell you something.' He stopped, looking for the words, and Annie understood that Steve was as vulnerable as she was herself. He shrugged then, almost like a boy, and said in a voice so low that she had to strain to catch what he said, 'You know that I love you, Annie, don't you?'

In the silence that followed she heard the echoes in her head, *I love you, Annie*, and happiness fluttered against her ribs again. She lifted Steve's hands and looked down at his knuckles, touching them gently, wonderingly, with her thumb.

From outside in the corridor came the squeak of hurrying feet and a door swung open and shut with a hiss and a bang. In the distance a trolley rattled at the big doors of the lift.

It was so quiet in the room, and the noise outside sharpened her awareness of the difference between there and here. She was hidden with Steve in this little square box. Martin told her, *I love you*, and that was the truth too.

'I did know,' Annie said at last, thinking that the words fell gracelessly, like stones. She tried to cover them, saying too quickly, 'Steve, I didn't . . .' but he stopped her from going any further.

'That's all,' he said. 'I wanted you to know, before you go. Will you think about it, Annie?'

Very carefully, keeping her mouth steady, Annie said, 'I won't be able to think about anything else.' That was her admission. Her face crumpled then and she blinked to keep back the tears. 'I don't want to go, Steve. I . . .'

Not even Annie knew what she might have said, because he stopped her with his hands to her lips.

'Think about it,' he repeated. Steve moved his weight awkwardly against the edge of the bed, and Annie knew that he was thinking, *Bandages, crutches*.

'It won't be long,' she said. 'They'll let you go soon.'

'Until they do, will you come and visit me?'

'Like all the others?' Annie smiled suddenly as she copied old Frank's descriptive outline in the air, but Steve caught her hands and kissed them.

'Not like that at all. Will you?'

Annie knew that she would come. The prospect of it seemed now the only way that she could bear to leave him.

'Yes,' she said simply. 'As often as I can. I promise I will.'

'It won't be long,' he echoed, and they looked at one another soberly.

'What will you say to Martin?' he asked, because he couldn't help it.

Annie let go of his hands. She turned her head to look at the window, and then walked slowly across the room. Dozens of other windows faced into the dark well. She saw the edges of curtains, cupboards, and through one window opposite the crimped edge of a sister's cap as she sat at a desk.

Painfully, she said, 'I won't tell Martin anything. There isn't anything to tell, yet, is there? I don't want to hurt him.' Annie realized that she was rationalizing aloud. She didn't understand herself what was happening, not yet. 'I have to think,' she said softly. Steve nodded, accepting. Annie went back to him and rested her head against his shoulder. Out of the tangle of feelings, suddenly happiness was dominant again. They had come through all of it, and they had held on to one another.

With his mouth against her hair he whispered, 'We should go now.'

Annie wanted to leave this, too, at the point that they had reached. She let herself hold on to him for a moment longer, and then she slipped out of his reach. She stooped to pick up his hated crutches and fitted them gently under his arms so that he could walk again.

Watching her, Steve thought that he had never seen anyone as clearly, with such intimacy, as he saw Annie now. With her hand at his elbow he lumbered towards the door. A cramp gnawed at his good leg so that he swayed, leaning against Annie for support, and she almost fell under his weight. They struggled for a moment before they were steady, and then they stood upright. Laughter washed over them until Annie had to hold on to the door jamb for support. She found herself thinking, How can this have happened, out of pain and fear, this laughter, and the happiness of loving a stranger?

But it had happened. There was no going back now.

'It isn't funny,' Steve protested as their laughter died down. 'I'm incapable.' He saw the brightness of Annie's eyes.

'That's just as well. Think what might have happened otherwise.' She dodged past him, and went to smooth the hospital bedcover back into its rigid folds. 'There. Now Sister will never guess.'

'Don't be so sure. She's probably got a spyhole somewhere.'

'Now you tell me.'

Annie peered through the glass porthole. Her face was serious again as she turned back to him, and then leant forward to touch her mouth to his.

Neither of them spoke, because in that long moment there was no need to.

It was Annie who moved first. Slowly she opened the door. She saw that the corridor was deserted and so she went quickly away, without looking back, afraid that if she didn't leave him then she never would.

Martin came to collect her the next morning.

Annie had packed her bag, and she was waiting for him, sitting in the chair beside her empty bed, when Sylvia saw him through the open doors and called across to her, 'Here he comes, love.'

She stood up to meet him and he kissed her cheek, both of them aware of all the others watching them. Annie felt the familiarity of him beside her, and at the same time her fear of leaving the safe, small hospital world.

Martin picked up her bag. 'Ready?'

'I just want to say goodbye.'

The nurses and the other patients were already waiting, lined up in dressing gowns and uniforms at the ward doors. Annie saw the sister slip out through the doors. With Martin at her side Annie said goodbye to each one of the others. Their good wishes and congratulations made a lump in her throat, and she was afraid that she was going to cry.

She was reaching the end of the row when the ward door opened again. The sister was back and there were others with her, all the men from the adjoining ward who were well enough to walk. Frankie the newsvendor was at the head of them, with a big bunch of cellophane-wrapped roses in his arms. He held them out to her, beaming. 'Here you are, my duck. You're a brave girl. Good luck, from all of us.'

Behind him, taller than the others, she saw Steve's dark head. *Not brave*, Annie thought. For an instant she thought that the terrible pull, one way and then the other, would tear her in half.

She took the flowers blindly and kissed Frankie's cheek. There were other kisses too, but in all the press of people she felt a light touch on her shoulder and she knew that it was Steve's. She nodded, not trusting herself to look at him, and stumbled forward with her flowers. She felt rather than saw that Martin held out his hand to Steve.

They were calling out to her, 'Good luck, Annie. Think of us, still in here.'

Martin's hand was at her elbow now, guiding her. Steeling herself she turned to look back, seeing the cluster of faces as pale blobs, except for Steve's. Every detail of Steve's face was clear.

'Thank you,' she said as steadily as she could, 'for the flowers, everything. Take care of yourselves.'

As her husband led her away she felt Steve immobile on his crutches behind them, watching her go.

Outside, the world seemed to teem with people and reverberate with traffic. Annie sat in the passenger seat of the car as they threaded precariously through it. Martin was whistling softly as he drove, and then at a red traffic light he leaned across and kissed her on the cheek.

'How does it feel?' he grinned at her.

'Strange,' she answered, and feeling the coolness of that she added quickly, 'Wonderful.'

Martin glanced at her and then as the car slid forward again he said, 'You'll have to take it easy, even though you're well enough to be at home. Everything's organized for you.'

Annie put her hand out to touch the knee of his corduroy trousers. 'Thank you,' she said.

They began the familiar climb up the hill towards home, in the grinding stream of lorries and buses, under the span of the wrought-iron bridge that Annie often crossed with the boys, on their way to the park. She looked up at it, curiously, as if she were seeing it for the first time. At the top of the hill they turned, out of the traffic, into quiet streets. The corner shops were familiar here, and then they passed the tube station that Annie had hurried into on her way to do the Christmas shopping, six weeks ago.

A minute later they reached the end of their road.

She looked down the length of it and saw their house, red bricks faced with yellow, bay windows under a little pointed roof. The car stopped outside and Annie saw the boys' faces bob up at the bedroom window.

Martin took her hand. 'I didn't tell the whole world that you would be home today. Everyone wanted to be here, to welcome you, but I thought you might not like a big reception committee.'

Annie smiled at him, touched by his care. But Martin was always kind, in just that way.

'I'm glad,' she said. 'They can all come another day.'

Martin helped her out of the car and they went up the path hand in hand.

'Thomas and Ben have arranged their own welcome party. Ready?'

She nodded, wondering, and Martin opened the front door. The hallway was hung everywhere with hand-painted streamers, and huge, cut-out letters dangling from the ceiling spelt out the message WELCOME HOME MUMMY. There was a second's silence as Annie looked at it and different tears burned in her eyes. And then the children, unable to hide any longer, burst out and tumbled down the stairs into her arms.

'Did you like it? Were you surprised?' Tom demanded.

'I coloured the ribbons,' Benjy shouted. 'All these. They go right up the stairs. *Look*, Mummy.'

Annie looked, and saw Barbara coming out of the kitchen, smiling at her. Through the open doors beside her she saw a fire burning in the polished grate. The house was warm, lived-in and comfortable and happy. Her tears blurred the welcome sight of it and ran down her cheeks.

'Why are you crying?' Benjy asked and she held him so that his face was warm against hers.

'Because I'm glad to be home.'

Barbara hugged her, and then the boys took Annie's hands and she let them lead her upstairs. She found that the bedroom was bright with flowers, and the covers were turned down ready for her on the wide bed. Propped against the pillows was a small, threadbare teddy.

'I put my ted in, see, to keep you company,' Benjy announced.

'I told him that you probably wouldn't want his smelly teddy,' Thomas added.

'I do. Of course I do.'

She sat down on the bed, feeling the familiar sag under her weight, and the boys crowded anxiously against her.

'You won't have to go back again, will you?' Thomas's casual voice tried to hide his anxiety.

'No, darling, I won't have to go away again.' With her arms around her children Annie looked out of the window at the view, the unchanged composition of slate roofs and bay windows and bare tree branches, thinking.

Nothing was different, and yet the whole world had changed.

She rested her cheek wearily against Benjy's smooth head.

Martin brought in a glass vase with the hospital's red roses arranged in it. Their colour reminded her of blood, and of Steve, motionless in the hospital corridor, watching her go.

Martin crossed the room and touched his finger to her cheek. 'Are you all right?'

'Yes,' Annie lied to him. 'Of course I am.'

Six

Annie was cooking dinner. She moved slowly to and fro in the kitchen, opening doors and taking out pans, collecting ingredients from the larder. It seemed a long time since she had done anything of the kind. She had made suppers for the boys, and she had started cooking for herself and Martin within a few days of being home again. Barbara had done it to begin with, but after a few days Annie had taken control. It surprised her to recognize how much she minded the displacement from her own kitchen, and she thought, *I must be more like Tibby than I've ever realized*. But tonight was the first proper dinner. It had been Martin's idea.

'You haven't had your welcome home party,' he had announced one night. 'Now you're better, we should all go out to dinner somewhere. We could ask Gail and Ian.'

Enthusiastically he had named three other couples, old friends and neighbours.

'It'll cost a fortune to take all of them out,' Annie had said.

'Oh, we can all pay for ourselves.'

'You can't ask them out to celebrate and then make them pay,' Annie protested. It was so like a hundred other plans and discussions that they had had over the years that she smiled suddenly.

'Ask them here. I'll make chili or something.'

'Can you cope with that?'

'Yes,' she had said. 'I'm sure I can.'

'I'll help.'

Martin had put his warm hand out to cover hers, and then they had turned on the television to watch the news.

And so it had been arranged. Three couples were coming to dinner, and because she wanted to make everything the same as it would have been before, Annie had decided that it must be a proper meal. She was a good cook, and her dinners had a reputation amongst their friends. So she had planned an elaborate menu, and done the shopping this morning while Benjy was at nursery. Now both the boys were watching television in the sitting room. Annie put down the big casserole dish she had taken out of the cupboard and went to stand in the doorway to look at them.

Tom was sitting on the sofa with his knees drawn up and his chin sunk into his jersey, his eyes fixed on the screen. Benjy was lying on the floor with strands of fine hair fanning out around his head. It was much too long, Annie noted automatically. She must take him for a haircut.

'D'you want a peanut butter sandwich, either of you, before I start cooking?' she asked. Neither of them spoke or took their eyes off the television and she asked again, hearing herself on the point of shouting at them.

'Oh. Yes, okay,' Tom said and Benjy declared, 'I want the same as Thomas,' just as he always did.

Annie went back into the kitchen and made the sandwiches, took them through to the boys, and then started work.

She made a stuffing of spinach and calves' liver cooked pink and spread it in the boned shoulder of lamb she had stood over her butcher for this morning. She rolled the meat and trussed it neatly with string, then browned it in the frying pan. The smell of fatty meat made her feel slightly sick.

Annie looked at the clock. It was almost six o'clock. She had intended to make her own puff pastry to wrap around the lamb, but she realized now that there wasn't time for that. She opened the freezer and rummaged for a packet of ready-made, then left it to defrost while she began work on the starter. She had made the same mousselines of sole a dozen times before, but today the fish seemed full of tiny, hair-line bones and her fingers felt clumsy and stiff as she tried to pick them out with the slivers of grey skin that stuck everywhere.

The buzz of the blender sounded unnaturally loud, sawing through her head.

Thomas came in and asked, 'Can I have another sandwich?'

Annie was about to snap at him, 'Wait for supper,' when she realized that it was past time for that. She clattered amongst the dirty saucepans and chopping boards, making beans on toast and poached eggs.

She put the food on the table and Benjy groaned, 'I don't *want* this.'

'It's all I've got time to do tonight. Eat that or nothing at all, I don't mind which.'

The boys sat opposite one another, silently eating their beans, eyeing her. Just the vegetables to do now, and ten minutes to deal with the pastry, Annie calculated. She had made lemon syllabub the night before and it was ready, a pale yellow froth, in the glass bowl in the fridge. She was congratulating herself on that when she remembered that she had forgotten to buy any cheese. Martin would have to buy some at the deli on the way home. He should *be* home by now, Annie thought with weary resentment. As soon as she recognized that she did feel resentful, it grew inside her. She was on her way to the telephone when it rang.

It was Martin.

'I'm sorry, love. I had to stay late with the client. One damn niggle after another. I'm on my way now. Are you okay?'

'Wonderful,' Annie said.

There was a tiny pause.

'Oh dear. And it's supposed to be your party. I'll do everything else, I promise.'

'Get some cheese at the deli, will you?'

'Done.'

Annie went back to the sink and clattered the greasy saucepans. I don't want to do this, she thought, very clearly. I don't want to make dinner for these people, and sit through an evening's talking and drinking. Then a wave of fright washed through her. *These people* were her friends and her husband, and dinners together had been their pleasure, before. She felt cold as she recognized how much reckoning she did in terms of *before*.

Before the bomb? Or was it not the bomb at all, but Steve?

To postpone the thought Annie whirled around the kitchen, clearing the worktops and banging the doors shut on the chaos inside the cupboards. Miraculously the room looked tidy again and the sink was empty.

She took the boys' plates and said, 'I'm not cross, Ben. Just in a rush.'

She gave them fruit yoghurts, and while they were eating them she stood at the other end of the table and rolled out the defrosted pastry. She set the lamb shoulder in the middle of the rectangle then deftly parcelled it up, trimming off the surplus and crimping the seams with her fingers. She crumpled the leftover pastry into a ball and rolled it out again, then cut out leaves with the point of a knife. The decorations looked pretty and the job was soothing. She was brushing her handiwork with beaten egg when she heard Martin's bag thud down on the step, and his key in the lock.

'*Dad*,' the boys shouted in unison, and ran to meet him. He came in, swinging Benjy. Martin looked anxiously at Annie and then glanced around the kitchen.

'Mouthwatering smells and a scene of perfect domestic harmony,' he murmured. 'I was expecting something different.'

'If you had been here an hour ago you would have seen something different.'

'I said I was sorry, Annie. I got the cheese.' He held up the carrier bag, as if to placate her.

Annie's resentment was focused on Martin now, but she felt too tired to embark on an argument.

'Why don't you go and get ready? I'll see the kids into bed, and do whatever else needs doing.'

'Thank you,' she said, still angry and yet knowing that it

would make the evening worse if she and Martin were on bad terms.

She went slowly upstairs and took a shower. Wrapped in the blue dressing gown that made her think of Steve again she went into her bedroom and took her favourite dress out of the wardrobe. It was a swirly black jersey that clung in the right places. Annie pulled the dress on over her head and stared at herself in the long mirror. She was too thin for it, and it hung like a shroud from her shoulders. The black material made her face look sallow because she hadn't regained her natural colour yet.

As she looked at her pallid reflection Annie had the vertiginous sense that she was confronting someone else, and not herself at all. *Steve*, she thought stupidly, *you know who I am. Is this me?*

Then she snatched up the hem of the dress and pulled it off, struggling for a minute within the black folds of the skirt. She searched along the row of hangers and took out a bright red shirt and narrow trousers, and bundled the black dress into the farthest corner.

When she was dressed, Annie faced the mirror again. She began to make up her face, outlining her eyes with grey pencil and dabbing blusher on to her cheeks. She brushed lipgloss on to her mouth and then sat facing herself, with the little brush dangling in her fingers. The optimistic colours she had applied seemed to stand out against her chalky skin like a clown's make-up. Annie sighed, and taking a piece of cotton wool she rubbed most of it off again. To neaten the ragged ends of her hair her hairdresser had cut it much shorter than she usually wore it. Annie pulled at the ends with a comb, as if that would stretch it to cover her bare neck and throat, and then dropped the comb with a clatter.

Martin came in and stood behind her, and their eyes met in the mirror.

'You look very pretty,' he said, and touched the exposed and vulnerable line of their jaw with his fingers. 'I like your hair like that. It reminds me of when I first knew you.'

Annie tilted her head, just a little, away from the touch, and his hand dropped. She smiled, hastily, to cover the awkwardness.

'I don't feel very pretty. I tried the black dress on first, and it looked hideous.'

'Red's better,' Martin said.

He had turned away when she spoke, and now he was looking in the wardrobe for a clean shirt. Annie watched him in the mirror, thinking of the little nuances of gesture and expression by which they interpreted each other, surprised by her own detachment.

To negotiate the evening, that was the first thing.

'I'm sorry I was angry when you came in,' she volunteered.

'I would have been back earlier if I possibly could.'

'I know.' Annie took his shirt out of a drawer and handed it to him, turning her back on their reflections. 'I was in a flap. I was afraid that the dinner wouldn't be ready, and that even if it was it would be inedible.'

'Annie, darling.' Martin had put the clean shirt on and he came across to her, the buttons still undone. He put his arms around her and Annie felt the shape and the weight of him, perfectly familiar, strangely null. 'The food you cook is always good. And even if tonight it happened not to be, even if we gave them dry biscuits, do you think it would matter to your friends?'

'I don't suppose so,' Annie said sadly. 'It's just that . . . it's just that if I'm going to do it at all, I want it to be good, and special.'

Martin laughed and let her go.

'You know something? In your own way, you're as much of a perfectionist as Tibby is.'

'I think I am like her,' Annie said, very softly. 'I've only just realized it myself.'

She stood for a moment, looking ahead of her with apparently unseeing eyes.

Martin finished dressing and reminded her briskly, 'Benjy's in bed. I told him you'd go in and say goodnight.'

Annie jumped, almost guiltily, then said, 'I'll go now.'

Benjy was lying under his Superman cover, but Annie knew

from the way that his head jerked up that he had been listening, waiting for her. When she sat down on the edge of the bed he turned over, folding his arms comfortably on top of the covers, looking up at her. She felt the sharp, physical pull of love and the weight of unending responsibility that went with it, both sensations conflicting with another, newer feeling. She could have isolated that one, but she turned her thoughts deliberately away. She bent down to kiss Benjy and he put his arms up around her neck, not letting go. He smelt clean and babyish, and his fine, floppy hair was a child's version of Martin's.

'You won't go away and get hurt again, will you?' he asked.

Benjy's fears for her had expressed themselves in nightmares, and in sudden tantrums, and Annie was relieved to hear him put them into words.

'No.' She stroked his hair back from his face, soothing him. 'I'm not going anywhere. I'm staying here with you.'

'And Tom, and Dad.'

'Of course.'

Only she looked at the wall behind the little boy's head, where he had scribbled in purple crayon, and she thought, *Impossible*. But Annie didn't know in that minute whether it was impossible to change anything, or impossible for life to go on as it did now.

She settled Benjy's covers around his shoulders.

'Goodnight, pumpkin. Sleep tight.'

'Blow kisses at the door.' It was his nightly demand, and part of the ritual of letting her go until the morning. Obediently Annie stood in the doorway and blew kisses until, content, he burrowed his head into the pillows. She turned on his night-light and quietly closed the door.

Thomas was in his bath, and she called to him as she passed, 'Put your dressing gown on when you've finished, and come down for half an hour.'

Martin was already in the kitchen, setting out glasses on a tray. They moved around each other, practised, knowing what had to be done. Annie finished preparing the vegetables and then laid the table, polishing the pieces of cutlery hastily as she laid them in place. She took the napkins out of the dresser drawer, frowning at sight of the creases in them. She found the branched pewter candelabrum that had been a wedding present and stuck plain white candles into the holders. There was, as always, satisfaction in making preparations. Annie smiled crookedly as the thought came to her again, *Just like Tibby.* Yet for almost all her adult life she had been gently, amusedly dismissive of her mother's fondness of guest towels and matching soaps in china shell dishes.

'How are we doing?' Martin asked.

'Ready, now.'

'There you are,' he beamed at her, as though the effort had been all his. 'Nothing to worry about.'

There was no point in renewing the disagreement, Annie thought, if the evening was to be comfortable. She smiled, and went through to sit by Thomas on the sofa. His hair was wet and brushed flat, his face shone, and he was methodically working his way through a bowl of cashew nuts.

Five minutes later, exactly on time, the doorbell rang.

The evening's ingredients were exactly the same as for a dozen other evenings over as many years. The six people who came to dinner were all old friends. Martin and Annie had known one couple since their college days, Thomas had been best friends from toddlerhood with the children of the second couple, and the third was Martin's partner and his wife. Like all long-standing groups of friends they held loosely between them a net of memories and impressions, expressed in private jokes and conversational shorthand, the bric-à-brac of shared weekends and holidays and pleasures and occasional crises. As soon as the eight of them were together, Annie and Martin's living room filled up with talk and laughter.

All six of their guests had visited Annie in hospital, and they had sent her flowers and brought her presents and offered to take their turn at looking after the boys. She had seen them separately, too, since coming home, but there was a shared sense that tonight was different because it was her proper celebration. She felt their warmth reaching out to her. There was champagne, and Annie drank two glasses, trying to launch herself into her party.

But she knew that she was drifting, smiling but separate.

She watched Tom handing round olives and nuts, and then went into the kitchen to look at the fish. When she came back she was disconcerted by the circle of cheerful, expectant faces all looking up at her.

'Bedtime, Tom,' she whispered to him, to cover her unbalance.

He went, with the usual show of reluctance, with the other parents calling out cheerful goodnights. Annie went out with him into the hall and hugged him at the foot of the stairs. The light on the landing was dim and soothing, and Annie looked half-longingly at the darkness beyond the crack of her bedroom door.

When she went back to her seat on the sofa, Martin's partner Ian was reminiscing about a holiday he and Gail had spent with Martin and Annie in Provence.

'Ten years ago, can you believe?'

'Nine,' Martin said.

It had rained for two weeks, so heavily that when they went to the cottage's outside lavatory they had had to wear their wellingtons, and shelter under a golf umbrella. They had played bridge, interminable games, unsatisfactory to all of them because Gail and Ian were good players and Annie and Martin weren't. Annie was a sun-worshipper, and she had sulked at being deprived of her annual sun-tan. They teased her about it good-humouredly now, as they often did, and she did her best to smile back.

'I've got the pictures here, somewhere,' Martin said. 'I was looking at them the other day, when Annie was still in hospital.' He rummaged in a drawer and produced a yellow envelope folder. The photographs passed from hand to hand, bursts of laughter and recollection erupting over each one. When they reached Annie she looked down into her own face, and the others surrounding it, as if she were seeing a group of acquaintances, made long ago and half forgotten.

She gave the photographs back to Martin and went into the kitchen again. She lit the candles in their pewter brackets and watched their reflection in the black glass of the garden windows, little ovals of flame that swayed and spluttered and then burned up bright and clear.

'It's ready,' she called.

They came crowding in and sat down, joking and arguing. Annie decorated the fish mousselines with little feather sprigs of chervil, and handed them round to a chorus of admiration.

'Annie, you are amazing.'

'Just look at this, will you? You especially, Gail, my darling.'

Martin walked around the table, pouring more champagne. Annie took her place opposite his, at the foot of the table. The lamb was in the oven, cooking pink inside while the puff pastry case turned gold That much was under control, but with the champagne fizzing in her head Annie frowned, trying to pinpoint another anxiety. Perhaps it had been an unnecessary demonstration to cook a meal like this. Perhaps she was trying to prove that nothing had changed, while all along it really had, irrevocably, and dry biscuits would have been, at least, an honest statement.

Am I lying to them all? Annie thought wildly. At her right hand David, the father of Tom's friend, reached for the champagne bottle that Martin had left and filled her glass. He lifted his own and said, 'Here's to you, love. And many more dinners.'

'Many more dinners,' Annie echoed him, and drank.

The evening went on, in all its jollity, around her. After a while she found that the wine helped, because it took the sharp edges off her perception. She served the lamb and then sat back in her chair, looking at the faces.

The room was cosy in the candlelight, and full of the scent of food. One of the other women was wearing long, glittery earrings and as she leaned forward across the table, telling a story, the earrings swung and shot points of coloured light. As she delivered the story's punchline there was a burst of laughter, and Annie joined in.

'Not like our Annie,' David said, in answer to someone else's remark, and squeezed her hand warmly.

Annie's gaze moved on around the table. They were all pleasant, good-humoured people, she thought, well-fed and lubricated, sitting together in a warm, comfortable place. Through the nimbus of the candles she looked at Martin, and his face meant no more or less to her than the others. Equally familiar, and just as remote from her. Annie was cold, suddenly, so cold that she shivered in her red shirt. They were all strangers, even Martin. Chillingly she knew that the only person who was real was Steve. She felt his closeness to her, and at the nape of her neck the fine hairs prickled as if his hand reached out to stroke her. Very clearly she saw the hospital ward, with the lights already dimmed for the night, and Steve's face in the defined circle of light over his bed. She knew that he was thinking about her, and the thoughts were like a bridge, linking them. She longed for him so desperately that she clenched her fists in her lap, digging her nails into her palms to contain the pain of it.

The dinner party seemed to be taking place a long way off, and she was seeing it across a cold and empty space.

'Annie, are you all right?'

She saw the earrings sparkle again and she focused her smile on them, willing herself to sound normal.

'Yes, I'm fine. Do you think we should have pudding or cheese next?'

She pushed her chair back and went unsteadily to the refrigerator, glad of the chance to turn her back until her face was controllable again. She stared into the white interior, and at the lemon syllabub in its glass bowl amongst the humdrum family provisions. None of this was real. The only real experience she had ever had was in the darkness she had shared with Steve. The only real feeling was this, that she felt for him now.

'I'll carry it,' Martin said. He reached from behind her and lifted the pudding out, and he kissed her cheek as he eased past her. 'That was a wonderful dinner.'

'I'm glad,' Annie whispered. 'I wanted it to be.'

It was, and miraculously no one had seen or guessed how little she belonged to it. She was sitting in her place again, spooning out the creamy foam, when Gail leaned across the table. With her eyes wide open in fascinated dismay she said, 'I knew I had something to tell you. Has anyone else heard that the Frobishers are splitting up?'

There was a frisson of shocked surprise, and then of clear relief. *Not us. So far, so good.*

'I don't believe it.'

'Neither do I.'

'It's true. She told me. He's moving out as soon as he's found a flat. She said that they hadn't really been getting along for years, and it was better now that it had finally happened.'

'How odd. They always seemed so keen on each other. Holding hands, and dancing together at parties.'

Martin held up another bottle of wine. 'Anyone for this? Have I told you my theory?'

'A thousand times, probably.'

'*My* theory is that it's just those people who are at pains to look so wonderfully happy with one another who are, in fact, right on the rocks. Witness the Frobishers.'

'Whereas people like us . . .'

'Forever nagging each other, and arguing about money, and about who promised not to be late home, are the ones who are happy. The ones who couldn't live without each other.'

He looked through the candles' glow at Annie. He had begun lightly, but as he spoke he had been reaching out to her, trying to ask the question. Unspoken, it had been growing louder inside him ever since Annie had come home. He couldn't make himself deliver it when they were alone, and so he had wrapped it up and pushed it delicately across the table to her, under their friends' eyes.

Do you still love me? It was banal, of course. *But you don't really care about him, do you? Except for what you went through, together . . .*

Annie's face was a colourless oval, too far away from him, and her eyes were opaque.

In that moment, Martin knew for sure.

Annie had gone away, and he would have to fight to get her back.

He heard his own voice, talking, joking with their friends around the table to hide his fear, and suddenly their whole life was a similar pretence.

Martin emptied his glass, refilled it and then drank again.

No, Annie was thinking, still listening to Martin's words inside her head. It isn't like that at all. Not as safe and as comfortable as Martin makes it sound. We were happy, the two of us, weren't we? And then in a day, in an hour, everything changes. How has it happened, all this, and what can I do now?

The question ran round in her head, unanswerable.

At last, the evening was over.

The last cup of coffee and the last glass of wine had been drained, and their friends followed one another out into the black, icy night.

'Bye, everybody. It was lovely, Annie. You're a miracle, you know?'

'Don't do too much, though, will you? You look a bit weary, still, to me.'

'See you on Saturday, then? With the kids, of course.'

Goodbye. Goodnight.

The words rang around Annie, friendly and foreign, emphasizing her isolation.

Martin looked around the kitchen. 'You go on up. I'll clear all this.' He glanced at her, and when she didn't respond he ordered, 'Go *on*, Annie.'

She went, too lonely and too tired to do anything more. She lay down in bed, in the comfortable darkness, and listened to the sounds of the house. She felt like an interloper. At last Martin came up. He turned on the light and sat down heavily on his side of the bed.

'Still awake?'

'Yes.'

She didn't know what to say, now.

Martin stood up again and moved around the room, undressing. He was a little drunk and bumped into the corners of the furniture.

When he was ready, he slid under the bedclothes beside her.

There was a moment when they both lay still. Then, with an awkward, possessive movement, Martin put his arms around her. He fitted her body against the curves of his own, his mouth and tongue against her ear. To Annie he felt very warm and solid, and utterly strange. She closed her eyes. He was her husband. She was suddenly struck by a sense of how random everything had been, all the choices she had made in her life, up until now. She could equally well have married David, or Ian. It could be either of them, anyone she had met or never met, with his body pressed to hers, and it would make no difference.

Somehow, cruelly and yet with such potent force that even now it melted her, Steve had become the only man she knew. The only man she wanted, and he wasn't there. Annie lay quite still while her husband made love to her, and she felt nothing. And then when it was over she lay in the dark and listened to his breathing, like a stranger's.

Martin had half-turned away, but he didn't fall asleep.

Annie had been there in his arms, and in that sense she had been as generous as she always was, but for all the intimacy of touch he hadn't been able to reach her. He could sense her separateness now, and it silenced him. They lay with a cold space between them, holding their feelings painfully apart.

Suddenly, Martin was angry. A knot of it gathered inside him, focused on Steve. He couldn't be angry with Annie, not yet, because she had been through so much.

He saw Steve's face as he had been on Christmas Eve, his face dark and drawn against the hospital pillows. And he remembered the little space where Steve had held Annie, and where they had shared the terrible hours that he was ashamed to be jealous of. That space had seemed much smaller than the bed's hollow that contained Martin and Annie now.

Anger jumped inside Martin and his fists clenched under the bedclothes. He felt no sympathy for Steve, and the certainty came to him that Steve would be a formidable opponent. He would have to be an opponent, an enemy, of course, because Martin would have to cut him off from Annie.

My wife. Annie, in the bedroom's silence.

He thought she stirred, and he waited breathlessly for her to put her hand out to him. Nothing happened, and with his imagination fuelled by the wine he had drunk Martin planned in angry detail how he would drive to the hospital in the morning. He would stand beside Steve's bed, and tell him that he was to leave Annie alone. His anger and his determination to keep her were big enough and simple enough to crush any opposition, Martin was sure of that.

When he fell asleep at last it was to uncomfortable, ambiguous dreams.

In the morning the anger had evaporated. As he shaved and went downstairs with a slight, dry headache to listen to the boys squabbling over their breakfasts, Martin knew that he wouldn't go to see Steve. It wasn't in his nature to force a confrontation, even with Annie. Especially with Annie. He looked across the kitchen at her white, exhausted face and he felt ashamed again. She had barely recovered, and she must be feeling her own unhappiness.

When the time came for him to leave for work Martin put his arm around her and rested his face against her hair. She returned the warm pressure, although she kept her face turned away, and he left the house holding on to that brief affirmation.

The sense of apartness stayed with Annie. It cast a thin, uncomfortable light on the routine of every day.

Annie ran the house mechanically. She went out to buy food in the local shops, and looked at the familiar shelves as if she had never seen them before. She washed and folded clothes, and drove the boys to and fro, feeling herself physically stronger every day. She sat with Martin in the evenings, hearing the silence between them, afraid. At night the dreams of noise and stifling darkness still came. Annie woke up, shaking, to find him asleep beside her and as the pall of brick-dust lifted again in her imagination she put her hand out to touch the separate warmth of his skin. Annie went back to the hospital regularly, to see her specialists and to submit to more tests. She waited patiently in the various clinics, soothed by the way that the system temporarily took away her sense of responsibility for herself. And after she had gone through what was required of her in out-patients, and only then, Annie allowed herself to go upstairs and see Steve.

The first time was no more than a few days after Annie had been discharged, but it seemed already that they had been painfully separated for months. On the morning of her appointment she went upstairs and chose, very carefully, what she was going to wear. She made her face up, and her hands were shaking so much that she smudged the careful strokes. Annie looked at her reflection and thought, it's like being a girl again. The recognition and the strangeness made her laugh, but her heart still hammered in her chest. She left the quiet house and walked to the tube station, remembering the last time, the midwinter morning with the snowflakes spiralling after the wind. This morning it was just as cold, but there were snow-drops under the bare hedge in a square of front garden, and the pale spears of crocus leaves pointing up through the broken earth beside them. When she saw the flowers it was as if she had walked into a shaft of light. The same happiness in being alive that she had felt on the day they wheeled her out of intensive care came back and took hold of her. Steve had felt that happiness, and the return of it now drew her even more strongly towards him.

For a moment, standing in the littered street, Annie forgot her anxiety and guilt. She smiled and straightened her shoulders, thinking, *Whatever comes, will come*. Then she began to walk again, faster, feeling herself strong and complete in her happiness. The people who passed her saw her face and looked again, watching her as she went by, but Annie didn't see anything except the warm light and the first signs of spring.

When she slipped in through the doors of his ward at last, she saw Steve sitting in the chair beside his bed, his crutches propped up within reach. The reality of his being there made her catch her breath, because all the way up in the lift she had been preparing herself for what she would do if he wasn't. She saw that he was thinner and much paler than the Steve she had seen inside her head, and she thought that she must have been imagining him as he would be when he could walk again, fit enough to leave the hospital. Willing that to happen. She realized too that the sense of separateness had evaporated. She was simply Annie with her heart thumping and the mixture of joy and apprehension drying her mouth.

Then he looked up and saw her and she wanted to run forward and to hold back at the same time.

Steve watched her walk towards him and he thought, She's beautiful. I hadn't noticed that.

As soon as she was close enough, he stretched out his hand and Annie took it. They held on to one another for a moment, all they could do under the eyes of the ward. Then Steve moved to reach for his crutches and Annie said quickly, 'Don't move. I'll sit beside you.'

She brought a chair, and put it beside his.

'Six days is a long time,' Steve said softly. Annie saw the hunger in his face and she had to look away, over his shoulder. It was a little before visiting time, and most of the curtains were drawn while the men slept after lunch. Even so there were still one or two patients shuffling to and fro, and the nurses. One of the nurses glanced their way and then looked more carefully. She waved a belated greeting to Annie.

Did they all see what was happening? Annie wondered. They must do, of course. If it was written as plainly in her face as it was in Steve's.

She turned back to him, closing out the ward behind them. It didn't matter. Only Steve mattered, here.

'Today was my first appointment,' she said.

'And you won't come to see me unless you've got the excuse of an appointment.'

'Not an excuse,' she began, and then stopped. She was using the fact of having to be at the hospital as a pretext, telling herself that she could always say lightly to Martin, 'Oh, I went up to the ward to see Steve. Just for five minutes, as I was there, you know. He looks much better.'

But of course she wouldn't say anything to Martin. Nothing at all, beyond the facts like the queue at Haematology, and the reassurances that the doctors had doled out to her. She had stopped talking to Martin about what mattered to her, in case it came too close to this. And gave her away.

Annie's happiness faded a little. If Martin didn't know anything about it, it didn't matter when she came to visit Steve. The subterfuge was for her own benefit, Annie thought, because she lacked the courage to meet what was happening face-on.

'Don't look like that,' Steve said.

'I don't know why I'm trying to pretend not to see you,' Annie was frowning, unravelling her motives. What had been clear, before, was murky now.

Steve leant forward and touched his thumb between her eyebrows.

'Come when you can, that's all. It doesn't matter, so long as I know I'll see you sometimes. I don't want to make more demands on you.'

Steve shifted in his chair, trying to contain his impatience with his slow-mending leg and the public tedium of the ward while Annie sat so close to him. Her hair smelt clean, with a mild, lemony scent. And even the brief touch of her had made him sharply aware of the texture of her skin, and the masked outline of her body. Steve was suddenly aware of the weight of love, pressing and trying to force its way into the open. It was new to him, and it made him feel childish and helpless.

Annie saw his impatience and her face lightened with sympathy.

'Shall we walk a bit?' she asked. 'Come on. I'll help you stand up.'

Together, they levered him to his feet. Annie held out his crutches and Steve leant his weight on the metal legs.

'We could go to the day room.' He smiled at her, crookedly.

They went slowly down the ward. Annie nodded cheerfully and spoke to the people they passed.

'No, they can't keep me away, can they?'

Truer than you know, she thought.

Annie pushed the doors open and the stale, smoky air of the day room enveloped them. It was deserted, but the television still shouted in the empty space. Steve went to the window and looked down into the street, then leant his forehead against the glass.

'It's like being in prison,' he said.

Annie came to stand beside him and he manoeuvred himself awkwardly so that he could put his arm around her shoulders.

'It won't be long,' she said.

'It can't be,' he answered. He wanted to kiss her but he felt as awkward as a boy with his crutches and his heavy, plastered leg. And even if he managed to reach her and fit her against him, the doors would open at once behind them, bringing in Frankie, or sister, or the first phalanx of visitors eager for a cigarette and a talk about operations.

He whispered, 'Annie,' feeling his helplessness again, and she moved quickly, turning her face to his and kissing him.

'It won't be long,' she repeated.

I love you, he thought, and the weight of it was pleasurable now. 'Let's try a walk along the corridor,' he said. They went out again, passing the round window of the side-ward and smiling, sideways conspirators' smiles.

They moved slowly along the corridor towards the opposite wing of the hospital, close together, listening to the sound of their awkward steps on the polished floor. After a moment Steve asked, 'How is it, being back at home? Are the boys happier now?'

'It's fine,' Annie answered carefully. 'Tiring, sometimes. They're reacting to my desertion of them by being truculent and clinging, by turns. Copybook behaviour, which I should have been ready for, and wasn't. If I had the energy I'd have lost my temper with them days ago. I'm relying on a kind of weary patience.'

She grinned up at him suddenly and he saw how she must be at home, ordinarily. Jealousy of Martin and her children, and their life with her, gripped him viciously. He said something as neutral as he could, looking ahead to the patch of light through the doors at the end of the corridor, but he knew that Annie glanced quickly at him. They were silent for a few more steps, and then began deliberately to talk about their physical progress, safe hospital ground.

As they talked they were both aware of the two dialogues, spoken and unspoken, starting up again. They wouldn't talk about Martin, although he was as close as if he were walking alongside them, making a third pair of slow footsteps. Although they talked about the bones in Steve's leg that had to knit together before he could walk, before he could leave the hospital, they didn't ask each other, *What will happen then?*

They reached the far doors and turned back again.

'It helps, just to move about like this,' he said and Annie nodded, knowing that he meant it helped the knot of boredom and frustration.

'And you?' he asked. 'What did the kidney man say?'

'I'm fine. Luckier than you. It happens much quicker.'

'Do you still have the dreams?'

'Yes. Noise, and dark, and being afraid.'

'I know.'

They looked at one another then, hearing the sound of their voices, as if the sterile hospital light had suddenly been blacked out. That was it, Annie thought. He did know, and when she woke up in the night and reached out to touch Martin's warm, insensible skin she blamed him in turn because he didn't, and couldn't.

'The dreams will stop,' Steve said.

'Yes.' The dreams, but not the rest of it. Did Steve think that too? The talk, unspoken but still audible, as it had been at the end, before the firemen reached them. They reached the top of the stairs, midway between the two wings, leading down to the main hall. Voices echoed up the stairwell and then the first wave of visitors appeared, trudging upwards, with their bunches of flowers and carrier bags. They watched them pass and for a moment Annie forgot that she belonged to the world outside, too. The visitors looked separate, odd in their thick, outdoor clothes, and she felt her closeness to Steve as it had been when they lay side by side in the dark.

She wondered, with a little beat of despair, if she would ever know closeness like that again.

The group broke up, heading towards the different wards, and Annie and Steve heard more voices and footsteps following them up the stairs.

'Are you expecting anyone today?'

'Perhaps.'

Annie was jealous then, thinking of the glimpses she had had of his visitors in the past, and imagining streams of envoys now from his life outside. She pulled the belt of her coat around her and said, too brightly, 'I must go, anyway. Ben's with my mother-in-law. He only goes to nursery in the mornings.' *He doesn't want to hear about my children*, she thought painfully. What can I tell him? What ground have we got, except that terrible, random thing that happened to us, and the closeness from it that we can't escape?

I don't want to escape, she answered herself.

Steve was balancing awkwardly, trying to free one hand so that he could reach out to her. His face was very dark, almost angry. Now that the moment for leaving him had come, Annie wanted it to be over, quickly, before she could feel the wrench of it.

'I'll come next time. My next appointment,' she gabbled.

Steve wanted to reach out and hold her, saying, *Stay, you can't go yet.*

But she was already on her way.

'*Will* you come?' he asked, insistent because of his immobility.

'Of course.'

She smiled at him then, and he stood at the head of the stairs to watch her go. She looked small and thin inside her big coat and he remembered how unexpectedly lovely her face had been as she came towards him. Then she went down around the curve of the stairs and he couldn't see her any more. Steve rested his weight on the metal legs for a moment, looking at the place where she had been, and then he went on towards the cubicle in the ward and his empty bed.

The visits that came after that were just the same. Annie waited with contained, anxious impatience for the day to arrive, and when the time came her brief moments with Steve were like dislocated footnotes to her constant, internal awareness of him. They talked, and then they looked silently at one another, and Annie knew that they were only waiting again.

A little while after her visit Steve was moved from the old ward and taken downstairs to a long-stay orthopaedic ward. The other patients were either immobile, slung up in complicated supports, or else they moved painfully like Steve on crutches and walking frames. None of them knew Annie, and so she could meet Steve now without feeling that they were being watched with any particular interest. But none of the staff knew her either, and so she could only come in at visiting times, like everyone else. Sometimes she had a long time to wait after her appointments were over before the wards opened. On another day the queues in the out-patients clinic were so long that the visiting hour was almost over before she could come to Steve. He never asked her again if she would come without another pretext for being at the hospital, and even she could only guess at the importance of her visits in the monotonous procession of days. Annie was able to blunt her longing a little with the round of housework and cooking and caring for the boys, but Steve had nothing except hospital and its constant reminder that he was trapped in it.

He protected Annie's visits fiercely, by warning everyone else he knew not to come on those days. Most of them looked at his face and accepted the restriction, but just once, whether by a genuine accident or out of curiosity, Vicky came. Annie was already there, and when Vicky saw them they were not even talking. They were simply sitting together, drawing strength from being close enough to touch one another.

Their intent stillness stopped Vicky in her confident walk down the ward. But she only hesitated for an instant and then she went on, calling out to him, 'Hello, love, I came today instead of Thursday because . . .'

Then Steve looked up, and when Vicky saw his expression the words caught in her throat. The fair-haired woman glanced at him, and then up at Vicky as the visitor put her package of new books and magazines down on the end of the bed.

'I didn't expect you today,' Steve said softly.

'No. Well, I've got a conference on Thursday, you see, so I decided I'd . . .' The words stuck again as she looked at them. Even from where she was standing, Vicky could feel the current between them, deflecting her.

The fair-haired girl said, 'Come and sit down. I've got to go in a minute.' Vicky noticed that she had a warm voice, and her smile tried hard to be welcoming. The smile made the absence of one from Steve all the more evident. The girl made room for Vicky to bring up a chair, and while she waited for Steve to listen to what Vicky was saying she turned away tactfully to look at the shiny covers of the new novels.

'So that's why I came this afternoon,' Vicky finished crisply. She had regained possession of herself now. 'I'm sorry if I'm interrupting. Won't you introduce us, now I'm here?' She smiled at the other woman.

'This is Annie.' Steve held on to the name as he said it, as if he didn't want to let it go. 'And this is Vicky.'

'*I* know.' Vicky suddenly understood. 'You were . . . you were there in the shop, that day, too, weren't you?'

'Yes, I was there,' Annie said in her low voice.

'It must have been horrible.'

'I don't think I would have survived down there if it hadn't been for Steve.'

Vicky noticed that she didn't look at Steve as she said it. As if she couldn't trust herself to look at him as well, in case her face lost its composure.

There was a moment's silence before Vicky said, as lightly as she could, 'You were lucky to have one another.'

Neither Annie nor Steve spoke. It was left to Vicky to talk, and she did her best to fill the awkward quiet with snippets of gossip from her world and from Steve's.

In a little while, when she judged that it wouldn't look too much as if she were running away, Annie looked at her watch and then stood up.

Involuntarily, Steve's hand reached out to catch her wrist. He made himself let go as soon as his fingers touched her.

'Don't go yet.'

'I must. I'll call in next time.'

She picked up her bag from beside her chair, and as she stooped her face was level with Steve's.

Vicky sat still, knowingly watching for the goodbye peck on the cheek from which she could gauge how far their relationship had gone. But although neither of them moved for a second, they didn't kiss each other. They looked, and then the wings of Annie's hair fell forward to hide her cheeks. She scooped up her belongings and stepped away from the little group of chairs.

'Goodbye, Vicky,' she said formally and then, in a much lower voice, 'Goodbye.'

She can't even bring herself to say his name, with me listening, Vicky thought.

Annie went, not looking back.

Steve's face was dark and stiff, and for the first time since they had met Vicky didn't know what to say to him.

She tried, 'It must help, being able to talk to someone who went through it too.'

'It did.'

Summoning up her courage she asked, 'Are you fond of her?'

'Fond?' Steve turned to her, examining her expression as if he had never noticed her before.

'Yes,' he said, and the word fell like a hard pebble into black water.

Vicky's face didn't change because she was too self-possessed to let her feelings show, but still the words formed inside her head. *That's it, then.*

Annie walked back to the tube station with her shoulders hunched against the cold. Here in the middle of town the streets were littered and there were none of the tiny signs of spring that had triggered off her happiness this morning. She thought back to it in bewilderment as jealousy crystallized inside her. She could see Vicky's face in front of her, younger than her own, with clear, pale skin. Steve's girl had a clever, rather hard expression. She was the kind of ambitious, single-minded woman Annie had always found intimidating, and Steve had chosen her, hadn't he? He had talked about her in the darkness. *That was before Vicky came along*, he had said.

Annie made herself breathe evenly to counteract the panicky waves that rose in her chest. She thought, What right do I have to be jealous? I'm going home now to my husband and children. I don't have any claim on Steve. We can't claim each other.

But she wanted to be able to. That was the truth, and the significance of it made her shiver in the February wind.

It was on that day too, Annie remembered later, that Martin first showed that he knew something was wrong.

He came home earlier than usual. Annie was washing up after the boys' supper, and the kitchen was still untidy with dirty plates and scattered toys and crayons. She heard Martin's bag thud on the step, and then the sound of his key in the lock. As the front door opened Benjy, who had been lying on the floor watching television, suddenly rolled sideways and snatched at Thomas's Lego model. There was an immediate howl of protest and the children fell in a heap, shouting and punching each other.

Annie jerked her fingers out of the washing-up water. It was too hot, and she had thought that she was in too much of a hurry to cool it. She wiped her scalding hands on her skirt and pushed past Martin as he came in, without looking at him. She bent over her children and pulled them apart. She was trembling with anger as she shouted incoherently at them.

'Stop it. Stop. Fighting all the time. I can't stand it. I can't stand it. Do you hear?' She aimed an ineffectual blow at the nearest bottom as they wriggled past her. 'Upstairs. Both of you. Get ready for bed.'

'Dad . . .'

'Do as your mother says,' Martin said evenly.

They went, still squabbling. When the door had closed behind them Annie's shoulders sagged. Her anger drained away as quickly as it had come, and left her with the blood throbbing dully in her head.

'Hello,' Martin said. 'Remember me?'

Annie looked at him, seeing him framed against the closed door with its grey finger-marks, part of the family furniture in the oppressive room.

'How could I forget?'

She walked back to the sink and began to lift out the dripping plates. He followed her and took her arm so that she had to stop, standing with her head bent over the popping suds. From overhead she heard thumping feet, and then the splash of bathwater.

'Annie, we've all had enough of this. What's the matter with you?'

The bathwater was turned off again and in the sudden quiet the bubbles in the sink burst with the sound of smacking kisses. Suddenly, insanely, Annie wanted to laugh.

'Nothing's the matter.'

'Ever since you came home, it's been either silent martyrdom or frothing rage. I know that something terrible happened to you . . .'

Is it so very terrible, to fall in love with a man who isn't your husband?

'. . . but sooner or later you have to forget it, and start to live your life again. If you need help, Annie, have the sense to ask for it. And if it's something else, tell me and stop taking it out on the kids.'

He broke off, and the silence closed down again. He had given her the opening, deliberately. But Annie knew that she couldn't find the right words to deny what was happening, or to convince him that everything was all right, after all.

Martin sighed, and turned away from her. 'What needs doing now?'

'You could bath the boys and put them to bed.'

'Of course I will, if that's any help.'

He went out and closed the door behind him, and in a moment Annie heard the three of them talking and then laughing in the bathroom. In solitude she finished clearing the kitchen and then she scoured the sink until it shone at her.

Later, when the boys were asleep, Martin and Annie sat down opposite one another at the kitchen table and ate their evening meal together.

Talk, Annie willed herself. *Talk to him.* But she couldn't think of anything to say that might not touch on the dangerous things, and she was afraid that if they came close to the truth her fragile defences would break down, and all the misery and the guilty happiness would come spilling out. She knew how much the truth would hurt Martin, and she recognized that she was more afraid of hurting him than of anything else in the world. Even more than the darkness of her dreams, and the emptiness she discovered when she woke up and found that Steve was gone from her side.

And so they sat in silence in the pool of light spreading over the table, while Martin unseeingly turned the pages of *Architectural Review*.

After supper, when the washing up was done, Martin said that he had some drawings that needed urgent work. He took his bag and went upstairs to his studio at the top of the house.

Annie didn't know how long she had been sitting in her place, unmoving, before the telephone rang. She stood up automatically and went to answer it, thinking as she crossed the floor that it was sure to be someone for Martin, something to do with whatever he was working on upstairs. There was an extension in the studio, but Annie lifted the kitchen receiver from its hook on the wall and said, 'Hello?'

She heard the rapid pips of a payphone, and then Steve's low voice.

'Annie.'

She leant against the kitchen wall, her breath taken away with her relief that she had picked up the phone after all, and not left it for Martin.

'You can't ring me here.'

'I just have.'

She knew just where he was, seeing him more clearly than the kitchen tiles and the children's drawings thumb-tacked to the wall beside the telephone. He was in the long corridor outside the orthopaedic ward, where two grey plastic hoods shielded the public telephones. The lights would already be dimmed for the night, making shadows in the corners. She imagined the hated crutches resting against the wall, as he steadied himself with his free hand. And then the shape of his hand, the warmth of it.

'What would you have done if Martin had answered? Pretended it was a wrong number, or something stupid like that?'

'I had to talk to you. Annie, are you listening? I don't want you to be jealous of Vicky. I don't want you to be jealous or afraid about anything, or anybody, because there's no need.' He was talking very quickly, his voice so low that it was almost a whisper. Annie closed her eyes on the kitchen and strained to hear what he was saying. 'I wanted just to tell you, before you go to sleep. I love you. Remember.'

She remembered the little side room of the old ward, and the way that they had held on to one another. He hadn't asked her for anything in return, then. He had even stopped her from saying anything.

Now she had the sense that the old, silent dialogue had swelled in volume. It grew insistently loud so that her whole body reverberated with it and, at last, she had to give voice to it. 'I know,' she answered him. And then, helplessly, 'I love you too.'

She heard, at the other end of the line, his sharply exhaled breath.

There was nothing for either of them to say, beyond that.

The silent words had been spoken, and there was no point in voicing the others that came rushing after them into the physical distance that separated them. 'I wish I could touch you,' he said.

'Soon,' Annie promised him.

'Goodnight, my love.' He was gone then, and Annie stood with the receiver in her hand listening to the purr of the dialling tone. As she replaced it she looked up at the ceiling and then she realized that she had been whispering, as if Martin might hear her, although he was two floors above. Whispering, and pretending, and not talking in case the most innocent-sounding topic accidentally touched on the truth. Deceiving and lying, even though it was by omission. That was what this joy inside her had led her to.

With her hand outstretched, groping across her own kitchen as if she were half blind, Annie found her way back to her chair. She sat hunched over, with her arms wrapped around her chest. Just to hear Steve's voice, tonight, made her unbearably happy, and the assurances that they had given each other made her blood swirl dizzyingly in her veins.

But the same happiness stabbed her as she looked around the kitchen because she knew that it was hopeless, and that she was trapped here by Martin and their children and the layers of love and habit that they had built up and sealed together over the years.

Exultation and misery ran together and coalesced into a choking knot that lay like a stone underneath Annie's heart. At last, still moving like an old woman, she went upstairs and undressed ready for bed. She lay down and the sheets felt cold and clammy against her skin. She drew her knees up to her chest and hunched over the painful knot.

'I don't know what to do,' she whispered. 'I don't know what to do.'

Seven

Tibby had gone into a special hospital for her rest.

When Annie went to see her she was struck by its difference from the big general hospital where she had been treated herself. The rooms and corridors here were carpeted, there were pictures on the walls, and the sitting rooms were pretty and cosy. There was no medicinal smell, and even the nurses' dresses contrived not to look like uniforms.

Tibby seemed happy.

'It's just like home,' she smiled, 'without any of the responsibilities.'

Her face was bright, but in the depths of the big chintz-covered armchair that Annie had settled her in she looked shrunken and brittle.

'That's good,' Annie said cheerfully. 'It seems like a nice place.'

There was no doubt now about the progress of her mother's illness. The cancer was inoperable, and although the doctors' estimates were deliberately vague they were beginning to talk in terms of weeks rather than months. Tibby knew exactly what was happening to her, and she had accepted it with silent graceful courage. The hospice's aim was simply to make her as comfortable as possible, and to help her to enjoy the time that was left.

'When would you like to come home again?' Annie asked her.

The doctors had told them that, for a while longer at least, Tibby could choose whether she wanted to be in the hospice or in her own home.

'Oh dear, I don't know. It's so comfortable in here. But I feel very lazy, not doing a thing. I'm still quite capable. I'm just afraid that Jim won't be managing in the house without me, and I daren't think about the garden. There's the roses, you know.'

Annie thought of the big corner garden and the shaggy heads of the old-fashioned roses that sprawled over the walls. Tibby liked to prune her roses in March, and to begin her régime of spraying and feeding. It was quite likely that she wouldn't see this year's mass of pink and white and gold, or catch the evening scent of them through the windows as she moved about in the awkward, old-fashioned kitchen. Annie looked down at her own hands, turning them to examine the palms, as if she could see something that mattered there.

'Don't worry about the house,' she managed to say. 'Dad can cope perfectly well. I went yesterday, and it looks the same as it always does. And if you'd like me to do the roses I can, very easily. Or Martin will.'

Two dialogues, again, Annie thought. We sit here talking about the roses and the dusting, and both of us are thinking, *Why must you die?* Why is it Tibby, and why now? There are a hundred other things, a thousand other things to say. She began in a rush, 'Tibby, I want to . . .'

But her mother took her hand, squeezing it briefly before replacing it in Annie's lap. It was as clear a way of silencing her as if she had said, 'I don't want to talk about it. Forgive me?'

Aloud, Tibby said mildly, 'Well. Perhaps I'll stay here just this week. And then I think I should get home.'

'All right,' Anne acquiesced. 'Of course you must go home whenever you feel like it.'

They sat and talked for a little while longer in the pleasant room.

Tibby wanted, more than anything else, to hear about her grandsons. She leaned forward in her armchair, eager for the little snippets of news. Thomas had just joined a local cub pack and Annie described how he had gone off to his first meeting the night before, resplendent and full of pride in his new green uniform.

Tibby nodded and smiled. 'They're growing up so quickly, both of them.'

She's seen you grow up. Seen her grandchildren.

As she tried to fathom the real expression behind her mother's smile Annie heard Steve's words again. She remembered the blind fear that she had felt herself when she thought that she was going to die, but more vividly still she remembered the bitterness of having to leave so much unfinished. Did Tibby feel that now? And when Tibby looked around the sunny sitting room with its chintz covers and faint smell of polish, did she feel the same sharp sense of how precious and how beautiful all of it was?

Tibby looked smaller and frailer than before, but her hair was set and she was wearing her own neat, unemphatic clothes. She was still Tibby herself, yet for all the closeness Annie had believed there to be between her mother and herself she couldn't gauge what she felt or needed now. The careful, light conversation about the garden and the boys ran on, and Annie had the disorientating sense that neither of them was listening to a word of it.

She wanted to shout at her, Don't go. We need you, all of us. *Talk to me.*

'. . . But with the price of container-grown shrubs nowadays,' Tibby sighed, 'what else can you do . . .?'

'I know. But I've never had your luck or knack with cuttings.'

I talked to Steve, down there in the blackness. I still could, if I would let it happen, if there weren't so many other things, such immutable things.

Tibby leaned farther forward and touched Annie's arm.

'Are you sure you're all right, darling? You look a bit drawn in the face, to me.'

I've fallen in love, Tibby, with a stranger. I'd walk out of here and go straight to him if I could, if only I could.

'I'm fine. The specialist says it will take a little time before I'm thoroughly fit again, but everything has mended perfectly well.'

I do it too, of course. I don't talk either, not to Tibby, not even to Martin. Only to Steve, and he hears me whether I say the words or not.

I wish I was going to him now.

Annie smiled at her mother, with the conviction that they were both close to tears.

'I must make a move, darling.'

'Of course you must. Thomas comes out at four o'clock, doesn't he?'

When Tibby held out her hand Annie saw that her mother's sapphire engagement ring was slipping on her thin finger. Tibby instinctively turned it back into place with her thumb. Annie leant over and kissed her cheek, noticing the unfamiliar smell of lacquer because Tibby's hair had grown too sparse to hold her old style.

'I'll come in tomorrow to see you.'

'Couldn't you bring Tom and Benjy with you?'

'Won't they tire you too much? They wear me out.'

'I'd like to see them.'

How many more times will there be?

'Of course I will. Goodbye, love. Sleep well.'

Annie settled her mother against her cushions again and as she left she felt her eyes on her back, greedy, looking through her at the past and into the future that Tibby wouldn't see for herself.

Annie drove home with the hard brightness of tears behind her own eyes.

On the same evening, Martin and Annie went to do the big monthly shop at the supermarket. As they always had done in the past, they went on late-opening night and left the boys at home under Audrey's supervision.

It was the first time they had made the trip together since Annie's return from hospital. Along the clogged urban route she sat in the passenger seat watching the shopfronts flick past. Her face was turned away from him, but she sensed Martin glancing sideways at her, frowning in the silence that hung between them.

They reached the big supermarket and Martin parked in the middle of one of the long lines of cars. They walked side by side over the pitted ground towards the entrance, skirting the puddles and the empty, abandoned wire trolleys. Even the air seemed gritty, smelling of diesel exhaust fumes, and greasy onions from the hamburger stall near the shop doors.

Annie was tired, and her legs felt suddenly so heavy that she wondered whether they would support her up and down the crowded aisles with the shopping trolley. Martin's pace quickened and she had to hurry to keep up with him.

'Don't walk so fast,' she called and he snapped back, without slowing down, 'Let's get it over with.'

Annie felt his anger, and her own rose sluggishly through her tiredness.

Is this what it is? she thought. Is this what I'm trying to hold on to?

The automatic doors yawned in front of them, neon-lit, and hissed open. Martin reached for a trolley and swung it round with a vicious clatter. Without speaking they wound their way through the crowds and the piled-up shopping to the end aisle and began to work their way along the shelves.

The harsh overhead lights hurt Annie's eyes, and the colours of the endless lines of tins and packets danced up and down in front of them. She heard herself repeating a silent litany, eggs, butter, yoghurt, cheese. Love, loyalty, duty, habit.

Martin was moving along the opposite shelf and she saw his mouth set in a straight line and the stiff, angry tilt of his head. Suddenly, with a molten heat that flooded all through her, she hated him. She turned her back on him and stared blindly at the shelf at eye-level, where the red and blue and orange packs shouted their rival claims at her. She reached up, still with the heat of anger flushing her face, and took down a packet of breakfast cereal. She dropped it into the trolley and then another, and followed them with a packet of the sugary variety that Ben insisted on.

Fruit juice, skimmed milk. Routine, responsibility, today,

tomorrow. Endlessly. Groping through the fog of her anger Annie tried to recall the certainty that had possessed her under the rubble. She had been sure then that her life and its order was precious. The certainty had evaporated. Now, in the hideous supermarket with its tides of defeated shoppers, she felt the structure of her life silently crumbling. She stood in the rubble of it, as trapped as she had been by the bombed wreckage of her Christmas store.

Martin turned around with an armful of tinned food and saw her face. Annie knew that her expression fanned his own anger.

'Come on,' he said sourly. 'I don't want to spend all night in here.'

She moved again with a jerk and they worked on along their lines of shelving, not looking at one another and separated by the other loitering shoppers and their cumbersome trolleys.

At the far end of the shop they turned the corner to start the next aisle. Annie's pace was slower and Martin accidentally ran the wheel of the heavy trolley into her heel bone. The pain shot up her leg, so intense for a second that it made her eyes water.

'Sorry,' Martin said, still without looking at her.

The pain receded as quickly as it had come and in its wake Annie's anger intensified. She had to clench her fists to control her longing to lash out with them, first at Martin and then at all the tins and bottles and their jaunty labels, sweeping them all together into a broken pile on the supermarket floor. Her anger spread like hot spilt liquid to flood over the other shoppers who blocked her path and stared past her with blank faces, over the supermarket and the life that it represented for her, and everything that had happened since the bombing. The anger was so potent that the current of it sapped her strength and she found herself weak and trembling. She leant against the corner of the shelf to steady herself as it engulfed her and swept her along with it. Under the bald lights and the big orange banners that shouted, 'SAVE', Annie knew the first real anger and bitterness against the bombers for what they had done to her. In that instant she hated the world, and the life she led in it, and everything there was except for Steve.

And she was angry because she was separated from him.

As soon as she realized it the flood of her anger turned. The currents swirled and changed direction and then, as if it had been no more than a trickle that evaporated in the heat of understanding, it disappeared.

Annie looked in bewilderment at a row of jamjars, staring at the plum and dull crimson and speckled scarlet of the jam in the glass containers as if it were entirely new to her.

I can't stay here, like this, she thought with the painful clear-sightedness that her anger had left in its wake.

I'll have to go.

I'll have to leave Martin, and go to him.

The knowledge made her shiver. It brought her neither happiness nor relief. A few yards away, over the heads of the crowd, she could see Martin plodding down the aisle. His mouth was set in the same grim line.

Annie's legs felt as boneless as the jam in the glass jars but she made herself follow him, mechanically picking the family groceries off the shelves as she went.

At last they reached the check-out lines and they stood in silence, inching forward until their turn came. Martin unloaded the trolley and Annie packed the goods into boxes. Eggs, butter, yoghurt, cheese. To feed the family. Annie was shaking as if she had a fever.

Outside, the sky was rimmed orange-brown with the muddy glow of street-lamps. They picked their way past the puddles again to the car, and piled the boxes of shopping in over the tail-gate. Still they had spoken hardly an unnecessary word. Annie shivered convulsively, pulling her coat around her, and then slid gratefully into the car as Martin banged the door open for her.

Both doors slammed again, isolating them in the rubber- and plastic-scented box. The usual litter of toys and drawings discarded by the boys drifted over the back seat. Martin fumbled with the keys in the ignition and clicked on the headlights. The light reflected upwards and threw unnatural shadows into his eyesockets and the angles of his jawline. Annie waited miserably, without thinking, for the car engine to splutter and jerk them into reverse. But Martin sat still, with his hands braced on the steering wheel. He seemed to be staring ahead into the orange-tinged darkness.

And then, slowly, he turned to her and said, 'I want to know what's wrong with you.'

Annie shook her head from side to side, unable to speak.

Martin's voice rose. 'I want to *know*. Say something, can't you, even if it's only fuck off?'

'I don't know what to say.' Even in her own ears Annie's response sounded thin and pathetic. Martin's knuckles went white as his fists tightened on the wheel.

'Why don't you bloody know what to say? I'm your husband. Have you forgotten that?'

'No, I haven't forgotten.'

'Talk to me then. I've tried to be as patient and understanding as I can. I've waited, and held off, and hoped you might get round to mentioning why you look as though we all turn your stomach. Why your face never cracks into a smile any more, and why you can't even bring yourself close enough to me to exchange the time of day. Why, Annie?'

Martin's questions came spilling out, the words tangling with one another, and she saw a tiny fleck of spit at the corner of his mouth catching the light. His tongue darted it away.

'Why is it? I want to know where you've gone. I want to hear it from you. *Say something.*'

He was shouting now. Annie saw a couple passing the car turn back to stare curiously, their faces white patches in the gloom. She had no anger left, nothing to match Martin's. And she knew that she had no reason to answer his rage with her own, because she recognized the portrait that he painted of her.

'I'm sorry.' Self-dislike and despair muted her voice.

Martin spat again, '*Sorry?* Jesus, you're sorry. Look, I'm sorry that you were hurt, and so badly frightened, and that you were ill and in pain and subjected to all those things in the hospital afterwards. Bu that's all over now, Annie. You've got to start up again. Can't you understand? If you want me, and the kids, and everything we had before, you've got to do it *now*.'

Annie looked down at her hands in her lap, twisting her fingers together like pale stalks. Martin is right, and wrong, she thought. I should talk to him, of course I should, but there is nothing I could possibly say.

'*Annie.*'

His hands dropped from the steering wheel and they shot out and grabbed her. He shook her, and her head wobbled. Annie knew that he wanted to hit her, and she knew then how desperate he was for her reaction. She jerked defensively to face him and managed to whisper through stiff lips, 'Leave me alone, can't you? Just, just leave me alone.'

Martin's hands dropped heavily to his sides. They were silent for a long minute, looking at one another in the headlamps' inverted light. Annie was ironically reminded of the old days when they had quarrelled violently, like this, and then the passion of their reconciliations had reflected the violence back again. A wave of exhausted sadness and regret washed over her.

'Look. Are you ill? Do you need to get help? A psychiatrist, I mean, Annie.'

'No,' Annie said. 'I'm not mad. I wasn't, not while it was happening and not afterwards and not now. I don't need to have my head looked at.'

Martin exhaled, a long, ragged breath. 'In that case, is it Steve?'

Annie went cold. He had been thinking about it, about them, she realized. She had never mentioned his name, and if it was just a wild guess of Martin's, wouldn't he have qualified it somehow? Wouldn't he have said, Is it anything to do with the man you were with, in there? Steve? Is it to do with him?

Instead of that he had just quietly asked her, as if the question had always been there, waiting.

Tick, tick. Annie heard the seconds whispering around them in the vinyl interior of their car.

'No.' Until the word came, she didn't know what it would be. 'It's nothing to do with him.'

And then the sadness took her by the throat, so forcibly that she wanted to drop her head against the seat back, draw her knees up to her chest and let the sobs break out. But because she had said, *No* she kept her neck rigid, and went on staring with dry eyes out into the darkness. I've done it now, she thought. I have begun the lies. She saw a net of them, drawing in ahead of her. And would the net split open in the end and let the truth out, as she had envisaged through the flood of anger inside the supermarket?

To leave Martin, and go to Steve?

With sudden briskness Martin turned the key in the ignition and the engine came to life. He swung the wheel and the car nosed out of the car park before he glanced sideways at Annie again. Seeing her face he dropped his hand briefly on to her knee. 'I'm sorry I lost my temper,' he said. 'It hasn't been very easy for me, either, do you see? I thought you were dead, and then I was afraid that you would die. And now, when it should be all over, you've gone somewhere and left me behind.'

The car moved slowly forwards in a double line of traffic. Martin drove one-handed and took Annie's hand in the other. In a low voice he said, 'I don't want to be without you.'

Annie opened her mouth, afraid that her voice would crack, but she found the ability somehow to whisper, 'I know that.'

Martin drove steadily on. *I don't want you to lie to me, either*, he could have added. But strangely, the baldness of Annie's denial had come as a relief. He saw clearly through it, and saw that she wanted to protect him from being hurt. The carefulness and the irrationality of it touched him, and he felt a warm wash of affection for her that was nothing to do with anger or bitterness.

Nothing had happened yet, he told himself. Perhaps, even, nothing would.

They followed the familiar route, with Annie's cold fingers still gripped in her husband's warm ones. They reached home, and they went in and unpacked the shopping side by side in the kitchen.

And later, when they went to bed, Martin lay still for a moment in the darkness and then he reached out for her, as he had always done in the past after they had quarrelled. His hand stroked her shoulder, and then he moved to fit himself into the curve of her back.

'Don't be angry.'

'I'm not angry.'

She was reminded again of the times before. They had always made up their differences, and they had drawn closer because of them. Not now, Annie thought, because of the lie that they had already started. Martin's hand moved again, to her waist and the bony point of her hips, warming her. His fingers traced the ridge of bone under the skin and he whispered, 'Poor love. Come here to me.'

His hands coaxed her. Annie thought, He's good and generous. Truer than I deserve.

For all the weight of her sadness, it was a relief to turn inwards to him. Their bodies met along their full length and his mouth touched hers. Annie felt her husband stir against her. She let her head rest on his shoulder, her face turned to the warmth of his throat. His hands moved, patiently, coaxing her. Annie held herself still, feeling that the anxiety and guilt and sadness of the day were just contained within the leaky package of her body.

But Martin knew her body too. Slowly and gently he worked on it until her fear of his intrusion melted and became, at last, fear that he would draw back again. Her mind stopped revolving around in its tight, overworked circles as the warmth spread through her veins. Annie's mouth opened and she tasted his skin, following the line of his jaw with her mouth. Under the point of it she felt his pulse flicker against her tongue. A half-forgotten urgency sharpened itself inside her.

'Martin.'

'Not yet,' he whispered. 'Not yet.'

'Please.'

The note in her voice broke through his control. He took her wrists and held her so that she couldn't move. He looked down into her face for an instant and then he fitted himself inside her. It was easy, and certain, because they had known one another for so long. She forgot, as he moved and she lifted her hips to answer him, all the questions and their bleak answers. The ripples of internal pleasure were spreading and Annie let herself be submerged in them. Ever since she had come home to Martin she had felt stiff and cold and now, however briefly, the feelings were gone. She closed her eyes and let their bodies take her over. The peak she was struggling for reared for a long moment beyond her grasp, then within her grasp, and then she had reached it and conquered it and the sharpness of it stabbed within her until at last it melted and ran away down the steep slopes into the level plain of satisfaction.

Annie felt the tears melt too behind her eyes. They ran down her face and into her hair, hot against Martin's cheeks until he rubbed them away with his fingers and kissed her eyelids, and then he took her face between his hands and kissed it and whispered to her, 'We'll be all right, Annie. You see, we'll be all right.'

She held him in turn as he moved inside her again, until he cried out with his mouth against hers, and then they lay in a different silence, wrapped in each other's arms in the quiet room. Annie heard Benjamin in his bed across the corridor, turning over and then shouting out something in his sleep. She was very tired, and she knew from Martin's breathing that he was still awake, listening to her. The circular treadmill of her thoughts began to rotate again until she was forming the word, *Steve*, and the picture of him lying in the hospital ward, watching the ceiling.

I must decide, she told herself. I must think. Do whatever is for the best.

But she was drifting now, unpinned by exhaustion, almost asleep.

Not now. Soon, I will. I must.

For the first time since she had come home from hospital, Annie fell asleep before Martin. He held her for a long time, not wanting to move in case he disturbed her. The day of the bombing, when he had struggled with fallen masonry to try and reach her, had taken her away from him. It was only now, in this moment of closeness, that he realized just how far. He wanted her back more than anything in the world.

Nothing had changed, Annie discovered in the days that followed, except that the atmosphere in the house was easier. They tried to show one another, with little, unintrusive gestures, that there was a truce. On Annie's part it was no more than cooking a favourite dinner or buying a special bottle of wine from the off-licence on the corner, but she did her best to appear to be cheerful as they ate and drank, even when her heart was heavy. In his turn Martin brought home an armful of daffodils to fill the clear glass jug that stood on the kitchen dresser, or the latest copy of a magazine that Annie considered too expensive to buy out of her housekeeping. They thanked each other briefly, almost shyly, but they didn't try to go beyond that. There were still silences, but they judged separately that the silences were more companionable than hostile, and they didn't try to fill them artificially.

Thomas and Benjamin, with their childish perceptiveness, noticed the difference at once.

'I think you're better now, Mummy,' Thomas said and Annie smiled at him, happy with his confidence.

'I am better,' she answered, keeping her awareness of the other things at bay as far as she could.

The boys quarrelled and fought less, slept better, and went off happier in the mornings. Annie could almost have believed that her life might in the end return to the old, smooth pattern of before the bombing, if it had not been for her visits to the hospital, and Steve.

February turned into March. In the middle of March there

came a spell of clear, still weather, so warm that the bare, black branches of the trees looked incongruous against the duck-egg blue of the sky. In her garden Annie watched the clumps of daffodils turn almost overnight from sappy stalks, tipped with a swelling of green and pale yellow, into solid banks of miraculous gold. The earth smelt sweet and moist, and in the mornings the sun shone with unexpected strength on the dewy grass and turned the patch of lawn into a sheet of silver.

On the fifth sunny morning, Annie walked with Benjy to his nursery. Even though they made the same trip every day, it was slow because the little boy wanted to examine everything they passed, stopping to peer in through garden gates in search of cats that he had met there before, and at the parrot who sat autocratically on his perch in the window of the house on the corner. Annie walked slowly, patiently, while Benjy alternately dawdled and ran ahead, as bright as a slick of paint in his scarlet tracksuit.

After the customary delays and detours they turned the last corner, and came to the church hall that housed the nursery group. There was a knot of mothers with prams and pushchairs standing talking in the yard outside. Benjy pushed through them and ran through the open doors, and Annie followed him, nodding and smiling at the other mothers as she passed them. She knew them all, because she saw them doing the same thing every morning, and she knew their children and their problems, and their houses in the network of streets surrounding the church hall. Most of them lived lives that were similar to Annie's own, but in the last weeks she had felt so remote that it had been hard to find a word or a gesture that would bridge the gulf.

'Hello, Annie,' they called to her. 'Benjy's eager this morning, isn't he?'

'Feeling the joys of spring, I suppose.'

'Wish I was,' someone else chipped in. 'Sophie had us both up all night.'

'You look better yourself, Annie. The sight of the sun does us all good, doesn't it?'

In the past Annie had found the simple camaraderie comforting and even sustaining. She had felt, before, that they all shared the same difficulties and the same rewards. And these women had clubbed together to send her flowers when she was in hospital, then taken it in turns to invite Benjy to play with their own children, so that Annie could rest for an hour or two. She felt that she didn't know, now, where she belonged or what she believed in. Part of her was still here, amongst the women, yet so much of her was nowhere except with Steve. It made her feel lonely, to be together and yet apart. Annie went slowly inside, out of the bright sunshine, thinking of the random violence that had altered her perspectives so violently that she doubted whether she would ever look out on the same landscape again.

The hall was dingy, but that was hardly noticeable under the bright layers of painting and collages that the staff and children had stuck all over the walls. Children squirmed over the climbing frame and in and out of the Wendy house, and groups of them stood around the little tables deciding whether to paint, or squeeze dough or glue strips of coloured paper into necklaces. As it always did, the sight made Annie smile. They were so busy, all of them, fragile on their wobbly legs, and yet perfectly robust.

Benjy had made a bee-line for the dough table, and now he was squeezing bright pink coils of it between his fingers, with an expression of furious concentration. Annie went across to him and kissed the top of his head.

'See you later, then?'

'Unh,' Benjy said.

She walked out into the sunshine once again.

On the way back she took a different route, passing through the little local park where the daffodils would be followed by municipal rows of scarlet tulips. The council contractors were already repainting the swings and the conical roundabout that Thomas loved to spin faster and faster until Benjy screamed in giddy terror. Annie thought dreamily of the hours that she had spent in this park, from the days when Thomas was a tiny baby out for his first outings in the pram. Martin sometimes brought them here at weekends now, and played elaborate hiding and chasing games with them in the little plot of trees and shrubs enclosed by green railings. She crossed the grass, leaving shiny footprints in the wetness. Beyond the park was a line of shops. Thomas was bringing home a friend for tea, and Annie thought that she would make a chocolate cake.

She did the necessary shopping, exchanging pleasantries with the cheerful Indian family in the general stores. Then she turned towards home, swinging her purchases in a plastic carrier bag. She reached the house and the gate squealed on its hinges, swinging back against the hedge and releasing its dusty scent of privet leaves. Annie went inside, picking up a scatter of brown envelopes from the doormat. The hallway smelt of coffee and the potpourri in a bowl on a sidetable.

Without thinking of anything, her head comfortably empty, Annie walked into the kitchen and filled the kettle. Martin had left the radio playing when he went out, and Annie was whistling to the music, softly, through pursed lips, when the doorbell rang.

As she crossed the hallway she saw a shadow, unidentifiable, beyond the coloured glass. And then she opened her front door and saw that it was Steve waiting on the doorstep.

It was as if the colour drained from the accessible world. The two of them were left standing, face to face, the only moving, breathing things in a grey landscape.

It was Steve who spoke first.

'Can't I come inside?' he prompted her gently.

Annie looked out at the empty street and the windows of the houses opposite, her innocent front gate that Steve had closed behind him, and the crocuses that edged the garden path. Then, stiff-armed, she opened the front door a little wider. As he stepped into the house Annie saw that Steve's crutches were gone. He leaned heavily on a stick instead.

With the door closed against the eyes of the street they looked at one another in the dim hallway. Benjy's tricycle was abandoned at the foot of the stairs.

'How did you find me?' Annie asked, stupid with surprise.

'Were you intending to hide?'

'No. I didn't mean that. I'm just surprised, to see you here . . .'

Steve smiled at her, but Annie read the anxiety in his face. It had been a risk to come. But he must have wanted to, very badly.

'The telephone directory,' he reminded her. 'I looked you up.'

'Yes. Yes, of course. Come . . . come through, and I'll make you a cup of coffee.'

I'm talking to him as if he's someone from the PTA, Annie thought. Or one of Martin's clients. She picked up Benjy's bike and put it aside so that he could pass, and led the way into the kitchen. She tried to hide her awkwardness by rattling the coffee percolator, and the cups as she set them out on the tray. Her hands were shaking, and she was rawly conscious that his nearness overturned the mundane order of her kitchen, as she had known that it would. She longed for him to touch her, and she dreaded it.

'When did they let you out? You didn't tell me that they might.' Her voice shook, too.

'I let myself out. One leap, and I was free.' They smiled at each other and Annie turned quickly to the coffee pot.

'Do you take milk?'

'Please.'

'Would you like anything to eat? What is it, breakfast or elevenses?'

'No, thank you.'

Steve watched her as she moved economically from cupboard to sink. He had imagined her so often, just like this, against the backdrop of her kitchen. Yet now that he was here with her he couldn't see any of it, nothing except Annie herself. Her hair was growing again to frame her face. In her jeans and shirt, with her untidy hair and her soft, dazed expression, she looked almost like a young girl. As he watched her Steve realized that he had focused so hard on the way to reach her that he had hardly thought beyond the moment when she would open her door. It made him feel so like an adolescent, at a loss when finally confronted with a real girl, that Steve laughed aloud. Annie turned, and when she saw his expression the colour flooded into her face. She put the coffee pot down abruptly.

'Annie.'

Steve's stick squeaked on the polished floor as he went to her.

'Yes.'

'Annie, I can't start all over from the beginning. Not with you.'

'I know that.'

We needn't talk about what the doctors say, about the weather or the garden or whether he takes one lump or two, Annie thought. Not now, and not ever.

She lifted her head and Steve cupped her face between his hands. He bent and kissed her mouth and her throat and the corners of her eyes. Annie kissed him in return, giving herself up to him, until he took her in his arms and almost lifted her. Their freedom alone in the empty house was extraordinary, beckoning them. For a giddy, drowning moment Annie was just Annie, forgetting the rooms and the furniture that she and Martin had bought and the pictures that they had chosen and hung together. Steve's hand touched her shoulder and then her breast, and her mouth opened beneath his.

Annie forgot everything except her need for him. The ache of the weeks of separation from him sharpened now that he was here, and close enough for her to understand how he could assuage it. They might have been anywhere, or nowhere, because all that mattered to them was that they were together.

Steve whispered, with his mouth against hers, 'My love.'

And Annie echoed him, 'I love you.' They felt the curves of their separate smiles touching and becoming the same smile of joy because it was the truth, and because it wasn't time yet to remember what the truth would mean.

Annie had no idea how long they stood there, locked together. When at last they stepped back to see one another again she was giddy, and her mouth was bruised and burning.

They examined each other's faces, inch by inch, and it was then, seeing into one another's eyes, that reality intruded again.

Annie's expression changed but Steve took her hand, holding it tightly between his own.

'Don't,' he begged her. 'Stay with me.'

'I want to,' Annie said. 'What can we do?'

He put his arm around her again and Annie rested her face against his shoulder. With his cheek touching her hair, Steve stared over her head at the pine table in the bay window, and the stick-back chairs grouped neatly around it. There was an antique pine dresser too, with pieces of willow-pattern china and photographs of her husband and children arranged on the shelves. Outside the window he could see the facing houses. Annie and Martin would know the people who lived behind those doors. Probably their children played together, went to the same schools.

He understood, suddenly, the magnitude of what he wanted from her. He wanted her to leave this. Yet how could he ask her to walk away from all the accretions of a married life, and come with him? He wanted her to, with single-minded intensity. Steve understood quite clearly that, just as he had never loved anyone before, he loved Annie fiercely now. And the intimacy that they had shared, afraid, and blinded by the dark, stayed with him. It seemed more precious and more real than all the rest of his life.

He took her hand, very gently, and guided her to the table. He pulled out a chair and made her sit down. The coffee cups sat forgotten on their tray between them.

'I want you to come and live with me,' Steve said. She made a move to interrupt him but he held her hand tighter and went on, faster. 'Not today. Not next week, not even next month if you really can't. When you're ready to come to me, Annie. If you want to come.'

Annie thought, I *do*, and the enormity of it was like a tidal wave, submerging her. She looked at Steve's face and at the way that a muscle at one corner of his mouth pulled it downwards in anxiety. I should say, *I can't*. I can't leave my husband and children, or bring my children to you. But I can't be without you, either. I know that, after this morning.

'I don't want there to be half-measures between you and me, Annie.'

Not an affair, she thought, with me creeping away to meet you when I can steal the time from Martin and the boys. No, I couldn't bear that, either. It must be white or black, of course, with no murky shades in between. Annie remembered the evening in the supermarket, and the anger with Martin that had overtaken her. She had thought that a truce had reigned since then, but now she felt more as if they had been nursing themselves, separately, in readiness for this.

She jerked her head up suddenly.

'I don't want half-measures either. But whatever has to be done must be done gently, so that Martin . . . so that it doesn't hurt Martin more than it has to.'

It was only then, when she saw the relief rub out the sharp lines in Steve's face, that Annie realized how he had gambled, coming to ask her for everything, without knowing or even hoping for what her answer would be. His honesty and the love that she read behind it touched Annie's heart.

'And so?' he whispered. 'Will you come?'

She waited, listening to the little sounds of the house as if she might hear something that would stop her. But there was nothing, and she answered at last, 'Yes.'

Steve moved then, stumbling from his chair with such violence that his awkward leg caught it and tipped it backwards, banging to the floor. Neither of them even glanced at it.

They had reached out for each other, and they were as hungry as if they had eaten nothing since they lay together in the darkness of the store. Annie knew an intensity of physical long-ing that she hadn't felt for years and years. Not since Matthew.

She heard herself laugh, shakily.

'I was thinking of Matthew.'

'I know,' he murmured, and he tipped Annie's head back so that he could taste the hollow at the base of her throat. 'Don't. Think of me.'

That was easy. It was easy as he touched the pearly buttons of her shirt, and then undid them. He bent his head again and kissed the curve of her breast where the shirt fell away from it. As his mouth touched her nipple Annie closed her eyes and buried her face in his black hair.

She thought, for a longing, oblivious instant, of the bed upstairs. It was neat and smooth under its white crocheted cover. She had straightened it before she took Benjy to the nursery.

No.

And then she looked at the stripped boards of the kitchen floor, which Martin had sanded and waxed.

No, nor in any of the other corners of the house that they had created and shared.

Annie lifted her head, and with her fingers entwined in Steve's hair she made him look up at her. 'Not here,' she whispered.

Steve held her for another moment, and then his arms dropped stiffly to his sides. They were both looking at the dresser with its blue plates and framed photographs.

Steve made a little, apologetic gesture. 'Of course not here.'

They turned away, not looking at each other.

Annie put her hand on the coffee pot to feel if it was still hot enough. She poured each of them a cup and they sat down at the table. But it was painful to see Steve sitting in Martin's chair, and so she stood up again almost immediately. She carried her cup across the room and stood drinking the tepid coffee by the kitchen window, looking out at the garden.

Steve said in a low voice, 'I'm sorry, I shouldn't have come here.'

Annie slammed her cup down on to the draining board and went to him. She stood behind the chair and put her arms over his shoulders, resting her cheek against his head. He grasped her wrists, holding her there.

'Of course you should, if you needed to. I needed you to. I didn't realize how much.' After a moment she added quietly, 'It won't be very easy. Doing . . . what we've agreed.'

We haven't even begun to talk about what it will mean in pain and unhappiness for all of us, Annie thought.

'Do you think I expect it to be easy, Annie? I thought about it, all those weeks in hospital. I wouldn't have dared to come here and ask you, if I didn't believe it was . . .' There was a pause, and then he brought the word out, painfully, '. . . inescapable. Because we belong to one another, good or bad.'

There was another silence. Annie rubbed her cheek against his hair, moving it so that her mouth touched the thin skin at his temple. She felt a tiny pulse flickering there and was reminded of their pathetic, physical frailty under the mounds of rubble. But they had survived. Perhaps they were more resilient, all of them, than she gave them credit for. They would survive.

Would Benjamin? And Thomas?

She straightened up abruptly and began to walk around the kitchen, touching a spoon and a silver-plated toast-rack that Barbara had given to her, straightening the glass jars that held coffee and tea.

'What would you like to do now?' Steve asked her gently.

Annie looked at the oven clock.

'I collect Benjy from his nursery at twelve,' she said. 'Before that, perhaps we could go for a walk?'

He smiled at her. 'All right. A walk it is.'

'A very short, gentle one, because of your leg.'

His smile broadened. 'I'm faster than you think.'

They went out together into the March sunshine.

Steve's car was a big grey BMW, parked at the kerb at the opposite end of the road.

'I wasn't sure which was your house,' he said. He unlocked the passenger door and helped Annie into the plush interior. She was interpreting his words inside her head. *It was tactful to park a car like this a little way away. Someone might see it, and wonder who you are.*

As they purred out of the quiet street Annie stared straight ahead through the windshield. She knew that her face was pink and that her expression was unnatural enough to make anyone who knew her, and who might be watching, look just a little harder. She thought back to the moments of happiness that she had felt with Steve in the hospital, and wondered at her own naïveté in letting herself believe, however briefly, that loving him as she did was simple and natural.

Steve drove smoothly away from Annie's immediate neighbourhood. As they left the streets behind she began to relax. She let her head fall back against her seat, passively watching the shop windows as they rolled by. She felt somehow that now she had left the house and come with Steve, the first of a long chain of decisions had been made, irrevocably, and that was a kind of comfort.

It was a short drive to the north side of Hampstead Heath. Annie noticed that Steve seemed well-acquainted with the belt of expensive housing immediately surrounding the Heath. He turned briskly into an unmarked side-road that led directly to the open space. He raised his eyebrows at her and she nodded her assent. Steve took his stick from the back of the car and they crossed on to the grass, walking slowly, shoulder to shoulder.

Annie glanced back at the large houses standing half-hidden behind their high fences. 'Are you a regular in places like this?'

Steve shrugged and laughed. 'Here? Film-producer country? Not exactly. I've been asked to one or two private functions in houses around and about. And they are functions, believe me. There was a very stiff party, I remember, in one of those houses over there. The green-tiled one, I think. I walked across here afterwards, in the very early hours of the morning, talking to someone. It was so quiet,' he recalled. 'Like somewhere very remote, an island or a stretch of moorland. Not London at all.'

Annie wondered whether he had been with Cass, or Vicky, or someone else altogether. She knew that her retrospective jealousy was inappropriate, but it took a moment to overcome it. She put her hands in the pockets of her jeans, dismissing the image of some film woman in a 'Dynasty' dress. She concentrated on their path over the short, tussocky grass.

'Are you all right to walk like this?'

'Perfectly, if we don't go too far or too fast. If we do, I shall have to lean on your arm.'

'My pleasure,' she whispered.

They smiled at each other, suddenly warmed by happiness that was stronger than the sunshine, and Annie forgot her jealousy again.

'Why do you come to film-producer functions?' Annie asked. 'I don't know anything about what you do, do I?'

'I can tell you, if you really want.'

The open heath dipping in front of them was deserted except for stray joggers in their tracksuits and one or two solitary walkers whose dogs sniffed at the dead leaves still lying in the hollows: for Steve and Annie their isolation here in the empty space under the blue sky was comforting.

'I do want. Tell me everything.'

They walked on, absorbed in one another, talking about little things as they had done in the long hours in hospital.

It was Steve who looked at his watch and reminded Annie at last that they must turn back to the car. Their steps were heavier as they retraced them, and they drove back through the streets towards Annie's home in deepening silence.

Two streets away from the nursery Annie said abruptly, 'Could you let me out here?'

'Of course not,' Steve answered, unthinking. 'I'll take you right to the door.'

'No,' she said sharply. 'I . . .' She was thinking of the group of mothers on the church hall steps, watching her.

Steve glanced at her face and then he drew in to the side of the road. His hands stayed gripping the steering wheel.

'I'm sorry,' Annie said softly.

Steve was silent, looking out at the suburban street. Annie wanted to whisper his name, to lay her head against his shoulder, but she made herself sit rigid.

'When will I see you again?' he asked her.

'I don't know. As soon as I possibly can. Will . . . the daytime be all right?'

'Come at any time you want, my darling.'

'I'll . . . come to you, this time.' She said the words very quietly, almost with distaste. She was thinking, then we'll be committed to the lies. Or else to making all the hurtful steps towards the truth.

Oh, Steve, don't go and leave me.

Go now, why don't you, and leave us in peace?

She felt herself torn, the pain from all the ragged pieces as severe as any of the physical hurt she had felt in the darkness.

'All right, then,' Annie said wearily.

Steve took a little square of pasteboard from his wallet and gave it to her.

'That's my address. And my number. You can always reach me there.'

'Thank you,' she whispered. She opened her handbag and slipped the card without looking at it through a tear in the lining, where it could lie safely hidden.

She lifted her head to look at him then. His face was soft, and his eyes were clouded with sympathy. Not a despoiler at all, Annie thought. Why was I thinking that of him? She leant forward very slowly and touched the corner of his mouth with her own. For a second they held together, burning, motionless. Then, as stiffly as an old woman, she sat back again.

'Goodbye,' Annie said.

He nodded, his eyes fixed on her face.

Annie fumbled for the door catch and stepped out on to the kerb. She raised her arm in an awkward wave and then she began to walk, too fast, heading for the church hall nursery.

Steve watched her until she was out of sight, but she never turned to look back.

'Can I do this puzzle?' Benjy asked. He was sitting at the kitchen table, already tipping the pieces out of their box.

Annie glanced briefly over her shoulder. She was standing at the sink, peeling potatoes.

'All right. Remember that there isn't much time before bed.'

'I *want* to.'

'I said yes, Ben. Just don't get cross if it isn't finished before you have to go upstairs.' Annie's response was patient, automatic. She wasn't listening, because her thoughts were busy elsewhere. Benjy spread the pieces out over the table and stared fiercely at them.

'I want you to help me.'

'I can't, love. I'm busy now. You do it.'

Benjy reached out across the table and with a lazy sweep of his arm he tipped the puzzle pieces over the edge and on to the floor. They fell with a satisfying clatter.

Annie threw down her potato peeler, the second clatter like an echo. 'What did you do that for, Ben?'

The little boy gazed at her, his face a pucker of defiance. Then he asked, 'Why are you always busy?'

Annie stood still, holding on to the sink edge, staring at her children.

Thomas lifted his head from his drawing. He said, as if he were stating the obvious for his brother's benefit, 'Because she's a grown-up.'

They watched her, the two of them, accusing and vulnerable at the same time, their uncertainty clear for her to see.

'Oh, Thomas,' she said.

Annie went to them. Benjy slid off his chair and wrapped his arms around her legs. Thomas stood up awkwardly, his shoulders hunched, feeling that he was too old to run into his mother's arms. She held them out to him and then she hugged them both, burying their faces against her so that they wouldn't see her own expression.

'I'm sorry,' she managed to say. 'I'm sorry that I haven't been very much fun, lately.'

I'm doing this all wrong, Annie thought. I'm thinking about myself, and Steve, every minute of the day. Instead of my kids. It would be better for them if I weren't here. If I just went, and left them, would they be happier in the end, than if I took them away from their home and their father, to a stranger? Suddenly, she was almost overcome by the physical pull of her love for them.

She drew them closer, smelling their warm, grubby scent, her cheek against Thomas's hair.

I can't leave them, she thought. If I go, they must come with me.

'I love you both,' she whispered. 'You know that.'

She hugged them one last time, and then let them go. The button on her cuff caught against Thomas's ear and he clapped his hand to it, yelling, '*Ow!*'

'Baby,' Benjamin said sternly and then the three of them were laughing, the tension breaking up like mist.

'Come on,' Annie said. 'It's bath time.'

Another day negotiated, she thought, as they went up the stairs.

The boys were asleep before Martin came home. He was tired after a meeting with a particularly exigent client, and he came into the kitchen wearily rubbing his hand over his eyes.

'Was it a bad day, then?' Annie asked.

Martin pecked her cheek, reaching past her for the wine bottle at the same time. 'Mmm? Only fairly bad. Dinner smells good. How was your day?'

'Oh. Usual,' Annie said carefully.

Martin poured himself a drink and took the evening paper over to the sofa at the far end of the room. He cleared a pile of clean washing out of the way and sank down with a sigh of relief.

'Thank God for peace and quite,' Annie heard him murmur.

She stood at the stove, poking unnecessarily at a saucepan with her wooden spoon. She was thinking, If I say something now, will it sound as if I haven't been able to hold it back? If I don't mention it till later, will it come out sounding contrived? Annie frowned down into the bubbling casserole. Lying didn't come easily.

'Martin?' she said, too loudly.

'Yes?'

'I thought I might go shopping tomorrow. Down to the West End. The boys need some things, and so do I. Benjy's going out to play for the afternoon, and Audrey will come in at teatime . . .'

Martin looked up from the paper. It was a good sign that she felt safe enough to go into crowded stores again. He smiled at her, trying to gauge if it was anxiety or the effort of concealment that made her voice sound strained.

'Good idea. Look, shall I come with you? I couldn't manage all day, but I might take a couple of hours after lunch.'

'There's no need.' Look down into the saucepan. Stir in one direction, then the other, take a deep breath. 'It's boring things, like a new duffel coat for Tom.'

I hate lying to him.

Martin watched her averted profile for a moment. And then he said lightly, 'Okay. If you're sure you'll be all right. Take the joint account chequebook. There's a couple of hundred pounds in that account.'

'Thanks,' Annie said. And so, she thought, she would have to rush into John Lewis's on the way home, and buy things to make her husband believe that she had been shopping all day long. Annie realized that the sight of the food was making her feel sick. She wondered bleakly whether it was her love affair itself that was sordid, or whether it was the lying and the subterfuge that made it seem so.

She had telephoned Steve two days ago, when she knew that she couldn't go any longer without seeing him. Her hands shook as she dialled the number, but they steadied again as soon as he answered. His voice sounded very warm and confident.

'I can arrange for a whole day. Until the children's supper-time, that is,' she said.

'When?'

'On Thursday. Is that all right?'

'Of course it is. I'll take you to lunch somewhere.'

And so it had been arranged. Annie dropped the wooden spoon into the sink with the rest of the washing up.

'Dinner's ready, Martin.'

'Wonderful.'

Another ordinary evening. Annie slept badly that night,

restlessly turning between guilt and happiness.

In the morning, when the house was empty and quiet after the rush of work and school, she walked dreamily through the cluttered rooms. She put the cushions straight on the old chesterfield, and wound up the pretty little French clock that stood on the mantelpiece. Then she went upstairs. She touched the bottle of body lotion on her dressing table, then opened one of the drawers and looked at her underwear neatly folded inside. Annie owned an expensive set of cream lace and silk underthings, but Martin had given them to her for her birthday a year ago. Annie took out her plain, everyday things and slammed the drawer shut again. She lifted a blue corduroy dress off its hanger and put that on too, defiantly not looking at herself in the wardrobe mirror. When she was dressed she went into the bathroom and combed her hair into waves around her face. Almost as an afterthought she took out a pair of jet combs that Tibby had given her, saying, 'I won't need these now that my hair's so thin.' She pinned the waves of hair back, and stared into her own eyes. They seemed very bright, and there were spots of colour on her high cheekbones. She looked, Annie thought, as if she were about to do something very dangerous, and desperate.

At midday she put her grey coat on, bought to replace the blue one she had worn to go Christmas shopping, how long ago? She picked up the chequebook that Martin had left for her on the dresser in the kitchen, and put it into her bag. For a moment she stood looking at the telephone, thinking, *I could still ring. I could tell him that I can't come, after all.* And then she thought of Steve, waiting in his empty flat for her to come to him. *I must go. I can't not do it, not now.*

She left the house. She was going to slam the front door, but in the end she closed it behind her with a tiny, final click.

Steve lived at the top of an anonymous block not far from Harrods. Annie rode up in the mirrored lift, turning away from the unwelcome sight of her repeated reflection. When the doors opened on the top floor she stepped out into a long carpeted corridor. She hesitated, caught a last glimpse of her desperate, defiant expression, turned and marched smartly down the length of deep pile. She rang his bell and he opened the door immediately.

Steve kissed her cheek, his hand briefly lifting her hair from the nape of her neck. 'Come in.'

She followed him inside. The room was bare, surprisingly high, decorated in shades of grey and cream. The few pieces of furniture were black, or glass and chrome. A long black table at the far end was piled with papers.

'Have you been working?' Annie asked. In this environment, Steve suddenly seemed a formidable stranger.

Then he smiled crookedly at her. 'Trying to,' he said, acknowledging the longing and the apprehensiveness that they both felt.

'Would you like a drink?'

Annie remembered the conversation that they had had in hospital. Steve had said, 'We've never met for a clandestine drink. I don't know whether you like vodka martinis or white wine spritzers.' This is clandestine enough, she thought. Why didn't we understand before that it would come to this?

'Just white wine,' Annie said. 'No soda.'

Steve nodded. She knew that he remembered too.

He went into the kitchen and Annie walked across the room to the black sofa, looking at the chic emptiness. He poured her wine and she drank it, tasting the gooseberry richness.

'Why aren't there any *things?*' she asked suddenly. 'No ornaments, or mementoes.'

Steve looked around, seeing the room afresh. 'There aren't, are there?'

'It looks as if it came all together, in a package. Do you mind my saying that?'

Steve laughed. 'Not a bid. It did. An interior decorator's package. I suppose I haven't wanted to remember anything in particular.' His face softened. 'Until now.'

'Come and sit here,' Annie asked, turning her face up to his.

They sat side by side, their heads almost touching.

'It isn't very like your house, is it? Your house is full of memories.'

'Yes,' she said. 'It's easier to be here.'

They drank again in silence, and when Steve spoke again it was in a light, deliberately cheerful voice, about something quite different.

When they had finished their wine Steve said, 'I told you I was going to take you out for lunch. You'd better know that I can't cook a thing.'

'I thought you must have one minor failing,' she answered, on the same cheerful note.

But under the bright surface they were both thinking that they knew all the big things about one another, the momentous things that made them who they were. Yet they knew none of the little, everyday ones that would have marked them out to their acquaintances. It was strange to have everything, and nothing, to learn.

It was a short walk to the restaurant. Steve seemed to be moving more quickly, leaning less heavily on his stick.

'The leg will always be slightly stiff,' he told her. 'But other-wise as good as new. Look at us.' They stopped for a moment on the crowded pavement and the shoppers streamed past them in the sunlight. 'We're lucky. Remember?'

Annie looked at the light and the colours, and at the reassuring roaring traffic, and at Steve's face, and uncomplicated joy flooded through her. Their eyes met for a moment, and then they began to walk towards the restaurant again.

It was a small, discreet place, with tables occupied by prosperous-looking lunchers well-separated from each other so that conversation was no more than a low hum. One waiter pulled out Annie's chair, another unfolded her napkin for her. The menu was placed in her hands by the head waiter. She glanced at it and saw that it was very short and very distinguished.

After they had ordered, Annie sat back in her chair with a

259

sigh, looking around the room. 'I like it here.'

Steve raised his glass to her. 'I like it because you are here.'

It was a meal that Annie always remembered.

She forgot the details of the food, but she never forgot the sense of being wrapped in calm, unshakable luxury, or the way that the exquisite food and wine went together, or the happiness of being with Steve. She knew that her skin was glowing and her eyes were shining, and she knew that she was beautiful and clever. Everything that was good and important had come together, as it had only ever done before in dreams. As they ate and talked and looked at one another Annie stepped outside her ordinary self and became somebody magical, and superhuman; a woman in love.

Steve sat across the table from her, oblivious of everything but her face and voice, his own face reflecting his happiness and his pride in her.

Nothing could go wrong. Nothing must go wrong.

And then, so quickly, their coffee cups were empty for the last time, and Annie had eaten the last of the tiny, exotic sweetmeats that had come arranged in their dish like jewels in a casket. She blinked, and looked around the restaurant, and saw that it was empty except for themselves.

'Shall we go home?' Steve said softly.

'Yes, please.'

As they went outside they felt that they were separated from the crowds around them, and the high red buses grinding past, by the secure nimbus of their happiness.

'Thank you,' Annie said. 'I've never eaten a meal like that before.'

'Neither have I,' Steve said, not meaning the food. 'It was important, the first time that we sat down to eat together.'

He took her hand securely in his, and guided her back through the ordinary people.

In the bare flat there was nothing for Annie to look at, nothing to remind her. The afternoon sun shone through the slats of the blinds, laying bars of brightness on the grey floor. When Steve held the tips of her fingers and turned her gently to him the light and dark played over their faces too, and it was like moving through water. She was floating, weightless in the waves, and then the current caught her. It was easy to move with it, unthinkable not to.

Their mouths touched, lightly, and the watery light rippled in long rays, spreading away from them. There was a moment of sweet, dreamy stillness and then the current was much stronger. Annie's mouth opened as the waves caught her breath, crushing her ribs until her heart pounded against them. The kiss opened up unthought-of submerged caverns of love and longing. Annie was trembling, her skin burned and she heard her own voice, a low cry, drowning.

I love you.

'I want you,' Steve said, and Annie answered, 'I'm here.'

They walked together through the patterns of light and dark, and there was no leader or follower because their need was equal.

And in the bedroom, where the blinds shut out the light except for thin, broken beams, they undressed each other. There was no hurrying, because they were certain of one another now. Their clothes dropped around them, forgotten.

Even as a girl, Annie had never been proud of her body and after the birth of her children her flesh had begun to fall in loose, softening folds. During the weeks in hospital and afterwards the compensating roundness had melted away to leave the skin stretched too tightly over her bones and showing the net of blue veins beneath.

But now, as Steve looked at her, Annie stood upright, natural and strong. Gently he touched the raised, angry pucker of the scar across her belly and the pink junctions of new skin over her arm and shoulder. She saw the fan of fine wrinkles at the corners of his eyes, and the tenderness in his face. She knew that she was beautiful, as beautiful as she had been in the restaurant, and now she was powerful too, because they were like this together.

In her turn, she looked at him. She touched the flat of her hand to the hair on his chest, seeing the blackness of it over the white skin. There were the ladder-marks of lacerations over Steve's arms and chest too. At the top of his leg the flesh had reformed, knobs of it over the old gash, but the muscles were shrunk and wasted. He was thin, and she saw the pull of muscles across his chest and back as his arms encircled her.

The length of their bodies touched together, hard and soft, unfamiliar and imperious.

She kissed the corner of his mouth and he turned his face to meet hers, his tongue seeking hers out. Annie's hair fanned lazily over his bare shoulders. She felt him arch against her and she put her hand down to touch him, gently at first and then insistently until he breathed sharply and lifted her off her feet. He laid her down across the bed and knelt beside her.

He parted her legs and put his hand between them and then, with infinite gentleness, his mouth. The pleasure was like a knife, turning inside her, and she cried out to him.

They had been slow and patient before, but they were helpless in the current now. Steve lifted himself to look at her and then his mouth touched her thighs and the curve of her waist, then her breast. The waves seemed to break over them, deafening them with their roar. Annie's mouth formed a word, inaudible, as she reached her arms up to him. There could be no holding back any longer. He came blindly up against her and she guided him until he found the place and joined them together at last.

There was an instant of shivering stillness.

Annie opened her eyes and saw the bare grey walls and the gold threads of sunlight spanning them. The gold light seemed to spill outwards to lap over them. It was hot and sweet over her skin and inside it and she rolled in Steve's arm, finding him as he found her, question and answer. She was hungry now, ravenous with hunger, as Steve was, and they were the only way to feed one another. If he had seemed strange to her in that moment of stillness, Annie forgot the strangeness at once. He knew her, and he opened recesses within her that she had forgotten, or had perhaps never known. As her body moved against his, as she leaned over him so that her hair brushed his face, or as they lay side by side so that they could look into one another's eyes, Annie was as supple as a girl again, but she was as knowing as a grown woman too.

At last they had taken each other as far as they could go. Annie's head tipped back and her legs wound tighter around his. Steve was still for a moment, holding her there, and then he thrust again until she cried out and he felt the butterfly flutter of her muscles against him.

'My love,' he whispered. 'Oh yes, my love.'

He held her with his love like a stone inside him, and when she was quiet again he let his face fall against the hollow of her shoulder and he gave himself up to her.

Annie's eyes were languorously heavy when she opened them again. She saw the gold-flecked irises of Steve's eyes, very close, and she smiled slowly. Their bodies were still joined, sticky and sweet, and their arms wound round each other. The room was quiet, and the murmur of traffic from the streets below seemed far distant. She knew that they were happy, here and now in this narrow space and time. She closed her eyes again.

They slept for a little while, dreamlessly, and when Annie woke up the sun had gone and the room was almost dark. She raised herself on one elbow, soundlessly, because Steve was still sleeping. She saw from the clock beside the bed that it was five o'clock, and she must leave in half an hour's time. She let herself lie down again beside him for a moment, listening to his even breathing.

Something in the shape of the room, or perhaps the quality of the light, made her think of the last time she had seen Matthew, lying in the upstairs room of the house overlooking the square.

Memories stirred inside her, reality quickening again, and she moved sharply, blocking them out. Steve stirred and opened his eyes.

'I'm sorry. I shouldn't have fallen asleep.'

She kissed him. 'I did too. I must go home soon.'

But he reached up and put his arms around her neck, drawing her down on top of him so that the firm foundation of her resolve cracked wide apart.

'Not yet. I want to make love to you again.'

His hands touched her and she lay back, protesting and then acquiescent, and at last as her body took her over again she was as demanding as Steve himself. They were slower this time, more calculating because of what they had learned already, but the final shock that took hold of Annie went deeper and burned her more fiercely than anything she had ever known before.

When it was over, Steve rolled away from her and lay on his back, staring up at the shadows over the ceiling.

He reached his hand out to touch his fingers to hers as they lay side by side and the recollection flooded over them at once.

'Remember.'

She felt the pain of her injuries again, and the momentous joy of having escaped. For a moment neither of them was able to move, as if the weight of the wreckage reared up above them all over again.

'I remember.'

Annie turned her head towards him then, and saw that there were tears at the corner of his eyes.

'What is it?' she asked, bewildered.

'Now that you're here, Annie, don't go away. Don't go.'

She looked away. 'I must go. You know that I have to go home to my kids.'

There was a second's pause, and then Steve sat up abruptly, his back to her. When he looked round again, she didn't know whether she had really seen his tears. 'I'll drive you home.'

'No. No, there isn't any need.' He couldn't drive her home, of course. 'I'll go back on the tube. I bought myself a return ticket.'

Annie pushed back the covers and sat up. She collected her scattered clothes from the bedroom floor and went into the bathroom. When she came out again Steve was dressed too, waiting for her. He kissed her, lightly, on both cheeks and asked her, 'Will you come to see me again soon?'

'As soon as I can,' she promised him.

They rode down together in the mirrored lift and Annie thought that their reflected selves looked sad, and strange.

Out in the street Steve called a taxi and put Annie into it.

'Safe home.'

She nodded, suddenly distraught at having to part from him. She didn't speak and the cab door slammed between them. She looked backwards, with her land lifted, until the taxi turned the corner. And all the way home she sat stiffly on the edge of her seat, looking out at the lurid glow of the city's evening lights.

Martin was sitting in the kitchen, with the boys eating their supper. Their three faces turned to her as she came in, and Annie felt that her mouth was bruised and burning, and that her hair was wild even though she knew that she had smoothed it in Steve's bathroom.

'Where's all your shopping?' Martin asked. 'Shall I carry it in for you?'

Annie stared at them with the blood thumping in her head.

'I didn't buy anything,' she said. 'Nothing at all.'

There was a long silence, and Benjy's alarmed face turned from one of them to the other.

'I see,' Martin said, deadly quiet.

Annie knew that he did see. In truth he must have seen all along, while she had pretended to herself that he was blind.

She turned away from the three of them and ran up the stairs to her bedroom. She lay face down on the bed, stiff and cold and stony-eyed. She heard Martin putting the boys to bed, and then going downstairs again. She lay without moving for hours, hearing him moving about, and all the little sounds of ordinary life, but he never came up again. At last she fell into an exhausted sleep.

The dream of the bombing came again, redoubling its terror. In her dream Steve wasn't there and when she woke up, bathed in cold sweat and with the taste of blood from her bitten lips in her mouth again, she was alone still. She stretched out her hand, timidly, and found that the wide bed was empty.

Annie swung her legs off the bed, with her blue corduroy dress caught up in creases around her. She felt her way through the dark house to the spare bedroom. She opened the door noiselessly and stood there, her fingers curled around the handle, listening to the sound of Martin's separate breathing.

Eight

For a week, and then another week, Annie felt that she was being slowly drawn in half.

On the first morning after the day with Steve she came down to breakfast and found Martin already sitting at the breakfast table. His eyes were dark with shadows and the pain in his face made the guilt and regret twist inside her. Annie tried to say something, 'Martin, listen to me, I don't know . . .' but he wouldn't let her finish.

'Not now,' he said coldly.

He left his breakfast, picked up his briefcase and his coat, and walked out of the house without looking at her. Annie wanted to shout after him, or to put her head down on the table and cry until she couldn't cry any more, but Thomas and Benjamin were standing in the doorway watching her.

'Are you angry?' Ben asked.

'No, love.' She tried to smile. 'A little bit sad, today, that's all.'

Their round faces reproached her.

After delivering them to school and to nursery, Annie came back and wandered in aimless circles through the house. She watched the silent telephone, willing Martin to ring so that she could begin to talk to him.

When at last it did ring it was Steve. Annie gripped the receiver as if the strength of her fingers could bring him closer.

'Thank you for yesterday,' Steve said. Annie could hear that he was smiling and the love and elation that she had felt yesterday lifted her heart. 'It was one of the happiest days I have ever had.'

'I was happy too.'

As always, Steve could hear more than the words. 'Is something wrong?'

Rapidly Annie said, 'It has to be at the expense of other people's, our happiness, doesn't it? At the expense of Martin's, and the boys'.'

'What happened?' he persisted gently.

'Nothing happened. Martin knows. Because he guessed, not because I had the courage to tell him. I came back without my shopping, you see, and that was supposed to be my alibi. Perhaps he's seen it all along. We've known each other for a long time, Steve.'

'I know that.' The words were barely audible. At length he said, 'He would have had to know some time, Annie. Isn't it as well that it should be at the beginning?' He was right, of course. But he hadn't seen the hurt in Martin's face last night, or the coldness this morning. Annie's fingers wrapped even tighter around the receiver. Stop. She must stop feeling that Steve was to blame; that anyone was to blame. What had happened had happened, and now it must be faced. She took a breath, and tried to put a different, stronger note into her voice.

'I'm sorry. I won't pretend that what's happening is anything but painful, or that it won't go on being painful for a long time to come. Can you face that too, Steve?'

He answered her at once, as she had known that he would. 'You know that I can.'

'Yes.'

'Annie, I'm here if you need me.'

She knew that too. She wanted to go to him, but she was fixed here, and she was afraid that the unfixing would damage them all more viciously than the bomb could ever have done.

'Will you leave me for a few days to try to work things out here?'

'Of course.'

After he had rung off Annie resumed her aimless circling of the house. She watched the slow clock until it was time to go to collect Ben, longing to have his innocent company. She set off briskly for the nursery, and all the way back she listened carefully to his recitation of the morning's activities, trying to focus on him to the exclusion of everything else. When they were home again she cooked his lunch, laying out the carrots in the pattern he insisted on before he would even pretend to eat them, then sitting opposite him with a cup of coffee while he mashed the food up with his fork. Through the stream of Benjy's questions and observations Annie kept hearing her own questions, and the silence that lay beyond them.

'Why don't you listen?' Ben demanded crossly.

Annie felt the heat of unjustified irritation.

'I can't listen to everything all the time, Ben,' she snapped. 'I need to think sometimes.'

He looked at her, surprised, and then he stuck out his lower lip. 'I need a cuddle,' he said, acting, but Annie knew that at another level he wasn't acting, but telling her the truth. She pushed her anger and sadness ashamedly back within herself.

'Come and sit on my knee.'

He scrambled up triumphantly and she hugged him, then drew his plate of messy food across and spooned up a mouthful.

'Come on, finish this and then we'll watch your programme.'

Ben felt that he had won some undefined battle and so he willingly ate the rest of his lunch. Afterwards they sat on the sofa together, with Benjy's head heavy against Annie's chest. Annie stared unseeingly at the puppets on the screen and thought of the afternoon ahead of her, and the other afternoons of motherhood, and tried hopelessly to imagine them in another place, with Steve.

'Let's go to the park,' she suggested when the programme finished. She found Benjy's red suit and dragged his tricycle out of the tangle in the cupboard under the stairs. They set off, with Benjy trundling beside his mother, his face screwed up with concentration and the effort of pedalling.

The route was numbingly familiar, and the park itself. She followed Benjy from the swings to the roundabout, and stood at the foot of the slide while he hurtled down it. She felt too stiff and far-away to join in his game of hide-and-seek.

'Not today,' she told him. 'Perhaps Daddy will bring you and Tom for a game tomorrow.'

What else would happen tomorrow, and the days afterwards? Annie felt cold. She saw that the sky was streaked with long fingers of cloud. The warmth of the misplaced spring was over, and tomorrow it would be as icy as January again. She walked around the knot of trees that stood in the middle of the park.

'Come on, Ben. We'll go and buy some bread for tea, and then we'll get Thomas from school.'

Teatime came and went, and then the routine of the children's play time, supper and baths and bedtime stories. When they were both asleep Annie came downstairs and poured herself a drink, looked at the dinner in the oven, and then sat down to wait. She knew that she was waiting for Martin, as she had been waiting all day. She waited for an hour, and then another half an hour, and then she took her portion of the dinner out of the oven and ate it, not tasting anything. She washed up the single plate and put it away, and sat down again in front of the television. She remembered that there was a basketful of mending waiting to be done so she fetched it and began to darn a hole in the elbow of one of Thomas's school jerseys.

It was nearly half past ten when Martin came up the front path.

He had been sitting for hours in the corner of a bleak pub he had never been into before. Amidst the plastic and neon of brewery décor he had been thinking about himself and Annie, back over all the years that they had been together. He remembered her as they had been when they first met, and he recalled that he had fallen in love with her in a coffee bar, when she was still an awkward hybrid of *outré* student and shy school-girl. They had grown up together, from then. In two, perhaps three years? It seemed a short time to have accomplished so much, looking back at it with the speed of years' passing now. But it had felt then as if they had for ever, ahead of them. The memories went on, parading past him, while he stared unseeingly at his beer.

Was this what *for ever* added up to, then?

Everything that they had done together seemed much clearer, and precious, now. Because he was afraid that the end of it was coming?

He had never been afraid before, because he had been so sure of her. Even when there was Matthew, he had been sure.

Martin ducked his head over his unwanted beer, confronted by the spectre of arrogance.

Carefully, now, he made himself remember.

Matthew had materialized in the hot weeks of the summer before they were married. Martin had never even seen him, but Annie's friend Louise, and other friends, had talked about him. Martin remembered that he had understood what was happening, but he had simply waited for her.

He had even asked her, *Do I need to worry about it?* And she had answered, *No.*

His certainty that she would come back seemed unbelievable now. Had he been so convinced that he was right about everything else, in those days?

He might have lost her, then.

Instead of losing her now.

For all the noise and distraction of the pub, Martin felt that he was hearing and seeing with sudden, perfect clarity.

Neither of them was fixed, nor defined as themselves at any point in time, not in that Soho coffee bar, nor on their wedding day, nor on the day of the bombing. They both went on changing, and they changed separately as well as together. They were not just the welded, coupled unit that he had silently asked her to confirm on the unhappy night of their dinner party. They were both of them at fault, perhaps, for forgetting that. They had seen each other fixed in a frame, as Martin-and-Annie, or as Benjy and Tom's Mum and Dad, and when they slipped separately out of their fixed places, then they lost sight of one another.

How restless had Annie been, while he worked and concentrated on other things?

She was so good at giving all of them what they needed from her, he hadn't troubled to look closely enough. It was only on Christmas Eve, when she had already gone, that he had really seen the neat evidence of her loving care. And then he had thought, *Why didn't I see before?*

Or had Annie herself stopped seeing things, too?

Perhaps, Martin thought.

And if they were both at fault in their carelessness of one another, he had been wrong all the last weeks to heap the blame for what was happening on to the bombing.

The bomb was a senseless, terrible catalyst, nothing more.

The juke-box in the corner of the bar sent waves of meaningless noise washing around him.

If it hadn't been Steve, then, it might have been someone else. Sooner or later.

Through the noise, Martin made himself follow the painful threads of thought. Now that it had happened. *Think it.* Now that his wife had fallen in love with someone else, what could he do?

With the end of his need to blame the bomb, Martin's anger and bitterness against Steve drifted away too. There was nothing to be gained from going to find him, confronting him, as he had still half-imagined that he would do. To say what? Martin thought, and half-smiled at the picture that it conjured up. To ask for Annie back?

Martin sat for a long time, without moving, and then he picked up the pint glass and drained it.

There was nothing he could do. Nothing except wait, and by waiting hope to show her that he loved her, and wanted her, and needed her.

He stood up at last, stiff and with the bar music beating in his head. It was time to go home.

He drove back the familiar way, and parked the car outside

the front gate. The lights were on in the downstairs rooms, and the dim glow of Benjy's bedroom nightlight glowed against the drawn blind in the top window. The house looked just as it always did, and the sight made him long even more sharply for the old, ordinary times. If they came back again, he vowed to himself, he would keep them, rubbed bright, and never give them a chance to slip away.

He went up the path, and let himself in through the front door. Annie was sitting in the circle of light at one end of the old chesterfield. He saw the colour of her hair and the line of her cheek, and the mending lying in her lap.

They looked at each other without speaking, neither of them knowing what to say. Annie got up slowly and crossed the room to turn off the television news, and Martin stood rooted in the doorway watching the way that she bent down, straightened up again and walked away into the kitchen.

'Would you like your dinner?' she called back, tonelessly. 'It's rather dry, I'm afraid.'

'It doesn't matter. Yes, bring it in here, is that all right?'

A moment later she came in with a tray, a plate of food, ordinary things, like on any other night. Martin took it and began to eat, feeling the food settling on top of the gassy keg beer that he had drunk in the cheerless pub.

After a minute he said, 'I thought we might talk, Annie.'

She was sitting across the room, her head bent, her hands folded on her darning. 'Yes. I thought we might too,' she whispered.

Martin groped, wondering where to start. 'Tell me what happened.'

She looked at him then with a strange, almost supplicating expression. 'You know what happened.'

He shook his head. 'No, Annie. I want you to tell me, now. It's time.'

She put her hands up to her eyes. He wanted to say, *Don't do that. Let me see your face*, but he made himself keep quiet.

At last Annie said, 'We were a couple, you and me, living here

273

with our kids. It wasn't anything extraordinary, was it? Nothing exotic, or passionate, or enthralling, but it was working. It was, wasn't it?'

Martin nodded. 'Yes,' he said, very quietly. 'It was working. Better than we deserved, perhaps.'

She looked across at him then, for a long moment, and then she nodded.

'And then the bomb happened,' Annie whispered. Martin saw her lift one shoulder, and let it drop again, a gesture of bewilderment, as though the bomb was something she had tried and failed to understand.

'Tell me, Annie. You've never told me what it was like. What you felt.'

Annie stared at him, and he was afraid that she didn't see him at all. And then she began to talk, in a low, unemphatic voice. 'I don't know how to tell you. I don't know how to describe what it was like. It was dark, there was a terrible noise and then there was utter silence. I couldn't move, and I could feel blood in my mouth, and dust and grit on my tongue. And there was pain everywhere.' She shrugged again. 'You know all that. What can I tell you?'

'About fear.'

Annie thought about Tibby. She had come home from her hospice, to her husband and the roses, but she was too weak now to do her pruning. *She's seen you grow up. Seen her grandchildren.* Yes. But what else was there? How many patient compromises? 'I was afraid. I was . . . angry, too. I suppose it was anger. With the sense that everything was being cut short. That I wasn't to be allowed to . . . finish. What I was doing.'

Martin looked round the room. There was a wicker basket full of Ben's toys next to the hearth, a jar of daffodils on the mantelpiece amongst the clutter of china ornaments and candlesticks and children's party invitations. 'To finish what you were doing here, Annie? Was that it?'

'Yes. Being a wife and mother.' The words as they came out sounded strange to Annie, as if she had repeated them to herself

274

so many times that their meaning had begun to elude her. 'We were all right, weren't we?' she asked hastily. 'The four of us.'

The past tense hit Martin squarely now. He looked at his wife in the lamplight, feeling the anger and bitterness of the past few days briefly renewed.

'We were,' he said. 'We can be again, Annie, when all this is forgotten.'

As soon as he had spoken them, he knew that he had chosen the words badly. He shifted in his chair and the cutlery rattled on his plate. He glanced down and saw that the barely-touched food was congealing, and pushed it aside. Annie was still holding Thomas's school jumper, with the darning wool unravelling on the rug beside her.

'I can't forget,' she said, the words falling like clear drops of icy water.

'Annie.' He fought to keep his voice level. 'You can, if you let yourself. It was a terrible, hideous thing to happen. The only thing you can do now is to be thankful that you survived, and forget everything else.'

They were circling around the truth now, watching each other, waiting.

'If it were that easy,' Annie whispered at last. 'If only.'

Martin sat silently, feeling a vein throb in the angle of his jaw. The moment had come, and yet he could hope that it would somehow slip away again.

Annie went on, in the same low voice, looking down at the work in her lap. 'Without Steve, I don't think I could have survived. Steve made me hold on. He made me believe that we would get out. I'm not a very brave person. You know that. But he made me be.'

'How?' The word stuck in Martin's throat, like a croak. He was remembering the day too; the cold outside the jagged store front, the corridors of the police station and the smoky tension inside the trailer, and the roughness of the smashed masonry as he pulled at it with the rescue workers.

'We talked. We could just touch hands. We held on to one

another and talked. Some of the time I didn't know whether I was talking or thinking, but he heard anyway. And I listened to him talking. If you think you are going to die, it doesn't matter what you say, does it?'

'What did you say?'

'We told each other about our lives. Everything, big things and little things.'

There was quiet again. Martin was imagining his wife, as he had done so often before, hurt in the darkness, with her hand held in the stranger's. And her voice, a whisper like it was in the dark to him too, telling him the big things and the little things, only for him to hear.

'Did you think about me, Annie?' The petulance of the question struck at him at once and he thought, That's how we all are. Annie dropped the darning and came across the room to him. She knelt on the rug in front of him with her head against his knees.

'Of course.'

Martin said nothing.

'I told him about you and the children and how I couldn't bear the thought that our lives should be severed, abruptly, so violently, with the ends left fraying.' He put out his hand then, tentatively, and stroked her hair. The ends of it were still frizzy from the awkward cut that had tried to repair the damage to it. 'I told him about when we met, and after that. The ordinary things. The house, and the garden, and all the things we made and did together.'

Made. Did.

'And he told you the same?'

'Yes. Not quite such happy things.'

'And after that?' Martin asked gently, with his hand buried in her hair. He twisted his head so that he could see her face and then he saw that she was crying. There was a tear held at the corner of her eye, and the wet streak of another over her cheek.

'At the end . . . it seemed like the end, you know . . . he was, he had become, more real and more important than anything

else. He was all there was, then. He had come so close to me that
. . . that I didn't know any more where I ended and where he
began.'

Martin's hand tightened, just perceptibly, in Annie's hair. He
had looked down into the hole, under the arc lights, and he had
seen Steve still lying there. His arm had been stretched out to
where Annie had lain. There was a bitter taste in Martin's mouth
and throat. He was afraid of defeat. It had gone so far already,
he thought, that they seemed utterly beyond his reach. With an
effort at conviction he said, 'But then you were rescued. It was
over.'

Except that it wasn't, not at all. He had sat beside her in the
ambulance, and she had opened her eyes and looked at him with
a mixture of bewilderment and disappointment.

When Annie didn't answer he pushed on, trying in spite of
himself to force the admission from her by seeming to mis-
understand. 'I know that you must have shared the shock and the
reaction with him afterwards. No one else could possibly have
come close to understanding what it was like down there. Of
course you would have clung to each other then, while you were
still recovering. Like a prop for one another.'

Annie raised her head and looked into his face. 'Oh no,' she
said. There were still tears in her eyes, but there was a kind of
reflected radiance as well. 'It wasn't that. It was the joy of it. The
pure happiness of finding ourselves still alive. Can you
understand?'

Martin counted back the days to that time. He had been
preoccupied with the boys, with keeping the three of them going,
and with containing his fears for Annie. There had been no
opportunity for joy. The closest he had come to it was when the
doctors had told him that Annie would live. He had gone down
to see Steve, so that he would know too. Christmas Eve. He had
sensed it, even then, Martin recalled. Pain and the fear of loss
suddenly stabbed into him so that he almost doubled up.

'Oh yes,' he whispered, his voice so low that she could hardly
hear him. 'I think I can understand.'

I must tell him the truth, Annie thought. *Now that we have come this far.*

'Everything looked so beautiful. So new, and precious, and exact. Steve saw it too. I think that it was because of that same feeing that . . . that we loved one another.'

And so he had heard her saying the words.

Suddenly his resolution to wait, and to hope, seemed futile. He couldn't help the pointless anger that surged up in him, against the two of them, against every single thing that had happened since he had stared at the television news picture of the shattered store. He thought of Tom and Benjy upstairs and what the few impossible words would mean to them. And he knew that he loved his wife, and that he didn't know how to live without her love in return.

'Annie,' he murmured. 'Do you know what you're saying? Do you know the hurt it will mean to all of us?'

Unable to keep still any longer he stumbled to his feet, knocking into a low table and sending his dinner tray skidding. Annie watched through stinging eyes the blobs of food fall on to the rug.

'I know,' she whispered. 'Do you think I don't know?'

'What are you going to do?'

Annie thought of Tibby again, and the life that she had accepted for herself. Would her mother have made different choices if she had lived at a different time? Annie sensed again how precious life was, and how vital and miraculous its reopening had seemed to her in the hospital ward.

'I don't know,' she said hopelessly. 'I don't know what to do. That's the truth, Martin.'

He turned to the window, jerking the curtains aside so that he could stare into the street, then letting them fall again, a big man in a small space.

'Are you going to bed with him?'

'Once,' Annie said.

There was a long silence after that. Martin sat wearily down again and Annie stayed motionless on the rug, her legs folded awkwardly beneath her, too numb to move.

At last Martin said in a softer voice, 'People who have been together for as long as we have, what do they feel for each other? If you take away all the props of routine and familiarity and comfortable habit, I mean? They don't love each other, do they? Not the kind of love you're talking about.'

Annie thought of the wrenching intensity of her longing for Steve, and the crystalline happiness that she had known with him yesterday in the restaurant and in the shadow-barred flat.

'No,' she said painfully. 'Not that kind.'

'What is it then?'

She knew, and she searched for the words that wouldn't devalue it, but Martin was quicker and blunter.

'Friendship. Liking. We're old friends, Annie. We've achieved that.' He was unmoving, but she felt the anxiety inside him. 'Oh, I still fancy you. You know that. That part of me belongs to you as comprehensively as everything else. But it's not the first thing between us, is it? There's more. We were solid. Perhaps we . . . didn't look at one another, or hear one another, as carefully as we should have done. But we were happy, weren't we?' As he looked at her she heard the directness of his appeal. *It can't be different now. It can't disappear, after so long.*

And when she didn't answer he persisted aloud, 'Doesn't it mean anything to you?'

Annie held out her hand and then, realizing the inadequacy of it, she let it fall again. 'Of course it does. Martin, I'm still me. The years haven't gone anywhere.'

But yet they were looking at each other across a divide. Here, now, so bitterly obvious amidst the shabby warmth of home. Annie knew that she couldn't explain to him how the violence of what had happened had changed every cosy perspective, and how the same change of perspectives had jolted her into awareness, and then into love with another man.

It's too late now, she thought.

'What are you going to do?' Martin asked her again.

She lifted her head. 'I don't know how to be without him.' It was a simple offering of the truth, but she saw how the words cut into him. She wanted to close her eyes so that she need not look at what she saw in his face.

Martin might have shouted at her, let any of the ugly words that jumbled in his mouth come spilling out, or jumped up and snatched at her in a useless attempt to imprison her.

But with an effort of will he held himself still. When he could trust himself again he said very slowly, as if he had painstakingly learned the words in a strange language, 'I don't want to let you go. You're my wife. Their mother.'

Love. Dues.

'I don't know what to say.' He looked down at his fists, clenching and unclenching them, the knuckles white and then red. 'Just that I'm here, Annie. If you . . . when . . . if you do decide. I want you to think, that's all. Think what it means. Think quickly.'

All he could focus on now was getting away, out of this room, to hunch over the gaping hole that her words had left. *I don't know how to be without him.* He stood up awkwardly, almost falling. And then he went out, closing the door behind him.

Annie heard him going upstairs, and then his footsteps overhead, the door of the spare room closing against her. She sat staring ahead of her, breathless with the pain that she had caused to both of them. Then she drew up her knees and, with her head resting against them, she tried to do what he had asked her.

The two weeks were like a time out of somebody else's life. In the mornings when Annie woke up she had forgotten for a second or two and she felt warm and easy. But then the recollection came back and she had to climb up and out into the cold again, and live through a day that wasn't her own any more, until it was time to sleep again.

To live without it made her more vividly aware that friendship was truly what she had shared with Martin. Even Benjamin recognized it when it was no longer there. He came early one morning and stood in the bedroom door in his blue pyjamas, seeing Annie alone in the wide bed.

'Aren't you friends with Daddy any more?' he asked, and Annie couldn't answer him. She held out her arms instead, and even though he came she felt him holding himself a little away from her, as if he didn't know where to commit his loyalty.

That hurt her more than anything else had done.

And she carried her sadness with her to Steve, although she tried hard not to.

'I'm sorry,' she said. 'I told you at the beginning. Our happiness makes unhappiness everywhere else.'

Steve was gentle and firm. He sat beside her on his deep black sofa and put his arms around her. He made her talk and he listened and he held her until her frozen shell of anxiety and guilt began to melt. Then he took her into his bedroom and made her lie down beside him. He knew when to coax and when to be insistent, and he knew when to let Annie herself take the initiative. Her need for him surprised her. She sat astride him and the shock of pleasure as he drove upwards made her arch her body and then lean forwards, enclosing him more tightly, until their mouths met and they rolled over, locked together, driving one another further on, and then further still.

'You're very sexy, my Annie,' he told her.

'I know,' she said, unblushingly. 'You've shown me that.'

In the face of everything, still, they were happy in their short hours together. When they had finished making love they would get up and go out together. Steve took her to odd, offbeat places. They ate lunch at a Jewish restaurant in the East End, they went to a workshop production of a short, savagely funny, feminist play, and to an organ recital at a Wren church in the City. From the way that strangers stared at her in these places Annie knew that she looked unlike the other women. She was glowing and crackling and alive in a way that she had never expected that she would be again. She took the hours of happiness and held tenaciously on to them, because without them there was no justification for the coldness and blackness that spread through all the other hours like a disease.

Although they were quite different from the penniless days

that she had shared long ago with Matthew, her short outings with Steve often reminded her of them. She felt the same exhilaration, and the recklessness was all the more pronounced because of the weight of reason and responsibility that settled around her on the way home again.

And at other times, when she looked at Steve sitting across from her in a restaurant, or standing in the aisle of the Wren church reading the inscription on a marble slab, she could hardly believe that this handsome, faintly ruthless-looking man was anything to do with her at all. She would draw in her breath then, shivering, but Steve with his ability to read her thoughts would reach for her hand, and say something that drew her close to him again, and then the moment would be past. When it was time for Benjy to come home, or at the hour she had agreed with Audrey or whichever of his friends' mothers had invited him to play, Annie left Steve and went back to collect him.

The glow of happiness faded at once and the dull, enduring pain of being pulled in half took hold of her all over again.

In between the terrible shuttling to and fro, whenever she could, Annie went to see her mother. She was still at home in the old house, but she had grown so weak that she could hardly move from her bed to the wing chair in the corner of the living room next to the fire. Jim and Annie and a home help, with a visiting nurse, looked after her between them as best they could. Tibby still wanted to be dressed in her familiar heathery tweed skirts and woollen cardigans, and on most mornings Annie went to do it after she had taken the boys to school and nursery. The clothes when she took them out of the mahogany wardrobe or the tidy drawers still smelt of her mother's lavender scent, but they seemed huge when she slipped them over Tibby's brittle bones.

'The fit on this skirt is terrible,' Tibby would murmur as she pulled at a gaping waistband. 'It's a good one, too. They don't make clothes like they used to, darling. I'd like the pink cardigan with this. It's better, don't you think?'

As she helped her up and fastened her buttons, pinned the

loose folds of fabric and arranged her mother's thin hair, Annie found that she could hardly answer. Her mother had been the centre and the heart of this big house, and now it was as if a draught had blown her into a corner of it, depositing her in a chair like a cobweb or the dust she had battled against for so many years.

Annie settled her into her place. Tibby's hands on her arms looked almost transparent.

'Shall I turn you round today so that you can see into the garden?' she asked.

Tibby thought for a moment. Annie saw her glance at the photographs on the low table beside her. Tibby's wedding picture. Annie and her brother as children, Annie's own wedding, her brother's wife and children. Thomas and Benjamin, Tom with his top front teeth missing.

'Yes, I think so,' Tibby said.

Annie turned her chair and they looked through the French windows into the garden. It was the first week of April. Tibby's early daffodils were already falling, but the forsythia hedge behind them was a sheet of gold. Tulips in bud like green spears had come up in the half-moon beside the window, and the prunus showed the first delicate edges of pink blossom. Annie saw that the lawn needed mowing. It must have sprung up in the warm sunshine of March.

'I'll ask Martin to come and cut the grass for Jim,' she murmured.

Tibby nodded; but she didn't begin to talk about attending to her roses, as she would have done only a week or so ago. She looked at her flowers, and at the blaze of the resplendent hedge.

'I think the spring has always been the best time,' she said, almost to herself. 'I think I've always preferred the promise to the reality. Of summer, of course. The brighter colours, you know. Too bright, sometimes. Not like this pale green and gold.'

Go on, Annie implored her silently. Please, won't you talk about it to me? She wanted to kneel down in front of her mother and rest her head in her lap. Talk about the promise, and the reality, won't you? Because we haven't got very long, Tibby. We both know that we haven't, and there is such a lot to say.

She was suddenly overwhelmed by her own need to tell her mother everything.

Gently she asked her, 'How do you feel today?'

If Tibby could admit the truth. If they could just begin, she thought.

Tibby's back straightened in her chair. She didn't take her eyes off the gold of the garden, but she said, 'A little better, I think.'

And so they wouldn't admit that she was going to die, and that it might happen at any time, and that Tibby would be gone, leaving only the dust and the big house and the echoes of their talk about the roses.

Annie bent her head for a moment, so that Tibby would not see her sadness showing in her face. If that was how Tibby wanted it to be, of course Annie must let it be. She straightened up again and asked brightly, 'Can I bring anything in here before I go?'

'The magazine and the book from the table beside my bed, darling, if you wouldn't mind. Jim will be back from the shops soon.'

Jim always went out to buy the few things that they needed, every morning, at nine-fifteen exactly. As Annie walked back through the shadowy house she saw that the tallboys and the grandfather clock were dusty. But as Tibby had stopped worrying about her roses, she seemed to care less for her house now. She was withdrawing into herself, the battle lost. Had it been worth the fight at all? Annie thought savagely. Was anyone's fight worth it?

She gave her mother the book and the magazine, kissed the top of her head and fled blindly from the house.

At the end of the second week, Annie knew that she was lost.

Her bearings were gone, and she was groping through days that seemed increasingly to belong to someone who she didn't know or understand. To compensate for her sense of being adrift she held on as firmly as she could to the familiar, mechanical things. She ironed the clothes, concentrating fiercely on folding the shirts into neat, symmetrical piles. In the evenings Martin often didn't come home until very late, so Annie filled the hours by cooking casseroles for the freezer. She ladled the food into foil cartons and labelled and dated them in small, neat handwriting that looked quite unlike her own. But the little, domestic satisfaction that she usually gained from such things turned itself against Annie now. She thought bitterly that she was lining her family nest with food and clothes before abandoning it herself.

She caught herself wondering whether, after all, she might be just a little mad. School holiday time came, and the number of hours that she could find to spend with Steve dwindled almost to none.

'Do you think,' he had asked her on the telephone, 'I could meet your children soon?' She had stood looking across the kitchen at them until his voice in her ear had prompted her, 'Are you still there?'

'Yes. Yes, of course, you must. What shall we do?'

They had arranged it. It would be on Friday, for a hamburger lunch and then a trip to the cinema to see a film that Tom had been agitating about for weeks and weeks.

Annie put off from day to day the moment of telling the children about the expedition. She told herself that she would make it sound very casual, an almost impromptu adventure with a friend. Then Friday morning came. It was one of those days when Martin had got up and gone to work very early, and Tom and Benjy had hardly seen him. They had been asleep the night before when he came in.

'What shall we do today, Mum?' Thomas asked. He had cleared the breakfast dishes for her without protest, and he had spent a patient quarter of an hour doing Lego with Benjy while Annie swept the kitchen and hovered the living room. 'Can we ring Timothy and ask him to come round?'

Annie wound up the flex of the vacuum cleaner very carefully.

'I thought we might go on a trip today,' she said. 'We could go for a hamburger, and then to see that film of yours.'

Their eyes met over Benjamin's head. Annie saw the wariness at once. He's been waiting for something, she thought. He may not know what it is, or even that he is waiting and dreading something. But it's there, just the same. He can feel it in the house. See it in our faces.

'Just us?' Tom asked her.

'A friend of mine would like to come along too.' She tried to keep her voice steady and warm.

'Who?' The small voice was suspicious.

'His name is Steve.'

'We don't know him,' Tom said at once, with utter finality.

'Not yet,' Annie agreed. 'But I hope that you will like him.'

Thomas lowered his eyes. He turned back to the box of Lego and rummaged through it, making ostentatious noise.

'We should go quite soon, I think,' Annie continued. 'We'll have to go into town on the tube.'

Thomas sat back on his heels, but with his head still bent over his model. He turned it to and fro, looking carefully at it.

'I don't want to go,' he said.

Benjy's eyes went from one to the other. 'I don't want to go,' he echoed. 'Not at all.'

They had set themselves solidly against her, by instinct, closing their ranks against the stranger their mother tried to push forward as a friend. Annie was convinced that their refusal was absolute.

They're eight years and three years old, she tried to tell herself. You're adult, and their mother. You can persuade them. Bribe them, force them.

For Steve's sake? For her own? Not for their own, she was certain of that.

She went across and knelt beside Tom. 'Why don't you want to go?' she asked gently. 'You've been telling me for weeks that you must see this film.'

She had thought, not carefully enough, that their eagerness

for it would carry all of them through the first meeting. And after that, then it would be easier.

Thomas raised his eyes again, and the adult awareness in them made her feel cold.

What am I doing to my kids? she thought.

'I want to see the film with Dad,' he told her clearly. 'It's about space. Dad likes things like that.'

'Me too,' Benjamin said. 'I want to see the film with Dad.'

Annie took a breath, trying to smile. 'Okay,' she said. 'We'll leave the film for Dad. Shall we just go and have lunch with Steve?'

Thomas flung the Lego back into the box. His face went dull red, as it always did when he was upset. And then he shouted at her, 'I don't want to. I don't like Steve. I won't go. Benjy won't either.'

Annie was shaking. It wasn't any use insisting to Tom, *You don't know Steve.* He did, of course. From half-heard fragments of his parents' angry talk, from the unhappy silence of the house, and from his own fearful unconscious, Tom had made up his own picture of Steve. He knew the threat was close, and he had responded to it in the only way he knew.

As she knelt there Annie saw, with perfect clarity, how it would be.

There would be months, probably years, of times like this one. As she watched Thomas's red face and Benjamin's bewildered one she felt the pain of their divided loyalties, the sharpening of their premature awareness. There would be the ugly battles over their custody. Martin would fight her, lent strength by his bitterness, she was certain of that. She knew, as vividly as if she had already lived through them, what the bleak Sunday visits with the boys would be like, what they would be like for Martin, whichever of them won whichever portion of their children's lives.

Was her own happiness worth that? This strange, exotic happiness since the bomb, that seemed increasingly to belong to another woman altogether? What was Steve's happiness worth?

She saw his face, every line of it clear, and she knew that she loved him, and the hurt stabbed like a knife inside her.

At last she stood up, stiffly, with pain in her chest and across her shoulders.

'All right,' she said softly. 'That's all right. You needn't come, if you don't want to. I have to go, because I promised I would. I'll call Audrey, and ask her if she can come and look after you, just for a little while.'

The boys sat in silence while she telephoned.

'Audrey?' Annie said. 'I know I've asked you too many favours lately. This is the last, I promise.'

'You want me to come in to the boys?'

Audrey, Annie thought, with her grown-up daughters and her grandchildren, and her morose husband. Has Audrey got what she wants? Is she like Tibby? Annie's face felt hot, and her eyes were bright and hard.

'Just for an hour or two, this morning.'

'Of course I will, my love. I'd be glad to. Gets me out of the house, doesn't it?' While they waited for her, the three of them sat in a circle round the Lego box, pretending that they were playing together. It wasn't until he heard Audrey at the gate that Tom said hastily, anxiously, 'Is it all right, Mum?'

'I'll make it all right,' she promised him. *Whatever it costs.*

Audrey was in the hallway. 'Only me,' she called out to them, as she always did. Annie went over and put the kettle on. 'Hello, Audrey. Shall I make you a cup of tea before I go? It's kind of you to help out yet again.'

Audrey looked at her, shrewd under her perennial headscarf. 'You go on, love. Do what you like, while you still can.'

Annie turned away with the kettle heavy in her hand. 'This is the last time,' she whispered.

When Audrey was furnished with her tea in her special china cup and saucer, Annie put her coat on. She didn't stop to look at herself, and Audrey had to call after her, 'Your collar's all caught up at the back.' She came after her and straightened it, motherly. 'Are you all right, my pet?'

'Yes,' Annie said quickly. 'Yes, I'm fine.' From the doorway she looked at Benjy and Tom. They were absorbed in their game now. She had told them that she would make everything right, hadn't she?

'Bye,' she said. 'I'll be back as soon as I can.'

'Bye,' Thomas said absently, not looking up. Ben didn't make any response at all. Only Audrey said again, 'You do what you want, Annie. Don't worry about us.'

She almost laughed at that. The sound of it, beginning in her head, was hideous.

Annie had no memory of how she reached Steve's flat. She was aware that it took a long time, and that she was afraid that her resolve would desert her. But at last she was riding up in the mirrored lift. She stared down at her feet rather than confront her own reflection.

When he opened the door she looked straight into his eyes.

'I can't do it,' Annie said.

He took her arm, led her inside and closed the door. The black sofa in front of her was too close, too comfortable. Annie broke awkwardly away and sat on an upright chair.

'What can't you do?' Steve asked her.

Nothing, she wanted to say. There's nothing I can't do, so long as I'm with you. Her vacillating spirit shamed her. Outside, a long way beneath the windows, Annie could hear the traffic. The sound was incongruous high up in the enclosed room.

'I can't leave them,' Annie said. The words hurt, as if they were pulled out of her like splinters.

Steve turned his face away. After a moment he stood up and went to the window. He looked at the skeins of cars and taxis down below.

'Why now, Annie? Why have you decided this now?' His voice was cold with disappointment. Annie thought of the two weeks that had just gone by, and the weeks before that, all the way back to Christmas. It wasn't a decision made just this morning, arbitrary, as Steve must see it. It was simply, at last, the recognition of the bald truth that had confronted her always.

'I am a coward,' she whispered.

Steve snapped round to face her then. His black eyebrows were drawn together in anger with her.

'You are nothing of the kind. Don't use that as an excuse.'

She saw his hurt, and it made her own seem trivial.

'I'll tell you what happened,' she said. 'The hamburger lunch and film that we'd planned, remember? I offered them to my kids this morning. As casually, lightly as I could. And their faces closed up. They knew at once that here was the threat to them. You and me. Do you know what Thomas said?'

Steve listened motionless as she told him.

Annie said, 'And I knew then that I couldn't do it. I couldn't even begin. Whether it's weakness or cowardice, Steve, I couldn't contemplate it being like that, for years, perhaps for ever, until they are grown up.' Her smile twisted. 'If it hadn't been *now*. If it had been in ten years' time. Or ten years ago.'

Except that it had happened ten years ago, and she had taken the easy option then. *I don't deserve even as much as I have got*, Annie thought sadly.

'Do you think your children will appreciate that so much has been sacrificed for them?'

She smiled again, crookedly. No one with children of his own, no one who understood the everyday sacrifices of parenthood, would have asked that. 'I don't suppose so.'

'And Martin?'

Annie thought. 'Martin and I were friends. Perhaps we can put some of that back together, for the kids.'

Steve made a last attempt. He put aside all the angry complex of feelings and he told her the truth.

'I love you, Annie. You haven't given me a chance.'

She wanted to run to him. She ached to lay her head against his heart, to rest in him and to acknowledge the truth. But Annie held her head up. Now that she had come so far, she couldn't waver any more.

'I love you too. There never was a chance for us.'

They looked at one another then, and they were drawn

helplessly across the room. Annie put her hands out and he took them in his. She knew the touch of them in every mood now, and he seemed suddenly so physically warm and real that the idea of being without him was impossible. Annie had promised herself that she would leave before she started to cry, but the tears came now and she could do nothing about them.

She looked up at Steve through the heat of them and she said, uselessly, 'I'm sorry. I would give anything for it to be different.'

With a sudden, fierce gesture Steve rubbed the tears off her cheek with the palm of his hand and kissed the red mark that was left. He kissed her eyelids, and the corners of her eyes and mouth, and then her mouth itself. For a moment, a long moment that threatened to tear her all over again, Annie succumbed. She felt that after all there was a possibility, a possibility within her reach. But then it was gone again, and she was left to confront the same truth.

She felt a sob gathering inside her but she forced it down again.

'I've got to go home now,' she said. 'Tom and Benjy are . . . waiting for me.'

Steve's arms dropped heavily to his sides. 'Don't let me keep you from them.'

She couldn't blame him for the bitterness, Annie thought. She turned, uncertainly, and went to the door. She held on to the handle for a moment with her head bent, on the point of turning to him again. She felt that he was waiting and she told herself, *No. Do it quickly now.* She opened the door and closed it again behind her. And then she was alone in the empty corridor.

Steve stood unmoving for a moment, watching the door. He could still see her quite clearly, as clearly as his reason told him that she was really gone. At last he shook his head, painfully, as if he were trying to clear it. He went to the window and leaned his forehead against the glass. It reminded him of the hospital, and the day room windows high above the side street.

'Annie?' he said aloud.

He watched until he saw her come out into the street, her

shoulders shrugged defensively into her coat. She crossed the busy road, and then she was swallowed up into the crowd.

He didn't know how long he stood there, watching the oblivious surge of people. The telephone rang on the black table and he picked it up.

'I'm sorry to bother you at home, Steve. Bob needs a couple of words about Boneys. Can I put him through?'

It was Bob Jefferies' secretary. Steve frowned, looking at his table. It was littered with story-boards, reports and notes. Dogfood, he thought.

'Put him on, Sandra. I'm not busy.'

Steve went through the problem about the pet-food film with his partner, his mind working, just like it always did. When Bob had run off Steve held on to the receiver, weighing it, like a weapon. Then he stabbed out another number. His own secretary answered.

'Jenny? I'm going to be in full-time again from Monday. I've had enough time off. Fix up what needs to be done, will you?'

Jenny made a silent face across the office at the word-processor operator. She knew that tone of Steve's.

'Yes, of course. There are some messages for you. Do you want them now?'

'What messages?'

Even though it was impossible, Steve hoped for a brief moment. Jenny recited them, ordinary, routine requests and reminders. Then she added, 'Vicky Shaw has called once or twice. She rang again this morning, just to see if you were in.'

It took Steve a second to remember, it seemed so long ago. He frowned again, with the sense of something unwelcome, and then he looked around at the grey flat. Through the open bedroom door he could just see the corner of the bed.

He thought of Annie as she had been in bed, laughing, with her mouth close to his. With her eyes closed, crying out. Asleep, with her hair spread out over his arm. He understood, then, that she was gone. With the understanding he hated the empty flat and the silence, and he was afraid of his solitude.

'Steve?'

'Yeah.' He was gathering up the sheaves of paper with his free hand, cramming them into his expensive black briefcase. 'Listen, Jenny, if Vicky calls again tell her that I'm on my way in to the office now. I'll be ringing her later this afternoon. See you in thirty minutes.'

Jenny hung up. 'Here we go,' she sighed to the word-processor girl.

Steve finished packing up his work. He thought of his car down in the underground car park, the familiar drive, his desk in the urban-chic company office. The work would be waiting for him. Boneys, fruit-juice, washing powder, whatever it was that needed to be shown and sold. Lunch, dinner with Vicky, bed and sleep and work again. And so it would go on, just the same. As if nothing had changed, instead of everything.

Steve picked up his loaded briefcase.

'There never was a chance for us?' he echoed aloud. 'You're wrong, Annie. We had all the chances that there could be.'

The phone rang again. 'I'm on my way,' he shouted at it. 'What more do you want?'

He went out of the flat and left it, still ringing.

Annie told Martin.

'I went to see Steve today.'

She was clearing the plates from the pine table after dinner and stacking them on the draining board. Martin would wash them up after they had watched the television news. How odd it was, she thought. They had reached the remotest point of their life together, so far apart that she didn't know how they would come back again. But they still went padding through the familiar routines, almost silent, barely looking at each other. Like the heavy, neutered tomcats next door. The comparison made Annie want to laugh, incongruously, but she turned from the sink and saw Martin watching her. He looked wary, and exhausted. She went to him then, and put her hand on his arm.

'I . . . told him that I was going to stay here. With you and the boys. I didn't want to go, because . . . I saw how it would be.' How inadequate the words were. 'I'm sorry.'

Martin nodded.

He should have felt a rush of relief, a sense of the oppressive weight that had darkened the house lifting, to let in the light and air. But he felt nothing. He looked at Annie, trying to see behind her face, knowing that he couldn't because he hadn't been able to for so many weeks.

'It doesn't matter who was right,' he said at last. 'Can you live with it, Annie?'

'Yes,' she answered him, because she had to. 'I can live with it.'

And that was all they said.

They were old enough, and they understood one another well enough, Annie reflected, not to expect there to be anything more. There would be no reconciliation in a shower of coloured light. Instead there would be the small tokens of renewal, scraps, cautiously offered one by one. In time they would be stitched up again into a serviceable patchwork, and that was as much as they could hope for.

That night Martin came back and slept beside her. It would take time, of course, before he put his arms round her again. That first night Annie lay quietly on her side of the bed, trying to take simple comfort from the warmth of him next to her. She made herself suppress the voice inside her that cried out for Steve.

But the truth was, as Annie had been half-afraid when she had answered Martin, that she couldn't live with it. She had made her decision as honourably as she could, and she did her best to keep to it. But the days began to pile up into weeks, and Annie felt that she was building a house without windows. It was clean and polished, and there was food on the table and clean clothes in the chests, but there was no light in it anywhere. It was claustrophobic; the air tasted as if she had breathed it in and out a dozen times, just as she had done the things that she was doing a hundred or a thousand times before. She would have done them gladly if she had felt that their repetition was taking her anywhere – but she was uncertain that she would ever draw close to her husband, or that Martin would ever let her come any nearer. They were polite, and considerate, but they were not partners, or friends.

And Annie missed Steve. She missed him every day, in all the intervals of it. She heard the cadences of his voice in the radio-announcer's, she glimpsed his head in a crowd and walked faster to keep him in sight, and then suffered the disappointment when the stranger turned and she saw that he was nothing like Steve at all. She found herself thinking about him as she carried baskets of wet washing out to peg on the clothes line, and as she made the plodding walk with Benjy to pick up Tom from afternoon school. She wondered whether Steve thought about her too.

Two or three times, despising herself for her capitulation, she picked up the telephone and dialled his number. The first time, when Martin was away for a two-day business trip, she sat at her kitchen table for an hour, looking at the telephone, before she went to it. She picked out the number with a clumsy finger and listened to the ringing in her ear. There were only two rings, not long enough for him to have reached the phone . . . there was a click, and Annie heard his voice, and there was a painful beat of pleasure before she realized that it was only a recorded message. He repeated the number, and said his name. He sounded so close, and yet she couldn't reach him.

With her heart thumping guiltily, Annie listened to the conversational message. *I'm sorry, I can't take your call. If you'll leave your name and number.* After the tone, she hung up. She went back to her place and sat down, her hands loose in her lap, staring into nothing.

A week went by, and she called again. The message was the same, and it gave her the same eerie feeling of closeness.

I must be mad, she thought. *What comfort is there in listening to his recorded voice?* But there was a kind of comfort, and she rang again, a third time, as guilty and as furtive as an addict.

April went, and May, and June came. The early roses came

into bud and then flowered. Tibby was still alive, but she couldn't see them.

She had been taken into the hospice again, and Annie knew that she wouldn't be coming home. But for her mother's sake she still went regularly to the old house, to dust the polished furniture and fill the vases and wind up the mantelpiece clocks. Annie didn't think that her father would do it. He had retreated from the house, apparently in relief. He lived in the kitchen, strewing it with spent matches from his pipe. It was Annie who cut the roses and brought them in to arrange in Tibby's silver bowls. She listened to the echo of her own footsteps on the parquet, and remembered the house as it had been when she was a child. She had had the same memories after the bomb. Herself, in a green dress with white ribbons in her hair, running to Tibby. She had hurt herself, and her mother had taken her out of the sun and into the shadowy living room to comfort her.

As she stood in the squares of light that the sun spilt on the wooden floor Annie had a renewed sense of time, ribbons of continuity linking Tibby and her husband, Martin and herself, Annie's children, children's children. In the silent house, with the memories of her own childhood close to her, it was the thought of the boys that comforted her. She could hear them calling, as she had heard them in the stifling darkness of the bomb wreckage.

Mum, look at me.

Running in the garden, at home. As she had run in this garden, calling out to Tibby.

Love for all of them warmed her, family love, and all the complicated knots of anxiety, and pride, and relief that they were somehow still together, caught at her and held her. With the sound of their voices in her head Annie remembered the happiness of chains of ordinary days that she had shared with her sons, all the way to yesterday, the last link in the chain.

She had taken them to Hampstead Heath, to the little travelling funfair that arrived two or three times a year and spread its gaudy, temporary camp over a bare patch of hill. For years they had been visiting it whenever it appeared, usually with Martin too, but yesterday he had claimed some drawings to finish and so Annie had driven the boys over on her own. She had felt the dead weight of loneliness as she negotiated the traffic, but when they had left the car behind and the boys were scrambling ahead of her Annie's spirits lifted like the strings of flags flying from the sideshow tents. They loved the fair, all of them.

Annie caught up with the boys who were poised breathlessly at the outer ring of caravans and generators and pulsing machines.

'What can we go on, Mum?'

She took one hand in each of hers and swung them round. 'Everything.'

They plunged into the crowds and noise together. The tinny music and the barkers' shouts, the smell of candyfloss and frying onions and the whirl of colours swallowed the three of them effortlessly. Within the circle of the fair Annie felt suddenly no older than Thomas and Ben. The fierce pleasure of childhood excitement touched her, and it was intensified by the added, subtle pleasure of her adult capacity to indulge her children, and share their indulgence.

With Tom pulling ahead they stumbled to the giant Waltzers at the centre of the fairground. The rumble of cars spinning on the wooden track drowned out even the blaring music. The riders screamed joyfully from their seats as they were swept past.

Annie clutched at responsibility for long enough to shout to Tom, 'Benjy's not old enough for this!'

Tom turned for a second, his hands on his hips, the sudden, living replica of his father. 'He *is*. We can look after him. One on each side.'

'I am old enough,' said Benjy stoutly.

'All right, then.' They beamed at one another, colluding.

The huge machine was winding down and the riders' faces, laughing, sprang out of the blur as the cars swung slower up and down the undulating slopes. As soon as an empty car rolled past, Thomas was off up the steps. He squirmed inside it and fended off the crowds who swarmed around it.

'No, this is ours. Come on, Mum, Benjy.' They ran up the steep steps after him, hand in hand, and jumped into the padded tub. Annie wedged Benjy tightly between Tom and herself and drew down the chrome hoop for them to hold on to.

'Here we go,' Tom yelled, leaning with the car as it began to turn to spin it faster.

Faster, and then faster again, and then to the point where centrifugal force pressed them helplessly against the chair back and tore the shouts from their throats. Annie drew her arm tighter around them, feeling their thin shoulders rigid with delighted fear. Benjy's face was three amazed circles, and Tom's smile was pinned right across his face. They spun faster and the world blurred into a solid wall, and the boy who took their money came balancing along the spinning edge and whirled their car faster on its axis, grinning at Annie and then pursing his lips to whistle as the wind blew her skirt up over her thighs.

'*Oh boy.*' Thomas was shouting with joy and Benjy managed a faint, tiny echo.

Hold on to them, Annie thought. *Hold on. Forever.*

And then they were slowing down again, gasping and laughing, thrilled with their daring as the world resolved itself again into its separate parts.

'Wasn't it great?' Thomas demanded and Benjy screamed, 'Wasn't I brave?'

'Oh, it was,' Annie said weakly. 'And you were, both of you. How could I have gone on that without you?'

They struggled off with rubber legs, the ground's immobility strange under their feet.

'What now?' asked Thomas.

Seeing his face, Annie wanted to take hold of his delight and keep it, so that it could never fade. So that nothing would fade ever again. But she couldn't do any more than put her hand on his shoulder, just for a moment, to link herself to him.

'Something gentle,' she pleaded.

'I know the one you like,' he said triumphantly. He took her hand now, and stretched out the other to Ben. 'Come on. Don't anyone get lost.'

He threaded them through the crowds to the huge mirrored roundabout whose steam organ ground out a pleasing, wheezy waltz. Annie looked up at it. The ornate lettering around the canopy spelled out, as it slowly revolved, *The Prancers. H.W. Peacock's Pride.*

'The hobby horses,' she murmured. 'I do like the hobby horses best.'

'They're pretty slow,' sniffed Thomas. But he enjoyed the ride, whooping from his horse's slippery back and hanging on to the gilded barley-sugar pole, as much as Annie and Ben did.

After the hobby horses they rode under the musty green hood of the Caterpillar, and on the Dodgems with their blue sparks and thundering crashes, and on the Octopus, and all the others even down to the toddlers' roundabouts at the outer edges of the magic circle where Benjy swooped on the fire engine and rang the bell furiously as he trundled around, while Thomas squeezed himself into a racing car or helicopter and scowled at Annie every time he came past.

When they had ridden every roundabout they plunged into the sideshows, from the bleeping electronic games that all three of them adored, to the tattered old stalls where Annie and Tom vied with each other to throw darts at wobbly boards or shoot the pingpong balls off nodding ducks. Benjy was furiously partisan, pulling at Annie's arm and shouting, 'Come on, Mummy. Why don't you win?'

Annie laughed and threw down her twisted rifle.

'It's no good, Ben. I'm not nearly as good as Thomas is.'

'Here you are, baby,' Tom snorted, thrusting the orange fur teddy bear that he had won at Benjy. 'Is this what you wanted?'

'I just wanted Mum to win,' Benjy retorted. 'I don't want her to be sad.'

'I won't be sad,' she promised him. The outside reached in,

just for a moment, between the caravans and flags. 'I won't be sad. Let's go and see the funny mirrors.'

They lined up in the narrow booth and paraded to and fro in front of the distorting mirrors. The images of the three of them leapt back and forth too, telescoping from spindly giants to squat barrels with grinning turnip faces.

The boys roared and gurgled with laugher, clutching at one another for support. 'Look at Mum! Look at her legs!'

'And her teeth. Like an old horse's.'

Annie laughed much more at their abandoned enjoyment than at the gaping figures. Adults never laugh like this, like children do, she thought. Not giving themselves up to it.

In the end she had to pull them away from the mirrors to make room for the press of people coming in behind them. She hauled them out into the sunshine, blinking and still snorting with laughter.

'Are you hungry?'

'I'm *so* hungry.'

'And me.'

They picnicked on hot dogs oozing with fried onions and ketchup, and Annie bought them huge puffballs of candyfloss that collapsed in sticky pink ridges over their beaming faces.

'You're letting us have all the bad things, Ma.'

'Just for today,' she said severely.

When they had finished the repellent meal they turned to her again.

'Is it time for the Big Wheel now?'

By unspoken agreement, they had saved it until last. They crossed the trampled grass now and joined the queue in its spidery shadow. Benjy tilted his head backwards to peer up at the height of it.

'I was too little last time.'

Annie crouched beside him, straightening his jacket, an excuse to hold on to him.

'You're big enough now. After the Waltzers you're big enough for anything.'

They grew so quickly. They were here and now, together. Wasn't that enough? As they inched forward in the queue the cold fingers from outside reached in to clutch at Annie. She tried to shake them off, and hold on to the day's hermetic happiness.

It was enough, because it would have to be.

At last their turn came. The attendant let them in through the little metal gate and they climbed into the little swinging car, the boys on either side of Annie. The safety bar was latched into place and the wheel turned, sweeping them upwards and backwards. As they soared up they felt the wind in their faces, scented with grass and woodsmoke up here, above the packed crowds and the hot-dog stalls. When they reached the highest point the wheel stopped turning and they hung in the stillness, rocking in windy, empty space. Ben gave a little squeak of fear and burrowed against her, and Annie held her arm around him, hiding his eyes with her hand. But Tom leaned forward, his face turning sombre.

Beneath them spread all the tumult of the fairground, suddenly dwarfed. Beyond was the undulating green of treetops, rolling downhill, and the houses edging the heath, a jumble of slate and stone. London stretched out beyond that, pale blue and grey and ochre.

'It's beautiful,' Tom said.

Annie felt tears in her eyes, and ducked her head. She put her arm round him and drew him close to her.

'It is,' she whispered. 'It's very beautiful.'

They sat silent in the rocking chair, and looked at it. In that moment of stillness Annie felt that she loved her children more than she had ever done before.

And then the wheel jerked and began to turn again, sweeping them down towards the ground.

After the ride they stood in the shadow of the wheel again.

'What shall we do now?'

Annie took out her purse. She opened it and showed them the recesses. 'Look. We've spent all the money. I've got just enough to buy you a balloon each to take home.'

They peered into the purse, needing to be convinced. Then they sighed with reluctant satisfaction. They agreed with the logic of staying until every penny was spent, and then of having to go home. On the way out of the noisy, joyful circle they chose a pair of red and silver helium balloons, decorated with Superman for Tom and Spiderman for Benjy. And then with the balloons tugging and twisting above them they plodded back down the hill to the car.

When they were inside it, insulated from the people streaming by, Tom turned to Annie.

'That was so good,' he said simply. 'I can't think of anyone else's Mum who would have gone on everything, like you. Well, I suppose they might have done. But they wouldn't have *enjoyed* it, like you did.'

'I did enjoy it,' Annie said. 'Thank you.'

Benjy scrambled forward and laid his face briefly against her neck, stickily, his own form of thanks.

Then Annie started the car up and turned towards home. Martin would be waiting, and the ache of Steve's absence would be waiting for her too.

It was not many days after the funfair that Tibby's doctor took Annie and her father aside. 'If you were going to ask her son to come home and see her,' he said, 'I think it should be done quite soon.'

Annie's brother was working as an engineer in the Middle East. Annie and Jim put through the call at once, as they had agreed with Phillip that they would.

'I'll be home within forty-eight hours,' Phillip said.

Tibby lay in her hospice room, surrounded by flowers that Annie brought in from her garden.

'There must be a fine show this year,' she said politely, when Annie had arranged them.

Annie sat by the bed, watching her mother's transparent face. Tibby was usually awake, but she rarely spoke. When she did speak, it was about small things; the doctors or one of the other patients, or the food they brought her that she couldn't eat. She didn't even talk about her grandchildren any more. Annie knew that her mother's world had shrunk to the dimensions of her hospital bed.

It was hard for Tibby to be dignified under such circumstances, even though the staff who looked after her did all that was possible to control her pain. But she clung tenaciously to the silence that she had maintained about her illness. She didn't talk any more about getting better, but she wouldn't admit the fact of approaching death either. In the beginning Annie had seen the refusal as a kind of graceful courage. But as the months had passed her frustration had grown. She felt the silence now like a cold glass wall between her mother and herself.

She reached for Tibby's hand and held it. It felt as dry and weightless as a dead leaf. As she sat in the quiet, flower-scented room Annie was realizing that she didn't want her mother to die without acknowledging the truth, even if it was only by a word. As if to acknowledge it would be to tell her daughter, *It's all right. I know what's happening to me. I can bear it, and so can you.*

I'm just like Benjy and Tom, Annie thought. I want my mother's reassurance, even now that she's dying.

Love, dues. The ribbons of continuity, again and again.

Annie glanced up and saw that Tibby was looking sideways at her. Her glance was clear, appraising, full of her mother's own intelligence and understanding.

Annie thought briefly, *At last.*

But then Tibby's head fell back against her pillows. 'I'm tired,' she said. 'I think I'll go to sleep now, darling.'

Annie stood up and leant over to kiss her cheek. 'I'll come in again at the same time tomorrow,' she promised, as she always did.

Phillip arrived thirty-six hours later. Annie met him at Heathrow, and drove him straight to the hospice.

'They don't know how much longer,' she told him. 'I'm glad you're here, Phil.'

She glanced at him as she drove. Phillip was fair, like her, but he was losing his hair and his skin was reddened by the sun. He looked exactly what he was, a successful engineer just back from overseas. Annie and her brother had never been close, even as children. Phillip had always been the brisk, practical one, while Annie was slow and dreamy. He had been his father's son, always, while Annie and her mother had shared a friendship, she understood now, that had its roots in their strong similarity.

But she was genuinely glad and relieved to see Phillip now. She felt some of the weight of her anxiety shifting on to the shoulders of his lightweight suit.

The family bond, she thought wryly. Always there.

When she stopped at a red light Phillip put his arm round her.

'I'm sorry I haven't been here. Are you all right, Anne? You don't look as though you've recovered properly yourself.'

The car rolled forward again.

'How could you be here? There would have been nothing you could do, anyway. And I'm fine, thanks.'

'It hasn't been much of a year for you, has it?'

Annie watched the road intently. 'It has had its ups and downs.'

There was nothing else she could say to Phillip, however searchingly he stared at her. Not to this broad, red-faced man who had stepped briefly out of an unknown world, even if he was her brother.

They reached the hospice, and went upstairs to Tibby's room. Jim had been sitting by her bed, and he stood up now and hugged his son. Tibby opened her eyes.

'Hello, Mum,' Phillip said. 'I've got some leave, so here I am.'

Tibby looked at him, unmoving. For an instant Annie glimpsed the same clear awareness in her face, and it heartened her. Then her mother smiled faintly, and lifted her shrunken hand.

'Hello, darling. Come and sit here by me.'

Annie watched Phillip sit down, and take hold of Tibby's hand.

Her sense of relief intensified, making her feel light, almost weightless. Of course Tibby knew that she was dying. Her way of confronting it was natural, for Tibby. Admiration of her mother's bravery blazed up inside Annie.

'I'll call in later,' she whispered, and she left Tibby with her husband and son.

It was early evening when she drove back again and the houses and shops and parks glowed in the rich, buttery sunlight. Annie parked her car in the hospice visitors' park and walked up the steps past tubs of shimmering violet and blue and white petunias.

Tibby's room was shadowy behind drawn curtains. Annie thought at first that her mother was asleep, but she turned her head at the click of the door.

'Did I wake you?' Annie murmured.

Tibby shook her head. 'No. I was thinking. Remembering things. I'm very good at remembering now. All kinds of things that I thought I had forgotten for ever.'

Annie smiled at her. She knew just how it was. The fragments of confetti, precious fragments.

'Shall I open the curtains a little?' she asked. 'The light outside is beautiful.'

Tibby shook her head. 'It's comfortable like this.'

Tibby didn't want to see the light any more, Annie knew that. Her world had shrunk to the bed, and the faces around it. She nodded, with the tears behind her eyes, and for a moment they were quiet in the dim room.

Then Tibby said, 'Thank you for calling Phillip home.' Her eyes had been half-closed but they opened wide now, piercing Annie. 'I know what it means.' She smiled, and then she added, as if Annie were a child again, and she was comforting her after a childish misunderstanding, very softly, 'It's all right.'

The mixture of pain, and relief, and love that flooded through Annie was almost too much for her. She sat with her head bent, holding Tibby's hand folded between her own. They were silent again. Annie thought that Tibby was pursuing her own memories, piecing together the confetti pictures as she had done herself with Steve.

But Tibby said suddenly, in a clear voice that startled her, 'Is it something between you and Martin? Is that why you are unhappy?'

Denials, placatory phrases and soothing half-truths followed one another through Annie's mind. She had opened her mouth to say, *Of course not, we're very happy*, but she raised her head and met her mother's eyes.

I was the one who wanted the truth, she thought.

'I fell in love with someone else,' she said simply. 'A stranger.'

'When?'

'After the bomb. We were there together.'

Tibby nodded. 'I guessed that,' she said. The maternal intuition took Annie back to girlhood all over again. She tightened her fingers on her mother's. *Don't go, Tibby. I'll miss you too much.*

'What are you going to do?'

Annie looked at her hopelessly. 'Nothing. What is there to do?'

Suddenly she could see how bright Tibby's eyes were in the dimness. The corners of her mouth drew down, an economical gesture of impatience, disappointment, all that she had the strength for. Annie knew that she had given the wrong answer.

There was a long, long pause before Tibby spoke again. 'I did nothing,' she said. 'Don't make the same mistakes. *Don't.*' The last word was no more than a soft, exhaled breath. The confession hurt her. Tibby closed her eyes, exhausted.

Annie saw it all, the sharp outlines of the story, even though she would never know the details. Tibby and Jim had failed each other somehow, in the course of the years. Perhaps there had been another man. Perhaps a path of a different kind had offered itself. Annie remembered her mother's wedding picture, with Tibby in her little tilted hat, her lips vividly painted. Whatever had happened, the two of them had stayed together. For her own sake, perhaps, and Phillip's. Tibby had taken on the protection of the house and the big corner garden, and Jim the routines that commanded his days.

Annie felt the sadness of it, drifting and settling, as silent and as endless as the dust on her mother's furniture. What reason was there?

Don't make the same mistakes.

But no one's mistakes could be the same. They were all different, and the permutations of their mistakes stretched on into infinity.

Annie lifted her mother's hand, feeling the bones move under the skin. Some things were right. So many of Tibby's. Those were the ones to hold on to.

'You've got us,' she whispered. 'I love you, Tibby.'

Tibby smiled, without opening her eyes. Her head was heavy against the pillow.

'I know,' she said.

Annie stayed with her until she was sure that she was asleep. Then she laid her hand gently back on the covers and went out into the light again. The brightness made her blink and she stood for a moment on the steps, watching the intensity of it on the frilled trumpets of the petunias. Then Annie climbed into her car and drove back through the streets to Martin, and the boys who were waiting for her under the rucked-up shelter of their bedcovers.

Tibby died the same night, peacefully, in her sleep.

She left no will, other than the joint one she had drawn up with her husband years ago, for Annie and Phillip's benefit. There were no instructions about her funeral. Annie was sure that her mother would have preferred to be buried, but she said nothing when Jim and Phillip agreed on cremation.

'That seems sensible,' Phillip said briskly and Annie had turned away with her grief, unable to comprehend how anything connected with her mother's death could be described as sensible.

The arrangements were made, and Tibby was cremated after

307

a brief service in an ugly, modern chapel. The curtains that parted for the coffin to glide through reminded Annie of the thick velvet ones at a pantomime. She wanted to laugh, and cry, but she went on standing stiffly beside Martin and the organ played treacly music over their heads.

Afterwards, they filed out into the overpowering sunshine.

With Jim and Phillip, Annie had made arrangements for Tibby's family and friends to come back to the old house after the ceremony. Looking backwards, Annie saw the little line of cars draw out after Martin's. The sun glinted cheerfully off chrome and glass, sharp in her eyes, until she turned her head again. Jim sat in the front of the car with Martin, and Phillip was beside Annie. She felt the vacuum that Tibby had left so profoundly that she wanted to shout out, 'Wait! We've left her behind. Turn round, Martin.'

When they reached the house Martin parked a little way from it to make space for the following cars. In a sombre line the four of them walked towards the gate. As they reached it Jim looked up at the gables of the house.

'I'm going to put it on the market,' he said.

The green-painted gate swung inwards, with the same creak that had welcomed Annie home from school.

'Probably the best thing,' Phillip said. 'It's far too big, now.'

They went on towards the front door, but Annie stood still. Behind her she could hear the other cars drawing up, and muted, respectful voices. She looked at the front door-knocker that Tibby used to brass-polish, and at the windows, veiled with midsummer dust now, that she used to insist on cleaning herself.

It's only a house, she thought.

But it was more, too. It was Tibby's elaborate, respectable shrine to a family life that had long ago ebbed out of it. It was, in the end, her reason for being, and now it would be sold and the new owners would smile at the outmoded décor. As she had known that they would. As she stood in the sunshine amidst the scent of roses Annie felt the lustreless pall of compromise and disappointment, her own as well as her parents', heavy around her.

Martin had waited at the gate, and now he came and put his hand under her arm. 'It isn't the same house without Tibby,' he tried to comfort her.

'I know,' Annie said. After a moment she whispered, 'It's a waste, isn't it? A terrible waste.'

They went on inside.

Annie did what was expected of her, just as her mother would have done. She greeted her mother's friends, and exchanged sympathies with them. She made sure that they were helped to food from the cold buffet, and she poured out glasses of white wine and handed them around. And then, when there was a brief lull, she went up the stairs to her mother's old bedroom.

She sat down on her bed, and the smooth, pale expanse of the bedcover crumpled up at once beneath her. Annie stood up again and went to the wardrobe, opening the mirrored doors to look in at her mother's clothes, neatly lined up on their padded hangers. She turned again and went to the dressing table, where Tibby's old-fashioned glass scent bottles with their braid-covered rubber bulbs stood in exact shining circles in the film of dust.

As she looked down at the rings the voice, insistent in Annie's head, grew louder and louder. Suddenly, it took possession of her.

Steve. Steve.

She put the scent bottle down and went to the telephone that stood on the table beside Tibby's bed. She dialled his number and listened to the message once more and the warmth that he had stirred in her leapt up all over again. This time, she left her own message.

It was earlier than his usual time when Steve reached home. He had endured a lunch with an agency man he detested, and he had drunk twice as much as he wanted in order to pass the time. He had sat through a meeting afterwards in a stuffy room while the sun edged past the blinds, and the day had left him with a dull headache and a sour, metallic taste in his mouth.

The flat looked bare and neglected when he came in. He

dropped his jacket in a heap on the black sofa and went into the kitchen to make himself another drink. Then, with the full whisky tumbler in his hand, he came back to his desk and flipped the keys on the answering machine.

It was there.

The first time he heard her voice, he wasn't sure that he hadn't imagined it. He had done so, before, more than once, in all the time that he had waited. Now, lately, he had stopped waiting. Annie had gone, of course.

He pressed the buttons to hear it again. But she hadn't gone. She was here, talking to him, vividly and unbearably close, out of the little spool of tape.

'It's Annie,' she said. There was a pause and he saw her, quite clearly, the light and shade on the planes of her face. The words came quickly. 'I want to see you. It's not too late, is it? Say it isn't too late.'

That was all.

Steve closed his eyes. The whisky was malty and cold on his tongue. At last he smiled. It was a painful, crooked smile, but Steve didn't hesitate. He reached for the telephone and slowly, carefully, picked out the remembered digits.

And then she was there. As soon as he heard her voice, he loved her as much again.

'Thank you for ringing,' she said softly.

'What's happened, Annie?'

'My mother died last week.'

'I'm sorry.'

Annie turned her back to the kitchen and leant her forehead against the wall.

'It isn't that,' she said. 'Steve, it wasn't finished, was it? The way that we left one another . . .'

'No,' he answered evenly, 'it isn't finished.'

'I want to see you again.'

Steve saw the sticky rings that the whisky glasses had left on the tops of his tables, and at the corner of the unmade bed visible past the open bedroom door.

'I'm going away for a few days. Will you come with me?'

He could feel the happiness that jumped inside her because it matched his own, regardless.

Without a second's pause she answered. 'Yes. Oh yes, I'll come.'

Martin and the boys were in the garden. Annie saw them through the bathroom window as she took her jars of cream and cosmetics off the shelves and put them in her sponge bag. With the bag weighing heavy in her hand she stood by the window, watching them. The slats of the lowered blinds were like bars, cutting her off from them. She felt hard and dry inside her skin, and her heart thumped against her ribs. She turned away abruptly, so that she couldn't see the boys' heads and the line of Martin's shoulders.

She had told Martin on the same evening that she had spoken to Steve. The boys were in bed, and the house was quiet, almost as if it were waiting for something. She had let the words spill out, knowing that there was no softening them. Martin had sat for a moment with his head bent, and then he had looked up into her face. She saw that he was neither surprised nor angry, and suddenly she had wanted to crumple down against him and bury her head in his arms. But she held herself rigid, stiffened by the thought that she had made all this pain for both of them.

'Will you be coming back?' he asked her at last. Annie realized that in the panicky flood of longing she had barely thought beyond getting to Steve. It was impossible to think of going, impossible to think of coming back.

What am I doing?

'I don't know. Yes. I don't know.'

'When are you going?'

She told him and he nodded, almost abstracted.

'If you do come back, we'll be here. The boys and me.'

Annie had murmured something then, with the sobs choking her throat, and she had turned and run from the room.

311

That was all, until now, when she was picking her belongings out of the family jumble and putting them one by one into her suitcase.

What am I doing?

She piled in the last things haphazardly and snapped the locks. It was time to go. Steve would be waiting for her. Annie went slowly down the stairs, carrying her bag. She looked at the line of pictures on the wall, and put up her free hand automatically to straighten one that was crooked. She left the suitcase standing by the front door and went through the kitchen and out into the garden. Their three faces turned to her as she walked across the grass. They were so quiet, waiting.

Benjy moved first. He ran to her and clung to her legs.

'I don't want you to go.'

She put her hand on his head, holding the roundness of it against her. Tom didn't move from his seat beside Martin, but Annie saw that he was staring fiercely to hold back the tears that he thought were babyish. Martin stood up awkwardly and came towards her. Annie felt how much she was hurting him, and the pain of it was worse than anything else she had suffered from the bomb.

I love you, she thought helplessly. *All of you, I love you so much.*

Martin bent down and scooped Benjy up into his arms, setting her free. She knew that her husband was letting her go, as gently as he could. She ducked her head, like a coward, away from his generosity. She ran across the grass to Thomas and hugged him, but he turned his face away from her. Benjy's hands snatched at her as she kissed him, but Martin held him tightly.

'Goodbye,' Annie whispered. It would have been like a lie, or a taunt, or an empty promise to add, *I'll be back soon.*

Martin touched her cheek, as lightly as if her skin would still bruise at the brush of his fingers.

'We're here,' he said softly, reminding her.

She nodded, unable even to say, *I know.* She left them then, and went back through the silent house to pick up her suitcase, waiting beside the front door.

When she had gone, and even Benjy had stopped watching the back door to see if she would come out again, Tom burst out fiercely, 'Why does she have to go away? It isn't fair.'

Still holding Benjy, Martin went back and sat beside him. Benjy settled his head against his father's shoulder, his thumb in his mouth.

'Tom, listen.' Tom looked away, but Martin was sure that he was listening. 'Mum isn't just your mother. She's a person, too. We belong to each other, all of us, but we belong to ourselves as well. If Annie needs to go, I think we should let her, and do the best we can.' Thomas's face was still averted, but Martin knew that he was crying now. 'She'll come back to you, Tom. She'll always be your mother.'

The child rubbed his face with the back of his hand. 'Like always?'

They know what's happening, both of them, Martin thought. Somehow, however, they feel it and they know it. 'Like always,' he lied to them, for now, until he knew for sure. 'Like always.'

Of course they believed him. That was enough, for now. Tom sat quietly for a moment, and then he wriggled off the seat.

'Can I go and phone Daniel?'

'Good idea. Ask if he wants to come and play.'

Thomas raced away across the grass, and Ben broke out of Martin's arms and chased after him.

It was very quiet in the garden. A cloud crossed the sun and a line of shadow swept over the grass like a drawn curtain.

Annie.

Martin's head dropped into his hands. He hadn't cried for a long time, but there were tears hot and wet against his fingers now. He had known that there was nothing to do but wait, and hope for her, but he felt his helplessness, crushing him. The sense of impotence brought vividly back to him the hours that he had waited at the police barrier. He had thought then, *If it could be me down there instead of you, Annie.* He had been certain then of loving her enough to take her place, to take on anything if it would save her hurt.

313

The thought came to him now.

If he loved her, did he love her enough to let her go? To let her go, to Steve? If that was what she wanted, truly.

He said aloud in the empty garden, 'Yes.'

He wasn't helpless, then. He could do that for her.

Martin lifted his head. He looked up through the leaves of the pear tree at the sky. There were more clouds drifting towards the sun. It was going to rain. He waited until his eyes were dry, leaning back on the garden bench and watching the sky. When he was sure that the boys would see nothing unusual in his face, he got up and went into the house to look for them.

Steve wrenched the wheel sharply and the car swung out from behind a bus. He accelerated out of the range of a taxi, but the brief burst of speed only brought him up against the wall of traffic waiting at the next lights. He glanced at the clock on the dash. He was late, five minutes already. Impatience made him push the BMW faster still, weaving in and out of the messenger bikes and Telecom vans. He was to meet Annie outside King's Cross station.

'Why King's Cross?' he had asked her, and she had merely replied, 'Why not?'

He reckoned quickly, his fingers drumming on the wheel. Five more minutes. Eight at the most. She wouldn't give him up in that time, would she?

He came past the red and yellow pinnacles of St Pancras in a surge of traffic, and then he saw her. She was standing at the edge of the pavement by the station, perfectly still, with her suitcase beside her. She was wearing a plain cotton dress, with her hair brushed back. She looked as vulnerable as a truant schoolgirl. Steve stopped the car. Absurdly, she was looking the other way, against the flow of traffic, and he had to call to her, 'Are you going my way?'

She swung around then, and the sudden light shone in her face. A second later she was in the car beside him, her suitcase bumping them both. They sat amidst the stream of cars and put their fingers up to touch each other's faces, tracing the contours, like blind people. Annie leaned forward and kissed his mouth.

A taxi began its insistent hooting behind them.

'Where are we going?' she asked.

Steve slipped out into the flow of traffic again. The hooting died away and he looked sideways at her.

'We're going to the seaside,' he said.

Nine

It wasn't Brighton, as Annie had guiltily pictured it.

Instead, they drove through the unravelling skein of East London, and Annie was intent on Steve's face and voice, and she saw none of it.

But at last she asked dreamily, 'Where *are* we going?' and he laughed.

'I told you. To the seaside. And to an East End boy like me, the east coast is the only seaside there is.'

Annie imagined Clacton then, or Southend, but they drove steadily further north, into a wide, flat countryside of huge yellow fields that tipped away at the edges under the arc of the sky. She looked curiously at the unfamiliar place-names.

'I've never been up here before.'

'So it will belong to you and me, when you remember it.'

They didn't look at each other for a moment after that.

They turned off the main road at last, down a side-road that seemed to lead nowhere. There was rough, open land on each side of them, humped over with gorse bushes, and black outcrops of wind-sculpted pines. Annie knew that they were coming to the sea, and then the road dipped suddenly and she saw it. There was a low huddle of houses and beyond them the North Sea, grey-blue even in the sunshine, and dotted with white horses whipped up by the wind. The little town was at the end of the road, with nothing beyond it but the sea. Steve drove to the sea-wall and they left the car in the shelter of it. In winter the waves would smash against the concrete and soak the street beyond with spray, but in midsummer the sea was a flat, sparkling dish. Annie and Steve climbed out of the car and leant against the wall to watch it.

The beach was big, rounded stones, slate-blue and dove-grey, black and shiny where the waves tipped over them. People walked slowly along the water's edge, their shadows fractured in the moving water, and dogs bounded in and out of the foam.

Annie turned and saw Steve looking at her, and she breathed in the salt-fresh air.

The light slanting around them was clear and clean, painterly.

'It's beautiful.'

'I think so, too. And it feels very remote.'

That's right for us, isn't it? Cut off from the world. Just for now, just for now.

'Look.'

Steve turned her round to face inland. There was a little row of houses, painted pink and pale blue and eau-de-Nil, their wrought-iron balconies looking out over the sea. He pointed to a blue one, very trim with white-painted curlicues to the gable ends.

'We're staying in that one.'

'Really? Aren't they pretty? As if they're painted on a backcloth for an end-of-the pier show. Let's go inside and look at it.'

Steve produced a key from his pocket.

The little house had bare wooden floors and basket chairs that creaked, faded cotton curtains and a wood-burning stove in the room that looked out over the balcony to the shifting sea. It reminded Annie instantly and vividly of childhood holidays. She could feel the sand in her canvas shoes, and smell salt, and drift-wood fires and tar. The complex of sensations and recollections overwhelmed her, and suddenly she felt almost painfully aware, all her senses newly primed. She walked across the room to the windows, touching the sun-blistered paint with her fingertips and with the salt-spray and dust from the curtains strong in the back of her throat.

I'm alive, she thought.

She turned to Steve again. He was watching her from the doorway, half in shadow, one side of his face bathed in the light off the sea.

'Whose house is it?'

'It belongs to a friend of mine.'

'Have you been here before?'

'Not like this.'

'So it will belong to you and me, when you remember it.' She echoed his words, confirming them.

'Annie. Yes, Annie.'

They came together then, standing in the middle of the room where the brilliance from outside flickered over the ceiling. Steve took her face between his hands and kissed it.

'Better than a hotel,' he murmured.

'Better.'

Hotels were for adulterers, Annie thought. For furtive, stolen times, while this little house was clean and innocent with the sand swept into corners and the beach stones arranged on the wooden mantelpiece. Was she dressing up the reality for her own comfort? Annie wondered. Perhaps she was, but for today, here and now, she knew that it didn't matter.

'What shall we do?' Steve asked her.

She grinned at him. She felt like a child, excited, on its first day in a new place.

'Let's go out and explore.'

'Let's do that.'

They went out again into the intoxicating air. They walked along the beach, hand in hand, with their shoes crunching satisfyingly in the shingle. Annie stepped backwards to look at the houses along the front, and an unexpected wave washed around her ankles. She took off her shoes and poured the water out, laughing, and Steve carried them for her as they walked on. The ebbing tide uncovered runnels of glittering wet sand, and Annie left her footprints in them until the next wave came and left the sand smooth all over again.

Beyond the town there was a long shingle bank, and at the far end of it the high, round mysterious bulk of a Martello tower. Annie put her wet shoes on again and they walked along the track towards it. In the lee of the shingle bank there was a little yacht basin, and the dinghie's rigging drummed out a sharp tattoo in the wind against the steel masts. When they reached the tower they stood for a moment staring up at the smooth, massive walls, and then looked past it at the line of coast that it had protected. It curved away into the distance, to the point where land and sea were indistinguishable.

They were dwarfed by the tower's size and by the emptiness beyond it. Annie listened to the waves and the cries of the gulls, now amplified and now drowned out by the wind. She half-turned, away from Steve, and looked inland. Here there was empty marshland spiked with coarse grass and furrowed with muddy tide channels. Further inland, a long way off across the great flat space, she could just see the upraised finger of a church spire. The wind was cold on this exposed promontory, and she shivered. But she was exhilarated, too, by the remoteness of it, and by the noise of the sea and the wind that almost drowned their insistent thoughts. Under the vast sky Annie had a sense of their impermanence, a sense that they borrowed the majesty of their surroundings to reflect on their own small concerns. She knew that they were incapable of making even the smallest lasting impression. But the tower was solid, spanning the centuries, and the sky and the sea were everlasting.

And perhaps nothing else mattered so very much.

Suddenly the notion was comforting, even soothing. They were there, and then they were gone, all of them. *Remember this*, Annie told herself, *when the time comes*. She was smiling. Steve had been watching the melting line of the horizon, but he turned now and saw her, and their eyes met.

'I know,' he said. He heard her thoughts, as always.

They stood for a moment in the shadow of the tower, looking at one another while they could.

Then Annie shivered again, and she felt the wet bottoms of her trousers clammy against her bare ankles.

'Let's walk back through the town,' Steve said.

They walked slowly, hand in hand, looking in at the windows of genteel teashops and old-fashioned grocers'. There was an estate agent's in a pinkwashed cottage, but they passed that by, neither of them so much as glancing at the inviting, impossible invitations that it held out. The cosiness of the high street, with its back firmly turned to the sea, warmed Annie through again.

They went back to the little blue house and Annie made tea, carrying it up on a tray to the balcony room so that they could watch the light change on the sea while they ate and drank.

In the quiet isolation of the house they were suddenly almost shy together. Annie was conscious of the months that had gone by since she had seen him last in the chic greyness of his flat. They sat close together but they didn't quite touch, now, as if they were uncertain of what the other wanted or expected. For a moment, Annie wasn't sure whether she knew him at all. Steve took her hand and she jumped, bumping awkwardly against the wicker sofa arm. They laughed then, fracturing the tension, and Steve said, 'Come on. I'll take you out to dinner.'

Annie bathed and changed in the little square bedroom. She took her clothes out of her bag and laid them neatly on one side of the patchwork-quilted bed. She put her hairbrush and jars of cream at one side of the chest of drawers, and then glanced at the bag that Steve had brought, still standing at the opposite side of the bed. She unfolded her clothes and put them on hangers in one half of the wardrobe, feeling the strangeness of having only her own things.

Anne picked up her empty case. It was a battered, nondescript one, veteran of numerous family holidays and weekends. Steve's unopened bag was a soft black canvas-and-leather holdall, quite unlike anything Martin and she had ever owned. She touched it briefly with her fingertips, thinking with momentary sadness that it belied all the connubial intimacy of the room. She turned quickly and stowed her own suitcase in a cupboard.

Standing in front of the dim mirror, she made up her face as carefully as if she were going to the grandest function of her life. When she came back to Steve he was sitting on the balcony staring out to sea, but he turned at once to look at her with an odd, admiring expression, as if they had only just met.

'You look wonderful,' he said. He kissed her and she felt the sudden imperative beat of her response to him. He touched the corner of her mouth with his.

'Dinner,' he said.

The roads across the wide, flat fields were empty and he drove the big car very fast. The sun was setting, and the rays of light slanted from the west, behind them, in long, oblique bars. They swept through a dense forest of black pines, miles of it, and when they came out again the sun had gone down and the summer dark had thickened in the sky.

Annie felt that she had never been so aware of the landscape and its lightness and darkness. She thought that all the magnificent effects of it were just for Steve and herself tonight, and then she remembered their insignificance beside the Martello tower, and she laughed softly. Steve's warm hand closed briefly over hers.

They came to another little town, this one left high and dry on its river estuary by the receding sea. There was a square enclosed by old red-brick buildings that glowed in the last of the daylight, and a little restaurant on the corner. There were paper table-cloths and bright overhead lights, and Annie and Steve's table was crowded into a corner by other tables packed with yachtsmen and fishermen and a handful of holidaymakers.

The seafood was the freshest and sweetest that Annie had ever tasted, and after it came sea bass in a simple, buttery sauce.

The two of them ate as if they had been starved, and drank strawy-pale Chablis that tasted of stone and steel. Under the influence of it Annie's cheeks turned pink, and they talked and laughed about little things as if no world existed beyond the uncurtained velvet-black of the restaurant windows.

Much later, they drove back again to the creaking darkness of the house overlooking the sea. They blinked at each other when Steve turned on the lights, unwilling to let the precious evening slip out of their hands.

'It's cold,' he said. 'I'll light the stove, shall I?'

There was wood in the log-basket beside it, and soon the stove was glowing. The real scent of burning driftwood enfolded them. Steve brought out a bottle of brandy and two glasses. He gave a glass to Annie and she drank, feeling the heat of the spirit in her throat.

'Listen to the sea,' Steve whispered.

In the room's stillness the waves seemed to break almost over their heads. He drew aside the curtain and they saw the distant beam of a lighthouse, an arm of light that swept over the sea and withdrew, and then reached out again.

The shyness of the early evening had gone. They turned to each other naturally now, not impatiently, but eagerly, knowing that the time was right. Annie felt his heart beating under her cheek as she rested against him. She tilted her head back to touch her mouth against his, and then he bent over her. He blotted out the red heat of the stove, and the lighthouse beam. Annie's head fell back against the cushions and her mouth opened to his.

He undid the front of her shirt, touching the buttons one by one, and his hand and then his mouth touched her breast.

'I love you,' she said simply.

They were both conscious of the flood of words, held back.

Steve said, 'Come to bed now.'

They climbed the narrow stairs to the upper room.

Annie had no sense of separation now, no sense of anything except that they were here, and the importance of this moment.

With clumsy hands they took off one another's clothes, and the air was cold against their skin. They reached out and touched the healing scars with their fingertips.

'Almost better,' Steve whispered.

'Almost. Not quite, yet. Not quite.'

They turned back the patchwork cover, like a couple in their own bedroom. Then Steve lifted her up and laid her on the bed.

Annie felt the chilly sheets, and then he was beside her, his arms around her. They clung together and their bodies warmed each other, and they let their hands and mouths speak for them while they still could.

When her body cried out for him he leant over her for a second and they looked into each other's eyes. Steve smiled, but Annie could see the pain beneath his eyelids.

Oh don't be hurt, my love.

She reached up, drawing his mouth to hers. He came inside her and she cried out, inarticulate.

They made love slowly, very gently, without the urgency and desperation that had driven them in London. When Annie opened her eyes she saw in the faint changes of light over the beamed ceiling the invisible sweeps of the lighthouse lantern across the sea. And when Steve let himself go at last and called out her name, *Annie, Annie,* she cradled his head in her arms and kissed his eyelids, and afterwards they lay still together and the murmur of the waves broke over them all over again.

'Today, with you, has been one of the happiest days I have ever known,' Annie said, almost to herself. That it couldn't repeat itself, unfolding into other days until they were old, was both its sadness and its strength. They had known this day, at least. That was what Tibby had meant. Suddenly, with certainty, Annie knew that that was the truth.

'Remember it,' Steve echoed.

'Remember it,' she echoed, sealing the pact of the day.

She lay in Steve's arms with her mouth against the smooth warmth of his skin, and fell asleep listening to the sound of the sea.

Annie dreamed the dream again.

The blackness was not just dark, but a terrible weight on top of her. She was pinned by it, crushed and bleeding, and in a minute, in a second, the weight would collapse and she would be blotted out. She opened her eyes wider until they stung in their sockets and there was still only the acrid dark. She was utterly alone. She knew that, because she was shouting somebody's name and he couldn't answer her because he was gone, or dead. She was certain he was dead. Terror engulfed her as she heard the rumble beginning overhead and beneath her. Now the rocks would smash down, and the pain would destroy her. She struggled, with a last, impossible effort, and reached out into the empty darkness.

But it wasn't empty. She was calling his name, and he answered it. His arms held her as she sat up, gasping and sobbing.

'Annie. Annie. I'm here. It's all right.'

'Steve?'

'Yes. Yes, I'm here.' His voice was low, and calm, and she felt the terror falling away in ugly swathes.

'The dark.'

'I know. It's all right. Look, there's the lighthouse.'

And through the window she saw the beam of it, bright, and regular, and beautiful. Steve held her until her breath came steadier. He kissed her wet eyelids and brushed the matted damp hair out of her eyes. She shuddered and lay against him, letting the ordinary reality of touch and sight and smell lift her out of the black terror. 'Was it the same dream?'

'Yes. Exactly the same.'

With one arm still holding her, Steve reached out and turned on the light beside the bed. Annie saw the reality of the patchwork quilt and the beamed ceiling; their discarded clothes and her own belongings laid out on the top of the chest of drawers. Colour flooded softly back into the room.

'Look at me now,' Steve said. She turned her head slowly. He took her fingers and pressed them to his face. To Annie it was as if they were in the wreckage again, but she could see him now, and touch him, and she wasn't afraid any more.

'It's over,' he said. She listened carefully to the echoes in the words. 'You're safe now.' With their linked fingers he touched the fading scars on her arm and shoulder and the long one across her belly. 'We survived. We made each other survive. It's all over, Annie.'

She nodded, suddenly mute with exhaustion.

'Lie down again.' Steve turned out the light once more.

She did as he told her, and he drew the quilt around them. Without knowing that he was doing it, Steve put his arms around her and held her exactly as he had done in the worst moments, when he was afraid that she would die. But her breathing was regular now, warm on his cheek, and her face when he touched it was clean and smooth.

It's over, he told himself once more. He remembered when the rescuers came. He had let go of her in the end, under the arc lights in the icy air. Now, the dim sweep of the lighthouse beam was like the faintest echo of those same lights. Involuntarily, uselessly, he held her tighter. 'Are you still awake?'

Her cheek moved against his shoulder. 'Yes.'

'Are you still frightened?'

'No,' Annie said. 'Not any more.' She was certain now, as sure as she would ever be of anything, that the terrible dream was gone and that it would never trouble her again. 'The dream is over too,' she said. 'It won't come back any more.'

In the darkness, with only the faint grey shimmer of the lighthouse as a reminder, Steve smiled with his mouth against her hair.

They lay for a long time, holding each other, in the old position. And then, at last, they fell asleep.

The sun rose over the sea, and filled the rooms of the blue house with penetrating light. When Annie went to look out, yawning and wrapping herself in her robe, the fishing fleet was coming in, drawing after itself a double wake of silvery, foaming wash and black swooping gulls. The diesel engines chugged in the stillness. Steve came and stood beside her and they watched the wake from the boats fan out and reach the shore in ripples which rolled over on to the shingle with hardly a splash.

Remember it, Annie told herself. *Remember it*.

They stood in silence for a moment and then Steve said, lightly, as if it were any day, 'I think we should have a proper seaside breakfast. I'm going to the shops.'

Annie sat on the duckboards of the balcony, her knees drawn up and the sun warm on her face, and waited for him. The first of the fishing boats was winched slowly up on to the shingle, the rusty old engine on the beach painfully grinding.

She heard Steve come in again, and begin to clatter in the kitchen. She went downstairs, barefoot, padding in and out of the shafts of sunlight. She stood in the kitchen doorway smiling, but then Steve glanced sharply at her and her smile faded.

'What is it?' Annie asked.

She stared around the kitchen, seeing the box of eggs and the brown paper bag of groceries, the unfolded newspaper and the coffee pot waiting on the table.

Steve hesitated and she felt the cold pulse of her heart, and then he picked up the newspaper. He came to her, holding the front page for her to see. Annie thought, *Martin. Tom and Benjy*. What's happened to them, while I'm here, away from them? No, please. Please not that . . . not now, and here.

She looked down in bewilderment at blurred photographs, mugshots, two men and a woman. The meant nothing to her and the fear that had leapt into her throat subsided again. They're always here inside me, she realized. Wherever I go.

She knew, suddenly and with utter conviction, that there was no decision to be made. It had been made, long ago, with the times that had become memories whirling like confetti in the darkness.

'What is it?' she repeated stupidly.

'Read it.'

Annie forced her eyes to focus, skimming over the words. She saw, *Arrested in South London. In connection with the Christmas bombing.* There were names, absurdly ordinary, and aliases. Suspected political affiliations. *Continued on back page.* She knew that on the back page there would be a reminder of what had happened on that day. Perhaps a photograph of the bombed store.

She let the paper fall instead of turning it over. The gas ring was already lit, a circle of dim blue flame, and it hissed softly in the silence. They couldn't hear the sea, here at the back of the house. The only other sound, now that Annie was listening, was someone whistling. A milkman, perhaps. Ordinary things, going on all around them. She thought of her parents' house, and well-washed milk bottles put out on the back step.

'So they're caught,' she said at last.

She was trying to make herself understand what she felt now, and it dawned on her that she felt nothing. She had spent her grief and anger long ago, for those who had died and suffered injuries. And for herself and Steve, the newspaper photographs of those wooden, staring faces had no significance at all. The violence had gone. Annie felt the gentleness of relief. It softened the clenched muscles in her face and throat, and loosened the set of her shoulders. She was lucky, after all. Nothing had happened to Martin or the boys. It wasn't too late.

'We're here,' Martin had told her in the garden. Sharp joy out of the words sang in her head. Longing and love pulled fiercely at her. She turned her face to look openly at Steve.

'What do you feel?' she asked him. The oddness of the question struck them both. She had never needed to ask that before.

His eyes held hers for a moment, and then he looked down at the newspaper faces.

'Nothing,' he whispered. 'What are they to us, now?'

That was all, but unspoken words spilt through the silence.

The blurred newsprint had come like an exorcism. It laid the violence and the fear to rest, and with them a different kind of violence seemed to die too.

Steve took her in his arms and kissed her, and he saw her as he had done at the very beginning. A woman out shopping, with her hair tumbled over the collar of her coat. Annie stood with her head against his shoulder. She was thinking back to the old evenness of her life with Martin and her children. The bomb had blown that apart. She thought of the pain that followed, and the revelation of its obverse side, joy more vivid than anything she had ever known. The pain and, she understood now, the joy had both faded together. It had happened, and it was over.

It was Steve, and herself, and Martin and the children who were left. No different from anyone else, and with the same old human ties.

Love and affection. How deep those ties went, after the violent need had flickered out. Martin was half of her. She couldn't cut away half of herself, but even more certainly she knew that she couldn't cut out of Martin the half of him that was herself too. The thought of his pain, much harder to bear than all her own, filled her eyes momentarily with tears.

She bent down to hide them, picking up the discarded newspaper with stiff fingers.

Steve's arms were warm around her shoulders for an instant longer, and then he let her go.

Annie dropped the paper into the rubbish bin.

'Let's make the breakfast,' she said.

Steve laid the bacon rashers in the blackened pan, and the fat turned translucent before giving its salty, domestic smell up into the air.

They took their plates up to the sunny balcony, and ate looking out over the empty sea.

When they had finished, Steve asked her carefully, 'What shall we do today?'

Annie busied herself with the coffee cups, and they rattled in her fingers.

Just one more day, she thought. *We can allow ourselves that much, can't we, out of so many?*

'Can we walk inland?'

'Of course we can. We can go anywhere you like.'

Just for today.

They took the Ordnance Survey map off the shelf of tattered paperbacks and spread it out, planning a route. The practicality of it gave them something to focus on, and they deliberately gave themselves up to it.

'Can we go that far?' Annie asked faintly, and he grinned at her.

'Easily.'

It was a long way, but Annie knew that she would remember every turn of that walk together. She saw every path and lane with extra clarity, and every change of the wide marshland sky as the sun climbed and began to sink again.

They crossed the marshes where the coarse grass brushed rhythmically against their legs, winding with the tiny creeks that had dried into cracked mud. There were larks overhead, spilling out curls of song as they circled their invisible patch of territory. Beyond the marshes they climbed on to sandy downland dotted with huge clumps of coconut-scented gorse and undermined with rabbit warrens. They came to a forbidding belt of conifers, with a tiny church standing almost at the dark edge. They stood for a moment in the cool dimness of the church's interior, where the sun streaming through the one stained-glass window left pink and amethyst lozenges on the varnished pine pews. The dimness outside under the pines was oddly similar, and they found themselves whispering as they walked over the soft mat of spent brown needles. On the other side the sun was directly overhead, dazzling them momentarily with its brightness.

They ate lunch in a pub garden, made secret by high hedges and whitewashed walls, the only customers for bread and cheese and hoppy local beer.

They walked on again, down shady lanes now that skirted huge fields of corn and barley. The world seemed empty except for themselves and the occasional farmhand who chugged past with a wave, perched high above the ridged wheels of his tractor. And then they began to circle back again, with the sun behind them now, towards the sea.

All the way around the sunlit, empty circle they talked. They talked about simple things, small things that related to themselves and to the past, filling in the blanks that had been left as they lay frozen under the rubble.

Annie told Steve about Tibby, and her mother's imploring words that had brought her here to the little blue house overlooking the sea. He listened, with the lines showing at the corners of his mouth.

329

What they were doing was like the walk itself, Annie thought. It was as if they must draw the raw ends together, to complete the circle, before they could step away again along another route.

They didn't talk about the future. To contemplate the future would have been to tear the raw ends apart.

At last, walking very slowly now, they came to the point where the road dipped eastwards and the sea spread out in front of them, grey, with all the sparkle of the morning drained away. Steve took her hand and they walked the last part of the way in silence, to the end of the road.

The house on the sea-front was full of the evening's shadows. Neither of them would turn on the lights, yet. Annie sank down on the stairs, too weary to walk another step.

'Come on,' he said. And they remembered how they had kept one another going long ago, at the very beginning.

'I'll do it for you,' Annie said. She smiled, but her face was shadowed. She went heavily up the stairs.

Steve followed her and ran a bath in the tiny bathroom with its clanking pipes. He found a jar of salts and tipped them in, whisking the water up into a steamy green froth.

'You read my thoughts,' Annie said, and he turned to look at her through the steam.

'And you read mine.'

They undressed each other, and lowered themselves into the welcome heat. Annie wound her legs around his, holding on to him. They took the soap in turn and washed each other, gently, as if their scars might open again. Steve leant forward and kissed her mouth, and then her breast as the bubbles of foam burst and revealed it. He stood up abruptly, sending a wave of scented water on to the floor. He lifted Annie out of the bath and wrapped her in a towel, and carried her through into the bedroom. They lay down as they were, wet and slippery, and they made love with all the urgency and pain and desperation that they had held at bay all through the day. And they lay in silence afterwards, not

330

knowing, suddenly, what they could say to one another.

Much later, when they ate dinner together, it was with the spectres of the first afternoon in the restaurant watching them. Annie remembered that she had felt beautiful, and invincible, because of Steve. She looked at his dark face now with the weight of inevitability pressing down on her, and she pushed the unwanted food to one side of her plate, and drank too many glasses of wine. Instead of dulling her senses, the wine sharpened them. She could hear unspoken words and feel the touch of their hands, even though the rickety table separated them. Their hands were still clasped, as they had been at the beginning, but the real world was prising them apart and wrenching back the fingers, one by one.

Annie and Steve sat for a long time over that dinner. Not for the pleasure of it, because the silences that they were too careful of each other to fill were lengthening, but because they were like children, unwilling to let the day end. But at last Steve tipped the empty bottle sideways. It didn't yield even a drop. He laid it on its side and spun it, and the bottle came to rest with the neck pointing away from them, out into the darkness. He shrugged, but Annie saw through the protectiveness.

She stood up, scraping her chair in the soft quiet, and went round the table to him. She put her arms around him and rested her face against his.

'Don't,' she said. She was going to say, *I can't bear it*, but she stopped short. *You can*, she told herself, *because you must*.

'I don't want to sit here any more,' Steve said.

They looked at each other calmly. And then they went up the stairs, very slowly, turning off the lights behind them.

The wind was rising and the little bedroom was full of the sound of the sea. They lay down together once more, and they were glad of the darkness because it hid their faces. In the darkness they gave themselves blindly up to murmured words and to the touch of their hands, and then at last to the insistent tide that caught them up and carried them away.

When it had ebbed into sad silence they lay holding each

other and listening to the real waves breaking on the pebbles below.

When Annie woke up in the morning she reached out her hand to Steve. The hollow of the bed beside her was still warm, but he had gone. She lay for a moment while recollection knotted itself around her, and then she got out of bed and went to the window.

The sky was veiled with thin grey summer cloud, and the sea was the same flat colour, almost white at the far point where it met the sky. There were people on the beach, sitting on the slope of stones or walking in ones and twos at the water's edge. She watched them for a moment, seeing the more distant ones as little dark figures, matchstick people. One of them was standing still, staring out to sea. Annie saw that it was Steve. A couple with a dog passed by him, then a child, running, all arms and legs.

Steve was a long way off, diminished by the curve of the beach and the sky. He was a stranger amongst other strangers. Annie closed her eyes. When she opened them she saw him bend down to pick up a stone, and then pitch it in a wide arc into the sea. Abruptly Annie turned and went to the wardrobe. She began to take her clothes off the hangers, fumbling with them because the tears were blurring her eyes.

When Annie came downstairs Steve was at the front door. She saw him framed in the glass, a tall dark man whose face she knew as well as her own.

He opened the door and looked at her, startled for an instant and then seeing too clearly.

'You have to go home today.'

It wasn't a question, or a statement, but a confirmation.

The words spoken at last.

'Yes,' she said softy. 'I must go home.'

He caught her hands in his then, unable to let her go as gently as he had promised himself he would. Out on the clean wide beach he had believed that it was possible. Now he didn't trust himself any longer.

'Annie.' He tried for simple words. 'I've never known anyone like you.'

Steve knew that to say more would be hurtful, and clumsy, but he couldn't stop himself. 'I want you to stay with me. I love you. Please don't go.'

'Oh, my love.'

Her face was wet, and she felt the last pain sharper than any she had suffered before. 'I can't stay. If I could change anything, if I could change this small, little world of me and . . .'

He stopped her then, his mouth against hers. 'Don't. I know that you can't stay. I love you for that too, because you're strong and I can't be.' They clung together, helpless, and the sun seemed to have left the sea and the horizon was a dull grey line, suddenly finite and fathomable.

It was Steve who moved at last. He turned away, making a pretence of putting things down on the table, tidying a tidy space. Annie watched him, her heart tearing inside her.

He said, 'I'll drive you to the main line station. There are good trains to London.' That was all.

Annie nodded, and looked blindly away.

Now that the time had come they seized on the mechanics of preparing for travel, as if their busyness would keep it at bay. Steve brought down her suitcase and put it in the car while Annie telephoned the station. Within an hour, they had locked the door of the little blue house and turned away from the expressionless sea.

As they drove past the wide fields Annie commanded herself, *Remember*.

Remember the Martello tower, and the marshes and the skylarks, and the church by the pine woods. Remember the bedroom and the lighthouse beam sliding across the dim ceiling.

That's all I can do, Tibby. Is that right? What is right, for any of us?

The miles to the station rippled past, as fast as in a dream.

Steve left the car in the forecourt and they walked into the ticket hall. At the glass hatch Annie bought one second class single ticket to London. She put it into her bag without looking at it, and they went out on to the platform. It was crowded with shoppers going up to London for the day.

Steve jerked his chin impatiently. 'Let's walk up to the other end.'

They went, side by side, not quite touching one another. At the far end of the platform was the station buffet. Annie looked in through the glass doors at the hideous red plastic padded benches and steel-legged tables, at the perspex-fronted display cases with their curling doyley exhibits, and the smeared chrome of the hot water geyser. The little sign hanging in the double doors said firmly, CLOSED.

When Annie turned she saw the yellow snout of the diesel engine rounding the distant curve of the track.

When the time comes. The time had come.

Steve put out his hand, tilting her chin so that he could see her face. Their eyes moved, taking each other in, remembering how the darkness had denied them that.

Annie heard the hiss of the train's brakes, the roar coming up behind them.

'What will you do?' she whispered. She didn't mean *without me*. Her own days were mapped out now, with a clear, lucid appeal that she couldn't think about yet, and she felt the sharpness of the contrast for Steve.

To her surprise he smiled, a genuine smile with a warmth that touched her. 'I don't know,' he said. 'All I do know is that it won't be the same thing, over and over, like it was before. It changed everything, didn't it?'

'Yes,' Annie answered. The bomb had changed everything. The violence that it had detonated had gone, and the passion that had followed would fade too, as all passion did. The bombing was old news, and it left them as it had found them, separate. But yet they had changed everything for one another. It would be impossible, Annie thought wildly, here and now with the train snorting behind them, if she couldn't believe that it was, at least, change for the better.

Remember. She wanted to say, *I love you.*

The train rushed into the station, a hissing blur of blue and grey resolving itself into carriages, packed with people. Steve picked up her case and walked with Annie to an open door. She let the other passengers stream past her, her eyes still holding his. The last London-bound shopper scrambled on to the train and the doors began to slam along the platform.

'I'm sorry,' she said stupidly.

He took her face between his hands and kissed her. His mouth was very warm.

'Don't,' he told her. 'Don't be sorry.'

There was a porter beside them now, holding the door impatiently. Steve lifted her bag into the train and stood back to let her go. Annie went up the steps and the door slammed resonantly behind her. At once the whistle blew and the train began to slide forward. They watched each other still, as long as they could, not waving, as if all the power of the diesel engine couldn't pull them apart.

And then the train moved faster, too fast, until they couldn't see each other any more.

Steve stood and watched the train until the oblong tail of it vanished out of his sight.

Remember it, he told himself. And as if by the old telepathy, *Remember it, all of it, and keep it.*

And then he turned and walked very slowly out into the car park where his car stood waiting for him.

Annie walked down the length of the train, her eyes stinging with her uncried tears. She found a seat at last, opposite a large family wedged in with sandwiches and Thermos flasks. As the big yellow fields slid backwards past her she sat and listened to the children talking and squabbling and crowing with laughter, and the net of familiarity began to close around her once again. She felt the sweetness of it, and the warmth, like gentle fingers. And then, with sudden gratitude, she thought, *Home. I'm going home.* The thundering engine seemed too slow, and the distance that separated her from them too great ever to cover again.

But at last, in the afternoon sun that had turned hot, Annie rounded the corner into the old street. Her arms ached from the weight of her suitcase, but she walked quickly past the red-brick houses that seemed to glow with satisfaction in the sunlight. A handful of children were roller-skating on the pavement at the far end. Annie passed the garden gates, counting the numbers. The old man who lived next door but one to Martin and Annie was leaning over his gate, watching her. As she drew level he took his pipe out of his mouth and nodded at her suitcase.

'What did you do, run away from home?'

'Something like that,' Annie smiled at him.

She went up her own path, with the gate giving its perfectly-remembered creak behind her. As she found her key and put it into the lock she noticed that the front garden needed weeding. It was a job that she always enjoyed, tidying up the little square patch and raking the gravel into lines. *Home.*

The front door swung open.

Annie stood in the hallway, looking around her. The same, the same as always, and infinitely precious.

Then the silence grew heavy and she turned her head sharply. She dropped her bag at her feet and the thud was unnaturally loud. The house was empty.

Annie ran to the living room door and pushed it open. There was no one there, although the cushions were flattened and the pieces of a jigsaw puzzle were spread on the table. She whirled around and ran into the kitchen, seeing the scatter of bread-crumbs on the worktop, the milk bottle standing on the draining board. In the irrationality of her fear, the signs told her nothing.

They had gone, she thought. She had come home too late, and they were gone. Desperation gripped her.

Into the stillness she shouted, '*Martin!*'

Then, through the window of the kitchen, she saw the three of them. Martin must have been sitting working in the garden, with

336

the boys playing nearby, but now they had heard her. They stood close together, their faces alike, uncertain. Annie saw that they didn't know what to expect from her.

She fumbled with the door handle, turning it the wrong way in her haste. The door banged behind her and she ran over the grass, almost stumbling. She heard Thomas's shout.

'Mum's home. Oh look, Mum's home.'

But it was only Martin that she could look at now.

Let me ask you just one more thing. After so many. Let me come back.

Martin's eyes fixed on Annie's face. Even though the tears were running down her cheeks he saw the look in it, and he knew that it was over at last. He held out his arms to her.

'Annie.'

With her head bent, against his shoulder, she asked him, 'Can I come home?'

He put his hands to her cheeks, turning her face up to his. 'We're here. We've been waiting for you.'

He kissed the corner of her mouth, and with his thumb he wiped the tears from her cheeks, just as Annie would do to Benjy or Tom. Annie saw her husband then, his face as familiar to her as it had always been, but sharpened with differences and now, suddenly, with the knowledge of happiness.

I don't deserve so much. She knew it, and she knew that she would remember it. *Remember*, Annie told herself, for the last time.

'Thank you,' she said simply. 'I love you.'

He smiled at her, then. 'I love you too.'

The boys' shrieks broke through to her and she knelt on the grass to look at them, drawing Martin down with her. Benjy's fists caught at her clothes and she hugged him against her, reaching out an arm for Thomas too.

'Don't go away again,' Thomas shouted at her. 'Don't go away again ever.'

She held them closer, so that they wouldn't see her tears.

'I won't go away again,' she promised him. 'Never, never.'

The words closed round the four of them, and they made an unbreakable, invisible circle on the grass.

337

It's over, Annie thought.

She listened, straining her ears, but there was nothing. The last echoes of the bomb's terrible roar had died away into the stillness of the garden.

A Woman of Our Times

Rosie Thomas

Harriet Peacock has everything. What more could she possibly want?

Harriet Peacock has come a long way. From a small shopkeeper and betrayed wife she has made herself the City's darling, her name linked in gossip columns with film star Casper Jensen.

She has come a long way from Simon Archer, the man who invented a brilliantly simple game of chance and skill in a prison camp forty years ago, a game that is the foundation of Harriet's busines empire.

She has come a long way from her family, friends and former lovers.

But when things start going wrong Harriet finds that in love, as in The Game, the quickest way to a goal can also be the riskiest . . .

arrow books

ALSO AVAILABLE IN ARROW

A Simple Life

Rosie Thomas

Dinah Steward has a secret . . .

Hidden beneath the comfortabe family life she shares with her successful husband Matthew and their two sons lies a shameful secret that has haunted Dinah for fifteen years. She and Matt never speak of it or the impossible choice he forced her to make all those years ago; they think the cracks have been papered over.

But when a chance encounter brings the past into sharp focus once more, Dinah realises that she can no longer deny the truth. She decides to risk everything – her husband, her sons, her perfect lifestyle, in order to claim what was always hers.

arrow books

Other People's Marriages

Rosie Thomas

They were 'the five families' – the pleasant hospitable Frosts, the brash and sexy Cleggs, flirtatious Jimmy Rose and aloof Star, maternal Vicky and reliable Gordon Ransome, Michael Wickham and his perfect wife Marcelle. Old friends, their lives are interwoven in a comfortable pattern of school runs and Sunday golf, barbecues and shared holidays.

Until Nina Cort returns to the cathedral city of her childhood. Rich, sophisticated and newly widowed, Nina is an exotic thread in the pattern, whose intrusion reveals a web of hidden flaws.

In the course of a year from which none will emerge unscathed, the five families and Nina discover that you can never truly know the fabric of other people's marriages. Perhaps not even of your own . . .

'Hugely enjoyable . . . Rosie Thomas writes with beautiful effortless prose; she shows a rare compassion and a real understanding of the nature of love'
The Times

arrow books

Bad Girls, Good Women

Rosie Thomas

Together they broke all the rules . . .

To London, on the brink of the Sixties, two runaways plunge into the whirl of Soho nightlife.

Mattie faces the hard slog of repertory and a sleazy strip-club in search of fame as an actress. But, when it comes, stardom is not enough, and the love that Mattie desires seems to elude her.

Julia chooses marriage and Ladyhill, a beautiful Dorset manor house. Then, after the tragedy, she realises that to achieve true independence she will have to risk her marriage and her child.

Though each has to make her own choices, their friendship – despite the guilt and betrayal – endures over three turbulent decades.

arrow books

Follies

Rosie Thomas

They were three modern women. They came to Oxford University full of hopes and dreams and would leave forever changed:

Helen: shy, quiet and hopelessly in love with Lord Oliver Mortimore, the dazzling, self-destructive blond who lives for fast cars, drink and drugs.

Chloe: glamorous and confident, abandoning a high-powered career and broken affair, obsessively drawn to her philandering English professor.

Pansy: heiress and aspiring actress, driven to prove she is more than an irresistable magnet to the men who flock to her.

Together for one unforgettable year, they would share a lifetime of emotions and a very special friendship . . .

arrow books

The Potter's House

Rosie Thomas

Olivia Georgiadis has left her English roots far behind. She lives on a Greek island, married to a local man, mother to their small sons. Year on year, island life has followed a peaceful unchanging rhythm.

Until now. An earthquake ravages the coast, its force devastating the island. In the aftermath comes a stranger: an Englishwoman, destitute but for the clothes she wears.

Olivia welcomes the stranger into her home, the potter's house. But as Kitty melts into the family and the village community, so Olivia begins to sense her mysterious visitor threatens all she holds dear . . .

'Beautifully constructed and written . . . a treat'
Marie Claire

arrow books

ALSO AVAILABLE IN ARROW

Moon Island

Rosie Thomas

On a small stretch of untamed coast, five old clapboard houses gaze out to sea. Fourteen-year-old Mary Duhane, arriving with her father and sister for the summer, feels isolated and resentful. Leonie Beam, staying in the neighbouring house with her husband's family, shares May's isolation, for she is unhappy in her marriage. She confides in Elizabeth Newton, an ageing widow who keeps the beach's secrets.

Meanwhile, May has discovered the diary of a dead girl, her own age. To unravel its story, she must immerse herself in the past. As she does so, she begins to feel she is destined to follow in the dead girls' footsteps.

'A feast of a book, achingly true in parts and totally bewitching in others'
New Woman

arrow books

Order further Rosie Thomas titles
from your local bookshop, or have them delivered
direct to your door by Bookpost

Free post and packing
Overseas customers allow £2 per paperback
Phone: 01624 677237
Post: Random House Books
c/o Bookpost, PO Box 29, Douglas, Isle of Man, IM99 1BQ
Fax: 01624 670923
email: bookshop@enterprise.net
Cheques (payable to Bookpost) and credit cards accepted

Prices and availability subject to change without notice
Allow 28 days for delivery
When placing your order, please state if you do not wish to receive any
additional information

www.randomhouse.co.uk/arrowbooks

arrow books